DASH, P.I.

DASH, P.I.

THIS DOG FOR HIRE
&
THE DOG WHO KNEW TOO MUCH

Two Rachel Alexander and Dash Mysteries

CAROL LEA BENJAMIN

WALKER AND COMPANY
NEW YORK

First published in the United States of America, respectively in 1996 and
1997 by Walker Publishing Company, Inc.

Published simultaneously in Canada by
Thomas Allen & Son Canada, Limited, Markham, Ontario

ISBN 1-56865-577-0

Printed in the United States of America

THIS DOG FOR HIRE

For Judy Nelson,
wherever you are, honey.

Acknowledgments

Many thanks to:

John Douglas of Partners & Crime Booksellers, whose enthusiasm and encouragement helped me to sally forth into a new genre

Marty Berkowitz, Ph.D., Richard Siegel, M.S.W., Polly DeMille, R.N., B.S.N., M.A., Bonnie Wilcox, D.V.M., John Laub, Jan Bella Berkowitz, Larry Berg, and Captain Arthur Haggerty, who so generously shared their expertise, with a hug for Joe Celentano, M.S.W., whose genius was the inspiration for an important part of this book

The Bomb Dogs and their handlers at the Sixth Precinct, Greenwich Village

Alice Quinn, a friend in need

Evelyn Abrams, who taught me, by her sterling example, how to listen

Ann Loring, for her boundless enthusiasm and unfailing support

Los Angeles Food and Fiction Club and NYC's Loose Women's Book Club

Gail Hochman, my wonderful agent

Michael Seidman, Zen master with a blue pencil

with a hug for Job Michael Evans (you're still the favorite)

and love to my family, Stephen Lennard, my sweetheart, Victoria and Stephen Joubert, Jennifer Gutbezahl, Mimi Kahn and Dick Goodman, Flash, the Border collie, and Dexter, a stand-up dog if ever there was one

1

Ordinary Secrets

GREENWICH VILLAGE IS a place full of secrets, back cottages hidden from view behind wrought-iron gates and down long brick passageways and little Edens way up high, secret gardens growing not on the ground but on the roof, retreats concealed from the prying eyes of strangers.

There are other secrets here as well, sexual secrets, passages across the gender lines that I thought, once upon a time, were immutable facts of life. But in this neighborhood of writers and artists, the facts of life were long ago rewritten, familiar images redesigned.

And more and more of late, the secrets indigenous to this place, once visible only to willing participants, are coming out, out of the closet, out of the clubs, out in the open for all to see. Even those who'd rather not.

Still, it's usually a case of live and let live.

But not always.

We have our ordinary secrets, too, the kind every neighborhood has, envy, jealousy, greed, lust, anger, all seething unseen under the surface. And like the other secrets lying doggo among the twisty, tree-lined streets between Washington Square Park and the Hudson River, these too are invisible, until one day they fester up to the surface.

Secrets are what interest me, particularly the ones that eventually compel seemingly normal people to start obsessing about murder.

My name is Rachel Alexander. I'm the Alexander in Alexander and Dash, private investigation. I get first billing, but Dash, my partner, is the real teeth in the operation. He's a pit bull.

Before I got Dashiell, I worked as a sneaky, lying, low-life, underhanded undercover agent, betraying the confidences of people who befriended me in order to get the information I needed to solve cases. The work suited me, and I liked the odd hours, but after a couple of years I decided I was no longer willing to split the client's check with an agency. That's when I started my own business, doing all of the above and worse, but exploiting myself instead of having it done for me by strangers.

I don't know how to explain my occupation any more than I can explain anything else about my life. I just have always been more interested in what's in the hamper than what's neatly folded in the dresser drawer. It's not that I don't ask myself, particularly when Dash and I are out on an especially seedy stakeout, what's a nice Jewish girl like you doing in a place like this? but I tend to think it wouldn't be all that different had I gone to medical school. Only then I'd be asking it while delicately sticking a gloved finger up some poor guy's ass.

That's one of the few places I haven't had to look for evidence. So far.

It had finally stopped snowing, and I was getting ready to take my dog out for his afternoon constitutional. I had one of my Timberlands half on when the phone rang.

"Get that, will you?" I told him, hopping in the direction of the phone.

Dash took the phone off the receiver and walked toward me with it in his mouth.

"For *me*?" I asked.

He dropped it on my unlaced boot. Thank God for reinforced toe boxes.

I cradled the phone in my neck, barked "Hello," and kept struggling with my boot until I figured out the good news. It was work.

The caller identified himself as Dennis Keaton. He was a pretty unhappy-sounding guy, which isn't unusual: Happy people don't usually hire detectives. He asked if he could see me right away about an urgent matter.

I told him he could.

I had an urgent matter myself. I was dead broke.

I could never see the sense in wasting money on an office when most of the work I have to do is done elsewhere. In winter I meet new clients at James J. Walker Park, on Hudson Street. There's a ball field there where the neighborhood dogs gather to play when it's off-season. It seems to me the proper ambience for my work, even when people do scoop.

Dashiell was dancing impatiently at the door, so I told this Keaton fellow where to meet me, grabbed my coat, my camera, and a notepad, and headed downtown.

2

It Began to Snow

DENNIS KEATON ENTERED the park, carefully adjusted the gate so that a garbage can would keep it from blowing open, and looked around for a second, then, with a walk that announced his sexual orientation, headed in my direction.

He was tall and reedy, but not your typical what-a-waste, gorgeous gay guy. First of all, his nose was much too big. His skin was okay, but pale, even for midwinter in New York. His eyes, which according to the rest of his coloring should have been a to-die-for blue, were an unrevealing steely gray. His uncombed mop of curls reminded me of an apricot-colored standard poodle I had trained for a lady rabbi, the Reverend Janet, back when I was the Kaminsky of Kaminsky and Son Dog Academy. Bernie, the Golden I had then, was the son. That was before I got married, before I got divorced, and before I decided to go from getting growled at to getting shot at, escalating what my shrink called my rabid counterphobia.

"Rachel Alexander?"

As soon as he opened his mouth, I saw that his teeth were crooked, too.

I was leaning against the back fence and patted the spot next to me in response.

He wore a brown leather bomber jacket, a small loop of red ribbon, carelessly attached with a safety pin, a long white aviator scarf around his skinny neck, and, despite a temperature in the low thirties, no hat. The rest of his ensemble deviated from code—shapeless corduroy overalls and ancient brown oxfords, both dappled with spots of black paint.

He took a deep breath and let it go. "A friend of mine, Clifford Cole, has been murdered," he said. "I was told you might be able to help me find out who did it."

He looked to be in his mid-thirties, but who knows. In this neighborhood, there's more illusion than reality. For all I knew, I was looking at the aftermath of a face-lift, a dye job, a perm, and liposuction.

"That's police business," I said. "Why would you want to pay for something you can get done free?"

I glanced at Dash, who was doing the doggy two-step with a flirtatious husky bitch.

"It's been two weeks since Cliff was killed—perhaps you saw it in the paper, if you had a magnifying glass. There's been virtually no interest and no progress."

I nodded. Most people talk more freely if they have evidence that someone's actually listening. The more information I can get before I start asking a lot of questions, the more revealing it tends to be, though it could take a while to figure out precisely what has been revealed.

"Since . . . the body was found on the Christopher Street pier, the police are treating it as a gay bashing."

"And you say?"

"Cliffie never cruised the waterfront. He has, God, I'm still having a lot of trouble with tense, he *had* a lover, but even before Louie, he didn't. It just wasn't his style. Besides, there are other things that signal it wasn't a random killing. The hour, for one thing. The estimated time of death was between four and six in the morning. Cliff was a painter. He has the loft above mine. He was a day person, up with the sun and right to work. It always floored me, because I'm up early trying my best to avoid working for as long as possible. And I quit as soon as I can manage to without excessive guilt. But Cliff was one of those people who could go on and on. His stamina was phenomenal. The energy in his work was just enormous, but well controlled. After he worked, he'd get cleaned up and then he'd go out with Magritte, they'd go out for hours. That's the other thing," he said, his voice suddenly sounding as if he were in a movie on television from which off-color words had been bleeped. "Magritte is missing. He wasn't at the loft, and he wasn't with Cliff when he was found."

He took out a handkerchief and blew his big nose.

"Magritte? The train coming out of the fireplace? And the pipe? *Ceci n'est pas un pipe,* right?"

"Yes, but this Magritte is a basenji. The barkless dog?"

I nodded. Anyone who'd worked as a dog trainer would know basenjis, one of the two quintessential brat dog breeds. Until rottweilers got so popular, basenjis and fox terriers were two of the mainstays of the industry.

"I've been at the loft, of course. We had each other's keys since Magritte was a puppy. I had him a lot of the time. You couldn't leave him alone for more than an hour or two. He'd get really destructive, and he'd make an awful racket."

Tell me about it, I thought. But I let him keep on talking.

"Louie couldn't stand him. So Cliff never took him to Louie's. And Louie never stayed at the loft. He was so pissed when Cliff began talking about getting a dog, and it only got worse. I think he was jealous. So Magritte stayed with me whenever Cliff stayed over at Louie's. He's always been sort of my dog, too. Anyway, it was only natural, when the police came—they spoke to everyone in the building—to go upstairs and get Magritte. That's when I saw he was gone, and his collar and leash weren't hanging on the hook where Cliff and I always put them. I thought maybe Cliff had taken him with him. Maybe he ran away after Cliff was hit. Maybe he was stolen. He's an immensely valuable dog, a champion and a son of the top-winning basenji in the country."

I nodded, careful not to interrupt.

"It was never an issue for Cliff, the money, I mean. He kept turning down requests to use the dog at stud. He always talked about it ruining his temperament, you know, making him aggressive with other males. But honestly, I think he just didn't want the dog to love anyone but him. He got a gigantic kick about Magritte winning in the ring, so he'd let Gil handle him at the shows. Morgan Gilmore, he's the handler who's always shown Magritte, he's fabulous with the breed. But that was it. I mean, I don't think he thought about the dog loving *me*, because he had to have *someone* to take care of him when he couldn't. So I think he just accepted that. But no one else could get in there, could get between them. God, he just loved that little dog to death."

He began to talk faster, as if he needed to relieve himself of the burden of carrying this information all by himself.

"He didn't care about making money hiring him out at stud. He used to fight with his handler about it all the time, because he, Gil, said he'd take care of it, and Cliff wouldn't have to mess with it or worry about it. He said it wouldn't change him, Magritte, that he'd be the same. But Cliff was adamant. What I'm trying to say is that if someone stole the dog on purpose, like if *that* were the point, that would mean whoever killed Cliff knew about Magritte. Gay bashing, you live in this neighborhood, you know a lot about gay bashing, it's random. The event may be planned—after all, you have to remember to put the baseball bats in the car before you leave Jersey—but the victim isn't preselected. Anyway, if the dog were with Cliff, wouldn't he have been hit, too?"

"You mean beaten to death?"

"I'm sorry. I'm doing this ass backwards. I didn't tell you one of the most important things. Clifford wasn't beaten. This was vehicular homicide."

"He was run over?"

"Hit at high speed from behind about two-thirds of the way out onto the pier. At least, that's where he was found."

"Do the police think he was actually hit there or that the body was dumped there?"

"Oh, no, they found enough evidence, they said, at the scene to be sure it happened there."

"Well, I guess we can rule out your garden-variety hit-and-run. Cars aren't allowed on the pier or, for that matter, except for official vehicles, in that whole waterfront area. Did he have any enemies, that you know of? More apropos, do you know of anyone who might stand to gain from his death?"

"I don't know of any specific enemies, not someone who'd want to kill him. Are we talking sane or crazy here? As for money, he plain didn't have much, not that I know of. His art was barely selling. He would trade pieces sometimes, you know, with artist friends. But he didn't actually sell much, and when he did, the prices were really low, a thousand or fifteen hundred at most. Ironically, his first break was about to happen. I guess you'd have to say, *maybe* about to happen. He had just signed his first contract with a gallery weeks before, not a great contract, but still a contract. He was getting his work ready to be in his first group show when he was killed. As far as I know, the loft is mortgaged to the hilt. It's not as if he owned anything worth *killing* for. Except Magritte, I guess. But now he's gone, too."

I took the notepad out of my pocket and began to write down the things he was telling me. When I finished writing, I looked up at the dogs. Dashiell was humping a little Jack Russell who kept turning around and snarling at him. It wasn't a pretty picture.

"Look," Dennis finally said, "the case is open, but I'm as sure as I can be that nothing much is being done, because of the location of the crime, the hour, and the sexual orientation of the victim. But this just doesn't fit the pattern of a bias crime. Well, perhaps there was bias involved—when isn't there?—but I can't accept the conclusion that it was a random crime. Even the money in his pocket was peculiar. A thousand dollars, separate from the rest of his money. And left on the body. Not taken. The bottom line is, I need to know who did this. And I need to find Magritte," he said.

He looked away. Maybe to watch the Jack Russell trying to get even.

I waited.

"The longer he's missing, the less chance there is we'll find *him* alive."

"Hadn't we better get moving?"

He turned around, looking like a deer caught in the headlights.

"You'll take the case?"

I nodded.

"Oh, shit. I didn't ask what you charge."

"It's five hundred a day plus expenses for me and a straight fifty for the dog."

"Fifty a day extra for finding Magritte?"

"No. Fifty a day extra for Dashiell. And I absorb his expenses."

A line appeared between Dennis's gray eyes.

"You mean if I hire you without the dog it's only five, plus expenses, of course?"

"Right. But I don't work without him. It's a jungle out there, and I need to know at least one of the animals is on my side. Do you know what I mean?"

"I do," he said, making a sound with his nose that would have gotten a tsk-tsk from my mother, the late but, if possible, still perfect Beatrice Markowitz Kaminsky. "Precisely. Okay—let's do this. When do we begin?"

"How about now?" I slipped off a glove, put two fingers in my mouth, and blew hard, making the sound of air coming out of a balloon.

"Needs work," he said. He whistled loud enough to wake the dead.

It must be a sex-linked trait. And, Lord knows, I haven't had any of that in a while.

"Thanks. Anyway, I'll need access to Cliff's studio, if possible. I'd like to spend some time there with Dashiell. I have lots more to ask you, but we can do that on the way."

"Does Dashiell actually . . . *do* things, I mean, besides protecting you?"

I looked down at my dog. The top of his head had been slimed by one of the other dogs. His big meaty mouth was agape and panting, a loop of drool draped delicately over his worm-colored lower lip. And he was covered with dirt.

"You thought he was just a pretty face?"

Dennis Keaton's smile was nervous and lopsided, the left side of his mouth moving up at the corner, the right side staying where it was. I got a good close-up view of those crooked teeth.

"Let's go," he said, pushing off the chain-link fence. "We can stop at my place for the keys, and I guess you'll be wanting an advance, or do I see too many movies?"

"I have no idea how many movies you see, but I see too many bills. I require a thousand-dollar advance."

Now *he* nodded.

He seemed like an admirable fellow, my new client, taking on responsibility in a world where most people prefer to shirk it. It appeared he wanted to do right by his friend, a friend whose murderer he wanted found at any cost. And in the midst of his grief, he was even worried about a little basenji.

I wondered what the real story was.

"Suppose we find Magritte, what then?" I asked while opening the loop of Dashiell's nylon slip collar. "Who would he belong to now that Clifford is gone?"

"Why, me, of course. I thought I made it clear that he's always been sort of my dog, too."

"I see," I said.

So it wasn't quite as noble as it appeared, I thought. Then again, it hardly ever is.

I slipped the collar onto Dash, and when I looked up, Dennis was holding the gate for me. What next, I thought, is he going to place his hand in the center of my back and steer me across the street? How does anyone know how to behave nowadays!

It began to snow. Huge white flakes were falling on and around us as slowly as if we were in a dream, and suddenly all the sounds were muted. Even the Hudson Street traffic sounded far away.

I wondered if it had been snowing the night Clifford Cole had died.

"Can we make a detour?" I asked.

"Where to?"

"I need you to show me where Clifford's body was found."

I had a stack of bills waiting on my desk at home. A case was exactly what I needed, and now, thanks to Dennis Keaton, a case was what I had. If I had a normal occupation, I'd be happy. But I don't. And I wasn't. I'd have been a fool not to think that the homely man with the goofy smile walking quietly at my side might himself be the killer I was hired to find.

Hiring the PI to throw everyone off the track is not unheard-of, particularly when someone hires a woman in what's clearly a man's profession. Sometimes it's because they think a woman will fail, and failure is precisely what they're after, at any cost.

Whatever the truth would turn out to be, it would emerge as it always did, in frustratingly small pieces, progressing so slowly I'd want to scream, or give up, or get a job selling jelly beans in the five-and-dime. Instead, I'd keep picking away at things until the scab came loose and all the ugliness underneath finally showed itself.

My mother always told me not to pick at scabs because, if you did, you'd get a scar. I never listened then, and I never listen to the voice of reason now. I just have to find out what's under things, the secrets, the motives, the little twists and turns the human mind can take that make something repugnant seem plausible. And when I'm finished poking around where I don't belong, when the answer is finally visible, the crime solved, I think about Beatrice and what she told me, that the wound will never heal properly, that the scar will be permanent, and that chances are, I'll be even unhappier when I get where I'm going than I was before I began.

3

I'll Draw You a Picture

THE CHRISTOPHER STREET pier sticks out stiff and straight into the Hudson River like an accusing finger pointing at New Jersey, the state with the worst drivers and the highest cancer rate in the country. I unhooked Dash's leash and let him run while Dennis walked me to the place on the pier where Clifford Cole met his killer and his maker on a cold winter night two weeks earlier.

"It must have been here. The officer I spoke to mentioned that," he said. I followed his gloved finger to the spray-painted sign on the concrete barricade, a comical face with a sad expression, the mouth a wide *M*, the sparse, spiky hair like an off-center crown of thorns, and next to it, "Punk's Not Dead."

I looked around the pier. Where was the dog? I wondered. Was he alive, or as dead as his master? If I looked over the barricade and into the river, would I see him floating there, bloated beyond recognition? I decided not to, not with Dennis there.

Dashiell was marking the pier. He was never one to ignore masculine responsibility. When I turned around to look at Dennis, I saw that he was looking up to avoid crying. I wondered how many times he had been told that big boys don't cry, that part of *his* masculine responsibility was to avoid showing any vulnerability, as if he weren't part of the human race, such as it is. I took the Minox out of my pocket and snapped a couple of quick shots of the pier.

"Let's get out of here," I said. "I've seen enough for now."

Just before we turned off the pier, I noticed another spray-painted sign.

Beware of Muggers. Don't Be Caught Alone.

"What a place to die," Dennis said.

I didn't respond. I had seen too many worse places, places far from the fresh, fishy smell of the river and the sweeping, open views north and south, places that stunk of urine, feces, vomit, blood, places so dehumanizing and frightening they could have wiped out every decent vision the victim had ever seen, and perhaps the worst place of all to die a violent death, one's own bed, the place for the sort of sleep you wake up from.

I hooked on Dashiell's leash and we headed for SoHo.

One-sixty-three Greene Street was an AIR—Artist in Residence— loft, which meant that only qualified artists could live and work there and that the tax abatement would make the cost a little cheaper, but nothing in SoHo was what you could call cheap. A lovely five-story cast-iron building with Corinthian columns, it was painted white, un- like its drab neighbors. There was an art gallery, Haber's, on the street level and four floor-through artists' residences above. A fabric de- signer named KiKi Marr who Dennis said had been away since before Christmas was on two, Dennis had three, Clifford Cole's loft was on four, and a choreographer named Amy Aronson was on five.

We walked up to Dennis's loft, a deep, wide space, open in the front, facing east, where there would be wonderful morning light, and divided in the back for living.

Dennis's living room was separated from his studio area by a long, low bookshelf painted teal green and some hanging plants so that it would still get the light streaming in from the enormous windows facing the street. By now it was close to four, and the afternoon light was all but faded in the bedroom and kitchen areas.

Dennis turned on some lamps and went to put up the kettle for tea. We had come in frozen from that long walk in the snow. While he waited for the water to boil, he sat down to write me a check. I thanked him, slipped it into my wallet, and took out my notepad.

He hadn't said what sort of artist he was, and oddly, I thought, there was no clear sign in the studio area except that there were drawing boards and stools, three of them, rather than easels. The art hanging on the pale peach-colored walls was obviously done by many artists, and of those where I could see a signature, none were his.

"Was Clifford close to his family?"

"Well, his dad is dead. His mom lives in Maryland, in Frederick.

That's where Cliffie grew up. You should've heard his drawl when he did Barbara Fritchie." He smiled to himself at the memory. "I never used to think of Maryland as the South, you know," he said, "but Cliffie always said it was. He said it surely was."

I had no problem with that. To me, the South started below Canal Street.

"His mother's only been here once," Dennis said. "It was a couple of years ago. Cliff de-gayed the loft and brought everything down here. So I wouldn't say they were too close, no."

"Has she been here since his death?"

"No, only his brother has. He called the next night to ask when I could let him in. He was very quiet, you know, polite, and apologetic about bothering me. It ended up that I left the keys at Haber's for him because I wasn't going to be home when he could come by."

"You never met him?"

"No—never."

"And he didn't have a key?"

"I offered to make him a set, but he said not to bother, he'd just be there a short while and leave the keys back at Haber's. He kept saying that I shouldn't trouble myself. I said anything he wanted was fine with me, wouldn't be any trouble. Shit, the man had just lost his only brother. I didn't mind helping him out, but he said he didn't want to take up any more of my time and that I'd been too kind already. I guess he just wanted to be alone."

"What about the service? Did he say anything about that?"

"He said the service would probably be in Frederick because it was difficult for his mother to travel."

I made some notes, then noticed the silence.

"The truth is, I don't think they want to have any of *us* there. Peter didn't say exactly when it would be, and he certainly didn't ask if I'd come. As far as I know, he never even called Louis at all, not even to say he was sorry. Perhaps he was afraid if his mother met her son's friends, she'd finally have to wake up and hear the Judy Garland records playing. Some people would rather live in denial than know what's going on in their own family. Well, my dear, what would the neighbors say!"

"But Peter knew about his brother, didn't he?"

"How could he not know? He'd have to be blind. Mothers and fathers, especially fathers, that's different. I mean, you could show up for Thanksgiving dinner in *drag* and your parents could miss it. But not a brother. Even if they didn't talk about it, he must have known."

"But you don't know for sure? Clifford didn't talk about Peter, like after he'd seen him? He never mentioned anything they talked about?"

"No. But I didn't find that unusual. I never talk about my family to my friends. Just having to *see* them is more than enough."

Tell me about it, I thought.

"Families, oh, you know. I mean, *they*'re the ones who ought to be in the closet. They're so em*barr*assing."

The kettle had been boiling for a while. He got up and went to the kitchen.

"Dennis, had Peter come up from Frederick?" I asked when he returned with two mugs of tea.

"No, he lives in Jersey," he said, "the *Garden* State." He rolled his eyes. "Fort Lee, I think. He's a teacher, married, two kids, boys. You know, a *nor*mal life. That's all I know. I mean, do *your* friends know your family?"

I took a sip of tea.

"Cliff used to meet Peter uptown, for dinner, once in a while, just the two of them. But not seeing your family too often isn't so unusual. You don't have to be gay to find family relationships stressful."

"This is true," I said. "Dennis, can you give me addresses and phone numbers for Cliff's family and friends?"

"Cliff's address book is upstairs, on his desk."

"And Louis, his lover? Where does he live, in the area?"

"Mmmm, Louie. Louis Lane, believe it or not. He lives on West Fourth Street, near Washington Square Park."

"Is Lane his real name?"

"Is Alexander yours?"

"It is now."

He raised one eyebrow.

"I got it the old-fashioned way—I married it. How did Louis Lane get his?"

"Made it up, for all I know." He suddenly looked uncomfortable.

"Perhaps he wanted something more memorable than his family name."

"Or less ethnic."

"You don't approve?"

He looked away for a moment.

"It was Polski, not that it's any of my business. At least that's what Clifford once told me, but that was after a major row, so maybe Cliffie was just being a bitch."

"I take it you're not terribly fond of Louis Lane."

"Miss Thing? Talk to me after you meet her," he said, rolling his eyes. "I wouldn't want to color your opinion."

Yeah, yeah, I thought.

"What about the handler, that was Morgan Gilmore, right?"

He put his hand up to his forehead and leaned his head into it. "God, I have to call him. He doesn't know about Magritte. And it's what"—he looked at his watch—"the second, less than a week until Westminster. Magritte is entered. I hope he's okay, wherever he is, I just hope he's okay."

I made a mental note to walk around the waterfront area and look over the barricades the next day, but the idea of finding the basenji that way didn't thrill me.

"Who found the body, Dennis? Did the police say?"

"Yes, as a matter of fact, the officers who interviewed me said it was a homeless man who hangs out on West Street."

He proceeded to tell me about the derelict, Billy Pittsburgh, who occasionally earns five or ten dollars and a cup of coffee by wandering into the Sixth Precinct, just across Tenth Street and up the block from where I live, and giving them the location of a wrecked car, a broken store window, or, in this case, a body.

There was a lot more I wanted to know from Dennis, but it was time to see Clifford's loft. I closed my notepad, stood up, and picked up my coat.

"I better get going on this. We don't have any time to waste."

Dennis picked up a set of keys from the top of the bookshelf and handed them to me.

"The round one is for the downstairs door, and the square one is for the loft."

"Can I hang on to these?" I asked. "I'll need to come back here, and I don't want to have to bother you. I sometimes get obsessed with things in the middle of the night and have to check them out, and where I have to check might be Clifford's loft."

"This might help, too," he said, and he took out his wallet and pulled out a worn-looking photograph of Magritte.

I looked at it, nodded, and put it carefully into my wallet.

"By the way, Dennis, when was the last time *you* checked the loft?"

"Three or four days ago. You can't imagine . . . Well, anyway, I had those keys made for you. I figured you'd want to spend time there alone. Too many movies?"

"Probably not enough. Life's too depressing to deal with reality every minute of the day. Sometimes I hate reality."

"Me, too. That's probably why I do what I do. Wait up."

He went to the back of the loft and returned with a book in his hand.

"Here," he said, "for the next time you need an escape from reality."

It was called *Too Big,* and it was written and illustrated by Dennis Mark Keaton. The huge dog on the cover, an Am Staff, looked a lot like Dash.

"Thank you."

"So—how will I know what's happening?" he asked as I headed for the door.

"I'll send you a report, once a week. What's your fax number?"

"Believe it or not, I don't have a fax. I use a messenger service."

"Don't sweat it. I don't have a fax either," I said. "And I hate to write reports. It makes me feel I'm back in school."

I turned the book over and looked at the back cover. A little girl with straight brown hair and round glasses was hugging the big dog, and they both looked deliriously happy.

"Not to worry. I'll call you. Or I'll just draw you a picture from time to time."

I stepped out into the hallway.

"And Dennis, don't hesitate to call me—anytime—if you learn anything new, anything at all, or if you just need to talk. That's okay, too."

I reached into my coat pocket and pulled out a business card and some lint.

"Okay. Good," he said, looking at the card.

It was pretty stark as cards go. It said, "Alexander and Dash, Research Assistance," and the phone number.

"Research assistance?"

"Right. You need some information. We're going to do the necessary research for you."

"I thought you were a PI."

"Maybe you *do* see too many movies," I told him.

I turned to go upstairs, and Dashiell bounded on ahead.

"Rachel," he called after me. "Ditto about calling me. Anytime is okay, day or night. I can't sleep anyway."

4

We Rode Downtown in Silence

AT FIRST, THE blinking red light of the answering machine was the only thing I could see. After a moment, when I got used to the dark, I found a light switch and was startled to discover myself dwarfed by the immensity, power, and beauty of Clifford Cole's paintings, which were hanging and standing everywhere.

I rolled back the tape so that I could hear Cole's messages. There were only a few since Dennis had been here. The one from the National Dog Registry took an easy preference to the others. My heart began racing, even though the dog who had been recovered wasn't my own. In fact, I hadn't even seen him yet.

Or had I? He was the subject of some of the canvases that were wherever my eye went as I called the 800 number that had been left on the machine a day or two earlier.

I explained my relationship to Magritte and apparently said enough of the right things to be given the name and number of the man who claimed to have him. A few minutes later I had spoken with him, and Dashiell and I were on our way.

Henri Plaisir lived in a walk-up on West Nineteenth Street, in Chelsea. After buzzing us in, he and Magritte waited in the open doorway while Dash and I climbed the three flights trying hard not to breathe in too much of the musty smell of the old tenement stairwell. Henri extended his hand to shake mine. For a moment, Magritte stood still as a statue at his side. I had the photo of him Dennis had given me in my wallet and had seen several much-larger-than-life portraits of him at Clifford's loft, but none of this had prepared me for seeing him in the flesh.

He was immaculately clean, almost sparkling, a little foxy-faced boy with small rounded-at-the-top triangular ears and dark, alert eyes. He was a ruddy chestnut brown with white points on his face, chest, paws, and tail, handsome, elegant, and with an uncanny presence, especially considering he weighed not much more than twenty pounds. He was clearly the kind of dog judges say "asks to win," the kind of creature you somehow find yourself drawn to look at, no matter how many other dogs are around. It was no surprise at all that he was so successful in the show ring.

Henri, as he had asked me to call him on the phone, swept us in with a broad gesture of his arm. Magritte came to life. He play-bowed to Dashiell, and all four of us stepped into Henri's one small, neat room, kitchenette on one wall, pull-down bed on another, two bookshelves, a small TV set on top of one of them, a round oak table with two matching chairs, and two doors, one presumably the closet and the other the john.

Late on January 20, Henri's story began, the evening of the day Clifford Cole was murdered and less than a dozen hours after his body was discovered by Billy Pittsburgh, Henri had stopped at Metrometer, the taxi garage on Charles Street, just east of Washington, to have his meter checked. It was there that he first saw the little brown-and-white dog who, cold, dirty, thirsty, hungry, and frightened, had ducked into the open garage.

Henri was from Haiti but had lived here since he was in his late thirties. He and his brother had saved for years to buy a taxi medallion, and now they shared the cab, each working a ten- or eleven-hour shift. That way they got the most use out of it and usually didn't even have the expense of a garage, he said. He had just parked the cab half an hour before I got there, and his brother would take it out at midnight.

He appeared to be in his mid-sixties, a little taller than me which meant he was five-seven or five-eight, about 165 pounds, with close-cropped salt-and-pepper hair, rough-textured, clean-shaven, dark coffee-colored skin, and soft brown eyes. He was wearing a weimaraner-colored cardigan with pockets, the kind I remember from when I was a kid, like the one Mr. Werner who ran the candy store wore, and beige twill pants with a crease. He had just gotten home from parking the cab when I called from Clifford's loft.

"I wasn't looking for a roommate at the time. I just thought my meter was running awful slow, awful slow. But there he was, and the man, he say to me, what am I going to do with this little boy when I close? I don't want to put him out in the weather with his short fur and all this traffic. And I say to him, I only have another hour or two to drive. What harm can it do if he sit in the front with me? I bend down just so." He knelt to show me. "And he just come right up to me. He make this funny sound. Not a bark. He never bark once in all the time I got him. Like a trill in his throat, he make. And I just lose my heart to him right there on the spot. Can I offer you a cup of tea, Rachel?" he asked.

I nodded.

"I didn't see the tattoo right off," Henri said as I sat at the little table. "And there was no collar, so no tag. But I figured that if I was so taken with this little boy, someone else must be heartbroken. I never thought anyone had throw him away, but that he got lost somehow. So I begin to take him with me every day. I never got such good tips," he said, shaking his head. "No, sir.

"I put some signs up, near the garage in the West Village. But no one call me. On the third day I have him, I was not going to drive the cab, so I decided to give Jimmy here a bath. I been calling him Jimmy, and he likes the name very much, don't you, Jimmy?"

Magritte looked up when Henri addressed him. Then he went back to bringing all his toys to Dashiell. There were quite a number of them, considering how short a time the dog had lived here.

"So, that's when I found the tattoo, and I wonder why someone would tattoo numbers on the inside right thigh of a dog, so from then on, whoever I pick up in the taxi, I ask them. I figure someone will know, and then I will know.

"The day I called it in, Rachel, my fare says to me I should pull over, and he looks at the tattoo and he says, 'Nine digits, it's a social security number. You have to call the National Dog Registry in Woodstock. They'll have the name and address of the owner.' So I am so happy to get my question answered and to learn something new. And I am so sad that I will lose my friend Jimmy here. He's been good company for me.

"He even know the number, this man, 1-800-NDR-DOGS. His German shepherd, he say, is tattooed also. So I call it. And so here you are."

He sipped his tea, I ate most of the cookies he had placed on the table, and then we sat in silence for a while, watching Magritte wrestle with Dash.

"You wouldn't think that big one would be so gentle," Henri said. "Not even a growl when little Jimmy jumps all over him."

I nodded, my mouth too full of Pepperidge Farm Chessmen for me to speak. One of the reasons people are so afraid of pit bulls is that they usually don't growl, even when they have ample reason to do so. If there's anything scarier than a dog making a racket, it's a silent one, especially if he's not making a fuss because it's clear he knows he doesn't have to in order to get the respect he's after.

"Listen, Henri," I said when there was nothing left to eat, "I'd like to offer you a reward. My client is going to be so thrilled. I just can't tell you what this will mean to him."

I reached into my coat pocket for my wallet. There was a fifty tucked away behind the picture of Dash, for emergencies.

"I don't want your money, Rachel." He shook his head back and forth and reached his hand out to pat my other hand. "It's been a privilege to have little Jimmy here with me."

"It's not my money, Henri. As I told you, I'm not Magritte's owner. That young man was killed, and I work for the new owner. And he, my client, would be happy for me to give you something." Of course, I hadn't told Dennis what I had discovered yet. I wanted to have the dog before I got his hopes up, to see for myself that he was okay. And even though the call had come through NDR, I wasn't about to send him out to retrieve the dog when its disappearance might have been connected to a murder. Somehow, when I heard Henri's voice on the phone—I pay a lot of attention to the sound of people's voices—I lost most, but not all, of my caution.

"No, no, I couldn't take it," Henri said. "It would give Jimmy here the wrong message." At the sound of his name, Magritte, aka Jimmy Plaisir, jumped as sprightly as any cat and landed on Henri's lap. Henri began to scratch the dog's chest very gently, stroking him again and again, and I noticed how still Magritte stood on his friend's lap and how he closed his eyes to concentrate on the pleasure.

"How about expenses?" I asked. "That's certainly fair."

"Well, he did chew up some shoes for me," Henri said. He began to laugh. "I didn't tell you that part, did I? Oh, he can be a devil, this one."

"I know exactly what you mean," I said. "I used to train dogs for a living. We call these 'brat dogs.'"

"I like that," he said.

I lifted the saltshaker and placed the fifty and my business card under it.

"If you should hear anything that might relate to the murder, Henri, you can call me anytime. I should be getting him home now. I can't thank you enough. Who knows what would have happened to this dog without you?"

It was nearly eleven when I was ready to leave Henri's apartment with Magritte. Henri kept one toy, a bug-eyed green frog, "for memories," he said, "and in case he come back sometime to visit his friend Henri." He insisted I take the rest of the toys, as well as half a bag of Science Diet and two cans of Kal Kan chopped beef. Then he decided he had better drive me to SoHo, because how else was I going to get there with a bag of food and toys and two dogs? and anyway, he said, it would give him a chance to give Jimmy one more ride in the cab.

We rode downtown in silence. Henri and Magritte were in the front. Dashiell and I rode in the back. Of course, the meter was off, so every few blocks someone stepped out into the street and tried to flag us down. Henri had asked where I live, and when I told him I lived in the Village, he insisted on waiting for me and driving me and Dash home. It took a bit of work, but I finally convinced him that Dashiell needed one more walk anyway, that I'd be perfectly safe walking anywhere with a pit bull, and that, if worse came to worst, I no longer had enough in my wallet to worry about. At that he laughed and finally agreed to let me off at the loft.

I hadn't done any of the work I had planned to do at Clifford's loft, and I was too tired and much too hungry to start now. But as I hiked up the stairs with Dashiell and Magritte, I felt I had done well for my first day on the job. I hoped Dennis wouldn't be spoiled and think the rest of the work would go this well or this quickly. And I hoped he wouldn't catch on immediately that I hadn't done anything at all to recover Magritte except listen to the messages on Clifford Cole's answering machine, just as he would have done had he gone to the loft before me or even with me.

What is detective work if not, at least in part, doing all the obvious things, looking at mail and listening to messages, talking to people who knew the victim, talking to people in the neighborhood and in the area of the crime scene in the hope that someone saw something, even if, at the time, they didn't know if what they saw was significant, and just stabbing around in the dark, hoping to find something somewhere that will point you toward the light? Finding Magritte was wonderful and satisfying, but what, if anything, did he have to do with the murder? As for finding the answer to that and every other question, I hadn't even begun.

5

You Don't Know Me

IT WAS A cold walk home. I unlocked the wrought-iron gate and followed Dash down the narrow covered brick passageway between two town houses into the large, square garden, in the far left corner of which is the brick cottage Dash and I gratefully call home. Though it sounds grand, it isn't. What is grand is the deal I got.

Sheldon and Norma Siegal, who own the town house on the left and the cottage, are rarely around, so more than a tenant, they wanted a caretaker, someone to watch over the house whenever they're away. In exchange for services rendered, the rent I pay is nominal. Which is exactly what I can afford.

The cottage has two floors of living space and a basement for storage. There are two small bedrooms and a bathroom on the top floor, a living room with a fireplace and a small, open kitchen on the main floor, and one big room, with another bathroom, downstairs.

Downstairs is where I keep all the things I still haven't unpacked since I moved here four years ago. I simply haven't found the need for good crystal in my current lifestyle.

The house works well for us, storing all the books, files, and rawhide bones we need to keep us reasonably happy. But best of all is the garden, wonderful when it snows, because Dash gets to make the first paw prints, terrific in spring when the perennial herbs and flowers return as if by magic, amazingly cool in summer, especially in the evening and at night, and mysterious and sad in the fall when the cycle draws to an end in a blaze of beauty, all hidden from Tenth Street and the rest of the world.

I unlocked the door, flicked on the light, fed Dashiell, and went straight up to bed. I had the tape from Clifford Cole's answering machine in my coat pocket, where I had put it before leaving the loft, replacing it with a new tape I found in the drawer of the table the machine sat on. I had wanted to hear it again, but suddenly the day caught up to me and I could no longer think of anything but sleep.

There were only three messages on the tape, anyway. The National Dog Registry, someone selling home delivery of the *New York Times*, and a squeaky-voiced lady who wanted to mate her bitch to Magritte, that adorable little stud.

Dashiell was already asleep. I closed my eyes and thought about Dennis's reunion with Magritte. I had knocked on the door and when he asked who was there I had said, It's me, Rachel, I'm ready to draw you that first picture. When he opened the door, the basenji dog had squealed. Dennis had bent down, and the little dog had kissed him all over his face. I thought about the look in Dennis's eyes, when he finally could take them off his dog.

I also believed my dog to be the best thing since indoor plumbing. I had rescued Dashiell from some wrong headed, mean-spirited young entrepreneurs I had run into on a case, people who planned to make money fighting him when he grew up. I liberated him in such a fashion, let's say, that I didn't take the time to get his pedigree.

Sometimes when the right dog finds you, he has papers. Sometimes he doesn't. Hey, I have papers. My divorce document. It's not much to curl up against on a cold night. A dog is much better suited for that job.

Hugging Dashiell, I fell asleep happy, but I woke up in the middle of the night with a start. Was it a dream that woke me? I couldn't remember. All I could remember was that sign at the pier.

Don't be caught alone.

I almost always was, more and more of late. I was thirty-eight, suspicious, competitive, too independent on the surface for the taste of most of the men I met, and under the surface, much too frightened to suit my own.

Even if I could have fallen asleep again, it wouldn't have been worth lying there and rehashing my whole life before I finally got fed up enough to sleep. I got up and went into the spare bedroom, a little two-by-four job where I did my paperwork.

Dennis's book was on the desk where I had tossed it earlier. I took it onto the guest bed, slid under the blankets, and began to read about Antonia, who was five and who had always wanted a dog, ever since she was four and a half. When she finds Eliot, she is sure that he was meant to be hers.

"I guess it wasn't meant to be," I told my sister, Lillian, after the divorce.

"Well," she said, meaning "bullshit," meaning she thought I had fucked up again, "what are you going to do *now*?" meaning now that I had ruined my life, just as she always knew I would.

"Move back to the city," I said. "I never should have left. And get a dog!"

"You're not going back to dog training, are you? Why don't you get a normal job, Rachel?"

"I don't know," I said, thinking of how much I hated going backward.

I had closed the school and moved to Westchester so Jack and I could have a "normal life," whatever that was. What had I been thinking! But it was done, and now I'd have to go forward. But to what?

"Look, maybe until you think of something else, Ted could—"

Oh, God. I was filled with panic at the thought of working in the garment industry.

"Well," I said, wanting to make her as miserable as she had just made me, "I've always wanted to be a detective."

It was simply the most annoying thing I could think of on such short notice.

"Rachel, have you completely lost your mind!"

I had a strong suspicion it was a rhetorical question, so I didn't bother to answer her.

"You know, I can really see myself doing investigation work. Jack always said I was the nosiest bitch he ever met, or maybe that was just during the financial disclosure part of the divorce. Anyway, the hours would suit me, and I wouldn't have to wear panty hose."

"A *detective*," she bellowed, "so now that you're finished being Clyde Beatty you're going to become Dickless Tracy?"

Just like that, for the first time in eight months I started to feel like myself again.

"Oh my God, Rachel, tell me you're not serious."

"I can't. I am."

Of course I wasn't. Not yet, anyway. I was just having some fun for a change.

"Rachel!" She was fairly hysterical by now. "Rachel—you wouldn't. You wouldn't dare!"

That's when I knew it was *bashert*, meant to be. I never could resist a dare from Lillian.

I looked at Dennis's ink and watercolor wash drawing of Eliot, realizing as I did that the black stains on his pants and shoes had probably been made by india ink. I mean, was I a born detective, or what?

And what was Lillian carrying on about? This was only my second stab at what she calls the dirt-bag professions. She needn't worry about the other three. Selling insurance has never appealed to me. I'm more interested in who than how much. And on my worst day I'd never consider real estate or the used-car business. Sure, I follow people, eavesdrop, go through people's garbage and read their mail, snoop, distort, deceive, and misrepresent. I even do a little B & E if it's absolutely necessary. But, hey, I have my pride.

I looked at Eliot again, a mountain of a dog, big, square head, thick and stolid, uncropped flying-buttress ears, large, meaty mouth, closed and serious for now. I studied every part of him, the massive chest, the strong, straight legs, the neat, large, rounded feet, so like Dashiell in every way except for coloring. Eliot was a brindle. Dashiell, except for the black patch on his right eye, is white.

"Please may I keep him, Mommy, may I, Mommy, please?"

"He's too big for you to walk," Antonia's mother said, as sensible as my big sister, Lillian.

"He's too big for us to feed."

"And where will he sleep? He's much too big to sleep in your bed."

But there they are, on the last page, in Antonia's bed, and, see, they fit just fine.

Bashert, my grandmother Sonya used to say.

I closed Dennis's book and dropped it onto the floor.

"You don't know me," he had said when he called me.

Was that just this afternoon?

"I got your name from someone in the neighborhood, but you don't know her. You did some work for her cousin about a year ago. Ellen Engel? And now I need your help. I need it badly."

Jack had said it, too, the first time he'd called.

"You don't know me."

There was a silence then, as we both waited.

"I got your number from your brother-in-law. Ted."

"Oh," I had said, my voice catching in my throat.

I closed my eyes and thought about the last message on the tape from Clifford's answering machine.

"You don't know me," a woman's voice had said, "but I have a beautiful basenji bitch, pointed, she just needs one more major, and I was interested in Magritte, you know, if you hire him out at stud."

Sex, it can fucking ruin you.

6

It Looked Like an Enormous Bowling Ball

IT WAS SO cold when I got up, I could see my breath indoors. One disadvantage of living in the cottage is that I get to pay my own heat bill, and by necessity and nature I'm cheap. If Dashiell were a malamute, I could say I keep the place as cold as the inside of a refrigerator to prevent him from blowing his coat. But the truth is, if he were a malamute, he'd blow it anyway. You really *can't* fool Mother Nature.

I went downstairs and opened the front door for Dash. A moment later, he was back with the *New York Times*, which gets pitched over the locked gate in an electric blue plastic bag.

It was going to be cold and windy with a chance of snow toward evening, the homeless were causing safety and sanitation problems at Penn Station, Tiffany's was advertising a diamond bracelet for about the price of a one-bedroom apartment, and a man in Oregon had poisoned his wife, who, the *Times* reported, had survived to testify at his trial, in his defense.

I fed Dashiell, got dressed, and headed downtown to Clifford Cole's loft.

Where Dennis had warmed the cavernous space with color, Cliff's studio area was white—tin ceiling, walls, and wooden floor all done in a shiny enamel so that when I arrived, the sun was bouncing off whatever surface it hit, except of course the paintings, where the light seemed to become absorbed into the canvas. The paintings apparently had not been touched since the murder, and I made a note to find out who owned them now. Then I took some photographs of the studio.

All the paintings in the large room were Cliff's, all huge, some telling their story in three or even four canvases. There was one set of three canvases, hung so that there were only inches between where one stopped and the next began, that took up the entire north wall of the huge space. The first canvas showed a pale blue wall with a window. Out the window was a single branch with buds, a March branch, and on the pale wooden floor a yellow and black ball, the kind that squeaks when squeezed. The second canvas showed more of the same place, blue wall, no window this time, a single wooden chair with a black baseball cap with a red B on it hanging over the left-hand corner of the ladderback, a green frog under the chair, the same kind Henri had gotten for his Jimmy dog and then kept "for memories." The third canvas showed the blue wall, the pickled whitish wooden floor, and the back end of Magritte, as if he had been caught walking out of the picture. In the lower right-hand corner of the last panel of the triptych, Clifford had printed the title of the painting in small, neat letters, all lowercase: *out, damned spot.*

There was another painting of Magritte on the south wall, this one called *rising son.* It showed another underfurnished room. Even the paint was used starkly in these portraits. The color was rich, but the brush strokes were very even, and you could see the texture of the canvas as part of the painting. At the top of the portrait, you could see the white-socked feet of the basenji, as if this time Magritte were floating up out of his own portrait.

There were two paintings standing against that wall, both done at the beach. In one, an oversize close-up of part of a wooden beach house, painted in shades of gray: you could see through the large window that it was raining *indoors.* The small printed title read *home, sweet home.* The other painting showed Magritte leaning out the window, elbows on the sill, a cigarette dangling from his tight lips, like the lonely men you see looking out of tenement windows in the city. Even Magritte was done in gray, so that the painting resembled a black-and-white photograph. It was called *he never read the surgeon general's report.*

I began to wander around the loft, just to get a feel for the space and to see where things were. I wanted Dashiell to take a look at things, too, the way dogs do, with their noses. So as I walked and he sniffed, every once in a while, I told him, "Smell it, good boy!" to let him know he wasn't just being nosy, he was working. I never know what Dash will come up with, but I always know that it will be very different from what I can "see." I put the kettle up, took out a big white mug, and found a box of Earl Grey tea bags. It was a cook's kitchen—good equipment, lots of expensive, shiny copper-bottomed pots hanging above. There was no microwave, but there was a Cuisinart and a professional-size mixer.

Dash and I continued wandering while the kettle heated. Cliff's bedroom, facing west, was high enough to get good light even though it faced the back of a building on Wooster Street. There was enough space for the light to filter down, enough to give the room a lovely cast, but not enough to blind you when you were trying to sleep. The bed, unmade, was a double, and the sheets and quilt were white, as were the walls, the floor, the rug, and the long, low painted dresser.

There was a four-panel painting hanging over the bed, titled *up*. In the first three panels there was a man asleep in a bed, in the very bed beneath the portrait, down to the last detail. Those three pictures were identical but for one detail, a slight change in the position of the head on the pillow, a dark head of hair poking out from the white quilt, the face not visible. In the last panel, the bed was rumpled and empty. Somehow I was sure the mysterious man was Louis Lane, that in this way, he did indeed sleep over.

Above the dresser there was a smaller painting with a dark, brooding, and sexually suggestive look, a Diane Arbusy portrait of two young boys, one on each side of the canvas. The empty space between the boys gave the portrait a palpable tension. Both boys looked ahead, at the viewer, as if unaware of each other. They were nude. The boy on the left was a cherubic-looking six- or seven-year-old, with large, apprehensive hazel eyes. The boy on the right, the older of the two, a ten- or eleven-year-old, had a lewd expression on his face. In the usual spot, it said *les and mor*.

Cliff's work was more intellectual than emotional, more Magritte than Matisse. Even the disturbing pieces had a coldness to them; they were either fascinating or clever but kept the viewer at a distance rather than embracing him, rather than bringing him into the painting or into the heart of the artist. Whatever emotion was visible was well controlled, as if the hurt could be displayed visually but without the accompanying feeling. I wondered how the work reflected the man, but it's not possible to put together a person from the pieces of his life. You can't even come close.

At the side of the bed there was another Magritte, the Clifford kind, the chestnut-and-white dog flying over the rooftops of what appeared to be Paris, a basenji angel with creamy, feathered wings. I wondered if Louis had seen *good boy*, and if he had indeed been jealous of his demanding, adored rival.

I opened the drawers of the nightstands and pawed through the dead man's personal stuff—condoms, K-Y jelly, handcuffs, nothing unusual.

I opened the closet and looked at the clothes, good-quality pants and jackets and lots of them, not the kind of clothes I'd expect to find in a poor artist's closet. Jack, who dressed like a peacock when he wasn't filling cavities (no pun intended, the man is a dentist), had introduced me to designer clothes, and now I could tell without even checking the labels. Cliff was apparently slight; his butterscotch-colored suede jacket fit me perfectly.

When I heard the kettle, I put Cliff's jacket away and went back to the kitchen, adding up in my head the cost of what I had seen in the closet, then opening the cabinets and toting up how much Clifford had spent to outfit his kitchen. Poor artist indeed. Perhaps the man had a patron.

Louis Lane?

I took my tea over to a desk that sat in a little in-between area, open, of course, because it had no window. It was a cozy nook with a desk, a rich, red oriental rug, red walls, and a red velvet chair, some-place to read, listen to music, watch videos, pay the bills.

There were two drawings and a painting in the den that were not Cliff's—a lovely pencil sketch of Magritte, signed "Jan Bella," a pen-and-ink nude, male, signed "D. K." (the D. K. who was helping me pay my bills?), and a smallish watercolor head study of a sweetly hand-some young man with a halo of curly hair, signed "john."

I sat at the desk and began to open drawers, and what I found told me that there were some pretty important things that Dennis Keaton did not know about his friend.

The first file I found was the one for Clifford's Fidelity Corporate Bond Fund. His current investment was in the neighborhood of $200,000, give or take a few thou.

The next file was an IRA, with Dreyfus. That was only valued at $22,611.16, but hell, the man had only been thirty-two.

His checkbook—Chemical Bank Select Checking, which, according to the brochure of bank costs in the file, required a minimum balance of $25,000, entitling Cliff to free checking, free telephone transfers, the privilege of larger ATM withdrawals, and a shorter line when he had to show up at the bank in person—had a balance of $44,682.13 in savings and only $132.11 in checking after a cash withdrawal of $1,000 made January 18, the day before he died. Clifford had neatly recorded the withdrawal both in his checkbook and on the bottom of the previous bank statement. But I hadn't needed to see that to know he was an obsessive-compulsive personality type. I had seen his pots.

I had also found money in many of his pockets, along with small sandwich bags for picking up after Magritte. As with every other New York City dog owner, every pocket, including the ones in his tux jacket, had plastic bags in it, because even if you've been out to a black-tie event, you still have to walk your dog and scoop when you get home.

Magritte's papers were in the desk, too, neatly filed like everything else. He was four and a half. His health was protected by the Murray Hill Animal Hospital on East Thirtieth Street. He had, I noticed, been vaccinated against Lyme disease, which probably meant he was taken out of the city regularly, perhaps to outdoor dog shows, and his rabies shot was up to date. He was indeed a champion of record, American, Canadian Ch. Ceci N'Est Pas un Chien. Clever, Clifford, mighty clever, I thought, and then, when the next certificate was in my hand, I was filled with admiration. It seems Magritte had a C.D., a Companion Dog degree, which meant he had satisfactorily performed all the basic commands off lead at three different AKC obedience trials and under three different judges, no small feat for a basenji.

There were photos in the file, too. In all three, Magritte was stacked, meaning he was standing in show pose, and a handler, a tall man with a ponytail, presumably Morgan Gilmore, was holding the show lead taut and beaming. The judge was in the photos, too, holding the blue ribbon and whatever bowl or platter Magritte had won at each of the three shows.

I found Cliff's gallery contract, signed by Veronica Cahill. Most interesting, there was even a copy of his will in the file drawer, with a note saying the original copy was filed with George Rich, his lawyer.

The most recent check register showed regular monthly payments to a Dr. Bertram Kleinman. I checked the medicine cabinet. There was no AZT, DDI, Bactrim, or even Flagyl. It didn't appear Cliff had active AIDS. There was no Prednisone or allergy medication.

Was Dr. Kleinman a chiropractor or a shrink?

From the amount of the checks, and the little drawings on them, two men emoting in kind, my guess was that Clifford Cole was in some sort of interactive therapy.

A gay man in therapy—what a surprise.

After another thirty or forty minutes of poking around, I took Cliff's will, the gallery contract, his address book, and Dashiell and headed for the closest copy shop, returning everything to where we found it before heading back for another look at the Christopher Street pier. But when we left the loft, I decided to walk over to the gallery first, just to take a look around and see what I might find out.

The Veronica Cahill Gallery was on the fifth floor of a wide ten-story brick building on West Broadway between Prince and Spring. To get to the gallery, you take one of those elevators that open on either side, depending upon which side you push the button, which depends upon which of the two galleries on each floor you are going to. The elevator opened right into the gallery spaces, which, like most of the West Broadway spaces, were large and bright.

The current installation at Cahill was called Dots, and the most enigmatic dot for me was the single sculpture placed in the middle of the gallery's white floor. It looked like an enormous bowling ball, but without the holes. It was titled *Black Dot*. The price on the title card was $25,000, and amazingly, there was a red dot on the card, signifying that this lucky dot had found a home. The paintings were also fairly large, although there were a few small ones toward the back of the gallery. They consisted of various canvases painted either white with one or more black circles or, for variety, black with one or several white circles. Prices were all in the ten- to twelve-thousand range. Several of those were sold as well. To each his own.

Dashiell and I had been welcomed by a short young blond with the proportions of a twelve-year-old, no hips, no tits, dressed all in black but, happily, without a dot on her outfit. He was offered a dog biscuit, and I was told about how fabulously well this young artist was doing, asked if I knew "Tess," if I had been at the opening, which was fabulous, if I was a collector, and then followed around as I looked at paintings, as if I might, if not watched carefully, slip one into my pocket.

The more I looked, the more I began to wonder if the red dots signifying sales were all real or if perhaps the gallery put out a few to make people think their current installation was hot and start a buying frenzy.

"This is nice," I said, trying to look sincere, "but what I really love are paintings of dogs. I sort of, you know, collect them."

I gave her the perfect opportunity to hard sell me a Clifford Cole painting. She fumbled the dot, but made a slight recovery.

"I don't know what's going to be in the next show. But would you like to be on our mailing list?"

I signed a false name in the book, thanked the young woman profusely, turned down a second Snausage for Dashiell, and headed back to the Christopher Street pier.

7

I Began to Dig Carefully

I WANTED DASHIELL in a work mode, so I kept him on leash until we were on the pier. Then I pointed down the pier, told him, "Find it," and let him go.

I pulled up my scarf so that it covered my nose and mouth and walked back to the Punk's Not Dead sign, the one closest to where Clifford had been struck. The sad face with spiked hair was still watching over the place where he had lain until the police came to zip him into a body bag and take him away.

The wind was cold and stinging. Loose snow swirled in circles, rose up momentarily, and fell back to the surface of the pier. On a summer weekend, dozens and dozens of gay men would come here to lie in the sun. In winter, it was a lonely place.

Dashiell was working the southern side of the pier. He would work the perimeter first, then quarter the pier and work each quadrant separately, in each case looking for something that didn't belong. That meant he would not alert if he found a condom. The pier was littered with them, both over and under the snow. Nor would he stand and bark for me, his front feet popping up off the ground with each woof, his ears flapping up and down in the wind he himself would create in his excitement, for beer cans, broken glass, cigarette butts, even underwear. These were all local weeds to him, things indigenous to the area.

Two types of things would get him to "call me." He'd signal for anything out of place, like a button, a wallet, or, say, a gun. In this case, it was unlikely he'd find anything of value. It had been too long since the murder, and the pier was too open and too populated. But Dash would also be looking for anything that had a smell reminiscent of anything at the loft. He had nosed around Cliff's clothing and his shoes. I had even dumped the hamper for him, letting him smell crotches and arm holes, places where the scent would be the most powerful. He had picked up other scents as well, those he would find personally interesting.

I didn't really expect there'd be anything on the pier after all this time, but Dashiell had made some wonderful finds on previous cases, things too well hidden, intentionally or by accident, or too small for me to have discovered. After glancing back at him, now rounding the corner to work the far end of the barricade, I stood at the south fence and looked out over the Hudson.

I could see the Statue of Liberty, far to the south, and Jersey farther west. The water surrounding the pier where you first walk onto it was frozen, but out here the Hudson was flowing, the light giving it a lovely silver cast.

I began wondering about the money, all that money, and where it came from, and why Clifford's friend Dennis didn't know about it.

Well, as my sister would say, hands on her hips, if your friend was busting his butt to make it, unable to have the freedom to paint, as you did, would you rub it in his face that you didn't have to be concerned about expenses?

When I heard Dash signal, I began to run. He had made a find. It was probably nothing of significance to the case, a cigarette lighter or an old shoe someone had left on the pier. But I needed to get to him quickly and to praise him to the sky. He couldn't discern what would be important and what wouldn't. Sometimes I couldn't at first. The only way to motivate him was to praise for every find, and hope like hell, if there was something there of significance, eventually he'd see that, too.

He was at the most westerly point of the pier he could reach, the last few feet blocked off by the chain-link fence. The sign there, this one official, warned of danger—Area Unsafe, Keep Off—but I could see where the fence was cut. This was New York, where warnings went unheeded.

Dashiell was sitting now, facing a snowdrift that had accumulated against the fence, just to the right of the warning sign on the other side. He always waited for me, never trying to bring me what he found. If he retrieved the item, were there prints, he'd blur them. In a different setting, a field or woods, if he brought me what he found, I'd never see the site to be able to look for other signs and clues. Most important, because I loved my dog, if I allowed him to pick up what he found on a search, he might get hurt. He could pick up—and drop—a gun, which might go off. He could find something toxic, something sharp, something that, when disturbed, would leave nothing in its wake but a huge hole and the smell of smoke.

When he saw me running toward him, he stopped barking. As soon as I reached him, he was on his feet, dancing excitedly as he looked from me into the snow piled against the fence and back, again and again.

I began to dig carefully, cracking through the crust, then brushing away the snow, a little at a time, with my gloved hands.

I felt it before I saw it, and the moment I touched it, I knew. As I lifted a piece of it carefully free of the snow, I could hear it, too, a faint, metallic tinkle. I cleared the rest of the snow more quickly, and there, tied to the very bottom of the fence, was a red leather leash, now wet, stretched, and twisted. Still attached to the leash clip was a red leather collar, complete with a small bell, fairly intact, and in my estimation, just about the perfect size to fit around the neck of a twenty-pound dog.

I knelt on the pier and opened my arms for Dashiell, folding him to my chest as he came for his hug. I slipped the Minox out of my pocket and photographed the leash and collar where it was before untying it and stuffing it into my pocket with the camera. Dashiell danced around for more praise, which he got as I checked the area as carefully as I could and then headed for home.

If the collar and leash Dashiell had found were Magritte's, then Clifford had definitely taken him along to the pier. But why? As a pickup aid? Lord knows, more people talk to me when I'm with Dashiell than when I'm alone. So was Magritte tied to the fence while Clifford had sex? If you took a rough count of the condoms that littered the pier, it was certain that, despite the weather, Clifford wouldn't have been the only one having sex out here.

I needed to talk to Louis Lane and see how they were getting along. Was it spite that brought him here, or hunger? And what about all that money? Why did he come out here with so much cash in his pocket? Did he simply have so much he was careless? The money in so many pockets back at the loft would lead me to think that might be the case.

Suddenly, I was famished. Craving a ham and melted brie on sourdough bread, I headed for Anglers and Writers, across from the ball field.

New York's laws prohibit animals on public transportation and in places where food is served, but since Dash, who schmoozes the old people at the Village Nursing Home when I am between cases, is a registered service dog, and perpetually in training, the restriction doesn't apply to him.

Being a detective is a lonely life, but at least I never have to eat out without a date.

8

You Don't Really Belong in This Family

GETTING INTO BED with the copy of Clifford Cole's will, gallery contract, address book, and a yellow highlighter looked to be the most promising evening I'd had in a long time.

The original will, which dated back to when Clifford was in his mid-twenties, was mostly the legal jargon that makes what should be three or four sentences go on for pages. Most people that young don't write a will, especially if they don't have kids. Unless their money is family money, and part of the deal when they get it is that it stays in the family.

In the original document, Clifford left everything to his beloved mother, Adrienne Wynton Cole, and, should she predecease him, to his beloved brother, Peter David Cole. This could mean that his father had already died when the will was written or that the money came from his mother or her family in the first place. Of course, once he had the money, in whatever form he got it, lump sum, generous allowance, untouchable trust where he could draw a set amount of the interest, or whatever, no one could require him to leave it to a person of their choosing. So he was either young or very honorable, or both. Or perhaps no one he preferred to leave the money to had yet come along. Follow the money. It was the first law of investigation work.

I turned to the next document, one of two codicils, both much more recent than the original will. It left the little African basenji, Ceci N'Est Pas un Chien, who apparently was not yet a champion, to Dennis Mark Rosenberg, aka Dennis Mark Keaton.

People are usually most defensive, my shrink used to say, about things that hit too close to home. Now, Rachel, she'd say after an outburst of denial, what's *really* going on here?

Of course, Dennis could dislike Louis for any number of other reasons. It's not uncommon for people to be jealous of their best friend's lover. I wondered if Dennis and Cliff had been lovers before Louis came onto the scene. Or even afterward. I checked the date of the codicil, but it turned out the one I had just read was the second. Perhaps when I checked to make sure I had everything ready to be copied I had gotten them out of order. The first of the two codicils was two years old, and left Clifford's entire artistic estate to Leonard Polski, aka Louis Lane. The Magritte codicil was dated a year and a half ago, five and a half months later.

If Cliff wasn't accepted by his family, he still kept faith with them financially. He probably knew he had to anyway. His will would be contested if he didn't, that is, unless he had been leading one of those normal lives your well-meaning relatives always tell you about, a life with a spouse of the opposite sex and children.

Dennis thought Cliff's "problem" was a problem for his family. Had they told Cliff, the way families do, that he could change if he wanted to? Had they offered to pay for therapy?

Would they have wanted either Magritte or Clifford's paintings? I wondered if his mother or his brother would have come to his show, had he lived long enough for the gallery to actually install it.

I thought about the coolness in his paintings, perhaps because he felt apart from his natural family, felt Magritte, of *rising son,* and his other heirs, Louis and Dennis, were his real family. If he left the paintings to Louis, he must have felt good about the relationship, at least at the time the codicil was written.

I picked up the gallery contract. How much of the post-eighties art world bust of the pay-the-piper nineties was reflected in Clifford Cole's contract with the Cahill Gallery I didn't know. I had never read a gallery contract before. I knew that a lot of the SoHo galleries had closed, and the remaining ones were often empty, run by people as desperate as the woman who had followed me around the Dots installation at Cahill earlier in the day. I have always found it amusing when someone tries to talk you into buying a so-called piece of art that costs more than your yearly gross.

There were still some wonderful things to see in the downtown galleries, works like Clifford Cole's that would linger in memory, where the range and ability of the artist actually merited the space his work occupied. Unfortunately, much of what was on display for eighties prices made me want to call the bunko squad. But there's no such thing, other than for forgery, in the art world. It's not a crime to produce derivative, dull, or simply poor "works," as the contract calls what the artist produces. It's simply a matter of taste.

Clifford's first contract was surprisingly short and simple, free of the jargon of wills, mortgages, and divorce documents. The gallery would determine the price, and the artist could not sell comparable works for less. The gallery would receive 50 percent not only of the price of works sold at the exhibition it would install but of any sales made by the artist from his studio that were a direct result of the representation and the exhibition at the Cahill Gallery, and even any nonrelated sales made out of the artist's studio for the duration of the agreement, which was one year. It was sort of the same deal real estate brokers love home owners to sign, stating that if the owner sells his home during the time of the broker's contract, even in cases where the broker has done nothing but sit on her ass and never advertised or shown the house, she will still receive 6 percent of the sale price. Nice work if you can get it.

The Cahill Gallery got first pick of all of Cliff's art, which meant that Cliff—now Louis—couldn't sell anything without giving the Cahill Gallery half the money, even if they never gave Clifford a show. I wondered what Leonard Polski would do with his inheritance. I hadn't seen most of the paintings. They were draped and standing in a huge storage closet opposite the den, and the light in the closet didn't work. Next time I'd bring a flashlight and look at the rest of Leonard's loot.

I flipped through Clifford's address book. There were lots of names of galleries, other places he had probably sent a padded manila envelope with his résumé, slides, SASE, and lots of hope. I liked his work a lot better than much of what I see in SoHo, but there was no way I could judge if it ever would have become hot enough to sell. Often that has as much to do with an artist's life or who he knows as it has to do with his ability or originality.

I wondered if Clifford had gotten depressed about his inability to sell his "works." He had probably been elated the day he signed the contract. That had been November 16, which would mean he had been working on things for his show since then. There had been no date set, no promise of how soon it would be or how many of his works would be included. Most shows were up for a three-week period, during which there would be an opening, often stacked with the artist's friends and sometimes, like the invitations, paid for by the artist. But then you had the chance to hope, and who could put a price tag on what that was worth? There might be a sale, a visit by a critic, a positive line in the press. You might, after all, have a chance.

Peter Cole did not live in Fort Lee, but Woodcliff Lake. I found Morgan Gilmore's number, too. He lived in Greensboro, North Carolina. I marked it with the highlighter, then put it on the nightstand with the rest of the papers.

In the morning, I'd try to reach Louis Lane. After that, I'd start looking for Billy Pittsburgh, who, I suspected, was using a name other than the one he had been given as a child.

What did it all mean, all this name changing? I had even done it myself.

When I took Jack's name, I had thrown away my own. I had detached myself from my past and my family. When we split, I chose to keep his name, not my own, even though I had used it for less than a year. I had set myself adrift. I had even rejected my profession, taking a job with the Petrie Detective Agency on lower Broadway, run by two brothers, Bruce and Frank.

I didn't actually meet the older Petrie, Bruce, until I had been working at the agency for two and a half months. He was obsessed with electronic equipment for both surveillance and criminal activities. Every few months or so he'd surface from his windowless back office and show us the specs on the latest eavesdropping equipment, voice-changing telephone, letter bomb scanner, or microcamera in a key chain.

It was Frank who had hired me to work as a junior undercover agent trainee, meaning I would do the same work as the regular agents but for much less money, because, as he so wisely explained, what if you're following a guy and he goes into the men's room and there's another way out? And when I presented the same scenario with a woman being followed, he had shoved some papers around on his desk and said he couldn't sit around all day and waste his valuable time arguing with me, there was work to be done, and did I want the job or not? I said I did. When I got home, I called Lili.

Why do you want to put yourself on the outside looking in? she asked, one of her usual rhetorical questions. No, she said, changing her mind, for you, that would be an improvement. You won't have time to press your nose against the glass. You'll be too busy looking inside other people's garbage cans to even wonder about how normal people live. You don't really belong in the family, she said.

Family, Dennis had said, *oh, you know.*

Frank Petrie had put a tail on me right after he'd hired me, a real geek.

Hey, you never know, the Pinkertons could have sent me to find out all his secrets.

The tail was so ugly, you couldn't miss him from a mile away. It did not require a genius to figure out what was going on. I called Frank.

"Next time," I told him, "send someone less memorable."

"Good work, kid," he said. "You might not be a total loss after all."

Now, why couldn't anyone in my own family ever say anything that supportive!

9

You Can Never Be Too Paranoid

I WOKE UP to the sound of my own voice coming from the office. I hadn't remembered to turn down the volume on the answering machine, which I leave on high during the day so that I can monitor calls from anywhere in the house. Living in this city, you can never be too paranoid. At least that's what my shrink always used to say.

The next thing I heard was Dennis.

"Rachel, it's Dennis Keaton. Please call me. I have something important to tell you."

I picked up the phone. "Hey."

"Have you seen the *Times*?"

"Not yet, Dennis. I was asleep."

"Oh. Sorry. I forget other people do that," he said.

Great. My mother had been reincarnated as a gay guy.

"Can you hang on?" I asked.

"The C section," he said. "Page nineteen. I'll hold."

I went downstairs, opened the front door, and sent Dashiell for the *Times*.

To most people, a C section is a cesarean. If you live in New York City, it's the arts section of the *Times*, the part your husband the dentist hands you while he reads the international, national, and local news and checks the value of his holdings in the business section. I found the article on page nineteen and picked up the cordless extension in the living room.

"So—'*Not* the Death of Art. Murdered artist Clifford Cole's works will be on display in his first one-man show this weekend at the Cahill Gallery in SoHo, a posthumous installation of the artist's paintings, drawings and sculpture,' " I said, reading from the article that Dennis could probably recite by heart. "I guess Veronica Cahill finally figured out what installation is going to follow Dots."

"What are you *talking* about, Rachel?"

"I stopped by the gallery yesterday, just to take a look, and they had this installation called Dots, the most god-awful stuff you ever saw. Well, no, I guess we've both seen worse. Anyway, I told the salesperson I sort of collected dog art, I had Dashiell there, and she failed to sell me a Clifford Cole. She said she didn't know what the next show would be. But apparently Veronica Cahill figured out a good way to get some mileage out of the contract she signed with Cliff. The way it's put here," I said, referring to the article, "well, the notoriety will at least bring people in, maybe even critics. Death makes good copy, or so they say."

"Do you believe this?" Dennis said. " 'An up and coming star of the downtown art world, cut down by human hatred just as his career was taking off.' Where do they get this garbage? She never even guaranteed him she'd put *one* of his pieces in a group show. Now she's his fucking *patron*. Excuse me while I go get a bag to throw up in."

There was nothing but silence on the line for a long moment.

"Listen, Dennis, this is good, isn't it? I mean, wouldn't it be worse if no one ever saw Cliff's paintings? They're quite wonderful."

He didn't respond.

"Dennis?"

"You're right, I know it, it's just that . . ."

"I know. He didn't get the support when he was alive, and he won't get to hear the applause, right?"

"Right," he said, "and someone else will get the money."

"Louis."

"Louis?"

"Louis."

"I thought his family . . ."

"Louis."

"Now I'm really going to be sick. Rachel, I bet Louis is behind all this publicity, this exploitation. I bet he engineered it!"

"It's possible. It should certainly increase the value of his inheritance. Let's keep our mouths shut and our ears open." That's the second law of investigative work. But I sometimes have trouble with the mouth shut part. I thought Dennis would, too.

"Dennis, don't tell anyone you hired me or what I do."

"Oh, God."

"What? Or should I say *who*?"

"I told Louis."

"Shit. Anyone else?"

"No. I *swear*."

"Okay. Let's keep it that way. I have to lie sometimes. Do you understand?"

"I never thought about it. I'm not exactly experienced in this sort of thing. Sorry. I'll watch my mouth. I promise."

"It's my fault, Dennis. I fucked up. I should have told you. It just means Louis will be, well, more guarded with me."

"You're not thinking that *Louis*—"

"It's possible. He did gain from Clifford's death."

"Not nearly what he lost."

Now it was my turn to be silent.

"You'll be there, at the opening?" he asked.

"Definitely. I wouldn't miss it for the world. Would you?"

"Clifford would kill me if I did, no matter what it took. Sorry I woke you, Rachel, but you said I could call anytime, and, shit, it's ten-thirty."

"No problem. I was up late reading Clifford's address book. His brother Peter lives in Woodcliff Lake, by the way, not Fort Lee."

"Same difference. It's all Jersey," he said.

"Dennis, while I've got you on the phone, I need to ask you something. You said Magritte's collar and leash were missing, right?"

"Yes. They weren't on the hook, and I didn't see them anywhere else."

"What did they look like?"

"Red leather, thin, buckle collar, not a slip, four-foot leash. Oh, and Cliff had hung a little bell on the collar. He liked the way it sounded when Magritte walked. Why?"

"Dashiell found them, on the pier. The leash was tied to the back fence, way low, buried in the snow. So he *was* there. Dennis, I'm sorry, but it looks as if Clifford took Magritte and went out to meet someone. Why else would he be on the pier at that hour?"

"You mean, he took Magritte out to help him hit on someone and then tied him up while he was having sex? That's so cheap."

"It's done all the time, Dennis. Let's get real here. Well, it may not be done all that often with a dog in tow, but guys are out there fucking in all kinds of weather and at just about any hour after dark. Am I right?"

"Okay, okay, I hear you. You're right. The police are right. So he had Magritte with him, and Magritte carried on while Clifford had sex. Magritte wouldn't have taken this lying down, you know. He had this thing about not being stopped from what he was doing. So if you took him out to walk, you better keep walking, not tie him up and fuck. That wouldn't have been part of his agenda."

"Dennis, I didn't say Magritte was *happy* to be tied up on the pier. And I know you're not happy to hear this."

"Never mind that. We're after the truth, aren't we? So, the way I figure it, why take the dog? He only would have made a racket. He'd have sounded like *he* was being murdered. That's just the way he was when he was thwarted. People think these dogs are quiet because they don't bark. Trust me, they're not quiet."

"Dennis, I can't say for sure why Cliff took Magritte with him, but you have to admit, a dog is a great icebreaker. No pun intended."

"Okay, okay, I understand, but what about the money, the thousand dollars?"

"Clifford wasn't quite as poor as you thought he was, Dennis. There's apparently money in the family."

"And the thousand?"

"Maybe he was just careless about money, since he never had to worry about it. Or maybe, like a lot of guys, he liked to carry a lot of cash. I read once that women will walk around with twenty bucks on them and feel fine, but that a majority of men don't feel right unless they've got at least a hundred bucks in their pockets. Maybe he needed the money for something the next day and forgot it was in his pocket. He left cash in lots of his jacket pockets, Dennis, not a thousand dollars, but cash. There was a fifty in his jean jacket. He seems to have been careless with money. Not irresponsible, but careless. Again, maybe because it wasn't in short supply when he was growing up."

"None of this makes any sense."

"It will. Give it time."

"But we know Magritte was there. That's definite. And that he was left there. We know that, too," he said, trying to take comfort in the fact that we had learned something about the night Cliff was killed.

"Apparently. The money was left. The dog was left. Maybe something went wrong. Who knows? We don't know the point of this, do we? But it's my guess that Magritte was there at the time of the murder. From the looks of the leash, he jumped around and couldn't break it, but finally backed out of the collar. What if, let's say, Cliff had had a row with Louis, a big one, and maybe he went out to find someone for spite. It happens."

"Rachel, I—"

"Dennis, you know how people driving by always stare at the pier when they're waiting for the light to change. They hate what they're going to see, but they're compelled to look, like when you pass a car accident. Okay, suppose some nut job was driving by on West Street, no one's around, and he sees a couple of guys in flagrante on the pier and loses it. He turns his car around, shoots back uptown, drives onto the waterfront area and back to the pier. Maybe by then, the other guy has left. Cliff is on the way to untie Magritte, and this poor excuse for a human being drives onto the pier and runs him down. He wouldn't take the chance of getting out of the vehicle and checking his pockets. He wouldn't expect to find so much money. Money isn't the point, is it? He probably got the hell away as fast as he could. He probably never even saw Magritte tied up at the far end or heard him over the car's engine."

For the second time he made that sound with his nose that would have caused Beatrice, the perfect one, to hand him a clean, ironed handkerchief.

"I'm not ready to give up yet," he said. "Are you?"

"Of course not. I mean, even if it turns out to be that it is what it looks like now, maybe we can catch the bastard. Maybe I can find a witness. The opening is tomorrow night. Let's see what we learn there, okay? By the way, has the gallery been in touch with you about getting the paintings?"

"No. They're probably working with Louis. He's known Veronica for years. That's how Cliffie got past the manila envelope and slides stage. Louis introduced them. Anyway, the art is his now, isn't it?"

"Yes. And he can get it? He has keys?"

"He may be there right now, for all I know," Dennis said. "Yeah, he has the keys. God knows why. He almost never came here. He claims he's allergic to paint fumes. And dogs. Okay, so I'll see you at the opening?"

"You bet! Get to work, Dennis. You'll feel better."

When I hung up, I needed to do something to clear my head, so I climbed on my exercise bike and began to pedal rapidly. I had gotten the habit of working out when I was a dog trainer, hauling around dogs that sometimes weighed as much as I did. It's not really brute force that gets the job done. A great deal of getting through to a dog has to do with winning its respect, which is often done mentally, but it doesn't hurt if you can impress the dog physically when necessary, stopping him or moving him, if not with your irresistible personality, then with a little muscle and some swell timing.

I had told Dennis if he did something he'd feel better. But I had, and I didn't. I couldn't stop thinking about the Christopher Street pier, how lonely it must have been that night, how dark. I wondered if there had been a moon.

I thought about the sound of the place, too, the wind, the car, the little bell on the dog's collar, the sound it would have made as he pulled and twisted, trying to break free, and the mournful yodeling of that little dog, Magritte.

10

It Should Only Happen

DESPITE THE FACT that my mail assured me I had won seven million dollars and therefore no longer had to work for a living, Dash and I headed for the waterfront to try to find the homeless man known as Billy Pittsburgh. After all, back before I became filthy rich, I had given Dennis the hope there might be a witness, hadn't I?

When the last thing you want to see is a homeless person, like finally you met a guy who's appealing, interesting, single, straight, and uninfected—it should only happen—and you're wearing your black knit coatdress with the deep V neck and matching cigarette pants, your mother's sparkling marcasite pin, sheer black stockings, and witchy black suede, ankle-high boots with a small heel, and your hair for once came out perfect, and you're even wearing makeup, for God's sake, *then* you'll see homeless people. You'll trip over them. They'll hold their filthy hands out, nearly touching you, and ask for money. Or you'll pass one, asleep in a doorway, and for a long time afterward, you'll continue to smell the rancid odor of urine, wafting into your nostrils from your own clothes, which absorbed the stink as you passed it.

I knew it would take great luck to find Billy. It's not as if he had an address or a phone number. And even if I found him, it was doubtful he saw anything or could remember or relate what he saw if he had seen anything. Still, this, according to my mentor, Frank Petrie, was

THIS DOG FOR HIRE / 51

how you did investigative work. And since I didn't have a better idea at the moment, I figured I'd give it a shot.

Frank required a daily progress report that he could forward to the client so that, even when there was no progress, most days, you could outline where you went looking for it. According to Frank, the third law of investigation work is Look, kid, no one's paying you to sit on your ass and watch TV.

Dashiell liked the waterfront, and in nicer weather I did too. It was comforting to be near the river and expansive to let the eye rove far instead of being stopped every few feet by a building. There's more sky in the Village than there is uptown, because the buildings are lower here, more on a human scale than the skyscrapers in much of the rest of Manhattan, and at the waterfront you can see *really* far, to the Statue of Liberty if you looked to the southwest, to the twin towers of the World Trade Center south and slightly to the east. If you looked northeast, you'd see the Empire State Building, which to me is still the tallest building in the world. I'm always reluctant to edit the truths of my childhood.

I could see everything, including my breath, but I couldn't see Billy Pittsburgh.

We crossed West Street, walked a block to Washington, and headed uptown. A lot of homeless hang out in the meat district, a few blocks north from where we were. It was a long shot, but maybe someone would have seen Billy and might know where I could find him.

When we got as far as Gansevoort Street, we found a tattered woman slowly pushing her shopping cart full of possessions along the sidewalk. Poking out from inside her torn coat was the broad, striped face of a red tabby cat, and there were two small mixed-breed dogs, each wearing several sweaters, riding in the cart among her treasures. The homeless men usually collect deposit bottles. Many have become rather entrepreneurial, amassing large amounts of cans and bottles they can exchange for enough money for a meal. The street women seem far crazier than the men. Few talk to anyone. Many rave as they go. They seem more impaired than simply hideously down on their luck. At least, with this lady, her pets gave me a possible opening.

"Handsome cat," I said, the jowls telling me the cat was male, "what do you call him?"

She stopped, looked at Dashiell, then, to my surprise, looked at me. Perhaps Dash's presence signaled I was trustworthy.

"Tuna," she said. "Just use your nose, girlie. A nose, by any other name, would smell a rat. Something's fishy in Denmark."

"I see," I said. "I mean, I sniff, therefore I am."

She tossed back her head and cackled.

"Sure would like some coffee," she said, lifting her head and air scenting, as if I might have some in my pocket.

"I'll get you a cup, um, what did you say your name was?"

"I smell, therefore I call myself Bo Peep."

"Wait here. I'll be a minute, okay?"

"No skin off my cat," she said, getting busy adjusting the parcels in her cart. The dogs sat perfectly still, staring down at Dashiell.

We were across the street from Florent, the wonderful little French bistro smack in the middle of the meat district on Gansevoort Street. I ordered a coffee to go, and while I waited, I figured out the name. It wasn't Bo Peep. It was B. O. Peep! Accurate, too.

When I got outside, B. O. was down the block. Dashiell and I ran to catch up with her. I handed her the bag with the coffee.

"B. O., do you know a homeless man called Billy Pittsburgh? He hangs around West Street sometimes."

She opened the bag, sniffing like a dog. "Coffee," she said, "I smell coffee." She closed her eyes and inhaled.

"Have you seen Billy around lately?" I asked.

"Billy *Pee*," she said. "Smells worse than Shithead here," she whispered. The little brown Chihuahua mix looked up at the sound of his name. "He eats it," she said, her hand next to her mouth in a dramatic aside, dirty fingers poking out of her torn, gray woolen gloves.

"Has he been around? Billy?"

"He calls me Mary Perry," she said slowly to no one in particular. "Mary Perry. It rhymes. Mary Perry. Not my name, I tell him. My address."

She put the bag under Tuna's face, for him to smell the coffee. His eyes became slits and his lips retracted.

"Slow Black Billy," she said, laughing. "That's what I call *him*. He don't move too good."

She carefully took out the container of coffee and opened it, smelling it again for a long time.

"Do you know where I could find him?" I asked her one more time.

She began to push the heavy cart with one hand, and I could see the coffee sloshing out of the cup as she moved on. After going a few feet, she turned around.

"Haven't spotted him lately," she said. "But someone else sure did. Don't know who. Don't want to know." She was shaking her head as she began to make her way slowly down the block, still muttering. "Always making fun, that Billy. Always making jokes on *me*." She stopped, and it looked as if she were pointing to her chest. Slowly, the cart began to move forward again. "Now the joke's *on him*," she said, but then the wind came up and I could no longer hear her.

Dashiell and I walked uptown for a few blocks before heading back downtown, but I didn't see Billy or any other homeless people. It was dark by then, and the transvestite hookers were out, dotting the corners of Washington Street in the meat district like colorful birds, dancing in place, preening hopefully each time a car passed, singing to attract a mate, or at least the chance to earn a quick twenty.

When we finally arrived at home, the cottage seemed unusually warm, safe, and clean. I fed Dashiell, took a bath, and poured a glass of wine; then, remembering that the short version of the third law of private investigation says, At least *look* busy, I went upstairs to the office to play the other side of the tape I'd taken from Cliff's answering machine. As I waited for it to rewind, I hoped his messages wouldn't be as dull or annoying as most of mine. I hit play, then scrunched up against the pillows on the office daybed to drink the wine and listen.

"Baby, it's Imelda Marcos. I was wondering if you had time to go to Shoe Town today. I need pumps. Oooo. Call me, honey."

Beep.

"Clifford, it's Gil. I was wondering if I could enter Magritte in the Westchester County Kennel Club show in September. I just got the judging list, and I think our boy would do *very* well. Call me. The entry deadline is in two weeks. And, oh, thanks for the check."

Beep.

"Baby, it's Amy Fisher. I was wondering if you could recommend a good auto body mechanic. I need to get my dents pounded out. Oooo. Call me, honey."

"Oh, dear. CLIFFORD, IT'S MOTHER."

Beep.

"Osso buco tonight, you delicious thing. See you at seven, honey." It was the same voice as the Imelda Marcos and Amy Fisher calls. Louis?

Beep.

"Cliff, it's Dennis. Are you there? Cliff, pick up, damn it. Oh, shit."

Beep.

"Cliff, it's Mike. I can't take Magritte today. Sorry. Give me a call."

Beep.

"This is for Robert Sutherland. I'm at the Marriott, Bob. I'll be here through Monday. Oh, it's Stanley Salkin of Power Crest. Give me a call."

Beep.

54 / CAROL LEA BENJAMIN

These were among my favorites, wrong-number messages.

I've always wondered if I were morally obliged to call the people and tell them they didn't get who they thought they got. But I never did. I figure living with the consequences of your mistakes is part of being a grown-up.

"This is Margaret at Dr. Sobel's office. You have an appointment tomorrow at two. See you then. Have a good day, and don't forget to floss."

Beep.

"Cliff, it's Mike again. Are you there? Shit. Either you're fucking your brains out, or someone died. Jesus—I hope you're fucking your brains out. Okay—I can get him at four. Unless I hear from you."

Beep

When I woke up, I was still holding the tape recorder, but the tape had run all the way to the end.

I had dreamed I found Billy Pittsburgh and that he told me he had written down the license number of the car that had hit Clifford Cole, it should only happen.

But now that I was awake, I couldn't remember what it was.

11

Last Seen Flying West

THE FRIDAY *TIMES* had a large ad for the Cahill Gallery opening of Clifford Cole's work, white letters on a black field. Very dignified.

"A visual chronicle of the alienation of the nineties." Where do they *get* this bullshit?

I turned to the obits. Since I didn't find my name listed, I figured I better get my ass to work. I climbed onto the exercise bike, called Dash, and told him to find a ball. When he did, I tossed it out the door of the office, where it bounced off the wall and went noisily down the uncarpeted stairs to the living room, Dashiell in hot pursuit. Even after ten throws, there he was, eyes ablaze, ready to do it all over again.

I have days like that. Sisyphus minus the rock, but getting nowhere all the same. I was afraid today would be one of them. Nevertheless, by ten to eight, we were ready to begin another search for Billy Pittsburgh.

There was more of a chance he'd be in situ, asleep, if we hit the streets early, but then I might be waking up a lot of homeless men trying to find him. We headed for West Street, across from the waterfront, checking doorways and loading ramps, heat vents, alleys, any place where a person without a home might find some protection from the weather, which at this time of year was fierce.

It occurred to me that the only thing I knew about Billy was that he was black, but even if I had decided to let the Asian and Caucasian homeless men stay asleep, you couldn't tell who or what was under any particular pile of rags or which packing box was trash and which was someone's cardboard condo.

With the exception of an auto body shop, nothing was open yet on West Street. And I couldn't figure out where Billy might be, because the street got the full brunt of the wind off the Hudson. We turned up Christopher and found one crusty guy with a blanket draped around him holding out a paper cup from one of the ubiquitous Greek coffee shops, hoping for a handout. He was Caucasian, under a lot of crud. I dug into my pocket and pulled out a handful of change. Dropping it into the cup, I asked him if he knew Billy Pittsburgh.

"Not here," he said, shoving the cup in my direction, as if to ask for more.

"He doesn't hang out here?" I asked.

"No more," he said. He was shaking pretty badly.

I tucked a couple of singles into his cup.

"Do you know where he might be now?"

He shook his head. "Don't know much," he said. "God bless," and he walked away.

On the lamppost on the corner a handwritten sign with the word MISSING on it caught my eye. Underneath it said, "Blue and yellow macaw, last seen flying west on Christopher Street, answers (sometimes) to 'Arnie.' REWARD."

We started snaking around the streets between Washington and Greenwich, checking every doorway and pile of trash, but finding nothing. On Washington and Bank we saw two transvestites, probably left over from the night before. I could hear their deep voices as they walked by us. The taller of the two had done something wonderful with her scarf. I'd have to try that sometime. At least the morning wouldn't be a total loss.

Of course, I'd also have some news for Dennis, something other than that his friend was doing the outdoor version of being a toilet queen when he bought the farm. But I didn't think that the fact that I had looked for Billy Pittsburgh and failed to find him would make Dennis release balloons.

We spent about an hour walking around looking carefully at what seemed to be piles of garbage but which actually, sometimes, were someone's attempt to keep warm. I spoke to two other men. One began to rant and rave, making no sense at all. I think he was afraid of Dash, but I doubt he made sense when he wasn't frightened. The other guy, a much younger man than you usually see on the street, talked nonstop. He asked for money, for a job, for coffee. He told me how he lost his job and couldn't pay his rent. He said he got beaten up at the men's shelter and that it was worse than the street. He told me three places where he could get meals, but none of them were open on the weekend. He said he had never met a black man called Billy, but there was a black woman called Billie who slept in a loading area on Greenwich Street, near Charles. I thanked him, gave him a couple of dollars, and headed for Charles Street.

We found Billie asleep under a pile of filthy blankets and newspapers. I put Dash on a sit-stay off to the side so that she wouldn't wake up, see him, and get frightened. I called her name four or five times before she stirred. Slowly, a hand wrapped in rags pushed up a corner of the blanket, and I could barely see a face deep under the covers looking out at me.

"Are you Billie?" I asked.

There was no answer.

"I'm looking for the Billie who found a man lying on the pier a few weeks ago, the Billie who told the cops there was someone on the pier. Was that you?"

Still no answer. But the cover stayed up.

"You're not in any trouble. I can use your help if you know anything or if you know another Billy who might help me. It's worth a nice meal, if you can help."

The cover dropped.

By now I was freezing. I didn't know how these people survived outside in such cold weather. Of course, not all of them did.

I tucked a couple of bucks under the blanket, then stood there like an idiot waiting for a response.

Chilled and frustrated, Dash and I headed home, stopping to pick up the photos I'd taken at the pier and at Cliff's loft on the way.

Why didn't homeless people flock together, like birds? Or sleep together for warmth? Then maybe someone would know Billy Pittsburgh's whereabouts. I felt stupid spending my time looking for him; I even began to wonder if Mary Perry really knew Billy.

Sometimes the homeless talk like the Alzheimer patients I worked with at the nursing home, stringing things together that they hear and talking about them as if they were real, adding parts of TV stories and overheard conversations to their own experiences.

I felt as if I were in a fog, too. So when I got home, I went straight up to my office, where I have an oversize blackboard I picked up at the flea market on Greenwich Avenue. I began to list the people in

Clifford's life and to think about what each stood to gain from his death.

Dennis Mark Keaton, aka Dennis Mark Rosenberg.

Gain: one champion basenji, Magritte. Will he do anything Clifford didn't do, e.g., hire him out at stud? How much could you make doing that anyway? Find out. Loss: one best friend with whom he was possibly (hopelessly?) in love.

Louis Lane, aka Leonard Polski.

Inherits a previously worthless, now valuable art collection. Could there have been a long-term plan at work here? After all, Louis had hooked Cliff up with Veronica. Were there hard feelings, oops, between the lovers? A desire for revenge? A need for money? Loss: the love of his life? Or not.

Veronica Cahill.

Lots of SoHo galleries had closed and lots of others were in financial difficulties, so . . . Did Louis and Veronica, old buddies, team up? If yes, how could this connect with where the murder took place? If they planned to kill Cliff together, then use the murder to increase the value of his work, how did they know he'd be on the pier that night?

Why was I doing this? The man was killed at four in the morning on the Christopher Street pier, where he had gone with his dog to get lucky. Boy, did he not get lucky! The best I could hope for was a witness—talk about getting lucky—and one who was sane and sober enough to have gotten the license plate number. Fat fucking chance, as my grandmother would have said if there had been a Yiddish equivalent. Like on top of everything else, the guy would have had to have a pencil and paper.

I added the next name.

Morgan Gilmore, Magritte's handler.

Gil and Cliff argued about whether or not to breed Magritte, but what could Gil gain from Cliff's death? *He* didn't inherit M. Did he think he would? Is there more to this picture? Would Dennis keep up M's career, or was Gil now out of a job?

Adrienne Wynton Cole, Cliff's mother.

She gets the dough. But it was probably hers in the first place, and she probably has a ton more. Mothers don't usually murder their children by running them over. They do it slowly, using guilt and disappointment. Even if she didn't accept her son or really know him (what else is new?), she lost her *son*.

Peter David Cole, Cliff's brother.

He would have gotten the dough if Adrienne had kicked off first. If

Cliff was in his early thirties, his mother was probably somewhere in her fifties or sixties. Even if she would now leave everything *she* had to Peter, he'd have a pretty long wait. Not a terrific investment, killing your brother and waiting twenty-plus years for the payoff, unless she prefers a charity of some sort, other than her own son. That probably depends whether she approves of Peter David. Have to meet him. Maybe at the opening? Loss: his brother.

I began to think about Lillian and all the times I felt like strangling her. But I'd never actually *do* it. Even though you probably get angrier at your family than at anyone else, they're your history, too, the people who know every stupid story about you since day one.

Okay. Check out the lover. And the gallery owner. Hey, what they do is exploit artists, isn't it? Maybe murder comes under the heading of exploitation, furthering his career. After all, his stuff wasn't worth much when he was alive, was it? Check prices.

I tacked the photos onto the wall, lonely shots of the pier, Cliff's art, even his unmade bed, images to haunt me as I tried to make sense of what appeared to be a senseless crime.

I decided to check the main house before getting ready for the opening. Not bothering with a coat, I grabbed the keys off a hook in the kitchen and ran across the snow-covered garden, Dashiell leading the way straight to the Siegals' back door.

I unlocked both locks, stomped the snow off my boots, pulled the door open, and followed Dashiell inside. Once indoors, I signaled Dashiell to sit and watch me, then gave him the hand signal for go find, a flat, open hand first touching my right eye, then sweeping out forward as far as I could reach.

Dashiell headed for the front room. We always started downstairs and worked our way up. I followed along behind, making sure the doors were still locked, no windows had been broken, no gas was leaking, no pipes had burst. Dash made sure no one else was in the house.

Downstairs was where a burglar would be most likely to break in, even though some preferred access from above, coming from the roof of another building. In some places in the city, you could travel an entire block by running across the roofs.

In New York City, most accessible windows had bars on them. But Norma wouldn't hear of it. "They're ugly," she'd said when I suggested that window guards would help safeguard the house. "I will not live in a jail. That's why you're here." I was in no position to argue.

I followed Dashiell, telling him he was a good boy, checking to make sure the shutters were closed in the front of the house and open to let light in in the rear, those windows that faced the cottage. The thermostat was set at sixty so that the old house wouldn't take too bad a beating contracting and expanding as the weather changed.

We finished at the top without finding a single thief hiding under any of the beds or in the closets, double-checked the front door, shut off the lights, and let ourselves out the back.

Once, the first winter I was here, Dashiell had started to pace and whine, going to the living-room window that faced the main house and coming back to poke me with his muzzle and look into my eyes. I had taken my gun from the shoe box in the bedroom closet, and we had gone across the snowy garden in silence, my heart pounding as I opened the back door. Five minutes later we were face-to-face with the intruder, a homeless woman who had broken one of the front windows to get in from the cold. She was nestled under three blankets in the spare bedroom, trying to get warm.

This time, everything was as it should have been. By the time we got back to the cottage, stopping briefly to race around the big oak, it was time to get ready for the opening. I had planned to soak in the tub until I was as wrinkled as a shar-pei, but I couldn't. I was too excited about the thought of possibly meeting the killer in an hour or so and the question of whether or not I'd know him—or her—when I did.

In the Village, if your sweats are clean, you're dressed up. SoHo is another story. Not wanting to stick out like a bulldog at a field trial, I put on my long black coatdress with matching pants, wound my hair up, and clipped it at the back of my head. Then I stood by helplessly as most of it worked its way out of the barrette. Looking as if I'd just been Marlene Dietrich's stand-in in *Morocco*, I called my dog, and together we headed downtown to see if anyone smelled like a killer.

12

He Raised His Lovely Eyebrows

THE BIG BLACK dot was nowhere in sight, and the floor of the
Cahill Gallery had been painted iridescent chartreuse. The walls, still
white, were hung with Clifford Cole's paintings, which gave me the
same kind of pang I got when I thought about my father not living
long enough to see his grandchildren. Then again, who ever said life
was fair.

Despite the fact that this was a posthumous show, the mood was
festive. Artists turned out in great numbers, as they always do for
openings—and the free food and booze—and there were an unusual
number of collectors, especially for the shrinking art market of the
nineties. There was press, too, so there would be, it seemed, even
more articles in the papers and magazines about the young artist who
died so tragically just as his tremendous talent was about to come to
light.

God, did schmaltz sell. Then again, lurid sex crimes also sold. It was
just a matter of time before the rest of the story came out, which
would drive the prices even higher than the schmaltz had already
done. Louis Lane was going to end up a rich man.

Dennis was in the back, with Magritte.

"Honey, *you* look sen-sa-tional!"

"Yeah. Yeah." I leaned in as if to kiss his cheek. "What have you learned?" I whispered.

He leaned closer. "Well, apparently blue eye shadow is back!"

"Dog people," I explained.

He rolled his eyes. "And *Lois* is here." He indicated the location with a tilt of his head, and I turned to get a look at the new owner of the collection, prepared to loathe him on sight.

"She's doing an *in*terview," he sang. "Does anyone ask *me*—" he began, but I cut him off.

"I'll see you in a bit," I said, leaving quickly and pushing through the crowd with Dashiell at my side.

Leonard Polski was a few feet away from where I had been standing with Dennis, talking to someone who was taking notes. I squeezed in close enough to hear some of the bull he was tossing around, sure I'd be hearing about his always having had faith in Cliff's ability, about how he encouraged him to try his last series of grayish, oversize paintings where images took several canvases to be completed, and, richest of all, how pleased he was that Magritte was found and how much he loved the little dog.

What I heard surprised me. Even allowing for the distortion of the tape recording, this was clearly the same voice that left the warm and funny messages for Clifford that I had heard last night. That was as I had guessed. The rest was not.

Louis Lane was speaking softly about the rise of hate crimes, the resurgence of Nazism in the new/old unified Germany, the racial cleansing in Bosnia, and the rise in gay bashing here at home. Then he began to talk about Clifford, his painting as a kind of journal writing on canvas, the curiosity that drove him into his own psyche to troll for powerful material, his feeling that if he touched upon the things he felt deeply about, his paintings would touch others in some powerful way even though each person's history was unique and even though Clifford's own story was not fully expressed, just alluded to mysteriously. That, he said, the mysterious quality of Clifford's work, was what he, Louis, loved best.

"It was his way of expressing not only his own alienation and the alienation all gay men feel, but a far larger issue, the alienation of the nineties, the understanding that we never really know each other, and the question of whether or not many of us care for each other."

Of course, this made me wonder how well Louis Lane knew Clifford Cole, or why he thought this was a nineties concept. From the beginning of time, no one has ever known anyone. I mean, did Adam know Eve? I mean, *really* know her, beyond the biblical sense?

"He was very emotional," he continued, "yet in the translation to canvas, a kind of artistic flatness took over. I think without that, he couldn't have gone where he needed to go. The pain would have been too great. And in that, he was a strong voice for what is going on in the post-Bush era, the disappointment people feel resonating with the pain of childhood, as if Bush the father betrayed us just as our own fathers did."

In action, how like an angel! To coin a phrase.

The reporter nodded and kept writing. Behind him, there was a triptych I hadn't seen at the loft. In fact, looking around, I hadn't seen much of what was on display. I guess these were the paintings from the closet. Looking at the one behind Louis, this one *really* was from the closet; it was a middle-aged man in drag, but in each of the three pictures he had his back to the viewer. What was weird is that it looked like early TV, like Milton Berle in drag. It was even painted without color, in black and white and shades of gray. This was neither genderfuck, where there is a devil-may-care mix of male and female, say a guy with a beard smoking a cigar and wearing a strapless gown, his chest hair poking up from the bodice of the dress, nor was it cross-dressing, where the aim is to pass for the opposite sex. This was broad burlesque, but somehow creepy.

The dress was a cheap housedress. You should *see* what guys wear when they do drag. You should *have* the money they spend. But this was a somewhat heavy guy in a woman's cheap cotton housedress and a five-and-dime wig, ever so slightly askew, with a cigar in "her" hand. The cigar was the only thing to change in the three paintings. That is, in the third canvas, the ash was dropping onto the carpet. Unlike all the other paintings I had seen, this one had no title on the last canvas. In fact, when Louis moved a little, I saw that the card on the wall read "untitled oil on canvas." It was dated this year. Perhaps it was the last series he had painted. Perhaps he never finished it.

I waited for the interview to end and introduced myself.

"Louis? Rachel Alexander. I understand Dennis told you he hired me to investigate Cliff's murder?" I put out my hand. "Can we talk for a moment? Perhaps we can duck out into the stairwell. It'll be more private there. And cooler."

He nodded, and Dashiell and I followed him out the side door of the gallery and into the hall in the stairwell. Unfortunately, others had gone out there to escape from the crowd and the heat, but we brushed by them and went up a flight, where we could be alone.

"You don't have a drink. May I fetch you one?" he asked in that lovely voice I had heard on the tape. "I guess I shouldn't say *fetch*.

That must be his job," he said, indicating Dash with his wineglass. It seemed he had had a few before this glass. He stood a little too close, occupying some of the space I needed to have between me and any other being other than a baby, a lover, or a dog, but I didn't want to back up because I thought it would put him off.

"I'm fine, Louis, thank you. I wanted to offer my sympathy on your loss. I understand Cliff's family hasn't included you or any of Clifford's New York friends in their plans. I'm so sorry about that, but it's not an uncommon reaction, is it?"

He seemed taken aback at the abruptness and the personal nature of my question. This is definitely a problem I have. I am only semi-skilled at beating about the bush.

"No. Unfortunately, it's more commonly the rule than the exception."

"Are they here? His mother? His brother?"

"I expect not. We've never met, but I did get a call from Peter yesterday saying the memorial service was this evening. In Virginia. I'd left a message for him on Monday, to tell him about the opening. So I don't expect them here. More importantly, *we* won't be *there*. I assume that was the point. He was very polite, of course. He said he'd come by the gallery one evening next week, after he returns from Frederick. Anyway, it's all water under the bridge now, isn't it? The time to be supportive to Clifford is gone.

"So *that* family can and will handle things any way they like. I've talked to Dennis, and we're going to have our own service in New York after the show closes, for Clifford's *real* family."

"What a good idea. So what's your take on this, Louis? Do you agree with the police assessment of what happened to Clifford?"

"It makes no sense to me at all. Oh, please understand, I am perfectly able to believe a gay man would be mindlessly killed by a stranger for no reason other than that he appeared to be homosexual. But I cannot fathom what Cliff was doing on the pier at that hour. Or, to tell the truth, at any hour."

Have you ever noticed that people who interject that expression, "to tell the truth," are often lying?

"What I was wondering about, mainly," I said, "was the same thing. The night of the murder . . ." He stiffened slightly at the sound of the word. "Where were you when Cliff left for the pier at three or four in the morning? Asleep? I mean, did he talk to you, say where he was going? Or why?"

"I told all this to the police," he said. "We weren't together that night. He stayed at his studio. He usually came to my place in the evening, and I'd cook for him or we'd go out, he'd almost always spend the night and then go back to the studio early in the morning, most of the time before I woke up. There's living space there—he was living there before we met. But we—I should say, *I*—never stayed there. I have a sensitivity to paint. And I'm allergic to dogs."

"Oh, I'm sorry, is he a problem?" I asked, looking down at Dashiell.

"Not unless I sleep with him," Louis said. He sighed, looked away, and then took a small sip of wine.

He was tall and slender, young, about twenty-eight, I guessed, with lovely olive skin, thick, dark hair, an angular face, almost but not quite too delicate, like a swarthy Montgomery Clift. His eyes were dark and intense. He was the kind of person that gave you chills when he looked at you. No wonder poor, pale, cloddy Dennis was jealous. I wish *I* looked half as pretty as Louis Lane.

"Was it unusual for Clifford to stay at the studio?" I asked after a moment of silence. "Had you had some sort of argument?"

"No, he was painting, he said, and he wanted to stay with it. He sometimes did that for several nights in a row, just went with it. But this time . . ."

"Yes?"

"He sounded tense that night, Rachel, not high."

When he said my name, it felt the way it does when a lover whispers your name during sex. He was good, this Louis Lane, a sort of work of art himself.

"When the painting was going so well that he couldn't stop working," Louis continued, "he'd be on a high, he'd sound wonderful, excited, energetic. But Tuesday night, he sounded, I don't know, funny, like there was something he wasn't telling me."

"And you didn't ask?"

"We tended to give each other a lot of room in that area, Rachel. I knew he'd tell me when he was ready. He always had."

I wondered what Leonard Polski had invented, besides his name. I wondered if he had murdered his lover.

Never assume, meaning never assume anyone is innocent until you're absolutely sure who's guilty. You could get killed that way.

"So you have no guess as to what happened, as to why he ended up on the pier?"

"Not a clue."

"Well, thanks, Louis." I took a card from my pocket. "Here's my number, in case you think of anything else you want to tell me, anything at all."

"Research. Interesting. I can't *imagine* how you do whatever it is you do do," he said. "I don't know what happened that night, and I wouldn't know where to begin to find out."

"What do you do?" I asked him.

"I teach high school Spanish."

Unless he had a *relativo rico*, there was no way Louis Lane could afford his Gucci loafers on a teacher's salary. No fucking way.

"Well, *I* can't imagine how you—or anyone—does *that*. So I guess we're even."

He smiled and showed me his perfect, even white teeth.

"Dennis doesn't want to believe that this is a hate crime," he said. "But what else could it be?"

"That's what he hired me to find out," I said, looking up into Louis's fathomless dark eyes. "I was hoping to find a witness, actually."

He raised his lovely eyebrows. "Really?" he said.

As far as I was concerned, it was definitely a hate crime. The question was, personal hate or random hate?

At the foot of the stairs I stepped aside, and Louis walked ahead of me into the gallery, head high, posture perfect, his hair looking as if he had never even *heard* of a sandstorm.

I began to walk around and look at the paintings. I passed several of the ones I had seen at the loft. There were a few pieces of sculpture, too, painted wooden pieces. I stopped to look at one, a life-size Magritte, and found myself walking circles around it in the company of a woman my sister would describe as perky and a short-waisted, stocky man wearing gray sweats, red-faced and moist, as if he had just stopped in after a long run.

"Isn't this di*vine*," the woman said. "God, it's sold!" I looked at the title card and saw she was right. Next to the price of $8,000 there was a red dot.

"Eight thousand," I said aloud, to no one in particular.

The guy in sweats whistled, one long, bright, clear note, and shook his head.

I turned to look at him, but all I saw were his broad shoulders and his back as he moved off into the crowd. Eight thousand, I thought, watching him disappear. He looked vaguely familiar, but I couldn't quite place him.

I looked back at the price and the red dot. Clifford must be rolling over in his grave. Actually, Dennis had said the body was cremated, and I wasn't sure one could still do that under those circumstances.

"What's your breed?" the perky woman asked. "Are you in basenjis?" And then she sort of squealed. She had apparently just noticed

Dashiell. The funny thing about pit bulls is that sometimes they sort of disappear. Dashiell, who went everywhere with me, had a way of blending in so that, despite his formidable size, he often wasn't even seen, for example, lying next to the table at a restaurant. Until we got up to leave.

"I'm a collector," I told her.

I lied quickly and easily. Frank always assured me it was a useful skill, not a character flaw.

"Oh, I am too, in a way. I collect basenjis. I have eleven. Four are Magritte get," she said with great pride.

If I were a dog, my brow would have wrinkled and my ears would have gone up. A dog's get are his offspring. I had been told that Magritte had never been bred.

"Really," I said. "Did you get the dogs from Cliff?"

"Oh, I didn't *buy* the dogs. My Tiffany was bred to Magritte. She had a dog and three bitches."

"I see. Is this recently? I mean, are the puppies for sale now?"

"Oh, no. Are you looking for a basenji?" She looked down at Dashiell. Actually, she didn't have that far down to look. She was about five feet tall, sort of tightly packed, with the kind of hair and makeup I used to see on my Upper East Side dog-training clients. "They're wonderful with other breeds," she said, hoping to make a sale. Who's lying now? I thought. Most basenjis aren't even good with themselves. Magritte was a miracle of good temperament, partly good breeding and partly because Cliff had trained and socialized him so well. "Melisand is due in heat soon," she said, "and I was thinking of breeding her back to Magritte. She's his daughter, out of Windy Moment. That's Tiffany. I could put you on the wait list," she said, arching her neat eyebrows.

Exactly what I needed, an inbred basenji.

"Um, who have you dealt with for the breedings?" I asked.

"Gil, of course. I've known Gil for, what, seven years, ever since I got into basenjis. He's fabulous. I wish I could get him to handle one of my dogs, but he's much too expensive for me."

"Morgan Gilmore? I heard so much about him, uh, from Dashiell's handler, but I never met him. Is he here?"

She took another look at Dashiell, frowning. Of course, pit bulls are not AKC-registerable dogs, so if she knew the difference between a pit bull and an Am Staff, she would have wondered what the hell I was talking about. UKC handlers would be totally unlikely to also work at AKC shows, and if Dash had a handler, which he didn't, he probably would have no idea who Morgan Gilmore was.

"He's over there, see, red shirt, ponytail?"

"Great chatting with you," I said, and headed back to Dennis.

"Here," I said when I had squeezed through the crowd and arrived at his side. I handed him Dashiell's leash. "I'll be back soon and explain." I signaled Dashiell to wait, and began shoving my way to where Morgan Gilmore was standing.

When I got close enough to eavesdrop, I pretended to study *out, damned spot,* which hung starting to his left and continuing down that wall. He was talking to two men about Westminster, which was now only a few days away. It is always held on the second Monday and Tuesday of February, and the hound group goes up on Tuesday. Since Magritte had been found, he would, of course, be shown. I couldn't hear everything, only snippets. ". . . the best front of any dog on the circuit today." "Schedules are never a problem—" "—with *that* topline! Please!" "—very typey . . ." "—the epitome of his breed." All the usual dog show bullshit.

"Hi," I said when I could finally get his attention. I was now close enough to see that he was one of those guys who have five o'clock shadow by ten-thirty in the morning. He was oddly shaped, tall and thin, but you could see the bulge of a potbelly pushing out his shiny red shirt, as if he had swallowed a casaba melon whole. His hair was seriously receding, but he had let the back grow long, and he did indeed have a ponytail. And he wore a string tie and cowboy boots. My guess was that they were his signature.

"Uh, what's her name," I gestured into the center of the gallery, "Tiffany's mom—"

"Aggie?"

"Right! Aggie said you might be able to help me out. I have a basenji bitch," I said. Morgan Gilmore's smile cranked up to 150 watts, and he hunched his shoulders and head toward me in a mockery of sincerity and interest. "She's pointed, of course. She just needs one more major"—I bet he never heard *that* before man, if he could toss it, so could I—"but I think I'd like to breed her this spring"—I took an audible breath and let it out, the way you breathe when you're twelve if someone mentions the name of a rock star—"to Magritte. He's got the best front. Just perfect."

Morgan Gilmore beamed. "No problem," he said. He reached two bony fingers into his breast pocket and withdrew his card. The logo was a beagle puppy sitting next to a cowboy boot. Talk about non sequiturs!

"Do you specialize in the hound group?"

"I'll handle *anything*," he told me, and for once I thought he was telling the absolute truth. "So, little lady, just call me when your girl's cycle starts, and we'll arrange everything. *No* problem."

He had no questions to ask me. Not one. He didn't even ask for a recent brucellosis test, the very least thing you'd want before any breeding, since brucellosis causes sterility in both dogs and bitches and is nearly impossible to cure. But, hey, this is not to say the man wasn't careful. He probably only bred Magritte to "qualified bitches," as the ads always say, "qualified" meaning he'd get paid in advance.

"Well, what about his show schedule and all?" I asked. "Will scheduling Crystal's breeding be a problem?"

"Well"—he paused and laughed intimately, since we were such good friends—"you know basenjis. They can be a handful, can't they? They don't always get along that well, even males and females. I'm sure your, um—"

"Crystal."

"I'm sure your Crystal is a dream girl, but I've seen some nasty bitches, and I can't take a chance my little boy will get hurt."

My little boy!

"So I just avoid the dangers of shipping, possible dogfights, or missed breedings because of Magritte's show schedule. None of this is a problem," he said smugly. "I bank his sperm."

Bingo! I thought. Morgan Gilmore had just moved up to number one on my hit parade.

13

We've Locked the Barn

IF YOU'VE NEVER turned on a date with a detailed description of how semen is collected and banked, and you think you might like to give it a try, just say, "I was thinking of using frozen semen to breed my dog. Less hassle." And when they ask the inevitable, just roll your eyes and say, "Don't ask." Human imagination always makes things more interesting than they actually are.

With Morgan Gilmore's card safely tucked into my purse, I pushed and shoved my way over to the bar, snagged a glass of white wine, then shoved and poked my way back to Dennis. Before I got there, to retrieve my dog and tell my client the news, I overheard a voice so condescending and full of authoritative ignorance that it could only belong to a gallery owner. Veronica Cahill was briefing the press.

"—a little steep for someone who's hardly sold, never had a show before, never been reviewed?"

"It might seem that way, but this is all there is of Clifford's art, all there's ever going to be." Dramatic pause. Eyes lowered. "Forty-seven paintings and five pieces of sculpture. This is it." She waved a careless hand to indicate the sweep of the gallery.

She was tall, about six feet one, what my grandmother Sonya would have called a long drink of water. But to an immigrant who lived where food was not plentiful, it would have been said with pity.

Veronica Cahill was anything but pitiful looking. She was stylishly slim and elegant, not poor and underfed. Her red hair, red from a bottle but nevertheless gorgeous, was cut short, boyish on someone else, but not on Veronica. Her features were slightly oversize—large eyes, long nose, wide mouth—giving her a dramatic look that the cropped hair, the makeup, the big jewelry, and the constant use of her large, long-fingered hands only emphasized. She had a ring on every finger, several bracelets that made noise as she moved, piercing hazel eyes that gave each and every one of us a turn. She was some piece of work, this Veronica Cahill.

"How did you discover Cliff?" someone asked.

"Oh, I've known Clifford for ages. I've been watching his art develop and waiting for a large enough body of work so that I could do this," she said, once again gesturing around the room. She smiled for someone's camera. She was wearing a short green silk dress to emphasize her legs, which, if she were lying down, would reach from here to Hoboken. And shoes I couldn't sit in, let alone walk in.

I had lost the drift of the interview for a moment, but something brought me sharply back.

"—saw it all, that poor, dear thing. It's lucky *he* didn't get killed, too. You can see, in Clifford's work of the last few years, how the image of Magritte, *our* Magritte, of course, not Ren, is used to express Clifford's emotional turmoil."

Shit. Dennis had told Louis, and Louis had told Veronica. Was that before he promised to watch his mouth or after?

"How do they know he was there? I had heard the dog was missing," a pretty woman in skintight jeans asked.

"Oh, it seems Clifford's friends have chipped in and hired a detective. A retired *police* detective. This is off the record, of course. It's all very hush-hush," she said to reporters from the *Times*, the *News*, the *Village Voice*, *People* magazine, and the *New Yorker*, according to the press badges I could see. "You know, so many of these cases go unsolved. Well, Clifford's friends would have none of that. At any rate, Magritte's collar and leash turned up at the pier. Poor thing. You know, it's most amazing, his recovery. It was because of a tattoo—"

The note taking had taken on a furious pace when I decided the only rational thing to do was to find Dennis and murder him. As I began to work my way out of the group that had gathered around Veronica, I could hear her finishing her botched story about how the National Dog Registry works and I heard her say, "The little darling is here, if you'd like photographs."

Somehow I knew it was Magritte she was referring to, not me, a retired *police* detective.

I decided to look at some more of the pieces, not wanting to find my face in Saturday's paper, even as part of the background. My only hope now was that my fucking name wouldn't appear along with the rest of the information I'd rather not have as public knowledge.

I decided to take a philosophical attitude.

A fuckup. How unusual.

The paintings were actually arranged intelligently, earliest to most recent. Unless you headed straight for the bar, you would see the few pre-Magritte paintings when you first came in. Next you'd see the beginnings of the flat technique, the texture of the canvas as part of the painting. The very early works looked more decorative, and though they were certainly beautiful, they didn't have the punch of the post-Magritte paintings, nor the humor of the Magritte pieces. *Our* Magritte, not Ren. I was surprised to see the small painting of Magritte as an angel, talk about oxymorons, because it had to have been one of Cliff's personal favorites, but then I noticed the "NFS"—not for sale—on the title card. That pleased me enormously. I loved the piece. It was as beautiful and perfect as an old miniature.

The alienation grew as you proceeded toward the later works, and then there was a sudden, harsh change with the appearance of the untitled "Uncle Miltie" painting and several other of these recent works, all in black, gray, and white or in grays with one startling touch of color. For example, there was one called *s. b.* that showed a street-tough boy, around twelve, in a dress. Everything else was typically male: dirty high-tops, one sock up and one halfway down, even the basketball steadied with one hand and poised on his hip. Everything was in shades of gray, except the basketball.

I looked around for *les and mor*. It should have been with this group of recent work, but it wasn't. I wondered if Veronica deemed it too weird to include it. But certainly others were equally disturbing.

When I glanced around for Dennis, I panicked. I had forgotten that Dashiell was with him. If Dashiell showed up in the papers, I might as well be there too. It would kill the chance for me to work undercover again. This was serious. Deception was not only essential in this work, it was one of my favorite parts, sort of like improvisational acting, only sometimes life-threatening.

The photographers had finished with Magritte, and I got over there as soon as I could get through the crowd. If Cliff had only lived to see this day. Then again, had he lived, he might have gotten one piece in a barely advertised group show during the slowest time of the year, and three people, all relatives of the other artists, would have shown up. He wouldn't have made a dime.

I got next to Dennis and looked around. Dash was nowhere in sight. "*There* you are," Dennis said, before I had a chance to say a word. "My friend Roger took Dashiell for a walk. You were tied up with Gil, and Dash kept looking at pedestals as if they were fire hydrants. Maybe he was just too hot, I don't know. Rog should be back any minute. I hope that's okay?"

That's when it occurred to Dennis that it might not be okay. I could see the fear coming into his eyes.

"I did it again, right?"

But before I had a chance to describe the enormous knot in my stomach over the fear that a stranger had taken my dog and I'd never see him again (how could I be sure Rog wasn't the murderer!), I was thrown onto Dennis and nearly knocked him down. It was just Dashiell's way of telling me how happy he was to see me again. He often made his sentiments crystal clear with a head butt.

"Rog, this is—"

"Louise," I said, standing up and giving Dennis a look that if looks could kill it would have, "Louise Keaton. I'm Dennis's cousin." Seeing the look on Roger's face, I added, "Long lost. Which is why he may have never mentioned me." I was too distraught and angry to do a good job of this. I just shrugged, turned to Dennis, and said, "We have to talk, cuz."

"Roger, thanks." Then he turned to me. "You *know* Dr. Schwartzman said no more alcoholic beverages, Lou*ise*." And back to Rog. "I have to get her out into the air."

We retrieved our coats from the rack in the back room and headed for the stairs. Magritte jumped down each steep step, following Dashiell, who kept turning to see if he was coming. When we got to the street, I opened my mouth, and Dennis grasped the back of my coat collar and hoisted it, making me lose my train of thought.

"Not yet, Lou*ise*. We need a drink first."

I decided not to remind him that he had just finished telling Rog that I was under doctor's orders regarding alcoholic beverages.

We stopped at the first place we came to. I showed the waiter Dash's bright yellow Registered Service Dog tag. He didn't say anything about Magritte, so neither did I, and we were taken to a corner table.

"Two kir royales, please," Dennis said. "And keep them coming."

He turned to me, reached out, and covered one of my hands, covering his face with his other hand. "Give me a minute," he said. I decided to skip the several sarcastic things that popped into my head, and wait.

"Look. First of all, I'm sorry."

"You ought to be," I said angrily. "I don't make it a practice to lend my dog or my gun to strangers."

"You have a gun?"

"Do Hasidim have sheets with holes in them?"

Dennis rolled his eyes.

"Okay. I accept your apology."

"Except *that*'s not what I was apologizing for. It was—the *other* thing. But I fucked up before you told me, uh, not to fuck up. Okay? I didn't think. I didn't know Louis Leaky would tell Veronica." He held up his hand. "Yes, yes, I know about it. And then for her to tell the press. God! At least she got it screwed up."

The kir royales arrived. The bubbles looked pretty rising through the raspberry-colored creme-de-cassis-spiked champagne. I lifted my glass, clinked Dennis's, which was sitting on the table, and took a sip.

"I spoke to Louis. He spoke to Veronica. We've, uh, locked the barn. I'm sorry." He picked up his glass and chugged half of it down. "Are you hungry?"

"Starved! Let's forgive each other and eat. But not until we have a few of these." I could feel the drink going to my head and warming my body, all at once and all lovely. The fact is, as long as my name and picture didn't appear in the paper, the rest was workable. I told Dennis. He leaned over and hugged me and finished his drink. The waiter brought two more. I hurried to catch up.

"Okay," I said, "there'll be a few articles about Cliff, they'll say thank God his lost dog was found, the prices of the paintings will go up, and"—I gave his glass another clink; this time it was in his hand—"Morgan Gilmore has been stealing sperm!"

"What?"

"Morgan Gilmore has been banking Magritte, for who knows how long. Evidently he refused to take no for an answer. So Magritte has sired pups, my guess is a *lot* of pups, and it looks as if Gil has been pocketing the stud fees."

"Good grief. Gil?"

"On Monday I'll go over to the American Kennel Club library and check the studbooks for the last few years and see if I can get an approximate count of Magritte's get. This could be big bucks, all stolen from Clifford."

"Rachel," Dennis said. He took a long drink of his kir. "*How* could I have forgotten! Well, I know how. I mean, it was *ages* ago, he never explained it, and, well, nothing happened. You know how it is, your own problems are at the fore, and you, well, you get caught up, oh God, I should have remembered. I should have told you."

"What? What are you babbling about?"

The waiter put two more drinks on the table. I felt something brush my leg, and suddenly a basenji was on my lap.

"About three months ago, Cliff came over looking really upset. It was in the evening, sevenish. I was having dinner. I asked him to join me, but he declined. He wouldn't even sit down. He was pacing. I hate it when people do that, don't you?"

"Dennis—"

"Right. He had left Magritte with me and gone out late in the afternoon, said he'd be gone a few hours, then come back for Magritte. I don't know where he was. He never said. He just said that he had found out something about someone and it had to be exposed, at any cost. I asked him what he had found out and who he was talking about, and he just said, 'Wait and see, old buddy. Wait and see.'

"Well, I was worried about him when it happened, but he never brought it up again. I was having this huge problem with my publisher, so I forgot about it. I wonder if he was talking about Gil, if he had discovered what Gil was doing. He was really upset, and God, he loved that little dog to pieces. He would have been wild, absolutely wild, if he had known what Gil had done. And Rachel, he was wild that night."

"But he never mentioned it again? He never said another word about finding out about something that had to be exposed?"

"Not a word."

"Does that strike you as unusual, I mean, to be so upset and then nothing?"

"Actually, no. I do it all the time, don't you?"

"Sure. But this is different. It's not like getting dunned for a bill you paid. It's bigger. And ongoing. Why didn't it come up again, I mean, if it *was* about Gil?"

"Because of the way Cliff was. He'd get really angry, then he'd plot."

"Plot?"

"He'd let it simmer, and he'd figure out what to do to get even, to hurt the person who hurt him. He used to quote that saying, you know, revenge is a dish best served cold. I don't know if he ever actually *did* anything, but sometimes he liked to talk about what he *wanted* to do to someone he thought was an enemy, something sneaky, so they wouldn't know it was coming or, if they did, they still wouldn't be able to do anything to stop it."

"He wouldn't have been direct?"

"I don't think so. Even if he said something, he wouldn't necessarily have let it go, the hurt. You know what I mean?"

I nodded.

"You couldn't just apologize. You'd have to wait for him to get over it in his own time and his own way. Even if it was something trivial, like you forgot a date with him. Or you were late. He'd be friendly, then when you figured it was okay, he'd get real sarcastic. I feel so disloyal saying this to you, I mean, I . . . he was my *friend*."

Dennis was looking even paler than usual.

"The thing is, he was your friend despite his faults. That's nothing to feel bad about."

He nodded. "I guess."

"Here's something to feel bad about. You look like shit. Let's get some food, okay?"

"Sure, sure. You order for us," he said, and I did—osso buco, which I had been dying for since hearing Louis's voice on Clifford's old answering machine tape.

As soon as the waiter had taken the order, I put Magritte back on the floor. I was pretty sure that once the food arrived, he'd turn into a cat burglar, and I thought I might have a better shot at defending my dinner if the burglar weren't on my lap.

"Dennis," I said, tearing into a roll while we waited for the meal, "those paintings of that older guy in drag, the one with the flowered housedress?"

"What about them?"

"Have you ever seen them before?"

He shook his head.

"I was wondering about that one, because Cliff always put a title on the last panel, and that one doesn't have a title. It's the only one in the show that doesn't have one."

The waiter showed up with the food, which immediately captured the attention of all four animals at the table. But even though I was as hungry as the next omnivore, it's difficult for me to let go once I have a question on my mind. "And?"

"Probably just didn't finish it," he said, his mouth full of food. For a while, the only sound was the pitiful whining of a hopeful basenji. When I looked down to give Magritte the eye, the most powerful tool a dog trainer has, particularly when her mouth is otherwise occupied, I noticed that Dashiell, God bless him, was back asleep. He has this unshakable faith that if I have food with his name on it, I'll be sure to let him know.

When Dennis's plate was almost empty, he looked critically at mine. "What?" I growled.

Getting raised by Beatrice Kaminsky is sort of like passing a car accident every day. You don't want to know, but your curiosity always gets the better of you. So even before he answered, I knew that asking had been a mistake.

"Eat your veal. Some little baby cow suffered so you wouldn't have to sate yourself on boring chicken."

"Yes, Beatrice."

"Beatrice?"

"My mother. You keep reminding me of her." I offered him my most insincere smile.

"Oh," he said, his hand to his bosom, "I like *that*. One little touch of guilt and criticism, and already it's getting testy with me. Eat, don't eat," he said, "it's all the same to me."

When the check came, Dennis and I had a brief battle over it, but not wanting to bruise the delicate male ego, I let him win.

"I'll walk you home," he said when we got outside.

"You don't have to do that. I'm a detective."

"Okay, then I'll walk you as far as Houston Street."

"Deal."

"Rachel, I have to go to Boston right after Westminster, to see my editor and meet with the art director. I'll be gone until midday Saturday. I could never get another good handler this close to the show. And Gil really brings Magritte out. But no matter what you find out this week, I don't want Magritte with Gil for one more minute after Westminster. You know, it wouldn't have been the money that would have bothered Cliff. It would have been the lying, for sure, but more than that, the loss of control of what happened with Magritte. He would have hated that. So I need a gigantic favor. Could you take Magritte for me until I get back from Boston? Gil said he'd keep him for me, but I definitely don't want to do that, and I can't bear to board him. He won't be any trouble at all. He's got wonderful manners. Unless you don't consider licking his balls wonderful manners. Lucky mutt. I always have to find someone else to lick mine."

"That can be very time-consuming," I said. "That aside, we'll take him. Dashiell loves to have friends sleep over." As a show dog, Magritte would be crate trained, so if I had to leave him home alone, I could still come home and find my possessions intact. And if he carried on, no one would hear him. Shelly and Norma Siegal wouldn't be back from Florida for at least another month. "I'll be at Westminster anyway. I'll just take Magritte home with me after Best in Show."

Dennis sighed. "Clifford sold more paintings tonight than in the entire time he was alive," he said. "Maybe he'll even get a posthumous cult following, like Frida Kahlo. Weird how things work, isn't it?"

The light was green as we approached Houston Street, so Dash and I ran to make it across Houston Street. When we reached the other side, I turned and waved to Dennis.

In a world where appearances are everything, this proud oaf had loved a beautiful man. But now Beauty was dead, and the Beast was as lonely and miserable as ever. Sounds like one of the bedtime stories Lili used to make up for me when our parents were out and had left her in charge.

14

Let Sleeping Dogs Lie

WHEN I GOT home, I fed Dash, checked the answering machine, and got ready for bed, but I was as wide awake as if I had just run out of a sauna and jumped into a snowdrift.

There's a period in every case when I feel really confused. It's usually from right after I'm hired until I find out who did it.

Dog training is a lot easier. At least you know who the criminal is. Okay, *sometimes* it's the dog, but usually it only *seems* as if it's the dog. More often than not it's the owner, the so-called intelligent partner who thought it was cutesy-poo when little Killer growled for six months before he actually started putting his teeth into it.

The thing is, when you're called in to solve a dog problem, you get to meet all the players up front. You'd be surprised how clear things look when the dog is seen in the context of his pack. When a dog is an accident waiting to happen, you can see it, and when the problem is fixable, most of the time you can fix it.

With human beings, things are never so clear. Motives are more complex, behavior is more devious, and the histories are infinitely longer and more twisted.

Dogs live in the present. They're not capable of planned revenge. Alas, people are.

Had Morgan Gilmore been an accident waiting to happen? Was it only a matter of time before one of his clients found out what he was doing and confronted him? For surely, if he was doing this with Magritte, he could be doing it with any dog he was handling.

Did Gil murder Cliff because Cliff finally confronted him about the thefts? Had Clifford threatened to expose him? In that case, Gil would have lost more than a good client. He would have lost his occupation.

Still, the question remained, how did he know Cliff would be out on the pier so that he could try to pass off the killing as a gay bashing?

I was pacing now, the way Clifford did that night he told Dennis he had found out something and that someone had to be exposed. It went underground then, stewed and simmered in him. He couldn't rid himself of all the bad feeling, couldn't confront and forgive, or even if that's what he had decided to do, maybe Gil couldn't take the chance that people would find out what he had done.

The American Kennel Club library wouldn't be open until Monday. But I didn't have to wait to see if I could get more dirt on Gil. I had every Westminster catalog since I began studying dog training. I went into the study, pulled two recent catalogs off the shelf, opened the first, and found the list of basenjis. The catalog not only listed the name of each dog entered and the name of the handler showing him but listed the name of the sire, too. This wouldn't tell me how many litters Magritte had sired or how many stud fees Morgan Gilmore had pocketed. It would only tell me if any of Magritte's get had been entered in Westminster. It was only the tip of the iceberg, but it was the only thing I could do until I could get into those studbooks on Monday morning.

Two Magritte daughters had competed two years ago. By the dates of birth, as well as the names of the dams, they were not littermates. Last year, three of Magritte's get were entered, one of the same bitches from the year before and two dogs, not of the same litter as either the bitch or each other. Apparently the frozen semen business was brisk.

I thought about the message from Gil on Cliff's answering machine tape. He said nothing about needing Cliff to sign the entry form. I pulled out an events calendar from my pile of *Gazette*s, the magazine published by the American Kennel Club, and checked the form. It called for the name of the owner of the dog, printed, and his all-important AKC registration number, so of course Gil had to know that, but it could be signed by *either* the owner or his duly authorized agent. And Magritte's duly authorized agent was Gil.

But what about litter registrations? Those certainly needed the owner's signature. Then again, with thousands and thousands of litters registered every year, who was sitting around double-checking every signature to make sure it was the actual owner of the bitch or dog who had signed each form? Don't sweat it if you don't know the answer. It was a rhetorical question.

I had the feeling that even a false signature on a bank check would go undetected unless the amount was unusually large, in which case the bank might check the signature, or unless the owner of the account realized that a certain check had been written and signed by someone else when he or she got back a month's worth of canceled checks with the statement. As Joan Rivers would say, grow up. Stealing stud fees was no doubt even easier than collecting the sperm with which to steal them.

Dashiell was on top of the blankets with his head on my pillow, and being a devout believer in the adage Let sleeping dogs lie, I had no choice but to squeeze down under the covers from the top.

Clifford had told Dennis that he had discovered something that had to be exposed at all cost. Was the cost losing a top basenji handler? Was it losing someone he thought was a friend worthy of his trust?

It's a funny thing, trust. Like Humpty Dumpty, once it's been broken, you can never put it back together again.

15

I Have My Standards

DASHIELL'S WHIMPERING WOKE me. His feet were running in his sleep, his eyelids twitching. As I gently scratched the back of his neck to quiet him, I realized that I had been dreaming, too.

I was at a large table, a street map of the Village spread out before me, the twisty streets with their unexpected turns, the private mews, the alleys, all there, but without names.

I was trying to find my way somewhere, but each time I thought I had it, I looked again and found the map oriented a different way. Once again I'd find my starting place, and with my finger I'd trace the streets, trying to make my way to wherever it was I just had to go. And each time I thought I was there, I'd find myself more lost than the time before.

I got up, padded barefooted down to the kitchen, put up the kettle, and opened the front door for Dashiell. There had been a fresh dusting of snow during the night. The yard was as still as a graveyard, everything silent and white.

I went back to the kitchen and made tea, still trying to shake the disturbing aftereffects of the dream. Dashiell came in, the *Times* in its cold plastic bag hanging out of his mouth, dropped it on my bare feet, and tossed himself onto the living-room rug with a sigh. I was feeling grumpy, too. I was coming down with a cold. The weather wasn't going to help, frigid winds coming down from Canada, chance of snow late in the day, high of twenty-two.

I started looking at the paper, just turning pages, barely seeing what was in front of me, until I got to the arts pages. Suddenly, I was on the qui vive.

There was Magritte, an incredible head shot, wrinkled forehead, manipulative dark eyes, to-die-for black gumdrop nose, head held on that slant dogs have perfected that can melt the hearts of statues. The title was short and to the point: WITNESS TO MURDER.

"A witness has been found in the murder of New York artist Clifford Cole, 32, who was found dead on the Christopher Street pier early on January 20th of this year in what the police are regarding as a random bias crime. The artist's dog, a champion basenji, the barkless African breed, who was reported missing the day of the crime, was recovered through an identifying tattoo on his inner right thigh."

It went on to say that it had been learned that the basenji dog, Ch. Ceci N'Est Pas un Chien, known to his friends as Magritte, had been a witness to the vehicular homicide of his master, whose opening last night at the Cahill Gallery in SoHo drew a record crowd. Veronica Cahill, who characterized Clifford's work as "William Wegman meets Diane Arbus," remembered to mention to the press that she had extended the run of the show from the usual three weeks to five weeks. And then came the good part.

The article quoted a couple of ersatz experts, the first a "dog psychologist" named Rick Shelbert who talked about "memory and trauma."

"If Magritte were in the presence of the killer," Dr. Shelbert stated, "there's no doubt he would react with fear. Because of the trauma," Dr. Shelbert had gone on to tell the *Times,* "Magritte would remember the scent of the killer forever."

Mobil, unleaded? It was doubtful the killer got out of his car.

"Magritte should be taken back to the scene of the crime," said Tracy Nevins, a local dog trainer.

Leave it to the *Times* to interview not one but *two* blowhards.

"With several visits to the area of the murder, he could be desensitized. Then nonfearful behavior could be shaped and reinforced with food treats, the most effective of which would be the freeze-dried liver tidbits with which handlers customarily bait the dogs in the show ring."

As to whether or not Magritte could finger his master's killer, Nevins was quoted as saying, "Definitely."

I read on.

"Magritte's new owner, Dennis Kenton, who writes and illustrates books for children, said the plucky little dog 'seemed none the worse for wear.'"

Funny. That didn't sound a bit like the Dennis "Kenton" I knew.

"'We are still planning on having Magritte compete at Westminster on Tuesday,' Kenton added. 'Clifford would have wanted him to be there.' The show, the second-oldest continuous sporting event in the country, second only to the Kentucky Derby, takes place Monday and Tuesday at Madison Square Garden. A representative of the Westminster Kennel Club said there was enormous interest in the show, particularly now that it was a champions-only event."

I decided not to call Dennis. What was there to say?

I felt a sneeze coming and put the paper down. A moment later, I heard a familiar *pop*. Then Dashiell showed up with a tissue hanging from his big mouth. I used the half he hadn't chewed on for the next sneeze. It made me wish one of my dog trainer friends were here to appreciate Dashiell's grand trick. But dog training is a loner's profession, and even when I was still part of it, I only got to see my trainer friends once a year, during Westminster and all the posh award dinners that preceded it.

When I first got into training, I got a kick out of crashing the Ken-L Ration dinner. It was an invitation-only black-tie event and considered the big ticket of the weekend. So it was a coup to be seen there. No matter how you got in.

It was at the Waldorf then, and for years this other dog trainer, Chip Pressman, and I used to meet there and sneak in together. Like basenjis, we wanted to be precisely where we weren't allowed.

The raison d'etre for the dinner is to honor the top show dogs of the year and their owners and handlers, and, of course, get all sorts of nice publicity for the product. There's always a guest speaker, usually someone funny to warm up the audience before the long, repetitious award ceremony, and lots of opportunities for schmoozing up new contacts and work possibilities.

Gil would be at the dinner. Shouldn't I be too? It would be a good way to hear a little helpful gossip, and it might be fun to try my hand at crashing the dinner, because now you had to do more than just sign in. Now you had to present your invitation to the guardians at the door. Difficult, true, but this was New York, where everything is possible.

Some people think New York is only a great place to visit, but take it from me, it's also a great place to live and work. For example, if you ever get a craving for Glatt kosher take-out for a long, hungry stakeout or you're dying to see a Broadway show you can't afford and don't mind missing the first act, you'd really appreciate this town.

For the first yen, try Lou Siegal's Glatt Kosher Restaurant on West Thirty-eighth Street. They deliver, but for a stakeout you should pick up. Law number four says, Don't call undue attention to yourself.

You used to be able to get kosher Chinese at Bernstein on Essex on the Lower East Side or Moishe Peking in the thirties, and kosher Japanese, yet, at Shalom Japan in SoHo, except of course on Shabbos, but they're all gone now. Like it or not, things change.

Anyway, as to the play, simply walk in with the smokers after the intermission. The stories aren't that complicated, and they always save the best stuff for the second half.

You can also crash almost any large celebratory dinner, such as the Ken-L Ration award banquet, which I was now planning to crash, by waiting until it begins and entering as if you belong after the invitation collectors have closed up shop. You have to figure that with two to three hundred people there, someone didn't make it. So there will be an empty seat for you. But be sure you dress as if you've been invited, or you'll stick out like a Great Dane at a cat show.

If this method would make you so tense you'd feel as if you were digesting a piano, opt for the second one.

Don't go an hour late. Go an hour early. Begin the evening by crashing the press hour that precedes the cocktail hour. Simply walk in carrying an expensive camera—I use my Nikon—and be prepared with the name of a magazine or newspaper, particularly one that usually doesn't cover dog events. In that way, you're less likely to run into the reporter or photographer the magazine *actually* sent, and you won't be questioned, because who would want to offend, say, the *New Yorker*? You can even disarm them by complaining that you just heard about their event yesterday and would they *kindly* give you a little more notice in the future. Using this method, you don't miss the free drinks, and there's much more chance to circulate and eavesdrop.

I heard the familiar nasal twang the moment I entered the cocktail hour for the winners and the press.

"Kaminsky, you bitch, where have you been keeping yourself?"

I turned around to see Susan Samuelson, who writes about the fancy for *Dog World* magazine. The fancy refers not to people who fancy dogs, such as myself, but to people who show dogs, such as the people being honored at the Ken-L Ration dinner.

"On the coast," I lied.

"Miss New York?" she asked, raising her plucked eyebrows. She was a sixtyish elf in velvet leggings, ballet slippers, and a tux jacket, her white hair in a pixie cut.

"For sure."

"Back to stay?"

"Think so. I missed the humidity."

"Yeah. So where can I reach you when I need a quote? Are you listed or un?"

I wrote my number on the back of her press notes. Susan used to call me all the time for quotes when I was working as a trainer, which helped my reputation and the accuracy of her articles, making for a very serendipitous symbiosis.

"Susan, *I* need a little info. A client of mine got an unbeatable offer, sort of a half-price deal, for breeding to a top show dog—for cash. From the *handler.*"

"Naughty, naughty. Who?"

"Confidential?"

"Always. Unless you tell me otherwise. Cough it up, kiddo."

"Morgan Gilmore."

"Uh—no surprise."

"How come?"

"You don't read the secretary's pages anymore?" She scraped her pointers at me, just like in grade school. "Reprimanded by the AKC, once for disorderly conduct, twice that I know of for registration violations."

"And he's still handling? He wasn't suspended? How the hell does he get away with it?"

"Grow up, my dear. They don't call him the Teflon handler for nothing. And anyway, if we tossed out the people who cheat, there might not be enough people left to run a dog show, and I'd be out of a job. We'll talk?"

"Definitely."

"Great. Hey, Kaminsk, where's your tan?"

"Sunblock. I used a shitload of sunblock."

She nodded and turned away. A moment later, there was a hand on my shoulder.

"Where have you *been*, bitch?"

It was Mike Chapman, a dog trainer who wrote a newspaper column for the *Bergen Record*, a Jersey paper. I guess I should explain that, as a dog trainer, I never considered "bitch" a criticism, merely the proper nomenclature for the female of the species.

"The coast," I said. "L.A."

"Are you back for the show or back back?"

I always wondered how Mike did the work. He was about my height and as wide as a doorway, big belly hanging over his belt so that he could never button his jacket, hands and face red, and he wheezed when he spoke.

"Back back," I told him. "I missed the snow."

The waiter came by with skewers of chicken basted in ginger and soy sauce. We each took two.

"So, you're going to be training in Manhattan again? Or what? Were you working out on the coast?"

"Sort of. Got married and divorced since I saw you."

"Heavy!" he said. "You okay?"

"I'm great."

"Hey, I heard about Bernie. Sorry, kid. What are you working with these days, another Golden?"

My mouth was full of chicken. "Pit bull," I said as soon as I could. "And I have a nice little basenji bitch, pointed, I want to breed."

"Basenji? Rachel—"

"I know. I know. Anyway, I was thinking of breeding her to Magritte. I got this swell offer from Morgan Gilmore, his handler—"

"Morgan *Gil*more! Shit!"

"What?"

"Six, eight months ago, that SOB tripped another handler in the ring, guy from the coast, maybe you know him, Ted Stickley?"

I shook my head.

"Fucker fell and broke his left arm, got up, punched Gilmore right in the snout with his right. Got a round of applause, too. Don't deal with Gilmore, Rachel. He's a snake."

"I wouldn't have to send my bitch to him. He banks Magritte." I took the last bite of chicken and waited.

"All the more reason to be careful. He could be sending you *anything*. His *own* sperm, for all you'd know."

I made a face. "Thanks for warning me."

I walked over to the bar, asked for a glass of white wine, and stood watching everyone talk while I sipped it. Being called Kaminsky had instantly drawn me back to the suffocating bosom of my hypercritical family. Beatrice had been dead for over five years, but the memories lingered on.

"Where are you going?" she used to ask me.

"Out."

"Yes, but with your hair like that?"

Gotcha.

People were starting to head out, and when I looked at my watch, I saw it was time for the regular cocktail hour. The award winners and press moved to a larger ballroom, actually two rooms with several bars, tables full of raw vegetables, cheeses, and dips, and several hundred people who knew what and where a hock joint was.

Morgan Gilmore was a few feet from where I was standing, his neat ponytail resting on the satin collar of his tuxedo jacket, a glass of wine in one hand and a cigar in the other. He wore his string tie instead of a bow tie and cowboy boots. Black lizard. How fitting! He was as classy as a bowling trophy.

I intended to stick as close to Gilmore as gum on his shoe, but I was back in my old milieu, and every time I tried to eavesdrop, someone else had another story to tell me. When the dinner hour arrived, I trailed behind Gil, ever hopeful, and managed to sit at the table next to his. But once again the animated conversation close at hand precluded hearing anything from his table. So while I ate my steak dinner, I ended up listening to how many points everyone's dog had accumulated during the last year. Just when my eyes were about to roll permanently up into my head, the ceremony began. I angled my chair so that I could watch Gil watch the proceedings.

The fifth law of investigation work says, Don't jump to conclusions. I began to wonder if I had. Just because Morgan Gilmore was a thief and a distasteful, repugnant human being did not make him a murderer.

In fact, I was only dead sure that he was distasteful and repugnant. I didn't even know for sure that he *was* a thief.

Suppose Cliff had lied to Dennis. Dennis thought Cliff was close to broke. Was it part of Clifford's southern manners to hide yet another easy source of income from his hardworking friend?

How did I know that Gil wasn't giving the stud fees or some agreed-upon percentage of them to Cliff after all? What if he was just a tasteless slime, and not a thief at all, let alone a killer?

Suddenly all I could think about was Clifford Cole's cozy little den, where, among his other papers, he kept his bank records. A peek in there might let me know if Gil was sharing those hefty stud fees or not. I figured the stud fee for a good-quality champion basenji such as Magritte would be five hundred at the lowest, and up to maybe one thousand if Gil had a real sucker interested. I didn't know if I'd find anything that might possibly mean Gil was sending checks to Cliff, but whether or not he was became the loose thread of the moment.

I decided it would be too rude, even for me, to leave in the middle of the speeches. So I waited until the bitter end before air-kissing my table companions and then running off to beat them to the coat check. I have my standards. They may be low, but they're there.

16

Nowhere in Sight

I TOOK A cab to the cottage, changed clothes, draped Dashiell's leash around my neck, and headed for Greene Street. Twenty minutes later I was sitting at Cliff's desk, the small green shaded desk light making a warm, bright circle on the open file folder with Clifford's bank records.

One large deposit was credited to Cliff's account every month, probably from some trust fund. It was done automatically—there were no deposit slips for those amounts. In fact, there were no deposit slips, period. Unless Gil was paying Cliff cash, unlikely with a deductible expense, he was indeed pocketing Magritte's stud fees.

I returned the file folder to its place in the lower left-hand drawer and opened the other drawers again to see if something would register that didn't the first time around. The more you learn on a case, the more you can understand the possible importance of what you see, the significance of something ordinary that normally might not catch your eye.

I was looking at the odds and ends in the middle drawer, the place where people keep pens, paper clips, rubber bands, and loose change. First I found a receipt for slides from B & H Photo. I put it in my pocket. There can be nothing more heart-wrenching than looking at the last photographs someone took. It's like getting mail from someone after they've died. But I thought Dennis or Louis would want them anyway.

Next I spotted a penlight and remembered that I had wanted to look at the paintings in the storage closet, but the light hadn't been working. I wondered if there'd be anything left to look at, or if, like the rest of the loft, the closet too would be depressingly denuded of Clifford's art.

I flicked on the penlight, shut off the lamp, and walked across the hall. The closet door opened with a slight creak, releasing the musty smell of a place too jammed with stuff to have been cleaned. There was also a faint odor like that of raw wood in lumberyards, probably from the unfinished floor. I walked in, the penlight making the tiniest imaginable circle of light in the nearly empty closet.

Dashiell followed me into the closet and started sniffing the floor as I sent the small circle of light slowly around the walls, looking to see if any painting had been left by accident or design. After revealing nothing but the bare closet on three of the four sides, the light hit three stretchers that were leaning on the wall to my right. I walked farther into the closet to take a better look.

Each of the three was as empty as a gaping, toothless mouth. It was my impression that stretchers were made and canvas stretched onto them only when the artist was ready to use them. Materials were expensive, and if someone other than Cliff were making the frames and stretching the canvas, then it was likely one would be made at a time. When I looked closer, I saw that these weren't new stretchers at all. They were dirty, splattered with drops of paint, and there were staples and threads on the back of each, as if canvas had been in place, used, and then removed.

I was leaning them back against the closet wall when I heard a key in the front-door lock.

I hadn't ever put on the light in the front room, and when I left the study, I had turned off the lamp, good training from my grandmother, who had lived through the Depression. So except for the small light from the penlight, the loft was dark.

For the briefest moment, I thought of Dennis, coming to check the answering machine.

I heard the door open, there was a silence, then the door closed.

If someone had entered the loft, they were wearing sneakers. Or they were barefooted. I tried to stop breathing so that I could hear them, but the loft was silent. I slid my finger off the button of the flashlight. Then I remembered Dashiell. I could no longer see him in the pitch-black closet, and my own breathing seemed so loud now that I couldn't hear his.

Suddenly there was light coming from the front room. I looked behind me and then stepped back into the far corner of the closet. When I turned, I saw Dashiell at the closet door, standing absolutely still, his head cocked to one side. I could see his nose twitching, trolling for a scent. It would come toward him in the shape of a cone, strong and narrow where it left the person, wider and fainter the farther it traveled. I needed to get Dashiell's attention so that I could signal him to come closer to me and stay quiet, but a sick feeling in my gut told me it wasn't Dennis, and I was reluctant to speak. Instead I reached behind me to scratch my nails on the wall so that Dash would turn and look at me.

I heard a drawer open and close in the front room and some clicking noises, and then there was silence except for the small whoosh of Dashiell blowing air out of his nose, the way dogs do when they ride with their heads flying out of car windows, to clear the way for an interesting new scent. Then, just as my hand found the wall, I heard Dash sneeze, and I knew he had the scent he was after. Faster than you could say *Gesundheit*, he was, as they say in my neighborhood, out of the closet.

For a few seconds I heard only the sound of Dashiell's nails on the hardwood floor. He was walking slowly, as if he were going to meet an old friend.

Was I being too paranoid, even for New York? If Dashiell wasn't worried, it *must* be Dennis who came in to check the answering machine.

Of course. That's what the clicking must have been. The answering machine.

Dashiell sneezed again. This time it was the kind that could blow your house down. Someone inhaled audibly—okay, gasped—and then I heard the crash. The front door opened and, a moment later, slammed shut. I bolted out of the closet and ran like hell toward the front room.

The odor hit me first, a sickly sweet cloud of aftershave or perfume. Lately, they all seemed the same. A sort of nasal androgyny has taken over the scent business. Whatever it was, it made me sneeze, too.

I rounded the corner and saw Dashiell. He was standing in the light of the lamp near the front door, just wagging his tail. Next to him, lying broken on the floor, was Clifford Cole's answering machine. When I picked it up and popped open the cover, I saw that the spool on the left was empty. I looked around on the floor, but the message tape was nowhere in sight.

17

If the Shoe Fits

LILLIAN TRIED TO get her arms around me as I de-bused, but couldn't make it. Both my arms were wrapped around her bulky birthday present, and Dash was pulling me in the opposite direction, doing a great imitation of an untrained dog.

"How are you?" she asked.

I sort of nodded and grunted. I had arrived more in body than in spirit.

I had gone to the huge windows in the front of Clifford's loft, struggled to open one, and then hung out, despite my fear of heights, as far as I could, just short of what would make me tip forward a trifle too far, lose my grip on the frame, and plummet screaming to the street, where my head would split open like a ripe melon dropped from the roof. I tried like hell to see who was leaving the building, but the gallery, Haber's, had these colorful flags out front with their current artist's name on them, so all I saw was a glimpse of a tall man in a camel-colored coat, black beret, and white scarf quickly turning right and disappearing.

How many people had keys to the loft anyway?

"I said, 'Are you working?'" I heard Lillian say. She had taken Dashiell's leash, and we were heading for her Jeep Cherokee. Dashiell jumped up onto the backseat, and Lili helped me place Mr. Present next to him.

"Feels expensive."

"I don't want to think about that part."

"You must *really* love me," she said, pulling out of the parking lot. She was beaming.

"I got work," I told her. Then I gave her the bare bones of the case, skipping my visit to the loft late last evening. Hey, I was alone at a murdered man's residence in the middle of the night, and a tall man in sneakers, cheap aftershave, and a camel coat came in, broke the answering machine, and stole the message tape. What's the big deal? But my family has a low threshold of irrationality, forcing me to edit everything I tell them.

"You think this handler with the ponytail killed him?"

"Too soon to say."

Ted came out to meet us, wearing his white chef's apron with a wooden spoon in his left hand, and gave me a long bear hug. "Rachel has a new case," Lili told him excitedly. Then she frowned. "Is this one going to be dangerous?"

Lili filled Ted in on her version of my version of the case as we walked inside.

"Would this artist have threatened the handler over the money?" Ted asked. "How much is involved in these stud fees?"

"Could be a lot. Thousands, anyway. But I don't think it would have been the money. He would have been livid about losing a choice as significant as whether or not his dog should be bred. At least, that's how Dennis sees it."

"And you? What do you see?" Ted asked.

"I'm still collecting data," I told him.

"But tell me, Rachel," he said, "how did this Gil person get Clifford out onto the pier?"

"Don't get technical," I told him. It was a Beatrice favorite when she was caught in an inconsistency.

"So this we don't know yet," Ted said. He was bending over, reaching into the oven, so I could see his bald spot.

"Roast chicken! I don't know about you, but I'm starving."

"So," Lillian said, "she's starving. What else is new?"

Had the intruder followed me? I wondered. But he had a key. What was he after on the message tape? Was it a message he himself had left and didn't want anyone else to hear?

"So, are you seeing anyone?" Ted asked. He was taking baked potatoes out of the oven one by one with a long-handled fork.

"No one special," I said.

"Well, we've met this young man, a single man, very nice. He sells woolens, imported fabric from Scotland, it's his own company, and—"

I wondered if he wore those plaid skirts.

"—we thought you and he could come to dinner sometime. You might like him."

"I don't know, Ted—"

Half the guys in my neighborhood wore skirts. Why would I have to come here for that?

"We hate to see you—" His voice trailed off, leaving the obvious unsaid. My family *is* subtle. You've got to give them that.

"What about all those good-looking policemen at the Sixth?" Lili chimed in. "Aren't any of them single?"

"Probably."

"So? A man in uniform? With good medical benefits?"

I sighed. "Cops leave the toilet seat up."

"Rachel, don't you get tired of—"

"I'm not alone," I said, skipping the part where she told me I would be forever and ever if I didn't learn to compromise. "I have Dashiell."

"Mea culpa," Ted said. "I'm sorry I mentioned it."

Lili called the kids and opened a bottle of white wine.

We gathered around the big round table in the open kitchen, which was a huge balcony overlooking the living room below, the spectacular view of the Hudson River ahead. For a while the only sounds were of platters being picked up and put down on the bare, round oak table and Lillian asking her children why they weren't taking vegetables onto their plates. As if it were the first time this was happening.

Don't talk about yourself, she'd told me more than once. Give the man a chance.

When would I get the message and stop coming to dinner on the lost continent, where time stopped in 1952? I was surprised my sister wasn't wearing a circle skirt with a poodle on it.

I tuned them all out and began to think about my case. Sometimes I'd get a message I wanted to save for one reason or another. I'd flip the tape, or if I *really* wanted to save it, I'd take the tape out of the answering machine and put it away, putting a new tape in the machine. But what could be on Clifford's tape *now*? Didn't everyone know he was dead? After all, it had been in the *New York* fucking *Times*.

"Ma!" It was Daisy.

"Stop teasing your sister," Lili said without even looking. She had probably said it a million times. "And don't fill up on bread," she added.

"My God, Lili, they've turned into us!"

"Zachery, use a fork. What do you mean?" she asked me, looking at me with her large hazel eyes.

I just shrugged. People not only dislike it when you make suggestions about their kids and dogs, they don't like it when you criticize the behavior of said offspring, unless that's what you're getting paid to do. At least that's what my shrink used to say as she criticized my behavior without the least inhibition.

"I've got this case now," I began to tell Daisy, who was seated across from me, "where half the people have changed their names."

"Maybe the other half have, too, but you just haven't found that out yet," Zach said.

"You may be right," I said. He was the older of the two, fifteen, and used to look like a cherub. Now his feet looked five sizes too big, and he had zits.

"Lots of people, in my day, changed their names for business reasons," Ted said.

"Yeah. Yeah. You mean they got rid of Jewish-sounding names so they could blend in."

"Did you ever think of doing that, Dad?" Daisy asked Ted.

"In *my* business? Hardly!"

"Did the people on your case change their names so that no one would know they were Jewish, Aunt Rachel?" Daisy asked.

"I don't know."

Lili got up to clear the table. My family are all graduates of the Evelyn Wood speed-eating course.

Had Dennis and Louis wanted to appear to be more mainstream? Or less like pushovers? Except for the Israelis, Jews were often characterized as wimps.

Had I thought Alexander sounded more game than Kaminsky?

I looked out over the living room and beyond to the river. It had gotten dark already, and the bridge lights were on. You could see the traffic slowly snaking its way to and from Westchester County, across the Hudson. I took Dashiell out, and we walked up to the crest of the mountain. Despite the quiet and the beauty around me, all I could think about was the case.

Maybe Clifford Cole's death *was* the result of random hate. Louis thought it was. It was easy enough, wasn't it? You just got a few friends together, took some sticks or bats and drove through the tunnel, then headed for the Village. The latest trick was to stop the car, ask directions to a gay bar, and if the stranger you had stopped gave them to you, everyone would jump out of the car and beat him to a pulp, justifying the action with the belief that no one but a lousy faggot would know how to get to the Monster or Sneakers. It's sort of a modern-day Cinderella story, a bunch of Jersey princes going around looking for a princess, or, in this fairy tale, a queen. And when they think the shoe fits, wham.

But what about the man in the camel coat? Could there have been a ponytail under that scarf or stuffed into that beret?

When we got back to the house, Ted was sitting in front of the fireplace, a fire burning and the brandy out, picking up the glow of the flames. I sat next to him, and for a while neither of us felt the need to talk.

"Stay over," he said after a while. "You can drive in with me in the morning."

The brandy was burning in my stomach. I leaned against his shoulder and sighed. "I can't," I said, the warmth of the fire on my face.

"You don't have to work tonight, do you, little sister?"

"No. But it's too quiet here. If not for Dashiell's snoring, I'd think I was dead."

He reached behind him, but I jumped up and out of the way. Then, due to my extensive professional training and a quick wit, I managed to get the brandy snifter off to the side before the couch pillow came sailing at me and hit me square in the chest.

"You're lucky my pit bull is such a sound sleeper," I said.

But Dashiell had awakened. He ambled over and was licking up the drops of brandy that had splashed out of my snifter when I got hit. Lili joined us then, and we talked for a couple of hours before they loaded me up with leftovers and drove me back to Nyack to catch the late bus home.

18

He Barked Twice

I HAD JUST stepped out of the shower when the phone rang. It was someone from Bailey House, the AIDS hospice at the foot of Christopher Street, saying they had heard about me and Dashiell from a caseworker who visited the Village Nursing Home, and they had both agreed that Dashiell would be an absolute godsend for their indigent AIDS patients. Since their social worker was in that morning and had a terribly tight schedule, they wondered if I could come over with Dash, say, in an hour, for a walk-through and a discussion about my adding Bailey House to Dashiell's schedule.

It was nine-thirty. I had to get over to the AKC library, check the studbooks to see if I could get some idea of how big a business Morgan Gilmore was conducting with Magritte's frozen semen, drop Dashiell off at home, hightail it over to the Garden, and see what else I could dig up about Gil from his fellow handlers. I told the person on the phone I'd be there in half an hour.

Bailey House is on the southeast corner of Christopher and West, across the highway from the Christopher Street pier. The building that houses Bailey House used to be the River Hotel. The whole top floor, with its sweeping, spectacular river views, belonged to the expensive, chic La Grande Corniche restaurant. You can still see both signs, but now homeless men and women occupy the whole building, people dying of AIDS who have nowhere else to do it.

I approached with the mixed feelings I always had doing this work. Why the hell was I here? How could I say no? Perhaps that's why Zachery says I'm only a medium-boiled detective.

Mr. Sabotini said he'd like to watch me with a few patients and see what Dashiell did, and then we could talk about the feasibility of regular visits. He was short and small with annoying little hands that fluttered constantly as he spoke, and he did that—speaking—slowly and carefully, exaggerating the enunciation of each and every syllable as if I were retarded or perhaps suffering from dementia. He was bald across the crown but had cleverly combed some long hair from the side of his head over the top and glued it down with something that made it look wet and stiff, so that of course no one could tell. And he was one of those self-important prigs who often end up working in institutions, people whose personalities are so offensive that they could never make it in any sort of private practice or in any situation where people feel they have any choice. I was ready to split when one of the patients walked into the office where we were talking and noticed Dashiell.

"Oh, God, it's Petey," he said, falling onto his knees and embracing Dashiell without asking anything. Lots of people called Dash Petey, the pit bull with the line drawn around his eye that was in the *Our Gang* comedies.

"Hi," I said. He didn't look up. His head was bent down against Dashiell's neck, and his arms reached way around, squeezing as tight as he could.

"He's won-der-ful," he said, his face so thin it was barely more than a skull, his eyes shining with the look some people get shortly before they die.

"His name is Dash."

"I'm Ronald," he said, taking his arm from around Dashiell and pointing to himself. "Will he be coming here regular?" He sat back on his heels and tightened the belt on his robe. "I like him so much."

"Ms. Alexander and Dashiell are here to discuss that today, Ronald," Mr. Sabotini said.

"Rachel," I said. "Can we walk you back to your room, Ronald?"

"Sure. Really?"

I handed him the leash and told him how to get Dashiell to heel.

Ronald was beaming. "Can I do this? Yes, I can do this. This is the most fun I ever had here."

"Me, too," I said. Mr. Sabotini was taking notes on a very little pad as we walked Ronald to the elevator, and seemed to miss the joke that Ronald and I were sharing.

I will say this for Robert Sabotini. He hung back and let me and Dashiell do our thing. Ronald, not Sabotini, became my guide, taking me from room to room, filling me in on names and bringing me up to date on each person's latest opportunistic illness, which Ronald referred to as an OI. He held Dash's leash and then passed it on to those who wanted to walk the big dog, too. Anyone who could, did.

I was surprised at how much I was enjoying myself, even though that's a funny term to use about a place like this. But each time we entered a room, the occupants would light up, and though their evident pleasure was because of Dashiell's presence, not mine, I still got to bask in the results. After we had visited nearly a dozen patients, Sabotini said he had seen enough and we could go downstairs and talk.

"No, wait. She di'n't meet John yet," he said. "Gotta show John Petey, okay, pleeze, Mr. Sabotini, it'll just take a minute. You go. I'll bring her down. I know the way."

"Well, if Ms. Alexander has the time, Ronald," Mr. Sabotini said.

"It's fine," I said. "We'll be down in five minutes."

"If you're quite sure," he said, smoothing down a hair that had come unstuck.

"She is. She's quite sure," Ronald said.

We watched Sabotini leaving like two little kids watching the teacher leave the room. Ronald took my hand and pulled me down the hall to a room at the end, near the window.

"This is John's room. I love him, John. He's so funny. He could always cheer you up, no matter what he has." Then he put his hand at the side of his mouth and in a dramatic aside told me, "He has KS. Kaposi's sarcoma," he said, enunciating carefully in a witty parody of Sabotini. "That's *can*cer," he explained. "Don't say nothin'. It makes bumps and dark spots, you know, on your skin, and John's real self-conscious about looking ugly."

"Okay," I told him, "I'll be cool."

We entered the small, sunny room with only one of the beds occupied, the other stripped, meaning John's roommate had recently died. Here you checked in, but you didn't check out.

Even though he was under the covers, I could see that John was unusually tall. He was also unusually thin, a not quite gaunt mocha-colored man with a bad case of KS, his face as lumpy as a flophouse mattress. He wasn't as thin as Ronald, who had wasting syndrome, but he was no Refrigerator Perry either. When he spoke, I heard the unclear, raspy voice that meant he had severe thrush, another sign of a system going down.

"Who you brings, man? You brother?" he said to Ronald. Then he began coughing into a small towel that had been lying next to him on the bed.

Ronald lit up. "See, Rachel, I told you. Isn't he funny? No, John, it's *your* brother. Only kidding. It's Petey. From *Our Gang.*"

"Yeah. And who I be? Buckwheat?" he said, coughing again.

"This is Dash. And I'm Rachel." I put out my hand, but he brushed at the air instead of taking it.

"You wanna walk him? He walks real nice," Ronald said, holding out Dashiell's leash. But I could see that John was not up to getting out of bed.

" 'Nother time," John said. "I takes him next time. Shows him where I use t' live. He like it they. Be real spacious." Then he began to cough again. I began to feel he was beyond where a visit from a dog could interest him, but a moment later, he asked if Dash knew how to bark. I told him yes and he asked me if I would show him.

"You can do it yourself, John. Just tell him *speak*."

"Will he?"

"Yes. Try him."

He shook his head, then lay back and closed his eyes. "I'n wants t' *do* it. I needs t' *hear* it."

I said Dashiell's name and asked him to speak. He barked twice, a booming, deep roar, his front legs coming off the floor, his ears flying up, then flapping back down like a bird's wings at takeoff.

John's eyes stayed shut, his lips spreading wide into a smile.

" 'S true, what I hears," he asked, eyes still closed, "a barking dog don't bite?"

I opened my mouth to disappoint him with the answer, but I didn't get the chance.

"Wunt touch 'at sucker wit no ten-foot pole. Wunt bark no how."

"He just did," I said. I was about to signal Dash to bark again when John spoke again.

"You comes back. This dog I likes."

"I will," I promised.

"I will," he repeated, smiling.

Ronald and I headed downstairs to Sabotini's office to cut a deal. A few minutes later Dashiell and I were in a taxi heading uptown to Madison Avenue and the American Kennel Club library. Dashiell spent the ride making nose prints on the right-side passenger window as I watched the city pull by us on the other side.

Sabotini had given me a list of patient names and room numbers as well as a batch of forms so that I could take some brief notes for him, but I had only glanced at the pages before folding them and putting them into my purse. For now, I had to see what I could find out about the illegal activities of one Morgan "No Problem" Gilmore.

The American Kennel Club library is a place where no librarian would ever have to say *Shhh*; from what I have always been able to see, it's one of the best-kept secrets in New York. The only other person I've ever seen there is the librarian.

The studbooks register the pedigree, that is, the sire and dam, of a dog or bitch that has been used at stud or has whelped a litter for the first time. They also contain the name of the owner of each dog listed and the breeder of that dog. What I would be looking for would be Magritte's name, Ch. Ceci N'Est Pas un Chien, as a sire, to get an idea of how many of his offspring had been bred last year.

Not all the dogs Magritte sired would be on this list. Some would never be bred, some would still be too young to breed, or, if they had been bred before, they wouldn't show up because the list was for first-time parents only. Still, it would give me an idea of what Gil was doing, and it was also the best way of complying with laws one and three.

I made careful notes whenever Magritte's name showed up. In fact, by poring carefully over the register for the previous year, I found the listing of when Magritte was first used at stud. It appeared that Morgan Gilmore had been using Magritte at stud and stealing the fees for a little better than two years. With a bitch, that wouldn't mean much. But in the case of a dog, whose work didn't take much time at all, even less when his sperm was banked, it could mean a lot of puppies sired and a lot of money paid in stud fees.

When I had finished with the studbook registers, I opened my bag to put in the notes I had taken and took out the papers Robert Sabotini had given me. The forms to fill out for each patient were fairly predictable, mostly things to check off such as: patient was up and about, patient remained in bed, patient responded to dog, patient did not respond to dog. There was a small space for any comment I wanted to make, and supposedly these notes and comments would be used by Sabotini and the staff to make the patients I visited more comfortable or happier. In some places that was so. In others, the forms got filed unread. But either way, on some visits Dash might make the patients forget about their illness for a few minutes; on others he might help them talk about it, if that's what they needed to do. I was sure at least two of them were already looking forward to his next visit.

I put the pages one behind the other as I looked them over until I got to the list of patients Sabotini wanted me to see. There were only six names on the list, those, it seemed from my visit today, who were responding least to other stimuli. He was sending us to the most depressed patients at the hospice, even though the place was small enough for me to visit everyone. Ronald's name was not on the list, but I was sure he'd want to escort me again. John's name was given as John W. Doe. Very original, they gave him a middle initial. Perhaps they kept track of their John Does by coding them alphabetically, the way busy dog breeders code their litters, never mixing the Ivy, Iris, and Irving puppies with the Jack, Jake, and Jessica ones. That theory would make John the twenty-third John Doe, unless it was the second or third time around the alphabet.

Of the other five patients on Sabotini's list, only one was female, Sivonia LeBlanc. I hadn't met her yet. I wondered which of these names, if any, were real, if any of these people even remembered the names they had been given when they were young, healthy, and had homes of their own.

Sivonia LeBlanc. Yeah. Yeah.

I checked my watch. If I moved fast, I could be at the Garden by two, in plenty of time to ogle my favorite breeds. Then, after most of the dogs had been judged, the handlers would be available for dishing, rumormongering, and the purveying of vicious gossip. For this case, the world of purebred dogs might turn out to be just what the doctor ordered!

19

I Never Knew It Could Be Like This

IT HIT ME as soon as I entered, even before I showed my ticket to the uniformed guardians of the gates to dog-person heaven, hit the way the flu does, gradually, but all at once too. In no time I was trembling, sweating, anxious, no longer in control, my legs like over-cooked spaghetti. I could hardly navigate, but the crowd moved me along, swept me into the tunnel under the stands, on toward the benching area, my pulse rapid, my temperature rising like smoke on a clear day, until I felt like screaming, screaming out until I had lost my voice, yes, yes, yes, I never knew it could be like this.

Westminster! It's better than sex. And the way my life's been, more frequent too.

I took the escalator up a tier above the floor where the rings were, an old habit from my training days. I always liked to start out high up in the cheap seats, watching the rings from above. It was an interesting perspective on movement and gave one an overall look at all the rings at once. Amazingly, considering how vast the crowd was, I could usually spot my old friends, even from that lofty, distant perch. It wasn't difficult. Captain Haggerty towered head and shoulders above the crowd, his head shaved bald. And the other person I wanted to see was also head and shoulders above the crowd. In his own way.

I looked down at the rings, both in them and around them. Inside the rings, the breeds were being judged, the judge assessing the dogs to see which of each breed came closest to that breed's standard, to see which the nearly perfect Platonic pointer, puli, or poodle was. They looked at the dogs stacked—standing in standardized positions according to breed—and checked the angulation of their legs, the line of their backs, the width of chest, the breadth of skull, their proportions, balance, overall beauty of form. Then the dogs were gaited, running one at a time with their handlers in a pattern set by the judge or all or many at a time, circling the ring, some breeds at what seemed like breakneck speed.

It had taken me a while to understand movement, thinking it was different for each breed. It is. And it isn't. Though a saluki and a Westie move very differently, in each case you're looking for the dog to move like a beautifully made, well-oiled machine.

From the movement, which is different with different structure, you can see if the dog would be able to work at the task he was bred for, rousting a rodent from its nest, moving the sheep, treeing the raccoon, finding the fox, bringing the shot-down bird to hand, whatever. At least, that's the theory.

In practice, much of the breeding for the ring was producing empty-headed beauty queens who wouldn't last half an hour doing the work that breed was originally bred to perform.

I watched some of the dogs gaiting, heard some cheers from the far left corner as the judge there made her selection, and then began to scan around the rings, finally spotting someone I knew.

His head was tilted just a tad to the left, as if he were listening to something very important that was difficult to hear. He still needed a haircut. His shaggy brown hair covered half his collar. And he was wearing the same damn Harris tweed jacket he always wore to the Garden. That meant he'd wear a blue blazer and a red tie tomorrow, for Best in Show. Some things never change.

I watched him for a while and thought about coming up behind him and grabbing his cute ass, just the way I always used to, asserting my right to be just as vulgar as any man, but when I got up to walk down the stands, I reminded myself that I had work to do. So I went straight to the Am Staff ring, not to the bull-mastiff ring where Chip Pressman stood, his arms folded across his chest, his catalog dangling from his right hand.

American Staffordshire terriers are sort of elegant pit bulls, the differences minor enough that some dogs have dual registration. That, however, was no reason for the people in either camp to like or respect each other's dogs. Deep in their hearts, Am Staff people tend to think of pit bulls as scrappy, unpredictable, badly bred mongrels. And pit bull people regard Am Staffs as beauty queens, dogs no longer up to scratch. A dog who wouldn't face his opponent by approaching the line scratched in the dirt of the pit lost the fight. Worse to some, he was considered a coward: If you said a pit dog turned, it meant he had turned back from the line, that he wasn't game. But if you said a Doberman turned, it meant something entirely different. It meant he turned on his master. He wasn't a coward. He was an ingrate.

The handlers were stacking their dogs, lifting each leg, one at a time, and placing the paw carefully down in just the spot that would make the dog look best. The more confident handlers let their dogs free-stack, holding their attention with bits of dried liver or bait, which the handler might even place in his own mouth and soak with his own saliva to make it all the more appealing. Or appalling, depending upon your personal taste.

The bait gets the dogs to lean forward, making them look elegant rather than clunky, bringing them up on their toes, making their necks seem longer, giving the proper angle to their shoulder assembly and a nice extension to their rear legs.

The dogs focused on the liver. The handlers watched the judge. After walking down the line of stacked dogs, dogs always between the handler and the judge so that the handlers did not obstruct the judge's view, she gave the signal to move the dogs around the ring. The muscular beauties ran with their handlers. The judge watched carefully, occasionally whispering to the steward, who made notes in his book.

I left before the Best in Breed was selected. I'd see that dog tonight, when the groups were judged. It was seldom what I cared about. It is the behavior of a dog that interests me. To some people I've met over the years, behavior equals obedience. But while some compliance is necessary for the safety of the dog and the sanity of the owner, it is the delicious peeks inside a dog's mind that excite me, understanding how dogs learn, crack jokes, communicate, even how they can pick up the rules of a game and then change them, just as their human opponents can.

I headed for the benching area, stopping, as I always did, to buy a present for Dashiell, this time a new Flying Man because his old one was falling apart. It always amazed me to see a powerful adult animal playing with a faux-sheepskin gingerbread man with a squeaker in its belly, acting as silly and thrilled to pieces as any three-month-old. Dashiell would never find himself in therapy searching for his inner puppy.

I checked my catalog to make sure I wasn't about to bother anyone who was yet to go up and began to schmooze with handlers, first about their breed; then, if things went well, I'd progress to frozen semen and Morgan Gilmore.

There were two people sitting in the Akita area, and I knew the Akitas had gone up in the morning, so I admired one of the dogs, who was immediately removed from his crate and stacked for me in the crowded aisle. I guess I sounded like a potential puppy buyer and had found an owner. Her companion, a no-nonsense woman in the de rigueur ring outfit—longish A-line skirt, blazer, and thick-soled, clunky oxfords—I suspected was a handler. My suspicion was confirmed when she gave me her card, so that when the Akita puppy I was about to buy from her friend got old enough, she could handle it for me and make it a champion. Hey, if you want people to open up to you, you have to ingratiate yourself with a few appropriate lies.

As soon as I could, I slipped in my usual fable about a neat little basenji bitch—this time I said she belonged to my sister—and the wonderful deal we were offered. I tried to look as if I had just arrived from a farm in Kansas instead of a lair in Greenwich Village. The women passed a look between them, a combination of pity and alarm.

"Tell your sister that's not a good idea," Trish, the handler, said.

"Why not?"

"Well, uh, you should be dealing with the owner?" Margaret, the Akita breeder said, looking again at Trish.

"I think like the guy who owns the dog has the handler take care of the breedings. Anyway, he said the dog was banked, you know, like a sperm bank, so—"

"Look," Trish said, "it sounds fishy. You know what I'm saying?"

"You mean—"

"Right." She looked all around to see who was within earshot. "The guy's a slime," she whispered. "Never did anything in an upright way in his life."

"Oh," I said.

"Trish knows. She sees him at all the shows. I don't usually travel with Bomber," Margaret said. "Trish shows for me. But of course, for Westminster, I mean, I wouldn't miss this for anything."

"How'd he do?" I asked.

"*He* did fine. The judge prefers another type."

"There's more than one type?" I said. Gee, and here I thought there was only one AKC standard.

"She likes a finer-boned dog. Bomber is heavy boned."

Trish snapped the leash up and took a piece of liver from her pocket, and Bomber snapped to attention. "See?"

"Heavy boned," I said. "Well, about the sperm thing. Are you sure? I mean, what sort of stuff were you referring to?" I whispered after looking around, not that *I* would know who to watch out for.

Margaret slid over, and I squeezed in next to her.

"I understand he gets real close with some of the judges," she said.

"How close?" I asked.

"*Real* close," Trish said, rubbing her forefinger back and forth along the ball of her thumb.

I clapped a hand over my mouth to express my astonishment.

I thanked Trish and Margaret, made a point of carefully putting their cards into my purse, then headed over to see the miniature bull terriers.

I began to chat with a stocky guy, mid-forties, male pattern balding, flat nose, drive-in pores, small, pale eyes, named Larry Benton, "but my friends call me Speed." He showed me his dental implants, canines and all, and I hoped, for his sake, those friends weren't referring to his sexual pacing. At least he was eager to talk.

"They call him Liver Lips," he said when I mentioned I was thinking of having Gil handle for me since he was so good with basenjis, "because what he does, see, he holds the liver in his mouth and makes it real juicy. Then he holds it here," he said, pointing to the middle of his bottom lip, "and then spits it to the dog, see, and the dog catches it. Makes the dog look at his face, at Gilmore's face. The judges, they eat it up. They think it's rapport. Think the dogs actually *like* him. Act like he's fucking Jim Moses or somebody who can *really* bond with a dog. But get this, he also spits the pieces of liver as he runs, see, so it'll distract the other dogs, get them to break their gait trying to grab the treats. Going in the ring with him is a handler's nightmare."

"Is that *legal*?"

"Legal, schmegal. Boy, are you naive. You like minis?"

"Love 'em," I said. It felt weird to say something true.

"Willy Boy here's got the best head I've seen in the breed. You know they're a head breed?"

I nodded. "Who doesn't?"

He referred, of course, to shape, not content. A dog with the IQ of cement could still win Best in Show.

I looked beyond Speed to Willy Boy's crate and saw his blue ribbon proudly displayed. Apparently someone else agreed that Willy had a beautiful head, a funny thing to say about a bull terrier, if you think about it.

I took Speed's card: "Larry 'Speed' Benton, Professional Handler, when you care enough to get the very best." Original!

I needed to get out of the intense crowding of the benching area for a while, so I went back upstairs, high up, bought a soda and a hot dog, and went back to the cheap seats to observe from above, where at least there was some air. It was canned, but still it was air.

Looking down at the rings below, I watched the tail end of the judging, the bichon frises in ring one, the rotties in ring five, the giant schnauzers in ring six. The dignity of the Giants could be seen even from above, but from high up, the rottweilers moving looked like black pillowcases full of bricks being mysteriously thrust forward. The bichons were circling, too, just about ready for the final pick. I closed my eyes and waited for the screams.

I nearly jumped a foot when a hand touched my shoulder.

"Kaminsky! Is it you?"

"Hey, Pressman. Nice jacket. Is it new? How the fuck you been?"

"What's it your fucking business?" he answered.

We both started laughing, and he slid into the seat next to mine.

"Where've you been keeping yourself?"

"Um, the coast, mostly."

"Yeah. Someone told me you were in California for a while," he said.

"Did you say something?" I asked, after killing some time concentrating on the rottweiler judging.

"I asked if you'd been on the coast." He was talking slowly and too loud now, as if he were talking to one of the inmates at the old folks home.

"I guess so."

"You *guess* so? You guess L.A. or S.F.?"

"NYC."

"NYC?"

"Yeah. The *East* Coast."

"You mean you *weren't* in California?"

"Nah. I can't seem to tear myself away from the theater."

"Not to mention the museums."

"I didn't."

"What?"

"Mention the museums."

"How true. Well, glad you're back, so to speak."

"Me, too. Glad to *be* back. As it were."

"So, tell me, is it true? What I heard?"

"Was it something negative?" I asked, unscrunching myself from the orange plastic seat. "Then it was probably true. More than likely true, I'd say. Well, definitely true." I grabbed his shirt and pulled him into my face. "What did you hear?"

"That you're divorced."

I let go of his shirt and slouched back down into the seat. "Oh, that," I said, brushing away an imaginary insect with the back of my hand. "Who isn't?"

"Not me," he said. He was sitting next to me, making the kind of direct eye contact only the most confident dogs make, only his eyes were green, not blue or brown.

I wanted to say something, to comment or respond in either a cheeky or compassionate way, but the thought came to me that I may have completely forgotten how to speak in English, and that if I dared open my mouth, I might find myself speaking in Chinese.

Chip didn't speak either.

Anyway, the screaming from the bichon ring was so loud we would have had trouble hearing each other if either of us *had* spoken.

I could smell his musky aftershave, or was that just him? I had the urge to sniff him, the way Dashiell would have, but I decided to hold off. At least for the time being.

"So, what are you up to? Still training?" he asked, reaching for my soda and taking a sip.

"I wouldn't want to lose my hand," I said, putting my arms on top of the back of the seat in front of me, resting my chin on the back of the top hand, and looking down at the rotties being stacked.

"You mean, at *training*?"

"Among other things. A woman's got to know how to take care of herself these days. What with all the divorce going around."

"I noticed your ad is no longer in the Yellow Pages."

I sat back up and looked at him, but said nothing. He had those little flecks of reddish brown in the green of his eyes.

"Have you finally found an occupation more in keeping with the delicacy of your gender?" he asked, draining the drink and letting an ice cube fall into his mouth. "No. Don't tell me. Let me guess. You've opened a yarn shoppe."

I smiled. Inscrutable as a chow chow.

"Did I ever tell you—" Then he began to laugh. "Same old Kaminsky."

"It's a family thing," I said. "It's genetic. None of us ever change. You might say I'm just a chip off the old block."

I thought he was going to put an ice cube down my shirt or something equally immature, but he didn't. He just sat there looking down at the rings. The rottie people were going wild. One of the pillowcases had won.

"I woke up too late to save the marriage," he said, still watching the dogs. "I hope to hell it's not too late to save fatherhood. You'd be surprised how difficult it is to accept the fact that you're not the kid anymore. You're the parent."

I exhaled for the first time since Lincoln was shot and waited.

"We're doing joint custody. Ellen says I spend more time with the kids now than I ever did when we were married."

I nodded.

He nodded back.

We both looked down at the rottie ring and watched the winning dog getting his picture taken.

"How'd you know I was here?"

"Saw you walking up the stands. I'd know your—walk anywhere."

"Horse shit, Pressman."

"No, it's true. You have one of the great walks. I've always thought so."

"Be that as it may," I said, but then I shut up. I could feel my face getting hot.

The thing is, if you've been attracted to someone when he wasn't available, that fact could have made him more attractive than he really was. And because you knew you wouldn't let anything happen, because who wants to always celebrate holidays on the wrong day and just sit by the telephone with nothing to keep you company but your low self-esteem, you never looked at him as a viable mate. So you just have this tantalizing impression. Which has zero to do with reality.

"Just when it's getting interesting, I have to meet a client," he said. "But I—"

"Yeah. Yeah. I've got to get back to work myself."

"I tried to call you, Rachel. You're not in the book anymore? Not even in the white pages?"

"Not listed."

He raised his eyebrows in unison and waited.

"Jesus! What do you need to find an old friend, a fucking private detective?"

I thought from there I could cleverly segue into the story of my life, but I didn't. Instead, I took out a pen, slid his catalog off his lap, and on the inside back cover wrote my name and my unlisted phone number. He leaned toward me just as I was looking down to put away my pen. His lips landed on my nose.

"Was that as good for you as it was for me?" He was grinning.

"I never knew it could be like this," I told him. His eyes were the color of moss.

"Same old Kaminsky," he said, pulling out his wallet, fiddling with its contents, and finally extracting his business card.

"We're not at the same number either."

"We?"

He handed me a photo of a shepherd.

"Betty," he said.

"Davis?"

"Boop."

She had a dark saddle, a red chest, piercing, intelligent eyes.

Okay, so I only trust people who carry a picture of their dog in their wallet. But the photo alone wasn't enough reason to run out to Condomania and stock up. Was it?

The good part of sleeping with your dog is that he never, ever gets out of bed, looks back at you, and says, "You know, babe, you'd have a great body if only you'd lose ten pounds."

And he never goes back to his wife.

I thought I should tell Chip that my new career required Zenlike concentration and that I couldn't afford the distraction of a sexual liaison at this time, or just make some childish, offputting, hostile remark to cover up how nervous he had made me, but before I got the chance to do either, he left.

I watched him making his way down the crowded stands, then crossing the Garden floor. His gait was strong and smooth, with no sideways movement or wasted effort, as if he were a beautifully made, well-oiled machine.

The river of dogs was still moving in circles in ring six. The crowd near ring two cheered. I watched, waiting for my heart to start beating at its normal pace again. When it did, I felt so drained I could have curled up among the empty soda containers on the sticky floor and taken a nap.

I've always had trouble dealing with more than one thing at a time. And right now, I reminded myself, my time was bought and paid for.

The day's breed judging was over, and they were starting to tear down the rings and sweep in preparation for the group judging that came in the evening: the working, terrier, nonsporting, and herding groups on Monday night, the sporting, hound, and toy groups, then Best in Show, on Tuesday night. People were clearing out now to go for dinner and many to change to formal clothes for the evening judging. I stayed. I loved the Garden when it was empty.

I had once come with Art Haggerty to interview the three families

THIS DOG FOR HIRE / 113

who had dog acts in Ringling Bros. Barnum and Bailey Circus. We had come in the morning, interviewed and watched the acts all day and all evening, and then were invited to stay late, after midnight, to watch a new dog act being trained for the next season. We waited in the stands, whispering to each other. It would have seemed disrespectful somehow to speak out loud. After a while a young boy, his hair wet and slicked neatly back, came out and walked to the center of the center ring. The only light in the whole place shone down on him as he played the trumpet, which in this cavernous, empty space sounded so mournful and moving we could barely breathe. When he finished and left, a very tall blond woman came out, bowed to the empty stands, and then blew a whistle. With that the dogs appeared, one by one, running into the ring and jumping onto small, high stools, then turning around to face her with rapt attention. These were the Daring Dobermans. As we watched her put the six male dogs through their paces, we figured out and whispered to each other the separate commands that, when seamed together, made up each routine.

The circus families trained dogs the same way they trained wild animals, not the way dog trainers trained, and so Letitia swung a kind of small fake whip over her head as she cued the dogs to work, a reminder of the fruits of disobedience.

We had watched the acts during the day and evening from the floor, but from close up we could see things we would not have been able to see even from the first row. We could see the size and strength of the flat metal collars used to contain the chimps, the pain and anger in their eyes too. We could see the sharp hooks on the rods that seemed to merely tap-tap at the elephants to keep them moving, and we could see the scars all over their bodies. Backstage, chained in a long line, they rocked and rocked, the way people in mental institutions sometimes do. We could see something so frightening in the eyes of the big cats, it defied description. We could see the scars they had left on their trainer, too.

From the floor, we had seen everything. I hadn't been to a circus since.

The Garden was quiet now. I opened my bag and took out the list I had made at the AKC library. Or at least that's what I thought I was taking out. Instead, it was the list of names Sabotini had given me. I began to read it. James T. McEllroy, Michael Smith, John W. Doe.

I shoved everything back into my bag and ran like hell for the pay phones.

20

You Can't Play This

HERBIE SUSSMAN AND two of his cousins were lined up at the curb on the other side of the street with their penises out. One at a time, they urinated into the street to see whose stream could reach the farthest.

Lili and I wanted to play, too.

You can't play this, Herbie said. You're girls.

Can, too, my sister Lillian sang, chin up, eyes defiant.

She pushed me up to the curb, told me not to move, and came back a minute later pulling the garden hose behind her. She put the nozzle between my legs.

Hold tight, she ordered. Then she turned the nozzle.

The hose sputtered. Then the arc of water sprayed far into the street, almost to where the boys were standing.

We win, Lili shouted, head cocked, hands on her hips.

The cold water dripped into my sandals.

No fair, Herbie yelled.

He stood alone now, his pinkie of a penis pale and flaccid at the opening in his pants. His cousins had already turned around, shaken their members back into their pants, and were running for home.

I was only six at the time, but I learned two valuable lessons. First, if you really want to do something, don't waste your time waiting for someone else's permission. Boys always say "You can't play this." If you believe them, you'll end up a teacher or a nurse when what you really want to be is a dog trainer or a detective.

Second, sometimes you have the edge. Sometimes you don't. Either way, life's unfair.

It was the second lesson I was reminded of when I heard the voice on the other end of the phone say, "Bailey House. Can I help you?"

I had gone to the bank of pay phones on the higher tier, the ones hardly anyone used, and listening to the phone ringing on the other end, I had wondered who I'd ask for, but the moment someone answered I knew. I asked for Ronald.

Patients didn't have bedside phones, but Ronald was ambulatory and had no trouble coming to the phone.

"Ronald, it's Rachel. Listen, the list Sabotini gave me of patients to visit, it had John down as John W. Doe."

"Yeah. They do that when guys come in all drugged out from the street. He was, you know, a user. He couldn'ta said his name if he knew it. So they give him one."

"Does he know his name now? Does he at least remember his street name?"

"Now? Yeah, sure. But they ain't going to change the record. I mean, it's not like he's getting family or anyone visiting him, you know. And like we all got used to calling him John before he got cleaned up, so, you know, it's hard to change, Rachel. How's Petey?"

"He's fine, Ronald. I'll bring him by again soon if you like, to see you and John. But tell me now"—I closed my eyes and inhaled—"Ronald, what name does John remember?"

"His name that he had when he was a little kid. You know, when he was growing up. But he don't care if you call him John. He don't get upset or nothing."

"So, Ronald, when John was a little kid, what was his name?"

"Oh, I thought I said. It was William. Willy was what his mama called him. That's what he told me, Rachel. You know, when he could."

"Did he say where he grew up, Ronald? Do you know where he lived when he was little?"

"Yeah. Sure. He likes me, John. He tells me everything."

"So, where was it?"

"Oh, right. Pittsburgh."

My heart flopped.

"You know," Ronald added. "In P.A."

I was hyperventilating. He hadn't parroted me, saying "Will he?" He was telling me his name! And he had seen Magritte. That was why he wanted to hear Dashiell bark. Magritte couldn't, so he thought that meant he'd bite.

"Ronald, you're the best. I'll be there in the morning. What can I bring you?"

"A milk shake. Chocolate, Rachel. If you would."

"I would." Then I fairly shouted into the phone, "I will."

I *Will.* I had found Billy fucking Pittsburgh.

I made one more call, to my friend Marty Shapiro, at the Sixth. The Sixth is home to the bomb squad, and Marty handles Elwood, the yellow Lab whom Dash adores, which is how we met. Billy had been in such bad shape when he had come in, the guys had gotten him a bed at Bailey House. No way they were going to let him back onto the street like that, Marty told me, no fucking way.

Small wonder I hadn't found him, waking up the homeless in the dead of winter, talking to crazy people so I could feel justified I was earning my fee.

On the other hand, for all the good it had done me, Mary Perry *had* seen him, saw him with KS, *spotted* him. Wasn't her, she said. But someone sure had. Someone who had been kind enough to offer him the use of a needle most likely.

I sat with Dennis for the evening judging, but I had trouble keeping my mind on the show.

"Where's Magritte?" I asked Dennis after the last group was judged.

"At home. Why?"

"When and how does Gil get him, for the show tomorrow?"

"I bring him in the morning. I'm meeting Gil at the benching area at eight-thirty."

"What time does he go up?" The damn catalog was sitting right on my lap, and I had already looked it up at least twice, and now I couldn't remember the ring or the time.

"Eleven-thirty. Ring three."

"Look, I know this is going to be tight, but I need you to meet me at Bailey House on the corner of Christopher and West streets—do you know it?" He nodded. "With Magritte, before you bring him here."

"Rachel—you know the dogs have to be benched all day!"

"No, no, look!" I was paging through the catalog. "Here it is, 'Benching hours,'" I read aloud, "'eleven-thirty to eight P.M.' See?" I shoved it in his face. "Dennis, this is *really* important. Eight A.M. In the lobby. We'll be at the Garden before nine, by eight-thirty if we're lucky. Trust me."

"Okay," he said. I must have been ranting, because he looked at me as if I was. "Eight A.M. Bailey House. In the lobby. And you're not going to explain this, right?"

"Right," I said, grabbing my coat. "Not just yet."

And like a husky let off leash, I was gone.

21

You Can Recommend Me

RONALD WAS IN the lobby waiting. I handed him the milk shake.

"It's all set," he said, holding the shake with both hands. "To, you know, go upstairs and see John."

Dennis arrived on time with Magritte tucked under his arm. We headed for the elevator.

I walked into John's room alone. He appeared to be asleep.

"Will?"

He opened his eyes. "Oh, it the dog lady. Where he at?" He picked his head up to look beyond me.

"He's not here today, Will, but I have to ask you some questions about another dog, the one you saw on the Christopher Street pier. The one who frightened you because he didn't bark. Remember?"

"I'n't remember nothin' from then," he said, looking suspicious. "Why you aks?"

"Well, there was a young man murdered that night."

He looked away, toward the window.

"Billy?"

"Yeah, a young man murder'd."

"And you were the one who told the police that there was a body on the pier. Remember?"

"A body. Yeah."

"Billy, did you see the young man before he got killed? Did you see him walking with the little dog onto the pier? Think hard, Bill, it's so important."

"No," he said, "Ah di'n't see tha'."

"I have the little dog here, Bill. The one you saw. The one you were afraid of because he didn't bark, remember? The one you saw on the Christopher Street pier."

"Oh shit," he said.

"Now listen to me, Bill, this dog does not bite. He doesn't bark because he can't. Did you hear him make some other sounds that night, like cries?"

I ducked back into the hall where Dennis, Magritte, and Ronald were standing and lifted Magritte into my arms. I stepped back into the room but stayed right at the door. Billy didn't move. I bent and kissed Magritte on top of his head, and he lifted his muzzle and licked my mouth. I could feel the heat of his body where I held him against my side.

"He's a very gentle dog, Bill, or I wouldn't have brought him. I thought if you saw him again, it might help you to remember what you saw."

"I never forget what I sees tha' time."

"How come?"

"Be a hard night." Billy Pittsburgh squeezed his eyes shut. A single tear rolled down one cheek.

"Bill, was the young man already dead when you first saw him?"

Billy Pittsburgh sat bolt upright in his bed. "Does I look like a doctor? Hey, I'm not a doctor. I'm a fucking *dope* addict. How'm I s'posed to know if he alive or dead?" He shook his head. "No sir. I don't know nothin' about that. What you aksing me that fo'?" He fell back against his pillow, all his energy gone as suddenly as it came.

"Billy?"

"Okay. Okay. I hears you." He pulled the cover up to his neck, his hands shaking badly. "He 'live."

"But you said you didn't see him walking onto the pier with his dog, with this dog?"

"You aks me if I sees th' man goin' wit th' dawg. I di'n't. He go alone."

"Alone? Are you sure?"

"I sure. Man, I sure I do not wanna *do* this."

"Please, Bill. Please help us out."

"Okay. You aks me. I goin' tell it." He held up one trembling finger. "Car comes." Then a second finger. "A white man take th' dawg an' drag 'im out th' pier, t' th' end. He tie him they." A third finger, his thumb, the nail bitten short. "He go back t' th' car and he sit they."

His hand was shaking so badly he put it under the blanket.

"Th' young white man come," he continued. "Th' dawg, th' one you got, he carryin' on, somethin' awful. The young 'un, he hears 'im an he start t' run t' 'im."

Billy's eyes are now full, and tears, one after the other, slide down his cheeks.

"And th' first man, th' man in th' car, he start up the motor, he put the lights on and he drive after th' second man."

He lifts his hands and covers his face.

"He knock 'im down. He back out an' leave 'im they. He leave th' dawg they an' the dawg cry out for 'ours 'n I di'n't go look 'til he gots 'imself out o' th' collar and runs away, because I always hears if a dawg don't bark, it bite. Tha's what my mama tol' me. Yes, sir."

I felt a tear run into my neck and realized that I was crying, too.

I walked over and sat on the side of Billy's bed. Magritte was as still as cold water. Slowly, Billy Pittsburgh reached out his hand and let Magritte lick his long, thin, trembling fingers.

"Billy," I said, "did you tell this story to the police?"

"No," he said. "I di'n't."

"Why not?"

"They di'n't aks me nuthin.' I's on drugs 'n they figure I di'n't know nothin'."

I turned toward the door. Dennis and Ronald had moved into the doorway.

"This is Dennis, Bill. The young man was his best friend."

"I sorry, man," Billy said, "I so sorry 'bout you friend."

"Bill," Dennis said. He seemed unable to say anything else.

"One more thing, Bill. Do you remember anything about the car, anything at all?"

He shook his head.

"Thank you, Bill. We want to find this man. You've helped us a lot. Can I come back soon with Dash, you know, Petey?"

He nodded. I squeezed his arm and turned to leave.

"Black," he said.

I turned around and looked at him.

"New."

I nodded.

" 'Merican. Th's all I see."

He shrugged and turned back toward the window. There was a

pigeon on the sill, its head down, its wings tight to its sides, like an old man with his hands stuffed into his pockets.

"I di'n't know 't was goin' happen. Cunna stop't 't nohow. Not nohow."

"Nobody thinks you could have," I said. "This wasn't your fault, Bill."

He turned his lumpy face toward me.

"Then why'm I bein' punish?" he asked.

IN THE TAXI on the way to the Garden, the little basenji curled up on the seat between us, and Dennis was nearly rigid.

"He got Cliff out there with Magritte," he said.

"What do you want to do?" I asked.

"Kill him," Dennis said.

"Dennis, that's not your job. And we're not positive it was Gil. Let's take this a step at a time. First, what do you want to do now, about Westminster and Magritte? Should we even be going?"

"Oh God, Rachel, we have to. Clifford wanted this more than anything. Magritte has to go up today. But how can I give him to Gil?"

"Look, Dennis, even if what we suspect is true and Gil committed the murder, we have no reason to think he'd hurt Magritte. If that's what he had wanted to do, he had the opportunity the night of the murder. Besides, he's been doing pretty well with Magritte and he might just think things will continue along as they were, only with you the one he's cheating instead of Cliff. Let him think that. Be charming. For God's sake, Dennis, just act dumb. Okay?"

"Yes, but—"

"No buts. Here's what I want you to do. Just give Magritte to Gil, no problem, okay? Tell him you've changed your plans, the trip got canceled, and you're taking Magritte home right after the show. Eight-thirty, on the button, you'll get Magritte from the benching area and bring him to your box. Unless, of course, he takes the breed. In that case, you'll be able to keep your eye on him because he'll be in the group, right in front of your face.

"The rest is up to me. I'm going to hang out in the benching area. I'm a big fan of Magritte's, remember? Gil knows all about my precious Crystal. He's already offered to cut me a deal. So he won't find it weird to see me there. I'll ask a lot of questions. I'll even tag along when he goes to the grooming area. When he's with Magritte, I'll stick to him like peanut butter on the roof of his lying mouth.

"I'll be ringside when he goes up at eleven-thirty. I'll see you there,

122 / CAROL LEA BENJAMIN

but I can't sit with you. I can't sit with you tonight either. Gil can't know that we know each other. Okay? Then, after tonight, we'll figure out where to go with the case, okay? I still have to *prove* he did it, Dennis, *if* he did it. So far, the evidence is all circumstantial—mounting, but circumstantial.

"You still have your trip tomorrow. But I'll have Magritte. You'll give him to me tonight, just as we planned. And if I work my can off and we're really lucky, maybe I'll have something more concrete by the time you get back from Boston. So are you with me on this?"

The cab had stopped at Eighth Avenue and Thirty-second Street. Dennis just sat there.

"Dennis?"

He nodded, then reached for his wallet. "Sorry," he said, coming back to life. He handed the driver a ten and then turned to look at me.

"Rachel, what would I do without you? You're the greatest."

"Yeah. Yeah," I said, lifting Magritte and making sure I had a good grip on his lead before I opened the door, "if any of your other friends have a loved one killed, you can recommend me."

22

Take Your Time,
I Told Him

WE SHOWED OUR tickets, then Dennis and I began to bulldoze our way into the benching area, passing and being passed by a sea of handlers with dogs of every size, color, and possible shape, Afghans and salukis sporting silver-lamé snoods to keep their long, feathered ears clean and dry, drooly dogs wearing bibs to catch the saliva that would periodically stream down from their loose flews, Yorkies and silkies, their long coats sectioned, wrapped in paper, and rolled in curlers to keep it from getting damaged, let down only on the grooming table and in the ring.

Dogs of astonishing size were carried, some on the hip or high up over the shoulder, like babies, and just as passive. Some were so docile they allowed themselves to be cradled, back down, feet up, or just held close to the chest. They were amazingly pliable, having stood on a grooming table and been manipulated into position from the time they were weaned.

There were photographers, too, nearly one per dog it seemed, shooting everything, dogs sitting not in but on their crates, dogs with teddy bears, dogs that were all coat, resembling mops, and dogs that had no coat, hairless dogs, so vulnerable looking they made you want to cry.

Even before we got to row six, Dennis and I separated. He headed directly for Magritte's spot, and I turned the other way, meandering past the rows of benched dogs on one side and concessions on the other. The benching area, raised platforms covered in sturdy green outdoor carpeting where the dogs are assigned to stay when not in the doggy bathrooms, the grooming area, or the ring, was surrounded by booths selling books, magazines, food, jewelry, all for dogs or dog related. Going around the long way, I'd eventually come to the area where the basenjis were benched from the opposite side.

From that moment on, whether Morgan Gilmore liked it or not, everywhere he looked, for the rest of the day, at least, I'd be in his face.

By the time I had worked my way to Magritte's assigned spot, Dennis was gone and Magritte was asleep in his crate, his chin resting on one hind leg, his white-tipped tail uncurled. Photos of him taking the breed at other shows were propped on top of the crate, and alongside, a stack of Morgan Gilmore's business cards.

"Do you think he'll ask to win today?" I asked Gil's ponytail.

He turned, scowled, and raised his eyebrows. My face was becoming for him like so many had been for me all the years I'd gone to dog shows, someone you see at every event but have trouble remembering exactly who they are, where you met them, or why they're there. We had talked at Cliff's opening, and he had probably seen me at the Ken-L Ration award banquet, but he couldn't place me. He was one of those people who didn't really pay attention to anyone he deemed less important than he was, which in Gil's case was nearly everyone. I wondered what he was hiding under all that arrogance.

"Crystal's mom," I said. With considerable pride.

He nodded. "She's not—?"

"In heat? No, April, I think."

"No, I was wondering if she was *entered*?"

I hadn't given him a registered name, just a call name, and since he didn't know my name, he'd have slim chance of knowing if any of the bitches being shown in the Best in Breed competition were my precious angel. Unless he knew all the dogs, which, with only ten entries, was certainly possible.

"No," I said, looking down at the vicinity of his cowboy boots. "She needs one more major."

Gil nodded, looking vaguely bored and annoyed. He needed me hanging around like he needed Lyme disease.

"So, do you think Magritte is up for this today? Does he have that I-want-to-win attitude he's so famous for?"

"Always," Gil said. "Dog's never had a bad day in his life."

"I guess he had one or two," I said.

Gil smoothed back his hair and, holding on to his ponytail, pushed up the band that held it. He tightened his string tie, too. "I guess you're right. I guess he has had a couple of bad days at that. But today he's going to have a good day. An excellent day. You know," he added, "when you show your little girl next time out, don't be thinking about her bad days. Makes for bad karma. You people, you're all alike. Think you can do the job of a professional. Always looking to save a little money. And what does it get you? The dog picks up all your negativity and you find yourself with a self-fulfilling prophecy on your hands."

He leaned toward me, his back to Magritte's crate and one boot up on the bench.

"That might be Crystal's whole problem. What I'm saying is, *you* might be her whole problem."

"You mean—"

"Little lady," he said, standing straight now to show me his full magnificence, "I can *guarantee* you that major Crystal is missing. No problem. We even can get that out of the way, if you like, before she comes into season so that you'll be breeding not just a dog but a champion. Think about your advertising. Champion sire and dam. Sounds pretty good, doesn't it? You've got to learn to think ahead, think about marketing." He lowered his voice to a stage whisper. "You get some of these serious show folk won't touch a pup unless both parents have proven themselves in the ring. Now you know that's the good Lord's honest truth, don't you?"

"Well, I don't know, it's awfully expensive to have a dog campaigned, isn't it?"

"If you're interested, I feel sure, as reasonable people, that we could work something out. After all, you're talking short term here. Unless of course she turns out to be so good you want to special her. Then we're talking a whole 'nother story."

"Could you do it, like, if I met you at the shows? Or would you have to actually *take* her?"

"In order to give you that guarantee, I'd take her south, young lady. Where the winning is easy. A month. Two months at the outside."

"Well, how much would that be? I mean, exactly."

He leaned close enough now that I could smell the coffee he had had earlier that morning and the spicy smell of the pomade he used to slick back his thinning hair. "Twelve a month. Plus expenses, of course. Much less than you thought, am I right?"

I nodded.

"I can bring in that championship for under five for you. Do you believe that?"

"Why wouldn't I?" I said. Too harsh, Kaminsky, I warned myself. "I mean, that's incredible! Truly."

I walked around him, bent to look into Magritte's crate, and saw his lovely, almond-shaped brown eyes looking back at me. His paws were crossed, left over right, and he was calmly surveying the scene. When I straightened up, I picked up a picture of him taking the breed in Monmouth County. Gil, in cowboy boots and a light blue jacket, was holding the leash taut and looking proudly down at Magritte, who stood, as in all these pictures, perpendicular to the photographer, showing off his level topline, his lovely wedge head, his wonderful double-curled tail, and his burnished copper coat, which shone like silk in the sunshine. I put the photo back carefully among the others and picked up one of Gil's cards.

"I sure would love to see a picture of Crystal like that. Taking the group. And I sure would love to see her *here* next year." Now I stood on my toes and whispered into his ear. "That's my *dream*. Westminster."

It's not hard to intone *Westminster* as if you were in church. For die-hard dog people, it *was* church.

"You really gave me something to think about," I said, feeling smug. I had successfully established my presence in his face for the day. Magritte was safe.

Or so I thought.

"Look, if you want to go for coffee or something, I'll stay with Magritte. There's nothing else I want to do today but think over your, uh, offer, and watch Magritte take the breed." I held up both hands with my fingers crossed.

Gil brightened up. "Are you sure you wouldn't mind?" he asked. "Well, if you're planning on sticking around anyway—"

"Absolutely. There's nothing I'd rather do than be near Magritte."

"Okay, okay," he said, "if you're sure. I could use a coffee and a run by the rings."

Good, I thought, time to snoop.

"Take your time," I told him, and he took off without saying another word.

I peeked inside the crate. Magritte was asleep. I suddenly realized how vulnerable he was, left by his duly authorized agent with a complete stranger who could easily lift him out of his crate, carry him to the escalator, ride down, and leave the Garden without anyone noticing or saying a word.

Who the fuck was I that he could leave the dog in his charge in my care!

Dogs were stolen all the time, not all of them from backyards, cars, or where they had been left for just a half a moment while the owner ducked into a store to buy a Boston lettuce.

But in fact I hadn't taken the time to ingratiate myself with Magritte's handler in order to steal Magritte, not that that made this Morgan Gilmore's lucky day. Quite the contrary. I had weaseled my way here to protect Magritte, and while I was at it, see if I could find something that would make the evidence against his handler more concrete than speculative.

I looked behind Magritte's crate to see if there was a camel coat neatly folded and tucked back there, and noticed, right at the side of the crate, in plain sight, that Gil had left, in a small heap, a pile of change, his liver pouch, his calendar, and his card case.

I opened the calendar first to January 19, the day Magritte had been stolen. There was no notation. Nor was there any under the 20th, the day Clifford was killed.

Well, how unusual. It didn't say, "Tuesday, January 19. Call Clifford Cole and find out when he'll be out without his dog. Kidnap Magritte."

Nor did it say, "Wednesday, January 20. Murder Clifford Cole."

I put the calendar back where I had found it and picked up the card case, flipped it open, and found not only Gil's business cards but his credit cards as well. It was a wonder to me that someone so dishonest could trust in the honesty of so many strangers and leave his valuables lying around where anyone could take them. Or did he have the poor judgment to trust that I would protect his valuables for him?

There was only a raincoat behind the crate. Bummer. Not even a beret or a white scarf tucked into the sleeve. I reached into his coat pockets and, underneath a handkerchief and an extra show lead, found his key ring. After a quick peek around during which I discovered that no one was paying the least bit of attention to me and that Gil had not returned to find me with my hand in his pocket, I pulled out my own keys and checked the loft keys Dennis had given me against Gil's ring.

I slipped the keys back into the bottom of Gil's pocket and put the raincoat back behind Magritte's crate.

There would have had to have been times when Gil had to pick up or drop off Magritte when Cliff couldn't have been there. So Cliff did the only practical thing he could.

He made Gil his own set.

23

You'd Have to Wonder

"HERE'S OUR BOY!" I heard, close enough to startle me and loud enough for several aisles of people to hear.

I turned to see Veronica Cahill, stunning in a double-breasted black pantsuit with gold buttons, bending from the waist to look Magritte in the eye.

"You better win, you little *vantz*," she told him. "You're costing me a fortune."

I got a wad of pretty good-looking tissues out just in time to catch a sneeze. Magritte sneezed back, as if I were playing his favorite game.

Just behind Veronica, Louis Lane was standing and waiting, but clearly not waiting his turn to greet Magritte. He spotted me and opened his mouth, but I shook my head in time to close it for him.

Veronica straightened up, making me feel like a troll. She was even taller than Louis.

"He looks wonderful, darling," she said, her hand on Louis's chest. "There's not another to equal him. I never get tired of looking at Magritte." She winked at Louis, whose neck reddened.

Perhaps it was his allergy acting up.

"Come on, Veronica. Oughtn't we try to get ringside now so we don't miss anything?"

"No, no. I want to see the others, the ones he's up against, those scruffy little interlopers." She turned down the aisle to check out the other basenjis, leaving Louis to follow or not.

Louis's mouth opened, then closed. Neither of us said a word.

He was wearing a white sweater with a charcoal-gray jacket over it, a long white silk scarf draped around his neck. I wondered exactly what kind of game he was playing with Veronica. I wondered if, at least on this occasion, he had stretched a point and considered the virtues of bisexuality. For business purposes.

"Naturally she'd be interested in what happens here with Magritte today. Considering"—he paused, but didn't take his eyes off mine—"her investment."

I heard Magritte resettle in the crate and, without looking, poked my fingers in for him to sniff.

"It can only help Clifford's name. If Magritte wins. And"—he got his handkerchief out just in time to catch a triple sneeze—"you know what this would have meant to Clifford."

"You don't have to explain anything to me, Louis," I said. "I'm only the hired help."

"Life is for the living, Rachel," he said. Then he turned and made his way down the aisle to Veronica.

Lots of people were making their way up and back in the benching area, and whatever their reason for being at Westminster, they didn't want to miss the chance to see Magritte. Some thought a barkless dog would be perfect for apartment living. No complaints from the neighbors about noise. Others were just attracted to anyone or anything important enough to be written about in the papers.

Most of them just stopped by quickly, checked their catalog, poked their fingers at Magritte, then headed for the concessions or down the next aisle. Short-attention-span disease was rampantly on display. I was sneezing back and forth with Magritte to keep him amused when I became aware that yet another spectator had stopped in front of us. I looked up.

"Pardon, is this Magritte?" His voice sounded hoarse.

"Yes, it is," I said.

It was the stocky man from Cliff's opening, now spiffed up in a navy suit, white shirt, and maroon tie. He bent to look into the crate.

I wondered if he was a reporter. I looked for a press ribbon, de rigueur at Westminster, but there was none. Nor was there a Nikon or a Hasselblad hanging from his shoulder. Not a reporter.

Maybe he was a dog trainer. He had a ruddy, used-up sort of face. Working outdoors, training dogs, can do that to you.

Especially if when you finally come indoors, you do a shitload of drinking.

"Is he going to win?" he whispered in his raspy voice. "He really got some fabulous press, didn't he?" He hiked his tan leather backpack higher onto one shoulder.

"Maybe he'll get the sympathy vote."

"Oh," he said. "Maybe he will. Are you—?"

"A friend."

"A friend of *his*?" he asked.

I merely smiled.

Most dog shows attract serious dog people, professionals who earn their living training or showing dogs and breeders who need to prove their stock and see what the competition is producing. This one, because of its location and the fabulous press it gets, even when none of the dogs competing have recently murdered owners, attracts a broader audience, families dragging their kids through the crowded aisles, hoping by looking and asking questions to select the perfect breed, the curious, the lonely. Rich or poor, the bored take in Westminster. They come to see Nanook, Rin Tin Tin, and Lassie, for a once-a-year lively alternative to the museum or the movies.

He bent and looked at Magritte again, putting his face close to the cage. His dark hair was so even in tone, I wondered if it was natural.

"He's so quiet," he said. "Is he always this quiet?" He straightened up. "Funny, isn't it? It's so hard to tell them apart. I wonder how the judges know which is which."

A detective listens, Bruce Petrie used to tell me. I thought this might be a good time to practice keeping my sarcastic mouth shut.

"Unless, of course, the color is different."

I nodded.

I wondered if he had used that stuff on his hair you comb in and no one's supposed to notice that in three days your hair is suddenly the color of a desk.

"I'm enjoying the show," he volunteered.

I nodded. I figured it might seem rude to ask. The whole idea is to fool people, isn't it? I mean, even if you're in your eighties and your hair is solid black, like enamel paint, or if, like Tony Bennett, you have a hairline considerably lower on your brow than it was when you were younger, no one's supposed to know it's not a result of Mother Nature's glorious and perfect design.

I checked my watch. "He's going up at eleven-thirty," I said. "Are you going to watch him in the ring?"

"Eleven-thirty," he repeated to himself. "I wasn't going to stay, but I guess I shouldn't miss that. Where would I go?"

Despite the fact that he had a catalog and could have looked it up himself, I told him the ring number.

He nodded, then turned and made his way through the folds of humanity clogging the aisle, stopping and squatting low to look inside the other basenji crates as he had done with Magritte.

"Here he is. So what's the big deal!"

There were two women in front of Magritte's crate now, one tall and thick, built like a tree, hair shorn short in front, the rest pulled back and tied with a scarf, the other short and soft and round with breasts that began under her chin and ended somewhere around her pillowlike stomach. The tall one clutched her catalog to her chest. The other kept methodically pulling pieces of rice cake from her pocket and putting them into her mouth.

"This *is* Magritte, isn't it?" the short one said.

I nodded. I was going to have a neck like a nose tackle by the end of the show.

"The *News* says he's a shoo-in," she said, a real edge in her voice. There was a thin mustache on her upper lip that she apparently hadn't had time to wax or bleach.

The tall woman checked her catalog and then bent to look into Magritte's crate.

"Orion has a better ear set," she said to no one in particular.

"They say he'll take Best in Show," the short woman said.

Her skin was doughy and pale, with small scabs on her cheeks. Her short, curly hair was dyed aubergine. I've always thought that color looked better where it belonged, on an eggplant.

"Well, he hasn't taken the breed yet," I said. "There are lots of other good dogs here today."

"But none as brave and *famous* as this one," she said, sarcasm dripping off her tongue along with a fine spray of rice cake.

In 1984 rumor had it that the Newfoundland Ch. Seaward's Black-beard would take Best in Show before he had even drooled and rolled his way into the Garden to compete in the breed. And he did. But that kind of successful second-guessing was rare, and even though some people assumed BIS was already a done deal at this show, I wasn't one of them. I refused to make assumptions about Magritte's chances.

I supposed they had a basenji entered and didn't care for the edge Magritte had picked up when he lost his owner and gained Veronica Cahill's publicist. I was going to ask which dog was theirs, but not wanting another rice cake shower, I decided not to. Instead I picked up Gil's catalog, hoping they'd take the hint and go away.

You wouldn't have to be a detective to figure out which dog was theirs. Ch. Turkon's Heavenly Hunter, a male, four years old. That would make them Poppy O'Neal and Addie Turkle. But which was which I couldn't say.

Once they had moved on, Poppy or Addie leaving a trail of puffed rice, like Hansel or Gretel in the woods, I got up to stretch, then stood up on the bench where I had been sitting to see if I could spot Gil. It was getting close to the time for Magritte to go get brushed, go potty, and present himself ringside. But Gil was not to be seen.

I remembered a story Chip had once told me about a famous handler. She had arranged to show a boxer the owner thought had great potential but was herself unable to win a major with. The handler met the owner and dog outside the ring the very moment the dogs were called. The owner had been standing and waiting, afraid the handler wouldn't show. The dog, absorbing all her anxiety, stood next to her, his head low, his tail down. As the handler took the leash, not saying a word to either of them, the dog's head came up, giving his neck an elegant arch, his dark eyes danced, his tiny, docked tail shot straight up and began beating rapidly from side to side. He won the breed, finishing his championship, and later on, with the same handler holding the leash, all know-how and confidence, he took the group.

If Magritte took the breed today, wouldn't it be a bittersweet victory? Like Clifford's soaring career, you'd have to wonder if all the great press, the sympathy, the sheer drama of recent events, would have made for a win that in the normal course of events wouldn't have happened.

I saw Gil approaching from the opposite way he had left. He was walking with another man, who was small and thin, his hair and skin the same dead-looking steely gray, a cigarette apparently stuck onto his dry lower lip despite the fact that there was no smoking allowed and that this was announced over loud-speakers with predictable regularity.

"—should go up. After today," the little man said in his gravelly voice as they got near enough for me to hear them.

"Without a doubt," Gil said. "You can bank on it." He smiled at me but didn't bother to introduce me to the little man, who ignored me so completely at first that I thought perhaps he hadn't seen me sitting next to Magritte's crate. When he finally took notice of me, he merely tossed me a hard stare, then turned back to Gil.

Gil reached in and took Magritte out of his crate, tucked him snugly under his arm, picked up his tack box, checked his other pocket for a show lead and his armband with Magritte's number on it, pulling them each out and then carefully replacing them, and headed for the grooming area, the little man at his side, me trailing behind like an obedient puppy.

"The chances are good. Is that what you're saying?" the gray man said, one eye closed to let the smoke drift by.

"Excellent," Gil answered. He found his spot, put Magritte up on the table, and, taking a brush out of the tack box, began to brush him. "You just leave it to me, Doc."

Doc reflected on what he had heard, standing next to the grooming table and puffing on the stub of his cigarette. When it finally got too small to smoke, he held it between two dry yellow fingers, took another from his pocket, popped it into his mouth, lit it with the stub, and despite the fact that there were dogs all over the place, dropped the stub on the floor without bothering to step on it. "I'll be ringside," he said.

After Doc had left, Gil reached into the tack box and took out an electric nail grinder. Magritte backed up a step, but the noose on the grooming table kept him from retreating any farther. Like every other dog I've ever met, he hated having his nails done. Gil plugged in the grinder, reached into his jacket pocket, felt around, and came up with a piece of dried liver. Magritte's tail began to wag, but to his dismay, the treat went not toward his own mouth but into Gil's. Liver Lips began to make a series of revolting slurping sounds, making me wonder if in another incarnation he had been a construction worker. He turned on the grinder and, lifting one paw at a time, began to work on Magritte's nails. When he finished the last foot, he leaned his face right into Magritte's and let the dog ever so gently take the moistened piece of liver from between his lips. Here was a man who truly lived up to his nickname.

That finished, Gil went on with the rest of Magritte's grooming routine, wiping him down briskly with a mitt to bring out the shine in his coat, powdering and wiping off his paws, and finally, spraying Show Foot paw tack on his pads to prevent him from slipping in the ring.

"Make yourself useful," he said, handing me the tack box. He hoisted Magritte and headed for the nearest exercise pen, the doggy bathroom, where we silently waited our turn on line, standing in the red cedar chips that spilled out as each satisfied customer emerged. The chain-link pens were hung with plastic sheeting, not for privacy, though an occasional dog *did* care, but to protect passersby from getting what in my neighborhood is called a golden shower.

When Magritte had finished, Gil lifted him again. The crowds were much too formidable to walk a small dog through the benching area and onto the floor where the judging took place.

Gil pushed his way through a constantly reappearing wall of people, me following along behind as usual. We stopped at Magritte's bench, where I dropped off the tack box and Gil handed me Magritte just long enough to strap on his bait pouch and secure his armband with a single rubber band around the middle. After pushing and shoving for another two minutes, we were finally ringside.

24

For No Apparent Reason

GIL WENT AROUND to the side just below the stands, where only handlers with their dogs were allowed. We had arrived ringside just as the basset hounds were finishing up, so, having manners more suitable for the IRT than any place aboveground, I elbowed and kneed my way around to the far side, where there was a single row of padded red folding chairs, and snagged one. Of course, there were plenty of seats in the stands, but those didn't place viewers nearly as close as they'd be sitting or standing ringside on the Garden floor.

Within moments, the basset people were replaced by basenji fanciers, catalogs open, ready to mark the wins.

Poppy and Addie were on the end of the row, to my left, funereal expressions on their faces. Beyond them, down the left side, I spotted Dennis. He was standing against the lavender velvet rope that demarcated the parameters of the ring, staring straight ahead.

When I turned to scan the opposite side, I saw the object of Dennis's gaze: Louis Lane, standing so close to his companion you'd have trouble slipping a foil-wrapped latex condom between them.

Veronica was whispering in his ear. From where I was sitting, her features looked too big after all.

Especially her nose.

Doc was up in the stands. He looked as dehydrated and gray as if he had died ages ago but no one had bothered to bury him.

I spotted Aggie too, standing ringside, near where the handlers entered. She was wearing a fuzzy aqua sweater with little faux pearls sewn all over it, perhaps to coordinate with her faux hair color. Even from where I was sitting, it seemed she had put on her makeup with a steam shovel.

The judge, ready to begin, nodded to the steward, who signaled the handlers. Gil placed Magritte down onto the floor, gave ever so small a pop to the lead, and that quickly, Magritte came to life. The ten basenji contenders, led by their handlers, entered the ring to great applause from the ringside fanciers and lined up inches from where I sat, to be stacked in show pose as a group and then examined, one at a time, by the judge.

Watching Am Staffs, Goldens, shelties, or Chinese cresteds does not prepare you for the basenji ring. Wherever basenjis are, they need to be elsewhere. It's just their nature.

Three of the ten dogs simply tried not stopping when they got to the far side of the ring. Two continued on under the velvet rope until they were pulled back by their handlers. One put its paws on the rope, perhaps contemplating trying out for the circus that would be back at the Garden come spring.

After stretching like cats, deep into their backs, two of the dogs, a brindle and a tri, began batting at each other with their front paws. A lot of the dogs stood up against their handlers' legs, begging for food, and were simply pushed off with a small movement of the knee. But one, a black-and-white, added humping to the routine and annoyed his handler enough to get a smack on his rump.

Gil knelt next to Magritte, reaching into his jacket pocket and placing a piece of dried liver at the ready between his teeth, then lifting each of Magritte's freshly powdered white feet and replacing it carefully in just the position necessary to show off the dog's conformation at its best—level topline, straight forelegs with well-developed sinews, straight flexible pasterns, moderately well bent stifles, hocks well let down. Magritte did not move. Head high, tightly curled tail quivering with excitement, his farseeing dark eyes looking straight ahead, he remained poised and still, his wrinkled forehead giving him the intense, intelligent, brightly curious expression so characteristic of the breed.

After the judge walked down the group and back, stopping to study each dog in turn, she motioned for the handlers to take them around, and the merry-go-round began, handlers and dogs trotting swiftly around the ring. The judge's forehead became as wrinkled-looking as any basenji's as she studied the dogs in motion, looking for the quick, tireless gait deemed desirable in the breed.

Despite the fact that the basenjis were held so tight they were just short of choking, the fine little two tricolor dogs behind Magritte still managed to pull sharply into the center of the ring, breaking stride in the process. His handler gave him a sharp pop with the show lead, quickly getting his attention back. No matter. The damage had been done.

While I didn't actually *see* Gil flip or spit a piece of bait as he was moving Magritte nicely along, I couldn't swear he hadn't done just that.

I looked to the left and saw that Addie or Poppy's pasty complexion had turned even less healthy looking, and she was popping rice cakes into her mouth double-time. I checked the number on the handler's armband against the catalog listing. It had been Orion who had fallen for Gil's trick. And what an effective piece of work it was! Basenjis hunt by sight *and* scent. If Orion hadn't seen precisely where the liver had landed, he certainly could have found it by its odor, a property Gil always augmented by rehydrating the liver with his own saliva.

Gil had his back to me for the moment, but I noticed that right after the tri broke, his hand went fishing around in his jacket pocket and, finding nothing there, went into the small leather pouch he had fastened onto his belt only moments earlier in the benching area, the pouch in which he kept his supply of liver treats.

The judge signaled the handlers to stop. Once again, each knelt on the mat and fussed with his or her dog, stacking, brushing, baiting, trying to get each to show at his best.

Gil pulled out the small brush that was sticking out of his back pocket and ran it over Magritte's back. Then he stood and dramatically took a few strokes with the same brush in his own hair, showing oneness with his little charge.

He stacked Magritte and stood again to face him, a piece of bait held shoulder height in his hand, seizing Magritte's attention with it, teasing him into leaning forward so that his shoulder assembly would be bent rather than straight, so that he'd be literally and figuratively up on his toes, so that his neck would look graceful, so that he might even look good enough to win. Gil kept smacking his lips to remind the little dog precisely how yummy the treat would taste when he had finally earned it.

Finally the judge asked each handler in turn to take the dog around once more in the prescribed pattern while the rest of the handlers kept their dogs in line, pretty, stacked, and waiting, some letting them chew on the bait as they held it in their fingers, others moving the bait in a mesmerizing pattern as if to say, See what you'll get if you do this right.

Gil was third in line. I watched him look back and forth between the dog-and-handler team moving across the ring and Magritte, making sure his own dog's attention was still crisp. Gil's face was shining with perspiration, and I noticed that twice he swapped Magritte's lead back and forth so that he could wipe his hands on a handkerchief. Finally, it was their turn. I felt something small as a bit of paper flutter and rise in my chest.

First the judge examined Magritte on the table, feeling his body, making sure there were two testicles, both fully descended into the scrotum, checking his bite, and looking carefully at his quizzical expression. Afterward, he was placed back on the mat and Gil was asked to take him around.

Gil began gaiting Magritte down the far side of the ring, going quickly at first in a well-practiced lope, his eyes on Magritte as he ran. When he got to the side opposite the judge, he turned, as the two handlers before him had, crossing in front of where Addie and Poppy sat, Magritte trotting beautifully between Gil and the judge.

With all eyes on him and Magritte, Gil approached the final turn that would have taken him diagonally back toward the judge, whose body language revealed her keen interest. (This, after all, was serious *business*.)

Gil never made the turn.

Instead, face flushed pink, he slowed his pace. And stopped. For no apparent reason, or so it seemed, he lost his balance, going down hard onto his right knee, the knuckles of his right hand bracing him on the floor.

There was a gasp from the crowd and, almost immediately, the nervous laughter of people grateful that what has happened to someone else hasn't happened to them.

We sat waiting for Gil to get up, grin sheepishly, put a crease back in his pants, put a snap into the lead, and continue like a trooper. After all, Morgan Gilmore wasn't the first handler to slip and fall in the ring. Nor would he be the last.

But he didn't stand up.

He lifted his right hand to his collar and scratched at it, as if he were a dog. It was almost comical, until his left leg skidded sideways and, with all the grace of a forty-pound sack of Eukanuba tipping over, Morgan Gilmore, now the color of skim milk, pitched forward, facedown, onto the mat.

25

Everyone Wants to Win, You See

THERE WAS AN enormous cry from the crowd, people who had been seated standing up. I felt my catalog slide off my lap and heard it land with a dull thud at my feet.

Then it was all movement again, not dogs and handlers going around, but the judge, the steward, and a rush of uniformed security guards, all surrounding Gil so densely that in a moment he was no longer visible to the crowd. One of the security guards stood on the outside of the circle, speaking urgently into his walkie-talkie.

Magritte was outside the circle, too, the end of his leash apparently still in Gilmore's hand, because twice he pulled to get away—basenjis do not take interruptions lightly—and twice he failed. He sat instead, a major no-no in the ring, his back to where his handler was down and surrounded by noisy strangers.

I heard the walkie-talkie crackle.

Magritte was frantic. He wasn't looking anxiously from side to side the way a German shepherd or a Dobie would. He was in an almost Zenlike trance, staring straight ahead. Except for one pretty white paw raised and doing the dog paddle in a heart-wrenching gesture of supplication, he was still. But I could see that his sides moved in and out too rapidly, and he was opening and closing his mouth as if biting the air.

Two men in white came running into the ring with a stretcher. Between the judge's legs and the steward's, I saw one of the technicians bend and take Gil's pulse at the neck. They closed ranks even more after that, moving quickly and efficiently while we all stood and waited to hear what had happened, having somehow forgotten the basics of breathing.

An elegant man, tall, thin, in his sixties, a flush across his cheeks as if he'd been running, appeared center ring. He lifted his hands and rode them down once, then twice, through the air, signaling us to sit, which we did, as tractable as the dogs in the ring, still frozen in show pose as they had been before Gil fell. Poised, calm, and eloquent, he began to speak.

"There's no reason at all to be alarmed. Mr.—"

He paused, and the steward whispered in his ear.

"Mr. Gilmore has fainted."

He smiled and looked down at his expensive, polished shoes. "As many of you know, and others can guess, this is tense, hard work."

He smiled again.

"Everyone wants to win, you see."

There was the laughter of recognition from a dozen or so in the audience.

With one long-fingered hand, the gentleman in center ring smoothed his trim, white mustache, his starched white collar, his red silk tie.

"There's absolutely nothing to be concerned about."

Again, his hands rode down the air in front of him.

I turned to look at Dennis, who was whispering with the steward, right at the place where the handlers enter the ring.

"Please," the man with white hair said. "Keep your seats, ladies and gentlemen, so that we may continue with the judging."

I looked up in the stands in time to see Doc's back as he tore up the steps to the third tier.

When the speaker's hands returned to his sides, I could see they were trembling. Yet he soothed us with his voice, jollied us with gentle dog show humor, and when he had finished speaking and had nodded to the judge, we saw that Gil was no longer lying there. He had been circled, hidden, and spirited away.

I saw the judge nod and gesture for the handlers to take the dogs around. And there was Aggie, in her aqua sweater and thick-soled dog show shoes, standing in third place, Magritte at the end of the lead, high-collared and nearly choking. The ten handlers popped the ten leads and, along with ten basenjis, just as before, began to run around the ring.

I turned to my left, then my right. People had opened their catalogs to the hound group, to the basenjis. They sat quietly, pens poised to mark the win, as if Morgan Gilmore had never been there, had never teased and baited his client's dog into posing for the judge, had never gaited him across the garish green indoor-outdoor carpet, praying for a win, had never fallen, face pale, struggling for air, and then been carried away, as if he were an injured player at a football game.

Morgan Gilmore, in his cowboy boots and string tie.

Was I the only one wondering if he was alive or dead?

I practically knocked over my chair getting out of it, pushing my way to get into the aisle where I could move. I was going to go get Dennis, but decided against it. Instead, I ran for the medical office, which was tucked away deep under the stands across from the basenji ring.

I moved as quickly as I could, sideswiping several people and spilling at least one woman's bathtub-size soda, but never stopping to apologize. This was New York. I didn't have to.

The security guard standing in the exit tunnel tried to stop me, but when I told him the man who had just been carried past him on a stretcher was my handler, reluctantly he let me go by.

I know. I know. I just wish to hell I knew what a handbasket was.

Cheering and screaming echoed down the tunnel after me from one of the larger rings. Perhaps one of the harriers or an Ibizan had just taken the breed, making everyone but his owner and handler absolutely positive the judge was as blind as a mole.

Good sportsmanship, like chivalry, had gone the way of fins on Buicks.

Even before I got to the medical office, I heard the engine of the ambulance and turned to run for the ramp where it stayed parked and ready for emergencies. I saw the back of it going down the dank, dark ramp, where smokers more law-abiding than Doc gathered periodically to turn the area into a gigantic ashtray.

I heard the faint wail of the siren as the ambulance hit the street and listened to that lonely sound until it was out of earshot, and other noises, the closer sounds of the Garden, were all I could distinguish.

When I turned around, I saw the security guard with the walkie-talkie who had called for the stretcher.

"He's my handler. Where are they taking him?"

I lied so emotionally, I almost believed myself.

"They go to St. Vincent's, lady. You can call there later."

He turned away and, hands linked behind his back, rocked a little on his heels.

"Was he conscious, awake?"

"I couldn't say, lady. They had an oxygen mask on him, so he wasn't saying nothing to nobody." He looked around, stepped closer, took a meaty hand, and patted his chest. "Looks to me like it was his heart," he whispered. "All that running, all that tension. Don't you worry now," he said, patting my arm lightly. "They'll fix him up, your friend."

I headed back to ring three, to find Dennis.

Orion was stacked on the table the judge used to examine the basenjis individually, and she was baiting him herself, to see his expression. He was a beautifully made little boy, but not as flashy as Magritte.

"How'd Magritte do?" I asked. When in Rome. The only heart problems at a dog show are the breaks and tears you get from losing. There's no world news here. No family obligations, holiday blues, overdue bills. There are only dogs, and the question of who will win and who will lose.

"Not so hot," he said. "Aggie had him choked so short his front feet barely skimmed the ground. How's Gil?"

"They took him to St. Vincent's. The security guard said it looked like a heart attack. I don't know how bad it is. Maybe you can call later. How did Aggie come to take Magritte?"

"You know these show people. All that counts is that the dog gets his shot. They don't care *what* happened to Gil. Well, neither do I," he said. "Anyway, she volunteered. I went to get him, and she was already talking to the steward. I figured, oh"—he sighed—"let him have his chance."

We stayed ringside, standing across from Louis and Veronica, watching each of the basenjis in turn get examined on the table and then gait in the pattern Gil had nearly completed before he fell. I tugged at Dennis's sleeve and told him to bring Magritte after the judging and meet me back in the benching area. His mouth opened, I guess to ask me why I was leaving, but then he turned back to the ring, figuring I probably wouldn't tell him anyway.

Gilmore's coat was still behind Magritte's crate, his calendar beneath it. I opened it to the front, where compulsive people fill in the lines under "In case of emergency, call." He had: "Marjorie Gilmore," and an address the same as the one above. I checked my watch. It was still too soon to call and find out my husband's condition.

I took Gil's stuff, including the crate, to the medical office and signed Dennis's name on the receipt they gave me. I went to the pay phones and left a message for Marty Shapiro to make sure he'd remember to walk Dashiell. Then I got a huge Coke. Since I had miles to go before I'd sleep, caffeine seemed a good idea.

Dennis looked downcast coming down the aisle, carrying Magritte under one arm. "He made the cut, but he didn't win," he said. "Aggie can't handle the way Gil can."

Maybe Gil was right. Leave the showing to the pros.

"Where's the crate and all Gil's stuff?"

"I turned everything in to the medical office. I figured it was only a matter of time before they'd think to come for it. I looked in his calendar first and got his wife's name. I can use that to call the hospital, try to find out how he is."

"Magritte is supposed to stay until eight-thirty. Where are you going to keep him?"

I patted my lap.

Dennis sat next to me, but he held on to Magritte.

"Do you think I should call Marjorie and tell her?"

"Maybe we should call the hospital first, see how he's doing."

He nodded, glad, I figured, not to have to do anything.

We sat quietly, Magritte asleep on Dennis's lap. After a while I went to call St. Vincent's, and on the way to the pay phones I decided that instead of making things more complicated, I would simply tell the truth.

"I'm sorry, Ms. Alexander," the attending from the ER said, in a voice more weary than sad. "He arrested in the ambulance, on the way here. Everything was done that could have been done. We weren't able to get him back."

He paused, but I said nothing.

"Would you like us to try to contact Mrs. Gilmore, or would Mr. Keaton prefer to do that?"

"Thank you, but we'll take care of it," I said.

I headed back to the benching area to tell Dennis.

26

You'll Only Have
Yourself to Blame

"WHAT WAS IT? His heart?" Dennis asked, his pale complexion looking gray under the harsh lights.

"I guess. He just said he arrested in the ambulance and they weren't able to resuscitate him."

"Well, that's that," he said. "You know, it's difficult to feel happy, even satisfied. I wanted to kill him myself, Rachel. Now that he's dead, I just feel, well, nothing. Empty. I'll go call Marjorie."

We slid Magritte onto my lap. He barely opened his eyes. His tail curled partly and then relaxed again. He was back to sleep before Dennis was out of sight.

Dennis came back, carrying a five-pound bag of Nutro Max kibble.

"He really loves this shit. You'll still take him, Rachel, won't you? It's too late for me to make other plans."

"Of course. Did you get Marjorie?"

"Thank God, I got Chris, the kennel manager. She's going to tell Marjorie. This way Marjorie won't be alone when she hears. I gave Chris the number of the hospital, and the number here. She has my number at home, of course, in case there's anything I can do. I said that. In spite of everything. I mean, Marjorie didn't do anything wrong. Except marry badly."

I barely listened as Dennis told me how much food to give Magritte, and when. He gave me his hotel number in Boston, just in case I had a problem with Magritte. At the dinner break, I insisted he go out and sit someplace nice for dinner and eat something other than a greasy hot dog. After he left, I walked around the benching area with Magritte, got myself a greasy hot dog, and went back to Magritte's bench to eat.

As it got closer to the groups, people began coming in who had been at home or in their cars when they had heard about Gil on the news. The story spread quickly around the benching area. I was glad I had finished my hot dog before hearing all that talk about heart attacks and everyone's theory on why.

"He was a smoker, you know," a short guy with thick glasses said.

"Weight's not everything," a really fat man said, "it has more to do with how many high-density lipids you have, whatever a lipid is anyway."

"All that running in the ring," a young man with long, blond hair holding a black-and-white whippet said, "you'd think heart disease would be the *last* thing a handler would get."

A woman in red said that *Live at Five* had reported that Gil had fallen in the ring at 12:11 and had arrested at 12:14, in the ambulance. They mentioned Clifford, of course, and went on to dub Ch. Ceci N'Est Pas un Chien "the bad luck dog." They had showed his picture, but hadn't had one of Gil. Now when people passed where I sat with Magritte, they did so silently, shaking their heads. Or they were careful to look anywhere but at us. Poor Ceci!

At eight Dennis and I went to his box seats to watch the evening judging, Magritte with us. I had gotten my coat from the coat check on the way so that after Best in Show I could make a hasty exit. I draped the coat over Magritte so that he could curl up on my lap and still be out of sight. Too many people were staring. Besides, there were TV cameras and press photographers everywhere, and I didn't want to see my own face on TV or in the paper. They'd probably dub me the bad luck bitch and report that I had once married outside the species.

As if they were perfect!

I wasn't sure why we were staying. We no longer cared who'd win, and considering the circumstances, Magritte could have gotten excused, but leaving would require energy, and energy was something neither of us had.

Dennis finally left right before Best in Show. I stayed; I was there already, and it seemed as good a place to be as any. With Magritte asleep under my coat on Dennis's vacated seat, I watched Mark Threl-fall handle the springer spaniel Ch. Salilyn's Condor to the win.

I even stayed in my place to watch all the reporters and photographers rushing out onto the floor to take pictures of the pretty springer with his huge blue ribbon and sterling silver Tiffany trophy, his humans behind him, beaming.

For just a moment, I let myself think about how much Dennis would have loved to have stood there with Magritte, and I got so sad, I nearly cried.

The Garden was half empty by the time I woke Magritte and walked him toward the ladies' room. Crates full of dogs, stacked three high on dollies like doggy apartment houses, were being wheeled out by grim-faced handlers. Better luck next time, I wanted to say. But I didn't say anything. I thought they were pretty lucky already. *They* were still alive.

I was only paying enough attention to where I was going not to step in some dog's "accident" and not to trip over a leash, an empty dolly, or a very short dog, when something in front of me slapped my brain awake.

I saw him from the back, only his shoulders were too narrow, his feet too slim.

It wasn't a him. It was a her.

She was wearing a long camel coat, her hair tucked neatly into a black beret so that I couldn't tell what color it was or if it was long or short.

She took a step and turned toward me so that I could see not only her profile but her companion as well.

It was Veronica Cahill, bending her long, graceful neck so that Louis Lane could take the white silk scarf he had been carrying for her around his neck and put it around her own.

Too bad the case was closed, I thought as Magritte and I continued on our way to the ladies' room. It would have been deliciously satisfying to pin something on those two.

I still had questions I couldn't answer. There was one less now. It had been Veronica Cahill who had come to the loft to remove the tape from Clifford Cole's answering machine. Her perfume had made me sneeze a second time when she had come to see Magritte in the benching area. And one more. Why?

Suddenly I found myself thinking about Beatrice and the time I had gotten stitches on my arm right after getting my first two-wheeler.

"Don't touch those," she'd said as I poked around under the bandage. "Leave well enough alone."

"They're my stitches," I told her, "and I'll do as I please with them."

"In that case," she said, turning her back toward the sink and away from me, "whatever happens, you'll only have yourself to blame."

Maybe the case was closed for Dennis, but I never had learned to leave well enough alone.

27

You Can Send Your Dog

THE CRUCIFORM LADIES' room, swinging doors on two sides, was nearly empty when I walked in, schlepping my heavy coat, Magritte, and Magritte's Nutro Max. Two handlers, armbands still in place, were at the sinks washing their hands. The aisle where the stalls were was deserted. There was no line of patient, chatting women, making friends while waiting their turn, no purses visible on the floor of the stippled gray stalls, no ugly crepe-soled, laced-up dog show shoes, facing forward, visible under the doors, no cries for toilet paper, hands fishing around in the neighboring stall, no toilets flushing, no one humming, laughing, or sobbing because their dog hadn't taken Best, no nothing. When the handlers left, Magritte and I were alone.

I went two-thirds of the way down the aisle, hoping for a cleaner stall that way, took Magritte in with me, hung my coat on the hook, and propped the bag of dog food against the front left pilaster. The moment I sat, Magritte on my lap and licking at my face, I heard the door open, the one on the side that led to the benching area, the one I had used.

I was doing nothing but wishing I had thought to use the handicapped stall at the far end of the aisle, where I could have put Magritte on the floor and peed in peace, when I heard the sound of stall doors opening and closing, one, then the next, then the next, coming toward me.

I wondered if they were about to close the Garden and wanted to make sure they weren't locking anyone in the john, but I checked my watch and it was much too early. I was sure the cleaning staff would be here for hours.

Maybe the first few stalls were out of toilet paper. It was late in the day, after all.

Two more doors opened and closed, getting closer to me.

Maybe she had inadvertently left her coat on the hook behind the door and was looking for it.

I don't know why, but I leaned carefully forward and picked up the bag of dog food, squeezing it onto my lap in front of Magritte. I lifted my legs, too, stretching them straight out in front of me and bracing myself with my feet against the door.

Then the oddest thing happened. The doors stopped banging open and everything was very quiet. Too quiet. Until the lady began to whistle, a sweet, clear little tune, just four notes, a pause, then those same four notes again.

As if she were calling a dog.

And again, four notes, a pause, the same four notes, only an octave higher now, the sound echoing off the tiles, reminding me just how empty this place was so late in the day, and how isolated.

Magritte stiffened, his hackles going up. And he growled, a low rumble in his throat I could feel as I quickly hooked his collar with two fingers just in time to prevent him from jumping down and disappearing under the door.

When he discovered he wasn't free to do as he pleased, he began to whine.

Suddenly the bathroom doors opened again, this time from the side that led to the passageway under the stands. I heard a woman's voice.

"God, it's late. Even the bathroom's deserted."

Immediately the door to the stall next to me opened and closed. Only this time, the lady who had lost her coat was in the stall.

"Do you have a comb? Dotty, a comb? Thanks."

I leaned down and away from that side, careful not to dislodge Magritte and his food, until I could see the shoes of the lady who had finally found a stall to her liking.

I saw white leather sneakers.

Big white leather sneakers.

Facing the wrong way.

Unless she was about to throw up, the lady next to me was not using the john in the usual way.

I waited hopefully for the sound of retching.

No such luck. She was using the stall as a place to hide.

"So, where to next?" I heard from the area where the sinks were.

"I'm off to a cluster. The South, thank you. Isn't this New York weather something? How do they live here?"

I took another peek at those shoes.

My sister Lillian wears a size eleven, and these feet could make her look as if she were Cinderella.

In my neighborhood, no matter *what* someone is wearing, feet that big can mean only one thing. The person in the stall next to me was no lady.

A chill went through me that precluded nearly all bodily functions, including the one I was there for.

The sixth law of investigation work says, Don't get caught with your pants down.

Quietly putting Magritte and the food down for a moment on the side opposite Big Foot, in one move I covered my ass, literally at least, slipped into my coat, and, hoisting Magritte but ditching the bag of Nutro Max kibble in the stall, bolted out of the ladies' room, almost knocking down Dotty and her friend.

"What's *your* problem?" I heard behind me before the swinging door closed.

But I never stopped to answer. I ran down the moving escalator, Magritte now under my coat and snug against my chest, and kept running until I was on Seventh Avenue.

There were people everywhere, all waving frantically for cabs. Not wanting to stand around vying with the crowd for too few taxis while whoever had been in the bathroom got the chance to catch up, if indeed that was his agenda, I headed for Thirty-second Street.

Carrying Magritte, exhaustion pressing against the backs of my eyes, I turned the corner and began walking rapidly toward Eighth Avenue.

As I walked west, I was more and more alone. Except for a sense of peril I couldn't shake.

I stopped once and pretended to check my pockets, but I didn't see anyone else stop and wait, nor did I spot a particular person behind me or across the street that I remembered seeing near me earlier.

Still, I couldn't shed that funny feeling, one that made the hair on my arms stand up. I began to run.

When I reached Eighth Avenue, the wind was whipping around, blowing dirt off the street into my eyes. I stepped off the curb into the street, one hand on the outside of my coat propping up Magritte, who by now felt as heavy as a semi, the other up and out like a flagpole, hoping to attract a vacant cab.

Watching the empty street in front of me, I found myself wishing I had my attack-trained pit bull at my side so that I could feel smugly safe instead of terrified.

My imagination can really get out of hand when I'm this tired.

Why would I be followed if the man who had killed Clifford Cole was dead?

Hey, relax, I told myself. It was probably just a pervert in the john. New York is full of them.

Or some guy who couldn't read English, made a natural mistake.

"Not to worry," I said out loud, to Magritte. "This case is closed as tight as a Brittany's lips."

But the feeling of being followed stayed with me. Even when it's baseless, it can be more frightening than being followed.

When you are sure you are being followed, you can do something about it, step into a store, jump on a bus, get lost in a sea of humanity or traffic.

Except it was nearly midnight in a deserted part of the city. There were no open stores, no buses, no sea of humanity. There wasn't even a fucking cab.

Okay, still.

You can draw a gun. (Mine was home.)

You can turn around and shout, "I see you, you cowardly scumbag, hiding in the shadow of that building. What are you doing there, jerking off and thinking about your mother?"

You can pretend you're going home and lead him to the Sixth Precinct.

And, if there's absolutely no other choice, you can send your dog to talk some sense into the bastard.

Unless the only dog you happen to have with you at the time is a lousy basenji.

In which case you're nuked.

That's when I turned around again, just in time to catch the man who was hanging back partway down the block step quickly closer to the building line where he'd be less likely to be seen. I could see the fronts of his white sneakers shining in the moonlight.

I was just about to succumb to the most hideous feeling of helplessness, a feeling I loathe because it's always easier when you can actually do something, when a cab pulled up.

I wrenched open the door and told the driver my address.

And had I not looked out the back window as my cab pulled out into the street and seen the man who had been standing in the shadows run to the curb with *his* arm up like a flagpole and immediately get a cab, the creep, I would have thought I was okay.

Safe.

But now I knew I wasn't. The signs were in place that someone wanted to know where I was going. As clearly as the toilet paper that might be stuck to the bottom of his sneakers would have told the world where he'd just been.

All I could think of was how good it would feel to be home with the door double-locked and my own dog at my side.

There was only one thing to do. I offered my driver an extra five if he'd get me home in five minutes, and he nearly left my head on Eighth Avenue making the turn on West Thirty-third Street, past the north side of the main post office, to go downtown.

And all the way home, all I could do was hope that the man who had been following me hadn't thought to make a similar offer to his driver.

28

Who Wouldn't Make a Face?

WHEN I WAS putting the key in the front-door lock, I heard the phone and nearly broke the key in half trying to get inside.

"Rachel, thank God you're okay."

Magritte had run in. Dashiell had run out. Now they were both in the garden, the door open, the warm air flowing out and the frigid night air coming in.

"Dennis?"

The dogs came barreling in and headed for the food bowls.

"Hang on a sec," I said, slipping off my coat and tossing the Flying Man into the living room.

"Hey, where were you raised," I asked Dashiell, "a kennel? Close that door."

He came from behind it, butted it once with his cinder block of a head, and then did a neat paws-up. The door slammed so hard, the house shook. I turned the lock and put on the chain.

"That's better." He and Magritte were tugging on the new toy.

"I'm back," I said into the phone, "what's up?"

"Thank God you're okay. I've been worried sick."

"What's wrong? What happened?"

"You're not going to believe this. Gil didn't die of a heart attack. He was poisoned!"

"What? How do you know?"

"When I got home, there was a message from Marjorie, saying it was urgent she speak to me as soon as possible, even if it was in the middle of the night. So of course I called."

"And?"

"A technician was moving the body, you know, Gil, because the ME has to autopsy to determine cause of death, and when he was getting him onto a rolling stretcher, he smelled bitter almond."

"Cyanide."

"Right. It wasn't a heart attack. It looks as if Gil was *murdered*."

"Have they done the autopsy yet?"

"Hey, we're talking New York here. There's a major backup in autopsy. But get this, the technician starts checking everything, you know, really looking at the body carefully and checking all the clothes, the pockets, whatever, and finally he opens the pouch. Well, as you might imagine, it stinks to high heaven."

"Of course, that's what liver's supposed to do," I cut in. "That's why it works so well as bait."

"But this liver smelled like bitter almond. This is where the smell was coming from."

"So how come Gil didn't smell it?"

"Maybe because he was working, you know, concentrating really hard on what he was doing with Magritte. Anyway, he was a smoker. Cigars. Dulls your sense of smell."

"And taste," I added. "Not only that, once he popped it in his mouth, by the time he might have realized anything, it might have been too late. Cyanide is fast. You don't get an awful lot of time to react."

"Rachel, doesn't that mean Gil put the poisoned liver in his mouth while he was in the ring? Right in front of us!"

"Yes. And not only that, it means not all the liver was tainted."

"How do you know?"

"Because I'm pretty sure he spit a piece to trip up the tri. So he would have died then if it was all laced with cyanide. And so would the tri if he'd spit it out before he went down."

"But the toxicology lab said all the liver in the pouch was poisoned."

"It was. But the liver in his pocket wasn't. That's how this was done, Dennis. Someone swapped the liver in the bait pouch for the doctored liver."

"How? When?"

"While Magritte was being groomed."

"You're kidding!"

"I'm not. Look, the pouch was where Gil kept his supply of liver, but he took some and put it into his jacket pocket so that he wouldn't have to wear the pouch until he was in the ring. He left the pouch with his stuff, in back of Magritte's crate. It was there, unattended, when we all trooped off to the grooming area. In fact, Doc left before we did. He also beat it away from the ring when Gil went down."

"Who's Doc?"

"This hideous little man Gil was talking to when he came back to get Magritte ready for the ring."

"Do you think *he* switched the liver?"

"All I'm saying is he *could* have. Dennis, *I* could have. Gil left all his things there when he went for coffee. But he had some liver in his jacket pocket, untainted liver, because he gave some to Magritte when he cut his nails. So, that means—"

"Magritte. Oh, God, you mean he could have—"

"No, Dennis, it went into his own mouth first, for a while, too. He kept swishing it around in his saliva to get it all juicy, and he teased Magritte to distract him from the indignity of getting his nails cut. That means the liver in his pocket was okay. That explains why the tri is okay, and why Gil wasn't poisoned in the group run."

"So you're saying that when he took liver earlier from his pouch, it was okay. And when he used liver later, from the pouch, it wasn't."

"Right. In fact, a moment after I saw him fish around in his pocket and then go into the bait pouch, I saw him make this awful face. I figured, shit, who wouldn't make a face, putting liver in his mouth. But, you know something, he didn't make a face in the grooming area, and he practically *ate* the fucking liver while he was grooming Magritte."

"But when he got a piece with cyanide, he did notice it was bitter."

"Apparently."

"My mother used to make me eat liver when I was a kid, you know, for the iron, and I still remember that some of it was sort of sweet and some of it was really bitter."

"So Gil could have thought he had just gotten a normally bitter piece. It's not like he had time to taste-test the whole pouch. He was in the ring, working. And anyway, he didn't have time for another reason."

"The cyanide. It's too fast."

"Exactly."

"Do you think the killer planned it so that it would happen in the *ring*, right in front of everyone?"

"I don't know. But if he did, it would mean that whether or not he was there, he'd hear the results of his handiwork on the news that night. There's no way something this dramatic would go unreported."

"Damn clever of him."

"Or her. What else did Marjorie tell you?"

"That the technician sent the pouch to the lab for testing. Once there's suspicion of murder, there's no delay, and two hours later the toxicology results were in and, big surprise, the liver had been laced with enough sodium cyanide to fell a fucking horse. That's what they told Marjorie."

Something was nagging at me, holding a part of my attention captive, but I couldn't get a grasp on what it was.

"They're sure it was cyanide poisoning?" I asked him.

"Pending autopsy results. But the doctor was sure enough of the cause of death to call Marjorie. Not his heart, he said. *Cy*anide."

"Dennis, you said you hardly knew Marjorie. Why did she call *you* right away?"

"I told her to call if she needed me, Rachel. She asked me if I would talk to the police, see what I could find out. She said she'd given them my number, and she hoped that was okay. I mean, she's so far away."

"Is she coming up?"

"I don't think so. You know how most people are. They figure if you just set foot in New York, next thing you know, you'll be murdered."

"Where could people get an idea like that?"

I thought about Big Foot in the ladies' room.

"Dennis, I—"

"I guess *he*'s off the hook," he said.

"What did you say?"

"Well, if someone killed him, doesn't that let him off the hook?"

"We don't know for sure the two murders are connected, do we?"

"What do you mean?"

"Suppose someone killed Gil, and it had nothing to do with Cliff's death?"

"Who would want to kill Gil? Well, except me?"

"How about anyone who had been in the ring with him? Didn't you see what he did to the little tri? There was also this handler he tripped in the ring. Ted Stickley. He fell and broke his arm. You can't handle dogs with a broken arm. Dennis, I wonder if he was at Westminster. Maybe he was biding his time, waiting for a way to get back at Gil. Did you save your catalog?"

"Of course."

"Check it for me."

"Hang on. Stickley, Stickley, Stickley. Yes. Ted Stickley. He handled a saluki."

"Well!" I said, as if handling a saluki were proof of his guilt. "There are a lot of people who hated Gil. Everyone knew his habits, Dennis, I mean everyone knew that liver went into his mouth."

"So you're saying maybe the person who hated him enough to kill him had nothing to do with Clifford's death?"

"Dennis, Gil's death doesn't *solve* this case. There's too much we can't explain."

"What next?"

"Sleep. It's been a long day. I'll call you tomorrow, in Boston. Everything changed today. I need some time to think."

"Be careful, Rachel."

"Yeah. Yeah," I told him.

But I hadn't even looked down the block when I'd gotten out of the cab, carrying Magritte, my keys ready in my right hand. I was just so happy to be home. Was I kidding myself to think we had really lost Big Foot?

When I hung up, I looked over at Magritte. He'd had three close calls, two the night of Clifford's murder when he could have been intentionally killed by whoever killed Cliff or accidentally killed crossing West Street after he'd gotten free of his collar. And another at Westminster, had Gil had the time to spit the tainted liver to him before he went down. That he hadn't may not have been an accident. Most show people care much more about dogs than they do about people.

Three close calls. Yet here he was. The *good* luck dog.

Magritte began washing himself, like a cat. Perhaps he had nine lives, too. If so, he was going through them mighty fast.

I poured a glass of wine and began to think about the loft and those three empty stretchers. Had Clifford changed his mind about three paintings, ditching them because they weren't good enough? I'd read that Picasso worked that way, painting quickly, creating many works, and keeping only the ones he liked.

Or was there some other reason those canvases were gone?

Who was Mike? *He* must have had a key to the loft, too, since he had left a message about picking up Magritte.

More important, who was Big Foot?

It had been easy to assume that Morgan Gilmore had been the

killer. He had the motive and the opportunity. He had keys to the loft. He knew Cliff would do anything to get Magritte back.

My head was aching, the questions I couldn't answer eating at me. I picked up Marty's note, which, as usual, was on the green marble table, just outside the kitchen.

Rach,
Dash played with Elwood and had dinner at the precinct, two slices of pizza, a burger without the bun, and a cinnamon doughnut. Sorry. You know how the guys are with dogs.
Marty

I stroked my hand over Dashiell's big, round belly, then scratched the base of Magritte's tail. They were heaped in a pile, sound asleep, Dashiell's head on the Flying Man, as if it were a pillow. Suddenly sleep seemed the perfect idea.

29

Tunnel Vision

I NEVER MADE it upstairs. I woke up at seven-fifteen, covered with my coat, the grayish light of winter slipping through the shutters, making stripes on everything.

I let the dogs out and watched them chase each other around, taking turns being hunter and prey.

Now that I knew it had been Veronica Cahill at the loft, I didn't need to check the *Young Detective's Handbook* to figure out why. But law seven says, Confirm your hunches.

I decided to catch Louis Lane before he left for school. That I most certainly did. He worked the late session and didn't have to be in until ten forty-five.

"Louis," I said, not bothering to apologize for waking him, "I was at Clifford's loft one night, and someone in a camel coat, black beret, and white scarf came in and took the tape from the answering machine."

Ba da boom. I never beat about the bush before I've had my first cup of tea.

"Oh, that was Veronica. She's so paranoid about people trying to cheat her out of her commission."

"But—"

"I told her that it couldn't happen because *I* own the art now, and of course *I* wouldn't cheat her, but she still had to go and get the damn tape. I guess it means she doesn't even trust *me*."

"She told you about going?"

"Of course. But only *after* she did it. She said there was some man-eating *beast* there and it nearly scared her to death, and I—oh! *You!*"

"Right. We scared each other."

There are always people who try to get around the gallery commission by buying directly from the artist, and few people, if any, would know that Louis, not the Cole family, now owned the art. Perhaps Veronica was right to worry—some people will do anything for money.

I wondered what else Veronica Cahill and Louis Lane might have done for it.

"Louis, there's something else, it's about Cliff's art and the way he worked. Did he sketch on paper before he painted?"

"Sometimes. But not always. Oh, he'd scribble on napkins in restaurants and stuff them in his pocket, on matchbook covers, anything at all when he got an idea, just little quick reminders. Then he'd sketch right on the canvas. In fact, when he got into his noir period, those gray paintings, a lot of the way he worked changed. *He* changed."

"How so?"

"He began working long, long hours. Sometimes he wouldn't even take Magritte out in the afternoon. He'd ask Dennis to do it. Or he'd use a dog walker. He just kept at it, painting until late at night, not coming here for days at a time."

"Did you worry? Did you think something was wrong?"

"Not *really*. He'd done it other times, I mean, get on a streak and paint almost around the clock. But never quite like this—"

"Louis, what about the piece at the show without a title?"

"He probably didn't get a chance to do the last panel."

"That's what I thought," I said quietly. "But wouldn't there be a partial fourth panel? A sketch on canvas? Something? The first three are clearly completed paintings. Is that how he worked when he did a multiple-panel piece? One at a time?"

"Actually, no. He worked on all the panels at once."

"Even so, you think the last panel never got done?"

"I don't know. Does it mean something?"

"It could. Louis, by any chance, do you know the name of the dog walker Cliff used?"

"Mike. I don't remember hearing his last name."

"Great. Thanks."

"I heard about Gil," he said.

I waited.

"Rachel? Are you getting anywhere?"

"It's too soon to say," I told him, wondering what his shoe size was and if he ever wore anything but Gucci loafers. "But I'll keep you posted," I lied.

I opened the door. The dogs were digging and burrowing in the snow. I let Magritte in and sent Dash back to the passageway for the *Times*.

The piece about Gil was in the sports section, adjacent to Walter Fletcher's piece about the springer's win, not with the obituaries. It was small, but dramatic.

Death at the Dog Show

Morgan Gilmore, handling the basenji Ch. Ceci N'Est Pas un Chien, whose owner, Clifford Cole, had been found dead on the Christopher Street pier late last month, fell in the ring and died just minutes later in the ambulance on the way to St. Vincent's Hospital, a representative of the Westminster Kennel Club said. Pending autopsy, the presumed cause of death was heart failure.

Mr. Gilmore, 47, of Greensboro, North Carolina, had been a professional handler for twenty-three years. He is survived by his wife, Marjorie, and his parents, Lloyd and Ellen Gilmore of Charlotte.

I called Marty.

"Shapiro. How goes it?"

"Could be worse. How's your case coming? I was going to give you a buzz, Rach, about that question you asked me, whether or not the victim had semen in his anus."

"And?"

"He didn't."

I knew I'd be looking for clues there one day!

"I saw in the paper Magritte's handler died of a heart attack. Bummer. Was he heavy?"

"This is why I'm calling, Marty. I got a call from the client, late last night. It wasn't as the papers reported it."

"So what else is new?"

"Marty, it was cyanide. He was murdered."

"No shit. Is this connected to your case, you think, or coincidental?"

"I thought he was our man until I heard how he bought it."

I told Marty what I had found out about Gil and the frozen semen business, and about all the loose threads that were driving me crazy.

"Be careful, Rachel."

"Hey, listen to you, playing with bombs day in and day out, the man tells *me* to be careful."

"You know something, kid, I feel much safer the seven years I've been doing this than I ever did the eleven I was on the street in uniform. At least no one's taking potshots at me now. Say, how's my boy Dashiell? He do okay on yesterday's menu?"

"Dog has a cast-iron stomach, Marty. Thanks for helping out."

"Hey, anytime, Rach. You know, the article upset a few of the guys. The heart thing. We fucking *live* on doughnuts around here. They're pretty high in cholesterol, aren't they?"

"What am I, a fucking nutritionist? Read the box. It's all there, in black and white."

When I hung up, I remembered one time when I was talking to Marty and he was gesturing with a powdered doughnut in his hand, the sugar falling everywhere, quietly, like snow. Dashiell's head followed the doughnut's every move, as if he were watching the ball at a tennis match.

Exactly the way the dogs in the ring watch the bait.

Now I knew what wouldn't stop tugging at a corner of my mind, like a terrier peeling a tennis ball. I ran upstairs to my desk and started leafing through the Cole file. They had even called the piece "Witness to Murder." Magritte's picture accompanied it, his brow wrinkled, his dark eyes so alert.

I read through the article quickly—artist dead, witness found, artist's dog, undiscovered genius, Dr. Shelbert, Tracy Nevins, bingo!

"As to whether or not Magritte could finger his master's killer, Nevins was quoted as saying, 'Definitely,' " giving the killer his motive.

" 'We are still planning on having Magritte compete at Westminster on Tuesday,' Kenton added. 'Clifford would have wanted him to be there.' "

The poison was in the *bait*.

I was so blinded by what I knew that I hadn't seen the simple truth.

Morgan Gilmore had been murdered by accident.

The poison had been meant for Magritte!

The article even included the whereabouts of the potential victim, giving the murderer a perfect blueprint from which to work.

If Magritte was the intended victim, whoever had tried to kill him knew by now he had failed. Gil's death, though the cause was misreported, had been all over the news last night and was in all the papers this morning.

That was no pervert in the john. It was the killer.

He was out to try again, and now he knew Magritte was with me.

It was tunnel vision, thinking the cyanide was meant for Gil. Just because *we* knew the practices at dog shows, it was the only way we were able to see the crime.

But the most logical and obvious conclusion, which we never thought of, was that if you want to kill a dog, you poison something he's going to eat. A five-year-old could have seen this clearly.

I added Mike's name to the blackboard. He had the key. Here was someone else who knew how Cliff felt about his dog. Maybe he had a motive, too. I'd have to call him. His number would be in Clifford's address book, which I had copied.

There were too many people I hadn't spoken to. Now was the time to change all that. I ran back downstairs, double-locked the door, and came back up to the desk where I could take notes. It was time to see broadly, to check every little detail out again, to consider every possibility and to avoid jumping to conclusions.

As Ida, my therapist, used to say, pushing up her sleeves and making two lines between her eyes, *finally* we're getting started.

"Mrs. Cole? This is Elaine Boynton, Clifford's friend. I was so sad to hear about Clifford. Yes. Yes. And so I feel just terrible that I missed the memorial service. Really? He said that? She's, uh, gone. Yes. A small, private one. Yes, I do. I'm sure they would. I understand. I was wondering where I could send a donation in Clifford's name. Does the family have a preference? Okay. Thank you."

30

What Would You Like to Say?

I HAD SPENT all day and evening yesterday on the phone. All I wanted to do today was get over to Cliff's loft and find the final few pieces of the puzzle. But there was one place I wanted to go to first, B & H Photo, to pick up Clifford's slides.

"This is olt," the pale, bearded young man in the yarmulke told me, examining the slip I handed him. "Vot made you vait so lonk?"

"I was busy," I told him.

Then he noticed Magritte, who had put his paws up against the counter to see what was on the other side.

"Oh, it's mine friend," the young man said, stepping forward and leaning over. "I'll get for you a kendy, vait, vait," and all in a stir, he reached into one of the candy dishes that sat at even intervals along the counter and pulled out a small Tootsie Roll for Magritte.

"He doesn't eat candy. It's not good for him," I said in protest. But I was too late. The Tootsie Roll was already in Magritte's mouth.

"He alvays eats a kendy ven he comes. Vot vould he t'ink if ve didn't give to him today a piece?"

But as I watched Magritte chewing, opening his mouth twice as wide as usual for each bite, all I could think about was the poisoned bait and how quickly and unexpectedly the whole world could change.

I put the yellow box into my pocket and headed downtown with the dogs. After I tossed the loft again, I'd sit down and look at the slides and have myself a good cry.

Walking downtown, Dashiell plodded along at his usual workman-like pace, stopping only when I told him to wait at street crossings where the light was red. Magritte kept pace, darting to the side occasionally to try to catch a bit of paper that was swirling about in the wind. But as soon as we crossed Houston Street, Magritte's demeanor changed. He began looking up at me and whining, as if he couldn't contain himself. When we got to Greene Street, he pulled straight for home, and once inside, where I unhooked both leads, he dashed on ahead, passing his new home and going straight for his old one.

I knocked. After all, there seemed to be more people with keys than without them, and I didn't want to cause anyone undue fright. Then I unlocked the door, Magritte impatiently jumping up and down at my side. He was the first one inside when I opened the door.

Dashiell headed straight for the kitchen, looking for water. Magritte walked to the center of the front room and sat. Head cocked, as if listening for a sign that his beloved master was home, a sound, a scent, anything to hang his hopes on, he stayed in place without moving, as I did, watching him. Suddenly, his muzzle tilted up, his mouth made a small circle, and he let out the most heart-wrenching sound, a keening howl, not long and smooth like a wolf howl, but a piercing *awoo, awoo, awoo,* a pause, then again, *awoo, awoo, awoo,* the second time joined from the back of the loft by Dashiell's guttural howl, honoring his friend's misery the way a second hunting dog honors a point.

For a while Magritte stayed close enough to trip me when I tried to walk, following me to the kitchen, where I filled the water bowl and put the kettle up for tea. He stayed close by while I poked around in the cabinets for snacks, even trying to join me on the step stool when I was checking out the shelves I couldn't reach. When he found he couldn't reach me, he whined and paced. I let him be. Dogs have as much right to the integrity of their feelings as people do.

After pulling down some unopened rice crackers and—God is merciful and all knowing—an unopened box of Mallomars, I felt an envelope on the top shelf, the one I could barely reach, even with the stool. I managed to pull it forward with one finger, sliding it along the oak shelf until I could pull it to the edge where I was able to grasp it.

The envelope was blank, but there was a letter inside it.

"Honey," I read, still standing on the top of the step stool, one hand on the cabinet, bracing me. "For so many years I pushed aside my desire to sleep with a man, not just the desire for sex, but to lie in a man's embrace, to feel his strong arms around me, his warmth and sweetness mine hour after hour. I never had that until I met you. And much as I want that, want to be with you, sometimes I can't.

"I'm driven by demons now. There's something I have to do, now, to get out, and I want you to understand that your love is my saving grace, my life, and to be patient with me while I work this out."

It was typed and not signed. Had Cliff written it to Louis? Or to someone else? "Honey" could be anyone. And why had it been hidden, not mailed, given, faxed?

After making tea, I decided I should do my best to really make myself feel at home, despite the empty spaces where art had once hung. If I got comfortable, I might get more into Cliff's head and be able to sort out some of the incredible things I had found out the day before. I decided that music would be the first priority. Having noticed a tape deck and drawers of tapes in Clifford's study, I put on the light and began to look at Clifford's taste in music. But before I had the chance to consider Diana Ross over Barbra Streisand, I saw just the tape I wanted to hear. It caught my eye because it was loose, sitting on top of the other tapes. Miles Davis. *Workin'*. I turned on the tuner and the tape deck, put the tape in, pressed the play button, and went to sit in the chair to drink my tea and listen while I thought about what to do next. Cliff had apparently made the tape himself, probably from a CD. There were other tapes he had made, carefully listing each cut in order on the paper in the box so that he would know what was coming and when. This tape, though, had no box. But Clifford was as obsessive-compulsive as you can get; even his copper-bottomed pots were polished. Why was this tape loose?

I went back to the drawer where the tapes were arranged not only alphabetically but by style of music, and looked for the jazz tapes, my finger running over the boxes—Chet Baker, Clifford Brown, Ray Charles, John Coltrane, Miles Davis, *Bag's Groove*, *Birth of the Cool*, and there it was, *Workin'*. I pulled out the box to read the titles of the cuts, but it wasn't empty. There was a tape in it.

I guess that's why he hadn't put the tape away, I thought, sitting back in Clifford's chair, at his desk, holding the box in my hand, turning it over to read the cuts. And while I listened to "It Never Entered My Mind," I began to think that the Clifford Cole *I* knew and loved was much too compulsive to leave a tape out where it could get dusty or to put a tape back in the wrong box.

For a moment I pictured the precise little lowercase letters with which he painstakingly titled his paintings.

I looked at the box in my hand, at the neat printing of each cut;

underneath the last one he had taken the time to put down the name
of each artist along with the instrument he played.

Was this a man who would leave a tape lying around loose?

I interrupted *Workin'*, popped in the unmarked tape, and pressed
play.

"I have Magritte."

It was a woman's voice.

But it wasn't really a woman's voice. You don't work for Bruce
Petrie for very long without being able to recognize the sound of a
voice-changing telephone. I even had one someplace, probably with
my good crystal, in the basement. Bruce had given it to me, "For
Hanukkah." And when I'd said, "Bruce, you shouldn't have," he'd
looked puzzled. "Why not?" he'd said. "It's your Christmas, isn't it?"

"I have Magritte," "she" said, enunciating carefully so that not a
syllable would be lost. "If you want him back alive, don't tell anyone
about this message. Come to the Christopher Street pier at four
o'clock tomorrow morning. Come alone—alone, you hear, or the mutt
dies. And bring a thousand bucks, you got that? A thousand, in small
bills. Yeah."

The money was an afterthought. The money was clearly not the
point of this. Which is why it wasn't taken.

I rewound the tape and listened three more times to the message
that signaled the beginning of the end of Clifford Cole's life. Afterward, I put "It Never Entered My Mind" back on, hoping that I was
finally on the right track and it wouldn't turn out to be my theme song.

Cliff had hidden the tape in the Miles Davis box. Did he think he'd
need it again later? He had hidden the letter, too. And one of the bills
I had found, a fifty, in one of his jackets, had been tucked into the
bottom of that long, skinny inside pocket that I always figured was for
carrying glasses.

He hadn't told Dennis the identity of the person he had found out
about. Hadn't told Louis about the kidnapping. It's only a dog, Louis
would have said. Why take chances?

He was secretive, even before the events that led up to his death. I
reached for the phone and called Information, to see if his phone
number was listed. That's when I got the next big surprise of the day.

It seemed everyone involved with this case was full of secrets, and
many of them were telling lies.

I took off my boots and padded out to the front room to make sure
the chain lock was on. Paranoia was in the air, and I didn't want any
surprises today, not from the ever lovely Veronica Cahill, and certainly

not from the person with the big feet who was my neighbor in the ladies' room at Madison Square Garden.

I wondered if he had the key, too.

If he was the murderer, apparently he did. After all, Dennis didn't say the loft had been broken into as an explanation for Magritte's disappearance, had he?

I went back to the little red room with its orderly collection of tapes, CDs, and videos and, opening each door and drawer, found the slide projector, a huge collection of slides, all marked as to content, three fat photo albums, and an ample collection of X-rated commercial videotapes, including two of my all-time favorites, *Scared Stiff* and *Honorable Discharge*.

There was another large collection of tapes, the homemade kind if you were to judge by the labels, all, oddly, with the same label, "The Cliff and Bert Show." I wondered if these were pornographic as well. I wondered who the hell Bert was.

Fortunately, I didn't even have to close the curtains to make the room dark enough. Since the den was an internal room, it was always dark.

Having determined to dig in and be comfortable, and since what's a movie without good snacks, I refilled my cup, took the box of Mallomars, and got Magritte settled on my lap. As I pointed the remote at the set and pressed play, I even answered my own question—who the hell Bert was.

Clifford Cole was on the screen, his round face tense, his smallish, close-set, brown eyes alert, as if he were waiting, his brown hair too long, my mother would have said, ringlets falling on his brow and curling around his collar, giving him an almost cherubic appearance.

"I watched the tape," he said, his voice nearly inaudible.

"And so what would you like to say?"

Bertram Kleinman's face wasn't on the video, only the sound of his voice, as seductive as bait.

"Well, when I was here last time and I talked about these feelings that keep cropping up, that come back from time to time—"

Clifford stopped speaking, and one hand went to his mouth, the fingers tracing his full lips from one side to the other, as if there might be traces of a meal he wished to wipe away.

"Well, when I viewed the tape," he said, drawing himself up, beating back what was coming, "that's just not true. It's not that they crop up from time to time. They're always there. Like weather."

"What does that feel like?"

"Like it's always raining. What I mean to say is, oh, it's so difficult to express, it's like the sun could be out, but it would be raining *inside*, inside *me*. I don't know why, but I'm carrying something around that makes me feel terrible. I know I'm not a terrible person, but I *feel* I am, do you know what I mean?"

"Yes, of course, Clifford. Can you tell me, when did this feeling begin?"

"Oh, it's been around as long ago as I can remember."

There was silence then, Kleinman saying nothing, Clifford looking down into his lap, as I had done so often, having arrived at Ida's office feeling blocked or sullen, not knowing what I was supposed to be saying or feeling, removed, as it were, for the moment, from my own self.

As I watched and waited, just as Bert Kleinman must have, suddenly the painful issue of the inability to create a human being from the clues of his life was no longer a problem. Here was the man whose murder I had been hired to solve, alive through the miracle of modern technology.

The technique had been around for ten years or so, predicated on the idea that watching the tape would let the patient see and understand things he had missed during the session, that seeing yourself respond, and not respond, would continue the process of education at home, between sessions.

Why not? Everything was on tape nowadays. People being born now would, in years to come, be watching themselves sally forth into life. What would they think, hearing those first cries at leaving the paradise of the womb for the harsh lights of the delivery room? What would they think, seeing themselves pop naked and greasy into the hands of a stranger?

I had pulled a tape from the middle, not paying too much attention to the dates. Waiting as patiently as Dr. Kleinman for Clifford to troll within and come up with something else to say—God, how I hated those blank moments early on in my therapy—I picked up the box and looked at the dates, four of them, four sessions on each tape.

Waiting, I began to think about Clifford's work, about the painting of Magritte at the window, the rain coming down indoors, inside Cliff. Those others, the gray paintings.

Now suddenly my mind was moving fast. I looked at the box in my hand, at the dates, then rewound the tape and looked for another, and another, all around the time that Dennis had said Clifford came to see him and he was wild, pacing, he had found out something about someone, wasn't that what Dennis had told me? And that it had to be exposed, at any cost.

Exposed.

I had to look at the film, too, the slides, it was dark enough in the den, but first I had to find the tape, I was sure there'd be one, where Clifford found out whatever it was he'd found out, trolling within, I was sure now that that's where the discovery had been made.

Three hours and twelve minutes later, the Mallomars long gone, the dogs asleep on Clifford's big white bed, I finally found what I had been looking for.

31

Man, I Couldn't Stop

HE WAS WEARING a navy blue turtleneck, the golden-brown curls like a halo around his face, his eyes no longer pinched and small but as round, open, and vulnerable as a child's.

It had been coming for months, for ages, hour after hour, talking about low self-esteem, about his lack of confidence, about feeling ugly, this beautiful child of a man, sweet-faced, sad, trying to make the bad feelings go away, trying to find out why, why some people could feel comfortable, even happy, but he couldn't.

"What would you like to say?" Bert asked as Clifford attached the microphone, pinching up a piece of his sweater and clipping it in place. "You look *so* sad today."

"I kept thinking about what you said, when I brought in the album, about how happy I had looked as a baby and as a young boy, and then the change, you saw the change, that later I never looked at the camera, only down, and that I looked so sad, almost frightened, you said. I kept thinking about that."

He wiped his palm over his lips.

He sighed.

"So I looked at the pictures at home, not the tape this time, the photographs," and his round, brown eyes began to shine with tears, his cheeks flushed, his nose and chin became pink, "and I kept seeing what you saw, I can see it now, I can't understand that I didn't *always* see it, and I kept asking myself why, and the more I did that, the worse I felt."

Clifford sat still for a moment, nothing moving except the tears running over his wet lashes and down his cheeks, falling onto his hands and lap.

"One day I'd paint for twelve hours, the next I'd stay in bed, keep my dog with me under the covers, not answer the phone, not go to Louie's house. I felt I didn't deserve to see him."

Clifford turned away, his lips pursed, brow knit, eyes closed. And waited. We all waited.

"That's how I feel," he said, his voice hoarse with emotion, "that there's something wrong with me, that I *deserve* to feel like shit."

Tears fell.

"But I don't know why," he shouted. "I don't know why."

"What are you feeling now?"

"Nothing." Sullen.

"You look angry now."

"I'm *not*."

Silence.

"That's not true. I am. Do you know what I did?"

"No, what?"

"I was taking out the pictures, so I could look at them better, first when I was happy, like you said, then later, when I was . . . not, like you said, when I was not happy anymore, when I was looking down."

Looking down now. Looking like a child. Pauses thick with emotion.

"I didn't mean to do it," he said, looking so young, so scared.

"What did you do?"

"I tore them."

"Which ones did you tear?"

"Mine. Me. But then Peter got torn, too. By accident. I tried to separate him out, so I wouldn't tear him, too. But he got torn. In half."

Now Clifford Cole was sobbing.

"I didn't mean to hurt him," he said. "I didn't."

And a hand appeared on-screen, offering a box of tissues.

Clifford wiped his eyes and blew his nose, and I watched as the sad face of a little boy was transformed and, like the sudden recognition of knowledge I'd never tire of seeing in the eyes of the dogs I used to train, Clifford Cole got the knowledge he'd been looking for, the full brunt of it, all at once, recorded on tape for posterity.

"I *did*," he said. "I did mean to hurt him. It was *Peter*. Peter was why I hate myself."

"Why is that?"

"Because he hurt me," Clifford shouted. "He fucked me. He abused me. I pushed it all away, but now it's back, now I remember what he did, that's why I began to rip him up!"

Triumph in his eyes, his eyes so old, so sad now.

"Tell me about it."

"All week it was coming back to me, weird, horrible feelings, and I'd be thinking about Peter or mad he hadn't called me, something stupid like that, only that wasn't it, wasn't the real thing, and I'd just feel like I was too ugly to go outside, I even hired this kid, Michael Neary, who walks dogs in the neighborhood to walk Magritte, and I stayed in bed, and then it came to me, like in pieces and I couldn't grasp hold of it, only see parts of it, but I knew it had to do with Peter, I don't know how to explain it, but I just did, and now all of a sudden I remember it all, what he did to me, when it was, everything.

"It started when I was seven and he was twelve, when my parents would go out and they'd leave Peter in charge of me, and he said he had things to teach me, because I'd be a man one day, and there were things I'd have to do, things I had to know, things he knew because he was older than me, and I had no idea what he was talking about, but I knew he was going to help me because he was my brother and I loved him. I trusted him. My parents, they always made this big thing about brothers, how you're loyal to each other, how it's forever, being a brother, that when they'd be gone, we'd have each other."

"And what did Peter want to teach you?"

"About girls. He said I had to know what to do about girls. That he'd *show* me. So he took me into our parents' room and he dressed me in my mother's clothes and he showed me."

"What did he do, Clifford? Tell me what he did."

"He hurt me." Sobbing now. "And when I cried, he said, Be a man, Cliffie, you have to know this, and Mommy and Daddy will never teach you, it's up to me, he said, because you're my brother and I love you, and I was so mixed up, because he said that, but he was hurting me, and after that time, he did it again and again, in his bed or in my bed or in my parents' bed, he'd put me in a *dress* and put lipstick on my mouth, all over my mouth and around it, big, grotesque, red lips, and he'd kiss me and he'd fuck me and he'd say, This is what you'll do when you get the chance."

He covered his face and cried, but when he took his hands away, his face had changed. He wasn't sad now, he wasn't frightened, he was angry, his face whole, open, strong, his eyes round and clear, sane, his demeanor adult, powerful.

"Then it changed," he said, strong in his knowledge, "and now *he* put my mother's dress on, and makeup, powder and rouge and lipstick, he looked so weird to me, but he said he was doing it so I'd know what to do, so I wouldn't make a fool of myself when the time came, so I could be a man. That's what he told me, so I could be a man."

"How awful for you."

"Gotta practice, he'd say. Gotta get ready. Gotta do it. That's what he'd say when I cried—Gotta do it. I was a *child*. I couldn't protect myself. I didn't know how. And there was no one there to do it for me. No one there to rescue me."

"That's what we're doing here, rescuing that child."

Clifford nodded, his gaze far away. Bertram Kleinman and I waited silently, watching Cliff see something from a long time ago, something only he could see.

"When I was little, before this, four or five, I guess, Peter used to make me alphabet soup, you know, from a can, of course. I still remember it," he said, his brown eyes glowing. "He'd bring the bowl carefully to the table, one of those flat, wide soup bowls with rims, and some of the soup would slosh up onto the rim of the bowl, and when it went back into the bowl, the letters that had washed up onto the rim would stay there, and he'd say, We need these, we need every letter, because there's a message in there. Where? I'd say, looking into the bowl of soup. In there, he'd tell me, there's a message for you in the soup. You just have to find it. And he'd hand me the soup spoon. Do you remember what a soup spoon felt like in your mouth when you were four or five, how huge it was?"

Kleinman must have nodded. Clifford smiled at him.

"That was my brother. Huge. I loved him. And he hurt me."

"What would you like to say to Peter now?" Kleinman asked.

Clifford sat still. I could almost feel the dizziness of his trying to think of what to say and the question of who you were, of how old you were, as you said your piece.

"He wasn't all bad," he said softly, almost inaudibly, his eyes down.

Clifford took a huge breath and let it go. He looked up now, toward the direction from which the hand with the tissues had come.

"I wouldn't like to *say* anything to him. I'd like to hurt him."

"That's a very disturbing thought. Tell me about that. Tell me what you feel."

Sullen now, Clifford sat staring, saying nothing, for what seemed like forever, until finally Dr. Kleinman said they'd talk more about it next time and the screen went black with thousands of swirling white dots on it.

In a moment the next session began. Clifford had on a flannel shirt, a deep rust, cream, and teal, his hair looked darker, it looked wet, curls on his brow, the rest smoothed back tight and straight, pulled into a ponytail in the back. He looked stony as he clipped on the microphone.

"I saw him. My brother."

He exhaled through his nose in disgust.

"And what happened between you?"

"I told him that I remembered what he had done to me."

"What did he say?" Kleinman's voice full of emotion now.

"He *said* I shouldn't make a big deal out it. You always were like that, Cuffie, is what he *said* to me. *What* a pain in the ass you always were. Imagine. *He* called *me* a pain in the ass!"

"How awful this must have been for you. How painful."

"You're so thin-skinned, he said. I can't even talk to you. That's just stuff boys do. You don't have to make a whole production about it now, do you, it was a million years ago, we were just kids, playing. That's how boys play, Cuff."

"And what did you say to him?"

"What *kind* of boys play that way, Peter? Tell me that."

"What did he say?"

"He got furious. *He* got furious. *Nor*mal boys play that way, he said. So I said, Yeah? How about *your* boys? Do your sons play that way? And he jumped up—we were in a fucking restaurant—and I thought he was going to smack me right in the face."

"What did you do?"

"I kept right on going. Man, I couldn't stop. He was putting on his jacket, and I was sitting there shouting at him, If it's so fucking *nor*mal, then I guess you wouldn't mind if everyone *knew* about it, would you? Like your *sons*. Or your *wife*. Or, and then I was laughing at him, the way he used to laugh at me, those nice folks at your school."

"What happened then?" Tension creeping into Kleinman's voice.

"He split. Ran out. Stuck me with the bill. You know, I remembered something else, Dr. Kleinman. I remembered that one time when we were kids, after he had started abusing me, I said I'd tell on him, and do you know what he did?"

Silence.

"He said he'd tell everyone *I* was a little shit-eating sissy. And they'd believe *him*, not *me*. And he laughed at me, laughed at his cleverness, at the trap I was in. After that, he used to call me that. In fact, in front of my parents, you know how kids always like to tease each other so that the parents don't know what's going on? Well, he just shortened it to SES, shit-eating sissy, then just SSS, and I'd know, SSS, like a snake. He'd whisper it at the table or when we were riding in the car, he threatened me with it, he shut me up with it until I felt so bad and so beaten that I shut away the whole thing, everything he'd done, and later, now, I just *felt* like a little shit-eating sissy, but I never knew why."

"Clifford, the word 'sissy'—"

"Faggot, fairy, queer, homo, you mean *that* word?" he shouted. "Yes, and let's not forget sissy. Sissy boy. He called me that, too. That, in fact, was another of his favorites."

"Do you feel that what your brother did had anything to do with your sexual orientation?"

"No," he said. "Of course not."

He sat quietly, his eyes filling, tears spilling out over the rims, not blinking, not catching those tears with a tissue, not wiping them away with his fingers. No, he just sat.

"Of course not," he whispered. "It had to do with my feeling like a little shit-eating sissy. It had to do with my always feeling inadequate, at fault, ugly, stupid, guilty."

I thought I heard Kleinman crying, too.

"But my sexual orientation is God-given. Peter didn't have anything to do with that. No matter what I thought when I was a little boy, Peter is not God."

I heard Kleinman ask Cliff if he was all right, and then static indicated that the session had ended.

A week later, Clifford needing a shave, Clifford looking as if he hadn't slept in days:

"I told him blood will tell. I told him that Morton was doing to Lester, his precious Lester, what he had done to me."

"You told him that over dinner?"

"No, I told him that by painting it."

Les and mor, for God's sake. Lester and Morton. Peter's boys.

That's why it wasn't at the show.

Peter had seen it the night that Dennis left the key for him. And after Louis had invited him to the opening, he'd done what any father would do. He'd gone back, to rescue his children.

"After that first confrontation, Clifford, what did you actually say to Peter?"

"I've been painting," he said. It was on his shirt, and in his hair. Orange, like the basketball the young boy in the dress was holding.

Peter. In a dress.

So that's how he would hurt him!

"What do you mean, Cliff?"

"I've been painting the truth, painting him the way he really is, the way he should be seen. Oh, he thought he made *my life* a drag! Wait until he sees what I can do to *his* life."

Bitter laughter.

"But you haven't tried talking to Peter again?"

Silence.

"Maybe in time, Clifford, you'll be able to. Right now, you need time to deal with your own feelings, with this terrible pain, so that you will be able to let go of it sometime in the future."

Snort.

"He needs time, too, Clifford. All he can feel now is defensive, but given time, if you tell him again how he made you feel—"

"I *told* him. I also told him I wanted him to *feel* how I felt. He's my brother, isn't he? So I want to *share* with him how shame feels, how fear feels, how it would feel to be threatened with exposure and humiliation, all the things that I felt. Thanks to him."

"You told him about the paintings? What did he say?"

"He laughed at me. Who cares what you paint? Who'll ever see what *you* paint? And then he hung up."

"Listen, Dennis," I had said late last night when he picked up, half asleep, "there's something bothering me."

"What?"

Well, to tell the truth, it was more like *wha?* It seemed Dennis had finally gotten over his insomnia. I forged ahead anyway.

"It's about those three missing canvases. Have you thought about them at all?"

"Sure. I figured Louis took them to keep for himself."

"Why take them off the frames?"

"A lot of people do that, roll the canvas so that it takes less space, you know, store it in a tube. Maybe he didn't have room for them. I understand his place is really small."

"But he had one painting at the show that was not for sale. Why hold three out?"

"He has that right. Maybe he didn't like them. Or maybe he loved them. Maybe they were personal. Who knows?"

"I'd like to."

"*Now?* Couldn't it wait until morning?"

I looked at my watch. It was after two.

"Sorry. I'll catch you tomorrow. I mean tonight."

I had wanted to tell him everything I had learned, but it could wait. At least until I was sure.

The catalog listed fifty-three works. I thought that's what Louis had said, too—or was it Veronica? Yes, she had said there were forty-seven paintings and five pieces of sculpture, and that's what was listed. Everything accounted for.

Except what had been on those empty stretchers. Two works in addition to *les and mor*.

I jumped up without bothering to shut off the VCR and went right for the photo albums, taking all three of them back to the desk. I opened the first.

The first album contained pictures of Cliff and Louie on a trip to Rome and Israel; from the looks of the other people occasionally in the photos, it was a gay tour.

The second album was a book of slides of Clifford's work. I took the loupe out of the middle drawer, took out one of the plastic pages, and, my eye to the lens, held it up to the light to see what was there. On this page, there were photos of *up* and *rising son*. Also the basenji sculpture, shot in various stages.

There were some shots of Cliff, in goggles and knee pads, painting, what looked like Saran Wrap around his watch, but it wasn't possible to be sure without projecting the slide.

The third album was the one I wanted to look at first, family pictures, the ones Bertram Kleinman had been shown, and yes, there was Clifford as a happy little boy, on a tricycle, with a litter of beagle puppies, holding hands with an older boy. A boy who was a little taller than he was and quite a bit stockier, even then. A boy holding a basketball against his hip. A boy whose head had been torn off.

I paged through the album slowly, studying Clifford's family, his mother and father, looking young and proud with their two sons, one, the younger, with blond curls, the other, the older boy, headless, and on and on, even until adulthood. Near the end of the book, I found Lester and Morton. In fact, I found the picture from which the painting in question had been made. In the photo, the boys stood close together, grinning falsely, clearly having been told to smile for the camera. Normal boys, like normal basenjis, not wanting to do as they were told. Not wanting to have their stupid picture taken when they could be playing war or climbing a tree instead. The painting, as I remember, was another story, a story of lewdness and fear, a story of incest and abuse, a story that said, Do your sons play that way? and Blood will tell.

Peter's wife, Linda, whom I had spoken to yesterday, was a short, square-looking woman with a round, flattish face, her hair neatly coiffed and sprayed, the hem of her unstylish dress landing primly beneath her knees, her children at her left, the ankles and feet of her husband to her right.

Bertram Kleinman's voice was coming from the television speakers.

Bert: "You said that to him?"

Cliff, crying: "Yes."

Bert: "You were able to get angry at him?"

Cliff: "Yes."

Bert: "This is marvelous, Clifford, a real breakthrough for you. This is what we've been working for."

Cliff: "But it didn't do any *good*. He just doesn't get it. The way he doesn't get that I'm an artist. Just because I'm his kid brother. I mean, even when I told him I had signed a gallery contract for my first show, well, my first *group* show, but still, he didn't get it. He didn't even congratulate me, Dr. Kleinman."

"What did he do?"

"He hung up on me. He said 'Shit,' and hung up. Do you see what I mean? What *good* did it do?"

Bert: "Clifford, we're not talking about changing Peter. Or erasing the past. We don't have the power to do either of those things. What we're talking about is *you*, we're talking about your ability to express what you feel. And toward that end, this has been a really positive step for you."

"I guess. I guess you're right."

So that was the Cliff and Bert Show.

I shut off the set and walked out of the little red room into the huge, hollow, empty studio in the front of the loft.

The light coming into the windows was from streetlamps, now, and when I walked over to the windows and looked out, I could see that it was raining.

It was raining inside, too. All around me, overhead, in every room, in the closets full of expensive clothes, in the kitchen hung with polished copper-bottomed pots, it was raining sadness. I had seen him now, heard him, felt him, listened as the secret of childhood abuse had bubbled up in therapy, but nothing I or anyone else could do would bring him back to paint in his studio, to wear his expensive clothes, to cook in those copper-bottomed pots, to walk his dog, to love his handsome boyfriend.

All I could do was make it as likely as possible that the person who killed him would be punished. I still had much to do.

32

Dashiell Was Ready

IT WAS AFTER seven and I was starving, so I went poking through the kitchen drawers for what every New Yorker has, menus. While I waited for my miso soup and tekka maki to arrive, I fed the dogs the last of Magritte's food and set up the slide projector in the studio, where I would be able to look at the slides on those huge, bare white walls.

When the delivery man buzzed, I salivated like Pavlov's dogs, buzzed him in, and waited hungrily for him to climb the stairs. I had the money ready. My dogs were ready, too. Dashiell was ready to lay down his life for me, or at least place his bulk in front of mine. Magritte, being a basenji, never wanting to be where he was supposed to be, was ready to escape.

I reached for the bag, handed the deliveryman the money, and felt something warm and quick brush by my left leg.

The deliveryman headed down.

Magritte headed up.

I figured, what the hell, the dog has a C.D. So instead of chasing him up the stairs while my soup got cold, I called him. And he came.

The food was wonderful, and I ate most of it. Ex–dog trainer or not, there was no way I was going to disappoint my companions. Even if my newest law of private investigation is Never put anything into your mouth that was meant for a dog, there's no law that says you can't do it the other way around.

I turned on the slide projector, and the first slide appeared on the wall.

Uncle Miltie. The stocky guy in the housedress and cheap wig. His back turned. The cigar burning.

Click.

The second panel. Ash accumulating.

Click.

The third panel. Ash dropping to the carpet.

(Stomach tightens.)

Click.

The fourth and missing panel. Otherwise known as the truth, as rendered by Clifford Cole.

The subject of the work, in a dress, a wig, and the kind of orthopedic stockings my grandmother Sonya wore, had turned around.

He was grinning.

He was wearing lipstick.

Lots of lipstick.

A garish amount, in my opinion. Especially with *that* outfit.

Genderfuck is done with wit. This portrait was done with malice. Be that as it may, once again we were face-to-face.

I had seen him first at the opening, even though he'd told Dennis he couldn't be there. He had been so impressed with the price of the basenji sculpture, he had whistled in amazement.

I had seen him next at Westminster, where he had wondered out loud how anyone could tell the basenjis apart. Where he had made dead sure he knew whose harmless bait to exchange for the tainted bait he'd meant for Magritte.

And when he'd heard on the news, no doubt, that a handler had died instead of a dog, that his clever ploy had failed to work, because after all he was not a dog person, didn't know the practices of the conformation ring, he had come back.

To try again.

Gotta do it.

He had followed me into the ladies' room. He had whistled then, too, whistled for Magritte, witness to murder.

My, I thought, studying his portrait, what *big* feet you've got.

Feet I'd know anywhere.

That is to say, feet whose *size* I'd know anywhere.

To the right of those big feet, there was even a title, neatly printed: *big shit-eating sissy*.

For once, without his head torn off.

33

Dead Ahead

I KNEW THAT Peter *could have been* at the opening before I learned that he *had been* there. I had learned that during one of yesterday's many phone calls.

"Mrs. Cole?" I had said when a woman answered.

"Yes. To whom am I speaking, please?" A voice like a dried magnolia petal, brittle yet still fragrant.

"This is Elaine Boynton, Clifford's friend. I was so sad to hear about Clifford."

"Well, of course you were, my dear. It was such shocking news, such tragic news."

"Yes."

"Were you close with my son?"

"Yes. And so I feel just terrible that I missed the memorial service."

"There was no service, Elaine."

"Really?"

"Why, yes. Clifford's brother, Peter, said he thought Clifford wouldn't want any sort of a fuss, wouldn't want to make his friends drag all the way down to Virginia. He said it wasn't necessary."

"He said that?"

"Well, it *was* basketball season, Elaine. His weekends belonged to the team. Don't even *call* me, Mother, he said to me. I'll call you when I get the chance. Both my sons are busy, busy men."

My bet was she didn't know Peter had moved out, had no number *to* call him at.

"Do you call your mother, Elaine?"

"She's, uh, gone," I said.

"I am so sorry, my dear. Was there a service for her?"

"Yes. A small, private one."

"I see. Well, I do feel that family and friends need the closure of a service. Don't you agree, my dear?"

"Yes, I do."

"Don't you think Clifford's friends would come to Virginia for a small service, once the weather gets a little kinder?"

"I'm sure they would."

"I'm so pleased to hear that, Elaine. I would like to meet my son's friends."

"I understand. I was wondering where I could send a donation in Clifford's name. Does the family have a preference?"

"Well, now, of course Clifford hadn't voiced such a preference. He was so very young." There was silence for a moment. "I'm sure any charity you pick would be just fine."

"Okay. Thank you."

"Thank *you*, my dear. Thank you for your affection for my son."

Ma son, she'd said. Delicate as a tank. I wondered if de-gaying the loft had more to do with Cliff's problems than his mother's.

More to the point, Peter had lied to Dennis about the service and had come to the opening to make bloody sure he hadn't missed anything when he removed the offensive canvases from the loft. He had taken *les and mor* and tossed the empty stretcher in back of the closet. Perhaps he'd taken another painting out, an older one, and hung it on the empty nail. He'd taken the significant panel of *big shit-eating sissy*. And he'd taken a portrait of himself, a portrait where his mouth was twisted and cruel, his eyes cold, his cheeks even more red and doughy than they looked under the unflattering lights of Madison Square Garden. That last one I'd seen when I watched the rest of the slides I had retrieved from B & H. It was called *helen*, the name gay men use for an old queen. It turns out it wasn't only his sons that Peter had gone back to rescue. It was himself.

My guess was that the only record of these paintings would be the slides that Clifford meticulously took and filed of all his work. I was so grateful he had done that. The slides of the missing paintings were enough by themselves to make me *suspect* Peter.

And my day on the telephone had all but eliminated everyone else. I'd found out from Louis that like so many other SoHo galleries, the Cahill Gallery had come close to folding when the art-buying frenzy of the eighties had ended so abruptly, but because Veronica has the scruples of a scorpion—*his* words—she'd managed, mostly with manufactured hype, to keep afloat. Now they were just making as much as they could out of what Louis had inherited.

"Can you blame us, Rachel?" he'd asked me.

Marjorie Gilmore had clued me in on Doc. He was Herbert Hanover, Ph.D., founder and owner of Hanover Cryogenics. Frozen semen. He not only stood to lose a lot with Gil gone, he and Gil were both at the Illinois State Veterinary Conference when Clifford was killed. So Gil was already dead when I found out he had a perfect alibi.

I had ruled out Michael Neary, the dog walker. He was only seventeen. And Addie and Poppy; had they tried to off Gil or Magritte with tainted liver, they would have jeopardized Orion. Anyway, they're dog people. They might have gone after Gil, but never Magritte.

In my back-to-basics mode of yesterday, I had even called information to see if Clifford's number was listed.

"I don't have a listing for a Clifford," the operator had said, "but under new listings, there's a *Peter* Cole."

That was interesting.

I called and heard his raspy voice on his answering machine, one of those no-name, covert messages—you know: "You have reached 989-2486. Please leave a message after the tone and I'll get back to you as soon as I can."

As if there were a person alive on the planet who didn't know to wait for the tone by now.

Next I called poor, shapeless Linda Cole, in Woodcliff Lake. Of course she didn't tell me he'd moved out. Why should she have? Who was I that she should tell me her sad story?

Whether or not he actually was abusing his boys would be her problem. And theirs, of course.

My problem was that I needed proof.

He had been *so* clever.

He had asked Dennis for a key, when in fact he co-owned the loft with his brother. I had discovered this by dropping in at the real estate office around the corner and checking the *Real Estate Directory of Manhattan*, volume two, which listed the owners of the loft as Cole, C., and Cole, P. D. Banks prefer steady income to lump sums of money, which, as anyone knows, can disappear. In fact, they are sometimes "placed" in the buyer's bank account by a rich, understanding relative and, subsequent to approval, "re-placed" back in the owner's account. A secure job always has more weight with the bank.

He had removed, and probably destroyed, the paintings Clifford made to shame him. I remembered that when I had looked at Cliff's will, the codicils had been out of order. Peter must have checked the will to see where Cliff's paintings were going. He'd need to know that. But he couldn't have taken them that night. He had to return the key to Haber's, and even rolled up, the painting would have been noticed. No matter. That is, until he learned about the show. Then he had to act fast.

But he didn't know that Clifford kept a meticulous record of all his paintings by taking color transparencies of them.

Neither did he know that Clifford's therapy sessions had all been taped.

I was sitting on the floor in the big, bare, empty studio, hugging my dog now, Magritte curled and asleep at my side.

He knew when Clifford went to therapy, when he wouldn't be home, when he could use his key, whistle for Magritte, take him away to use as bait to get his brother out onto the pier, to make it look like the sort of crime no one would bust his ass to solve.

Peter had evidently used a voice-changing telephone, ninety bucks from Sharper Image. Probably bought it, used it, and tossed it. Made his voice sound higher, like a woman's voice, to disguise his identity and maybe even to make it all sound less threatening to his brother.

But only a person who had never lost his heart to a dog could think that any scenario that put that relationship in jeopardy could sound less threatening. Less threatening than what—nuclear holocaust?

"I have Magritte." Three little words.

Sticks and stones will break your bones, they chanted in the school-yard when I was a kid, but words will never harm you. Another of the lies I grew up on.

What did Clifford do while he waited? What did he think?

When did he write and hide the letter?

Why had he hidden the tape? Had he planned that *after* he got Magritte back he would take it to the police?

Did he get the message in time to get to the bank before it closed? Of course, with Select Checking, he could have gotten the thousand from the ATM by making two withdrawals of five hundred each. He had noted the amount he had taken out, not how it had been retrieved.

I laid my face on Dashiell's neck, breathing in the comforting smell of dog, and closed my eyes.

Frantic. He must have been frantic, wandering from room to room—everywhere he looked, Magritte wasn't there.

Finally, it was time to go. He felt the money, a small lump, in his pocket. Not as much as it would be for a person. After all, Magritte was only a dog. That's what the police would have said. Louis would have said that, too.

He crossed West Street, the wind going through his clothes, and finally he heard him, heard Magritte, and his heart lifted like a piece of paper caught in a gust, swirling and joyous. He never saw the car, sitting there, motor off, he only heard Magritte. He began to run.

Peter sat across the seat waiting, watching out the back window of the rented car.

I had even found out where yesterday, by calling all the rental places as Mrs. Peter Cole, complaining I was overcharged. Thrifty Auto Rental, West Ninety-fifth Street, walking distance from his new apartment, assured me the bill was correct.

"We have the AMEX receipt, Mrs. Cole," they told me. "Shall I send you a copy?"

Difficult to rent a car without a credit card. Difficult to use a fake name when you need the credit card and driver's license.

Still, he'd planned so carefully. He knew he couldn't use his own car. Clifford would have recognized it. Had to think it out, think it through, find a way to stop the little shit-eating sissy from destroying his life. He had his name to think about, his reputation, his job. He had sons to protect.

His sons. How he missed them. There was another one who took things the wrong way, Linda, that cow, making a big deal over everything, couldn't even let him love his own kids in his own way, seeing faults in every little thing. Forcing him out.

The way his brother had forced him into *this*. Threatened him.

Both of them. Family! Well, fuck that noise.

It wasn't that he *liked* the idea of killing his brother, shit, he was no pervert, he wouldn't *enjoy* doing this, it just had to be done, Clifford running amok like he was, painting him as some old faggot, some helen, in a fucking dress, for God's sake, what would people think, and how would he earn a living, right, great, working with adolescent boys after *those* pictures were in everyone's face, his luck, the shit would end up in some museum, and then he looked up, and saw that his brother had passed the car, he was on the pier now, running, running toward that stupid dog of his, damn thing would be the death of him, and you know, he couldn't help it, he had to laugh at his own joke.

It's his own damn fault, the little shit, he just wouldn't let it go. I told him, Drop it already, I told him, that's how boys play, crying in the restaurant, his eyes all red, as if he were some girl, what would people think.

After the impact, he hit the brake.

Safe, he thought. I'm safe. Then, looking over his shoulder, he backed off the pier and was gone.

The car was coming out backward, quick as it went in, and Billy Pittsburgh ducked down, down, down, under his blanket and lay still as snow, stayed that way so long, maybe he fell back to sleep again.

When dawn broke, the gulls woke Billy, and, wrapped in his blanket, dragging his bag of bottles and cans, he walked partway out onto the pier, saw the dog was gone, saw the young white man lying on his back; and he turned around fast as he could, knew just where he could take what he knew, trade it for some coffee, a place to sit and drink it out of the weather.

Turning his back to the wind, he headed for Tenth Street, for the Sixth Precinct, passing on his way the wrought-iron gate that led down the passageway that opened into the garden in which my cottage sat and in which I lay warm as the coffee cup he'd soon be holding in his hands, sleeping like spoons with my dog.

I don't know how long I sat there brooding, but it was dark out, time to go. I had seen a leather backpack in Clifford's bedroom closet. I took the significant audio- and videotapes and the box of slides I had picked up at B & H, put them in the backpack, and locked up the dark loft.

Walking home from Clifford Cole's sad, empty loft to my own cozy cottage, I kept trying to figure out exactly how I could make sure that Peter Cole would get his just reward. I had to get him. Had to.

Though I did not want to be the one to have to tell Adrienne Wynton Cole that she had lost *both* her sons.

Still, it had to be done.

That he deserved to be got, I had little doubt. But so far all the evidence was circumstantial, none of it conclusive. I had to be sure that if he was charged, the charges would stick, because nowadays people got away with all kinds of murder.

34

I Know Your Secret

MAGRITTE BEGAN TO whine, anxious to run free in the garden. The lock on the gate seemed stuck—all these gates were so old—but I wiggled the key, and finally it clicked open. I unhooked the leads, and both dogs dashed on ahead down the narrow, unlit passageway. I locked the gate behind me and noticed how relieved and safe I always felt to be home.

Except for the path, where it had been worn down by our feet, the garden was still covered with thick layers of snow, crusted hard on top so that there was a sound like crinkling cellophane when the dogs ran. It was a clear night. I stood still for a moment, looking up at the stars.

It was quiet in the garden, the way it rarely is in New York. Even that hum that newcomers to the city are so conscious of, that unexplainable constant din of background noise, seemed to have abated. When Dashiell sneezed, it seemed as loud as a thunderclap.

Inside, I toweled off the dogs, filled their water bowl, and made a fire. I thought about calling Dennis, but it was after eleven and I decided against it. It would be better to call him when I knew for sure what I was going to do.

I thought about calling Peter Cole, too, but not then. I could call late the next morning, after he'd left for work, and leave a message on his answering machine. I could even use my own voice-changing telephone, if I could figure out which box in the basement it was in.

I know your secret, I could say.

Yeah.

Meet me at the pier. You know which one, and you know when. Don't tell anyone about this call, asshole, and bring five thousand dollars with you.

The price has gone up, I could say.

Right. I should wait alone on the Christopher Street pier at four in the morning for a guy who had already killed his own brother, like he'd have some compunction about eighty-sixing me.

He'd probably just rent a car and drive over me a few dozen times, just to make sure I didn't bother him again.

Growing up is murder. I'm glad I never tried it.

I decided to go to bed and figure it out in the morning, when I'd be seven or eight hours more mature.

But when I got upstairs and was taking off my snow boots, Dashiell began to pace and whine, going over to the window, pushing his nose against the shutters so that they rattled, then coming back to me and catching my eye.

I shut off the light, went over to the window, and, leaving the shutters closed, opened the slats so that I could see out. My bedroom window faced the main house, and as I looked across the deserted white garden, for just a moment I saw a flash of light.

It could have been from a car passing on Tenth Street, the headlights momentarily lighting up the dark house. Except that this light didn't flash across the house, appearing first in one room and then almost instantly the next, moving left to right from where I was, the way the one-way traffic did on Tenth Street. This light was only in the kitchen, nowhere else. It was an intense beam. The kind of light a flashlight makes.

I looked down at Dashiell and saw that his hackles were up, so I relaced my Timberlands and, keeping the lights off and not bothering with a coat, left the cottage and headed for the Siegal house to see what was going on.

I had only planned on taking Dashiell. Magritte was sleeping on my bed, and I had no reason to disturb him, but as usual he had ideas of his own. I felt him brush by me on the stairs, and he was first out the door, turning back toward us with his eyes afire, then play-bowing to Dashiell to start a game.

But Dashiell wasn't having any. His mind was elsewhere.

I followed him across the winter yard, the elongated shadow of the big oak flat on the snow in front of us, then crawling up the bricks of Norma and Sheldon's house.

There was light on the third floor now. I saw it swing across the back bedroom Norma used as a study.

I unlocked the back door as quietly as I could, pulled it open, and left it slightly ajar, going first, while I had the chance, toward the front of the house to find out where someone had gotten in. I signaled Dash to stay by me, but he kept looking toward the stairs. Still, he obeyed, and Magritte trotted alongside, stopping here and there to sniff the strange territory.

It didn't take a detective to see what had happened. One of the front ground-floor windows had been broken. But this time someone had used a glass cutter and a suction cup, silently cutting a circle near the lock rather than noisily smashing the whole window. Someone had planned this, had cased the house and returned with the necessary tools to do the job.

My heart picked up its pace, knees high, arms pumping. If a heart could sweat, mine was sweating. I had thought I'd find another home-less person, some hapless creature just trying to find shelter from the cold. A homeless person with a glass cutter?

Had Big Foot's cab followed close enough to my own to see approx-imately where I had disappeared after getting out of my cab? Not knowing the Village, Peter Cole wouldn't be likely to guess the secret of what lay beyond the wrought-iron gate. He would naturally assume I lived in the main house. Or had he tried the gate? Was that why I'd had trouble with the lock?

I decided to go back to the cottage and call the precinct. I didn't think it was a great idea to take chances when my gun was in its shoe box in the closet rather than tucked into my waist and there were a bunch of lovely policemen just across the street waiting for a little excitement to enter their lives.

I gestured to the dogs and headed for the open back door. But when I stepped out the door, Dashiell was nowhere in sight. He must have misunderstood; whenever we had come in the past, he had got-ten to search the whole house. And this time, his efforts would actu-ally pay off. Apparently he was on his way upstairs; when I stepped out onto the small back porch, there I was alone with Magritte.

I turned to go back and call him. After all, Peter's choice of weap-ons was pretty eclectic. This time around *he* might have a gun. But before I got the chance to take a step, the breath was squeezed out of me, a powerful arm around my throat, choking me, taking me off balance, and dragging me backward. I could smell the foulness of stale cigar smoke on his breath and clothing and smell the sourness of his sweat, even though it was below twenty and we were out-of-doors. I clawed at his arm and kicked back, but his grip only tightened, and when I opened my mouth, he clamped his other hand, in a leather glove, over it.

Suddenly he was dragging me closer to the house. I thought he was going to take me back inside where no one would have heard anything and he could have done whatever his beady black heart desired to me, but he didn't.

He did something far worse. He kicked the door shut, separating me from Dashiell. Once again, I was in danger and the only one there to help me was a twenty-pound basenji.

With the door closed and me under control, Peter began to whistle, that eerie little tune, four notes, a pause, the same four notes again.

That's when I remembered who it was that Peter Cole was out to get.

If I got it too, well, that would only mean he was being careful.

I could see Magritte in the center of the garden, keeping his distance.

Peter whistled again.

Magritte wasn't having any.

The choke hold tightened. Here was clearly a man who could do more than one thing at a time.

Maybe someone else had heard the whistle, I thought, but wasn't that just me whistling in the dark, so to speak? True, another garden backed up to mine, and beyond it was another house, one you entered from Christopher Street, one block south of Tenth. But those windows were so far away. And there was a wall at the back of the property, separating the gardens. What I loved about this place was the privacy, but just then I was thinking maybe I had too much of a good thing.

I was shivering.

I tried to tell myself it was because I hadn't taken my coat when I ran out.

Suddenly the hand on my mouth loosened and I heard his raspy voice, a guttural whisper right at my ear.

"If you scream, I'll hurt you. Will you be quiet?"

I nodded enthusiastically, and the hand slipped off my mouth but the arm around my throat held tight. It was then I had a hopeful thought. He didn't know I knew who he was. He was behind me, whispering. Maybe he didn't intend to kill me. Maybe I could get out of this.

"Who are you?" I whispered, not wanting him to think I was crying for help and cover my mouth again. "What do you want here?"

"Shut up," he growled. I could feel him moving behind me, but I didn't know what he was doing. Then he spoke again, but this time that rough voice was up in pitch. Because it wasn't me he was addressing.

"Here, boy," he said. He whistled again. Four notes. A pause. The same four notes, only an octave higher.

Magritte cocked his head and lifted one front paw. But he didn't come closer. Instead, he began to whine.

Even a basenji, not exactly my number-one choice as a protection dog, knew something was wrong. Magritte had grown attached to me, and he could smell my fear as well as he could sense Peter's malice.

Again, "Here, boy." Then I could see his hand moving, waving about. He had something for Magritte, and he was trying to tease him closer. The hand moved where I could see it, thumb and pointer holding something small, something hard, something grayish brown.

Liver!

Magritte took a tentative step closer.

I didn't know how far Clifford had gone with Magritte beyond the C.D., but if he had, it was my only hope.

I screamed at the top of my lungs, "Go out! Magritte, go out!"

And as I did that, I realized I might have just traded Magritte's life for my own. I could literally feel the rage surge in Peter Cole. A hideous sound came from me as the arm around my neck jerked back. My knees buckled, and I thought I was going to pass out. But two things changed all that.

One was Peter trying to force the piece of liver into my mouth. I never ate it as a kid, and I sure as hell didn't want to start now, not with the smell of bitter almond filling my nostrils.

The second thing that happened was that I saw something move off to the side. And realizing what it was gave me courage.

I jerked my head violently from side to side. You don't grow up with a Jewish mother without knowing how to refuse food. At the same time, I lifted one two-ton Timberland boot and kicked back as hard as I could. It felt as if I only glanced off his shin, but I heard an *oof*, so I knew I'd hurt him, and before he got the chance to get even, and then some—this was surely a vindictive man—we were both pitched sideways into the snow. Now instead of bitter almond, I smelled the comforting odor of dog.

I was able to roll away, and as I picked myself up, I saw Peter Cole, his face gray with terror, a gray not unlike the one his brother used to paint him as the revolting pervert he was, holding his arm now not around my aching throat but up in front of his own face.

Dashiell was standing over him, the sound of an outboard motor coming from somewhere deep in his massive chest. Then, his face inches from Peter Cole's, he barked twice. His tail was wagging. He was triumphant.

"Get him off me," he cried. But I ignored him. I turned to look at Magritte, and he was licking his lips. I panicked.

"Where's the liver?" I shouted.

Peter tried to move his arm, and Dashiell grabbed it in his jaws, stopping the movement.

"Don't move. Is it still in your hand?"

I could barely hear him. "No."

I turned back to Magritte, who was just sitting in the snow, watching us. Then I saw it, grayish brown, lying in the snow. I picked it up and walked over to where Peter Cole was lying on his back, terrified, under Dashiell, who never once took his eyes off his prey.

I wondered if he was as scared as he could possibly be. Or if there was room for improvement.

"Open wide, asshole," I said, holding the liver over his mouth.

For a moment, I saw what I had wanted to see. I could leave the rest up to the police. I pulled a plastic bag from my pocket and dropped the liver in, knotting it securely on top.

"Excuse me," I said to Peter. "I hope you won't consider me rude, but I have to use the john."

I turned and headed for the cottage and, after making the phone call I had to make, grabbed my sheepskin coat and went back out to the yard to wait for the police.

35

Up to Scratch

IT WAS SNOWING lightly on Saturday. In the morning Dashiell and I walked over to Bailey House to see Billy Pittsburgh and tell him the white man he'd seen commit murder was in jail. We saw Ronald, too, and we got to meet Jimmy McEllroy, who was only twenty-two and loved Dashiell, but we never did get to see Sivonia LeBlanc. She had died early on Thursday morning.

In the afternoon Dashiell and I went over to Dennis's loft to take Magritte home and collect our check.

"I still can't believe it was his own brother who killed him," he said after I'd caught him up on all he'd missed.

"Why not? It's the second-oldest crime. Right after stealing fruit."

If ever I'd heard an exit line, that was it. I stood and picked up my coat.

"Wait up," he said. "You never told me how Dashiell got out of the house."

"Dashiell," I said, and when he looked up from wrestling with Magritte, I pointed to the door.

He was up in a flash. He grasped the knob, turned his head, and, carefully keeping his grip, backed up.

"Only their door opens out, so he had to push instead of pull."

"Brilliant!" he k'velled.

"Yeah, yeah," I said modestly.

I had known Dennis less than two weeks, but it seemed I'd known him ages. I sometimes think detective work is like summer camp. You make friends and enemies in record time.

"I was at the Sixth yesterday," I told him as I put on my coat. "They have the tapes, the slides, and the piece of tainted liver Peter tried to shove into my mouth."

"We did so *well*, didn't we?" he said, sharing the credit as he leaned to kiss me good-bye. "We could be partners, Rachel, you know, a politically correct Nick and Nora Charles. And Dashiell—"

"Yeah, yeah. Dashiell could be fucking Asta."

"Exactly," he said with a grin, those lovely crooked teeth looking like piano keys after an earthquake.

But I already had a partner, I thought as I followed him down the stairs, his ears bobbing as he descended toward the street. One who had proven himself up to scratch.

Once upon a time I had saved his life. He had recently returned the favor.

THE DOG WHO
KNEW TOO MUCH

For Noah Kahn
I love you, Dad.

The author wishes to thank

The school of T'ai Chi Chuan, New York City, especially Pat Gorman for her giving nature and extraordinary ability to teach and inspire, George Fletcher for the lovely way he grew along with his students, and Jackie Harris, classmate and friend

For the generous sharing of information and insights, Joel Mc-Mains, former deputy sheriff; George Axler, graphologist; Larry Berg, cynologist; Detectives Joseph Barker, Daniel O'Connell, and Bob Moller of the Sixth Precinct; Barbara Jaye Wilson, fellow mystery writer; and Beth Adelman, whose interests and talents coincided in the most serendipitous way with the needs of this book

Mystery Writers of America, Private Eye Writers of America, Sisters in Crime, the Authors Guild, and the Dog Writers Association of America, professional organizations that help writers be considerably more savvy in a dog-eat-dog world

Gail Hochman and Marianne Merola at Brandt & Brandt

Michael Seidman, maven d'editing

My friends and family, especially my sister Mimi and Stephen Lennard, my sweetheart

And Dexter and Flash, because if there's Zen at the top of the mountain, some dog brought it there

1

If You Weren't Careful

DASHIELL STOOD MOTIONLESS on the dark, wet sand, his eyes cemented to the driftwood log I held up over my head. Just before I moved to send it spinning over him and into the ocean, as if he were able to read my mind, he turned to mark its fall; then, all speed and power, he ran flat out into the surf. Looking beyond him at the vast, gray-blue Atlantic Ocean, flattened under a bright spring sky, I remembered myself as a child playing fetch on this very beach with some other dog, now long gone.

I used to come to my aunt Ceil's house in Sea Gate, the gated community just beyond Coney Island, when I was a kid. I would race for the water the minute we hit the beach, shedding flip-flops and T-shirt as I ran, staying in until Beatrice, my mother, standing on the shore about where Dashiell stood a moment ago, hands on her hips, a line showing over the center bridge of her sunglasses, would shout to me that my lips were turning blue, and why didn't I come out and play on the sand like a good girl, as my big sister Lillian had long since done.

"I can't hear you," I'd call back, bobbing like the stick I'd just thrown for Dashiell.

"You'll be the death of me," Beatrice shouted, her voice like the roar of the waves from far away on the shore.

Playing on the hot, gritty sand under my mother's scrutiny held no charm for me. The ocean was the lure—all that power, beauty, mystery, and life. Even death, if you weren't careful. At least that's what Beatrice used to say, as if being careful could do the trick and keep you safe.

Beatrice found the scary side of everything, the don't instead of the do. That's why I grew up looking for trouble, just to defy her. At least that's what my shrink used to say. That sad fact, according to Ida Berkowitz, Ph.D., would explain what I was doing here today, even though my mother, like that pup I had played fetch with when I was a kid, was long gone.

Dashiell was riding a foamy, frigid wave back toward me, the driftwood crosswise in his mouth.

I had hesitated for only the moment it took for the guard to call ahead and make sure I had actually been invited to come to this private and protected community that occupies the point of land where the Atlantic Ocean meets Gravesend Bay. By the time he had lifted the barrier and motioned me to drive in, I knew I had a stop to make before keeping my appointment, for my sake as much as for Dashiell's. I'd headed here, to the deserted beach, so that my partner, the other unlicensed PI with whom I was in business, could dig in the sand, swim in the ocean, and roll in dead fish and used condoms, reminding me as he always did precisely how delicious it was merely to be alive. Soon enough I'd be immersed in less expansive feelings, because it was a case that had brought me to Brooklyn on this cool, clear April day.

Dashiell stood squarely in front of me, holding the stick dead center, eyes locked on mine, water running off his underside and down his legs, his one-track mind on the task at hand.

"Out," I told him. I have a way with words.

He dropped the driftwood heavily into my hand and, hoping for another toss, retreated to where the incoming waves could just reach him, washing over his feet from behind, then swirling in front of his ankles before returning, as eventually we all must, from whence it came. I gave him one last swim, sending the driftwood high and far over the waves, watching him watch it, electrified with pleasure. We saw the splash. Dashiell, the quintessential pit bull, charged forward with sufficient grit, strength, and tenacity to bring the damn ocean to its knees, if need be. Work or play, it was all the same to him. He'd use whatever force he deemed necessary to meet a challenge.

We ran around on the sand to dry off, then headed back to the black Ford Taurus that David and Marsha Jacobs, Aunt Ceil's neighbors and friends, had rented for me so that I could drive here to the quiet community where they had lived for forty-seven years and listen to them tell me about the sudden, unexpected, and violent death of their only child.

2

We Could Hear The Kettle Whistle

MARSHA JACOBS WAS one of those women who wear stockings and heels even in their own homes. She'd answered the door in a dark gray silk dress, the uneven piece of black grosgrain ribbon that signified a death in the family pinned to her chest. It would leave holes in the silk, I found myself thinking, then silently berated myself for the frivolous thought.

Driving home along the Belt Parkway, I couldn't get the image of Lisa Jacobs's mother out of my mind. For that's what she was, first and foremost, the devoted Jewish mother of a beautiful, blue-eyed, curly-haired thirty-two-year-old who ten days earlier, with no clues to foreshadow the act, had opened one of the oversize windows at the t'ai chi studio where she studied and taught and jumped five stories to her death.

"We want to show you our Lisa," Marsha had said, welcoming me into the living room time forgot. "Come and sit, Rachel. Can I get you some tea?"

"Thank you," I said, feeling chilled by the room and my wet clothes. Dashiell had body-slammed me several times right before we left the beach, and my leggings felt as if I had been in the ocean, too. I wondered if we'd each get a different pattern of bone china from which to drink our tea, like the cups my mother had collected.

David Jacobs was sitting on one side of the couch, a thick, leather-bound photo album on his lap. He patted the middle seat, and hoping I wouldn't leave a big, wet ass print on their sofa, I sat next to him.

"This has been very hard on her," he said as soon as Marsha had left to make the tea. "She—" he began, but then hesitated. "She's up all night," he whispered, "pacing, pacing. She's driving me *crazy*. She—" he sighed before correcting himself—"we, *we*," he repeated, "would like you to help us, Rachel. We cannot understand what could have possessed Lisa, what made her do this awful thing." He sounded angry. "We don't have a guess. Not a clue."

David placed the album on the coffee table, stood, and went to get his cigarettes from the top of the piano. His suit pulled across his potbelly and hung too loosely around his arms and shoulders, as if he had recently lost a good bit of weight, a supposition that, considering the circumstances, I would not have had to be a detective to make.

"Lisa never complained, never complained. She never spoke of any problems. She was always cheerful, kind, a happy girl. Ach," he said, stopping to light his cigarette, "how could this have happened? We gave her everything."

I could hear Marsha talking to Dashiell in the kitchen, where she'd suggested I stash him, even though he had already stopped dripping by the time we'd arrived. Dashiell's tail tapped out his answer on the tile floor.

"She was studying to be a Zen Buddhist priest, my Lisa," Marsha said, standing in the archway at the rear of the living room. "The study and the t'ai chi gave her peace. Peace. That's what she told her father and me. So why—"

"Sit, Marsha," David said, blowing smoke into the middle of the room. Marsha sat next to me. Now I had their grief on both sides. In our silence we could hear the kettle whistle, and Marsha left again to make the tea.

"Are you cold, Rachel?" David said, as concerned as if *I* were his daughter.

"No, no," I lied, "I'm fine."

"Are you sure? Marsha, bring her a sweater," he shouted in the direction of the kitchen.

"No, thank you, I'm fine. Really."

"It's no trouble," he said, half to himself. "We have plenty of sweaters."

He moved the album closer but didn't open it.

"Ceil said you used to be a dog trainer. Before."

I raised my eyebrows.

David looked at me and puffed on the cigarette, ashes dropping onto his suit pants. "Before your—before you were married." He brushed at his trousers, leaving a dry, gray trail where the ashes had been.

Marsha arrived with the tray and placed it carefully next to the photo album. She handed me a cup with yellow tulips on it and gave David one with purple irises, saving the one with the tiny red rosebuds for herself.

"Marsha—the sweater, the sweater," David said impatiently.

Suddenly I had the eerie feeling I was in some relative's suffocating home. I reached for a cookie. Marsha returned with a navy blue sweater and handed it to David, who handed it to me. I put it over the arm of the sofa.

"So—" David said. "You married again? Your husband approves of this kind of work, de*tec*tive work?"

Marsha was biting a small biscuit. She looked up, curious.

Ceil would have told them I hadn't married again, wouldn't she?

I reached for another cookie. "Lisa was single, wasn't she?" The eighth law of private investigation, according to my erstwhile employer and mentor, Frank Petrie, is, Don't *give* information. *Get* information.

"Lisa never married," her mother said.

"No, marriage wasn't what Lisa wanted," David said.

"Her studies were everything to her." Marsha gathered the crumbs from her silk skirt onto one hand and carefully brushed them off in one corner of the tray.

"The mother has a college degree, too. Did your aunt mention that?"

"*Da*vid." Marsha flapped a hand in his direction.

"Six years she studied, three at night, three full time, at Brooklyn College, competing with all those young hotshots. She got wonderful grades, wonderful."

I smiled at Marsha, and she patted my damp leg.

"She taught school, too. A very intelligent woman. That's who Lisa took after. Her mother. A bachelor's degree. Just like the hotshots."

"Is that how you met, at college?"

"Fourteen years," he said. He took a last puff on the cigarette and put it out. "That's how long we waited for Lisa."

"David, we shouldn't—"

"Rachel needs to know these things, isn't that so, Rachel? She came here to get the facts, so that she could help us. We never thought there would be a baby, not for us. Fourteen years it took."

We sipped tea for a moment in silence. Finally David opened the album. But I had already seen Lisa. Across from us, on the baby grand piano in a standing silver frame, was a photo of a pretty young girl smiling.

"She was an extraordinary child," Marsha told me as David turned the pages, "not average."

I looked at Lisa in her carriage, Lisa in the bath, Lisa sleeping.

"She did everything early, before the books said," Marsha told me, looking at me for approval.

"Everything early," I repeated.

"This was the summer she went to camp," I heard David say, "but we missed her. Marsha kept saying, 'David, we have the beach right here, we have the Atlantic Ocean at our beck and call, why does Lisa have to be in the Adirondacks with all those mosquitoes and no ocean?' So, what else, we went up on visitors' day and brought her home. At the end of July. Slow season. I could take her to the beach every day. No problem. She was some swimmer, that child. Like a fish."

"She was a varsity swimmer," Marsha said, "at Abraham Lincoln High School." She got up and brought over the medals and one of the trophies that sat on the shelves across from the couch.

"She was the valedictorian," David said. "She made a speech on graduation day. Smart. Like her mother. There was nothing that girl couldn't do, if she set her mind to it."

"When did Lisa get interested in t'ai chi?" I asked.

"While she was in college," Marsha said. "Just before she broke her engagement, the end of her sophomore year."

I could feel David tense. Marsha looked into her lap.

"You liked the boy?" I asked.

"He was going to be a dentist," she said, "like his father."

"Water under the bridge," David said.

Had Ceil told them *I* had been married to a dentist, that I too had let a professional man go?

"In her third year," Marsha said, "that was when—"

"China, China, she wanted only to go to China. To study. She was nineteen. What did she know? Imagine, running to China, a nineteen-year-old kid, alone, on the other side of the world."

"So, did she go? Did she study in China?"

"Go? Did she go?" David bellowed.

For a moment he looked as if he were on fire, red smoke swirling about him as his aura turned the color of his rage.

"You tell me if you'd let a kid like that go off on her own to a foreign country. What did she know, to do a dangerous thing like that, by herself? She stayed here. It was for her own good. Everything we did was for her, everything."

"She studied here," Marsha said. "At Barnard. Eastern philosophy and Chinese language."

"She spoke Chinese, what else, beautiful, just as good as if she had lived there, you should have heard her."

"After her postgraduate studies, five years at Columbia on a fellowship, that's when she met Avram, the director of the school where Lisa worked. She studied with him since then." Marsha picked up a napkin and held it to her mouth for a moment. "Avram adored her, you know. He said Lisa was his best student."

"Then she was here, living here with you?"

"Oh, no. She was at the Printing House," Marsha said. "On Hudson Street. Not far from you. She wanted to be near the school. To walk."

"She wanted the Village, the Village, so, what else, I bought her a condo," David said.

He took his checkbook out of his breast pocket. I began to protest, but his hand went up to stop me.

"It's just that—"

"The police have looked into our Lisa's death," Marsha said as David wrote, "but they're busy with many other things, there's so much crime in the city, so much."

David looked up. "What we need," he said, "it's not really police business, Rachel. They're finished now. But we're not. We're the parents. We have to know what happened, what went on. We need"—he practically bellowed—"to find out why our daughter took her own life."

"*David,*" his wife said, trying to calm him.

"Mr. Jacobs, I—"

"David. Forget this Mr. Jacobs. You could be Lisa's friend, you're so young. You could be my own daughter."

"And call me Marsha, Rachel. We know your aunt so long, we feel we know you, too."

"David. Marsha. To find out something so intimate about a person, it might take a long time. Often the victim's best friend, or her parents, had no idea she was depressed."

"Spend the time, Rachel. We can afford it," David said. "Now tell me your fee, please."

I did. And asked for a thousand in advance.

"Money I have," he said. I heard the sound of a check being torn from a checkbook. "A daughter I don't have, but money I have." He handed me the check. Without looking, I folded it in half and put it into my shirt pocket.

"Even if I do spend the time," I said, "I might not find the answers you're looking for."

"I can't think of anything more important to spend money on than at least *trying* to understand what happened to Lisa. Can you, David?"

But David Jacobs didn't answer his wife's question. He had turned his back to us, and I could see his shoulders trembling. With one hand he removed his bifocals. The other carried an ironed white handkerchief toward his eyes.

"I'll do my best," I heard myself promise. I called Dashiell and heard the jingle of the tags on his collar as he got up.

"We already know that," Marsha said, squeezing my hand.

"I'll have to speak to people—"

"Of course," Marsha said.

"I'll need Lisa's address book, her appointment calendar, and access to her apartment, if possible."

She slid her arm in mine, the way my mother always used to, to walk me out. There was a briefcase on the small table near the door. Marsha lifted it by the handle and gave it to me.

"There are some letters she wrote to us in here, so that you will be able to see for yourself the kind of person she was, how bright, how thoughtful. Her keys are in the zippered pocket. You know the Printing House?"

I nodded.

"Anything else you need, you just ask us."

Despite my willingness to travel as I always did, by foot or subway, David insisted I'd need a car for the duration of the investigation and had already paid a month's rent in advance on the Taurus.

Once out of their house and inside the car, I opened the briefcase and looked inside. There in the pocket, as promised, were Lisa's keys. Her apartment, Marsha had said, was undisturbed. As I was leaving, she'd urged me to go there, where there might be clues, something, anything, that might help me discover what I had to do in order to help her understand what had gone wrong in the perfect life of her perfect child.

Yeah, yeah.

I wondered what Lisa had *really* been like.

I started the car. Then I slipped the check out of my pocket to take a look. It was for three thousand dollars. I had been redefining hand-to-mouth for a month or so. Now if I found myself headed for the poorhouse, I'd be able to go by limo. Driving home, I thought about hiring a cleaning lady. And a gardener.

3

Don't Mention It, He Said

IN THE MORNING, after leaving a message for Avram Ashkenasi asking to see him about Lisa, I headed across the street to the Sixth Precinct to see if my friend Marty Shapiro was around. The officer at the desk said Marty was exercising Elwood and Watson, two of the bomb dogs he worked with. That meant he'd be in the wide alley that ran along the side of the precinct, between Tenth Street and Charles, where the cops parked official vehicles. I found him there, tossing a tennis ball.

"Look at El, Rach," he said as soon as he saw me. "No waistline, and a belly like he swallowed a cantaloupe."

"Too early in the season for melons. More likely it was a box of doughnuts. Maybe you ought to take him to Overeaters Anonymous, on Christopher Street."

Dashiell's nose was welded to Watson's ass.

"I'm taking *him* to Sniff Enders," I said, hooking a thumb toward Dash. He and Watson danced in circles, play-bowed, and began taking turns trying to hump each other.

"No kidding?" Marty said, the tennis ball poised over his head, then flying down the alley, a very overweight Elwood slowly running after it. "Why don't you just change his name to Bruce?"

"Very amusing, Shapiro."

Elwood, the fat yellow Lab, dropped the ball at my feet. I kicked it toward Charles Street.

"Marty, you know anything about the Lisa Jacobs suicide? Her parents have asked me to look into it."

"Look into what?" he asked, surprised.

"Oh, they want to find out what made her depressed enough to go out the window."

"Yeah, right. Good luck on that, kid."

"Why do you say that? I know it'll be difficult, but—"

"Look, Rachel, they're *par*ents. They wanna know it wasn't their fault, you know what I'm saying. Do them a big favor. Spend a few days in the park, catch a few rays, give 'em a call and tell 'em what they need to hear. It's a horrible thing to lose your kid. They don't need guilt on top of it."

"One thing was odd, Marty. They talked to me for ages, but they didn't say much about the incident."

"Not unusual. They don't want to think about it."

"So what was the deal? I heard she did it from the school."

"Maybe her place was too low for a guaranteed success. Maybe she hated her boss, you know, a passive-aggressive last act. Who knows?"

"Are they sure it was suicide?"

"Okay, you want the scene, right?"

I nodded.

He began ticking off the facts on his fingers as he spoke.

"She went out sometime after midnight. No sign of a struggle. The door was locked—"

"Chain on?"

"No chain. Anyone with a key could have locked up on the way out."

"Bingo," I said.

"You New Yorkers, always in such a rush, jumping to conclusions before you got all the facts." He tossed the ball for El, then looked around the alley to make sure we were still alone. "Okay," he continued, "you got a negative scene. No overturned furniture. No burning cigar. No smashed mirrors. No handprint on her back. You following this?"

I nodded.

"No one bent over and let his wallet drop out of his pocket onto the floor for us to find. In fact, there was no nothing."

I nodded again to show I was paying attention.

"You got your locked door, true, without the chain on. You got no one across the street seeing nothing. We checked it out. Maybe that was because the lights were off in the studio. Maybe it was because of the courtyard and all the trees blocking the view. Who knows? Then you got this poor woman coming home from St. Vincent's Hospital, a private duty nurse. She finds the body on the sidewalk. You got the dog upstairs in the studio—"

"Dog? What dog?"

"The victim's. A big Akita. No one's going to bother her with *that* thing around."

"Any big dog would offer a certain amount of visual protection, but—"

"And you got the note."

"Oh," I said, "no one mentioned a note. What did it say?"

" 'I'm sorry. Lisa.' "

All at once the dog was beside the point. True, the Japanese claimed the Akita Inu would protect its master with its very life. But as it turned out, it was only herself Lisa had needed protection from, and hometown hype aside, no dog could do that, not even the national treasure of Japan.

" 'I'm sorry. Lisa'? That's it?"

"What do you want, a memoir? She was depressed, right? She wanted out, so she's out. Young," he said. "And pretty, too. The parents must be real broken up."

"Her father's not eating. Her mother's not sleeping. Their worst nightmare came true."

"So, you're going to put them out of their misery, so to speak. You're going to tell them what good parents they were, right?"

"Right," I said, only half listening. "Where's the dog now?"

"*Now* you sound like the girl I know and love."

"The dog, Marty. Who's got the dog?"

"The guy who owns the school, Ashkenasi, he took her that night. He came to let the detectives in, and when everything was done, he took her home. I don't know where she is now. But if I know you, you'll find out. So good, now you have your work cut out for you."

"Did you secure the scene?"

"No need to put Ashkenasi out of business, Rachel. It was a suicide."

He tossed the ball toward Charles Street and it bounced under one of the police cars. Watson and Dash went to wrestle the ball out from under the car while Elwood stood by, so dopey looking he might have been drugged.

"Right," I said. "There was a note. Where is that now?"

"In the file, Rach."

"Could I see it, Marty?" I whispered, even though there was no one else around.

"Let me get this straight, you're standing there asking me to break the rules?"

Every cop lives by two rules, Marty had told me the first two hundred times I'd asked for information. Rule one, Keep your mouth shut. Rule two, Never break rule one.

"Just this once," I said. As usual.

He rolled his eyes.

"You're a pain in my butt, did I ever tell you that?"

"You did," I said. "Several times."

"Okay, as long as it's on the record. Wait a minute. Wait right here."

Information you don't *share*, he'd say, drawing out the significant word, can't come back to haunt you.

He opened the side door, the one that led to the kennels. Elwood and Watson ran inside, and then Marty disappeared, too. I waited in the alley, Dashiell at my side. In a few minutes Marty was back, a doughnut box in his hand, Elwood waddling along behind him.

"These are the doughnuts you accused me of feeding Elwood," he said. "Here, take this home and read for yourself. These are *fat free*, Rachel. No way Elwood coulda got fat on these. I think it's his metabolism."

I took the box and looked at Elwood, remembering that not so long ago he was thinner, faster, and *smarter*.

"You might have a point there, Marty. Have you ever had his thyroid function tested? He might be hypothyroid."

"Yeah? Gluck has that, the guy at the desk. Blew up to two-fifty couple of years ago. Slept ten hours a night, sucked caffeine all day, and he was always looking to take a nap. Now he takes his pills, he's just like normal. I'll get El checked out. Thanks, Rach."

"Thank *you*," I said. "For the doughnut box." I gave it a shake. "And the doughnut."

"Don't mention it," he said. Then he whispered, "I mean *really* don't mention it."

I nodded.

"You take care, kid, okay?"

I clipped Dash's leash to his collar and headed back toward Tenth Street. As soon as I had turned the corner onto Hudson, heading south, I read the box, then opened it. There were two things inside. I pocketed the folded piece of paper, ditched the box in the trash basket on the corner, and ate the delectable-looking, full-fat, chocolate-covered doughnut on the way to Lisa's.

4

She'd Called Her Penny

LISA JACOBS'S APARTMENT was on the second floor of the Printing House, one of many formerly industrial buildings that had been converted into high-priced condos or co-ops, only in the case of the Printing House, the prices were so high that a lot of the units had failed to sell and were rentals. Not Lisa's. Lisa had wanted the Village, the Village, so her daddy had bought her a condo, one with full-time concierge coverage, maid service, and a gym on the top floor. Lisa's apartment faced east, overlooking Hudson Street and, beyond that, James J. Walker Park, where kids played baseball in the warm weather and dogs played Who's Dominant? from December through March.

Dashiell went crazy smelling the odors left by Lisa's Akita as I walked around trying to get a feel for the place and for the woman who until recently had lived here. Straight across from the door was a wall of enormous windows, serving both the downstairs and the bedroom, up a flight, built as a balcony over the end of the apartment nearest the door and looking down over the living room. The place was painted white, underfurnished, clean, interesting—it looked as if it had been a cheerful place to live. There was a small, colorful rug in the area opposite the kitchen where the dining room table sat, and the *Times*, nearly two weeks old, was lying there as if Lisa had just gone to heat up her coffee. Or more likely, get another hit of herb tea. Over the table, hanging upside down from the ceiling, were dozens of dried bouquets of roses, still fragrant, and on the table was a teal blue vase, empty now. Near the vase were Lisa's appointment calendar and a small address book. I slipped them into my pocket.

The kitchen was small, utilitarian, and neater than mine. No big trick. On the floor, opposite the sink, were two bowls, one obviously licked clean by a large dog with a healthy appetite, the other with a small amount of water still in it. I picked up the water bowl, rinsed it in the sink, then let the water run until it got cold. It was a ceramic dish, cream with a rust-colored dog bone, rimmed in blue, smack in the center. On the outside, in the blue, was written "My Dog." I filled it and put it down for Dashiell. I could hear him drinking as I stood in the center of Lisa's living room and looked around.

On my left there was a wall of books, with photos of Lisa doing t'ai chi tucked between the volumes. All the photos were of Lisa, none of anyone else—not a boyfriend, not even her Akita.

Under the huge windows there was a comfortable-looking black couch, a small glass coffee table, and two black leather chairs. The rest of the room was empty. I tried to imagine Lisa practicing t'ai chi there.

Dashiell was on his way upstairs, his nails clacking on the wooden steps. I followed him up, then sat on Lisa's double bed. The *Tao-te-ching* was on the nightstand, with a piece of lavender string as a bookmark. I opened it and began to read. This was enough to make *me* want to end it all.

I had gone through a Zen phase years before, when I was nineteen or twenty. I wore black, studied t'ai chi, and for the hours between lunch and dinner one day became a vegetarian. But aside from an occasional line that made sense to me, most of what I'd read and heard was incomprehensible.

"Mystery of mysteries," it said on the page where Lisa had marked her place. She had not only underlined it but copied it in the margin in her small, neat handwriting.

How could you come to understand something that couldn't be explained and couldn't be taught? Moreover, when you finally thought you had a handle on it, you didn't. Give me a break, I thought, putting the book back on the nightstand. Life is difficult enough without Zen.

But then I picked it up again. Lisa had been reading it. Probably for the hundredth time. Maybe I ought to give it one more shot. I left it on the foot of the bed to remind me to take it home. I would put it on *my* nightstand. Beyond that, I couldn't say.

I looked at Lisa's clothes. Almost everything was black, soft cotton tops and pants you could wear when you practiced or taught t'ai chi. But there were a few cheerful touches in her neat closet, too—a pair of pink high-tops, a pair of red cowboy boots, a sort of patchwork quilted jacket, and silk scarves, lovely ones in nearly every color, long ones, the kind you could wrap around twice, knot, or play with seductively as you leaned close to chat. I pulled out a lavender one and draped it around my neck, smelling Lisa's perfume, which still clung to the fabric.

On the tall oak dresser, there was a wooden jewelry box. I opened it and pawed through Lisa's treasures. I looked in the dresser drawers, too, at her underwear and sweaters. I rifled the nightstands. I checked under the bed. Snooping was my profession, wasn't it?

If Lisa had been depressed, I couldn't see any signs of it. There were no clothes strewn around, no pile of neglected laundry or unpaid bills, no Prozac, Valium, or sleeping pills in the medicine cabinet of the upstairs bathroom. There weren't even dust elephants under her bed. Maybe Daddy had paid for a maid, too.

There was lots of makeup, bubble bath, body lotion, perfume, and some pretty necklaces hanging near the oak-framed mirror opposite the sink. She didn't seem to lack anything. There were even condoms in the nightstand drawer.

Perhaps there had been a sudden descent, something that made her feel she was falling down a bottomless black hole. Or maybe the change had been chemical. I thought about Elwood waddling down the alley.

I walked around the bedroom once more, touching Lisa's things, feeling that there was something missing. Of course. There was no dog bed. I undid the neatly made bed. On the side nearer the stairs, there was black fur on the sheet. The dog had not only slept on the bed, she'd slept under the covers.

Years ago, when I was training dogs for a living, I'd had a client named April Anton, a nurse, who had hired me to train a little dog she had rescued from the shelter. She'd called her Penny because the adoption counselor had told her the pup looked like a scent hound, and April, who had always taken advantage of her access to drugs, heard it as "cent hound."

But I never got to finish the course. One evening her brother called to cancel the last lesson. When April hadn't shown up for her shift and hadn't answered the phone, he'd been called. He'd gone to her house to find that his sister had reached the end of her ability to tolerate her troubles. He found her in bed, the cigarette she had been smoking burned down to her fingers, Penny pressed close against her side. After calling 911, he'd called the animal shelter and arranged to have his sister's dog euthanized.

I'd always wondered how she'd been able to desert Penny. Now I found myself wondering how Lisa had been able to leave her dog so unsafe. Lisa's parents hadn't even mentioned her. I wondered where she was and what would become of her. I sat on the bed, picked up the phone, and called Marsha Jacobs.

"Marsha? It's Rachel."

"Yes, dear," she said. "Have you learned something?"

"I'm calling about, um, well, you didn't say and I was wondering, was Lisa seeing anyone recently?"

"There was a young man she mentioned, a Paulie Wilcox. But we never met him, this Paulie person."

That made sense. Barring the use of torture or drugs, who would discuss their love life with their parents or sacrifice an innocent young man by bringing him home for the grand inquisition?

"Do you know if she was still seeing him at the time, um, recently?"

"I don't know for sure."

"Oh, okay, and one other thing I wanted to ask was about the dog, Lisa's Akita."

"Yes?"

I hesitated, afraid of what I might hear. "Where is she now?"

"With Avram, dear. Why? Do you want her?"

For a moment I listened to the sound of Dashiell breathing and the hum of the refrigerator from downstairs.

"I'm sure she's lovely, but I already have a dog."

"Maybe Avram will keep her. She's used to him."

"One other thing, Marsha, about the note, Lisa's note—"

"Her apology?" her mother asked.

"Um. Yes."

Now the silence was on her end of the line. I could hear some muffled conversation, as if the mouthpiece had been covered.

"We didn't mention it—"

"Yes?"

"Because we thought it was personal."

"I see," I said. But I didn't. I thought it was very queer that they hadn't mentioned the note. Then again, they hadn't said much else about the circumstances of the suicide, and Marty hadn't thought that weird at all. Still, I'd ask about the note again, but only when I could see them.

"Well, I'll be in touch, okay, Marsha, and thank you."

"No, thank *you*, dear. We feel so much better that you're helping us."

I put the phone back in its cradle and sat quietly on the edge of

Lisa's bed. A film of dust covered the top surfaces of all the furniture. I drew a small Akita head in it with my pointer. The only sounds now were the occasional noises of the traffic outside on Hudson Street, a horn honking or tires screeching because someone was in too big a rush to get to the next red light. Even the comforting smell of dog was no longer detectible by a mere human nose. Lisa's apartment was a lonely place now. It had been deserted.

I pulled the folded piece of paper out of my pocket. It had some chocolate stuck to one side, which I carefully peeled off and ate.

"I'm sorry. Lisa," it said.

There was no date, no To whom it may concern, no By the way, could someone please be kind enough to give my dog a home. Just "I'm sorry. Lisa."

Had Lisa, once upon a time, expected her dog to protect her? Then shouldn't she have protected her dog right back?

What could have made her abandon her dog?

What was it that troubled her so that it didn't seem reparable?

I surfed my mind for a possible explanation, but found none.

There is a Zen saying I had once read. *When you seek it, you cannot find it.* Would I ever understand why Lisa Jacobs had taken her life? Like Zen, it seemed to make no sense at all.

5

I Stood Behind Him

BY LUNCHTIME DASHIELL was shaking his head so much, I had to take him to the veterinarian. He had an ear infection, probably from getting water in his ear while he was swimming. I had neglected to dry his ears.

One guilt attack and one hundred and thirty-two dollars later, we were home and I was making room on the small kitchen counter for the Q-Tips, the ear cleaner, and the otic antibiotic. After listening to my messages, I headed back to Lisa's apartment to watch her t'ai chi tapes, look through her books and papers, listen to her music, and gaze out her windows.

Late that evening, still wearing Lisa's scarf, I walked over to Bank Street T'ai Chi to keep my appointment with Avram Ashkenasi. I took the elevator to five and tied Dashiell's leash to the railing at the top of the stairs, just across from a long, low shelf filled with pairs of black cotton shoes of all sizes, the kind you see for sale in Chinatown, only used. Since this was the top floor, and it was so late the building seemed deserted, I thought it would be safe to leave Dashiell in the hall while I spoke to Lisa's mentor and former employer.

He opened the door, looked us both up and down, then motioned with a sweep of his arm for me to follow him.

"Yes," he said as if I had asked a question. "Bring him, too."

He was a troll—barrel-chested, short waisted, long armed, his meaty hands, red and hairy, hanging at his sides, fat, clumsy, and useless looking, his yellowish white hair long and held in an elastic band, the scraggly ponytail reaching halfway down his back, his stern-looking face half hidden behind an untrimmed white beard.

Santa Claus. In a horror movie.

"Take off your shoes," he commanded before we walked onto the polished wooden floor of the studio.

He was cranky, too.

Most of all, he looked dangerous, like one of those professors the other girls would tell you not to get caught alone with.

Keeping my eyes suspiciously on him, I obeyed, taking off my shoes and leaving them, toes touching the wall, next to another pair, black cotton shoes, small, like mine, not big, as his would be.

He pointed one of his big hands to a spot against the mirrored wall of the studio. "Sit," he said, as if I were his dog. I did.

"You, too," he told Dashiell, who usually obeys no one but me unless I hand over his leash. Dashiell sat, too.

Turning toward the adjacent wall, also mirrored, he began the form, first breathing deeply, then finding shoulder width with his feet.

He raised his too-long arms as if they had been lifted by a string attached to his wrists. Next the fingers rose, and soon his body began to move, ever so slowly, as if propelled not by his own power but by another force. A weather vane, pushed by the wind.

Legs folded in front of me, Dashiell at my side, I watched as he moved silently through space, strong, smooth, and graceful, his body shifting direction, his arms and hands slicing through the air, decisive, deliberate, and painfully slow, like foreplay. Before my eyes the troll became beautiful, transformed by movement into something almost holy.

When he stopped, I stood, full of questions. I had come, after all, about Lisa.

"Mr. Ashkenasi—"

He stopped me with one finger to his lips. "Now you," he said.

"Look," I said, straightening my back, "I came about Lisa, not to learn t'ai chi. As I told you on the phone—"

"Yes, yes," he said, "you're a friend of the family. You want to know about Lisa. You have many questions to ask."

"A cousin."

"A cousin?"

"Yes. And I've promised my aunt and uncle—"

"Of course you did," he said. "I am going to help you, Rachel. *If* you'll trust me."

It was a question. Though it wasn't spoken as one.

"I—"

He smiled to himself.

"I know. It's asking a great deal of you, an enormous leap of faith on the word of a stranger. But you are asking a great deal, too, Rachel, to try to understand a person who—" He waved his hand in the air. "Has vanished from our midst. But, of course, you knew her, your cousin. So—"

"We weren't close," I said. "It's sad, when you think about it, living in the same city but being so wrapped up in our own lives—"

"That happens, of course."

"The truth is," I said, "I hardly knew her at all. I hadn't seen her since we were kids."

Had I been a wooden puppet, he would have been impaled on my nose by now.

I looked into his pale eyes. He seemed moved to tears.

Damn, I was good.

"You won't learn anything worthwhile about Lisa by asking questions," he said softly, so softly I had to lean closer to hear him. "The police have already done that, Rachel, and what have they learned? If you want to learn about Lisa's life, you must walk in her shoes."

He picked them up, the single pair of shoes that I had placed mine next to, little black cotton shoes with rope soles, like the ones I'd seen in the hall, only these had "Lisa" written in black Magic Marker inside each shoe.

He held them out to me.

I didn't move.

"What can it hurt?" he asked. "You're already wearing her perfume."

When I took the shoes from his hands and lifted one foot, I felt his large hand cup my elbow. I let him support me while I slipped each one on. His hand was as warm as the hearth of my fireplace after a fire had been burning all evening.

"They fit," I said.

He smiled.

"Does he need water?" he asked. "Come," he said to Dashiell, "there's a bowl in the office." A moment later I heard the slapping sound of Dash drinking. Good, I thought, he still has the Akita.

The huge windows on the north side of the studio opened out, which must have made it easy to see from the street below from where Lisa had taken her plunge. I wondered which one Lisa had gone out of and exactly what she was thinking at the time. I wondered how I'd possibly find out what made her so desperately unhappy that she had decided to take her own life. Was it in fact a decision? Or might it have been instead a thoughtless, spur-of-the-moment rush to make an end, once and for all, to her pain?

I tried to picture Lisa in pain, but I couldn't. All I could come up with was the lovely, smiling face I had seen on her parents' piano and in their photo album.

Not average, her mother had said.

Avram returned with Dashiell padding along at his side as if they were old friends. He took my hands in both of his.

"I am so glad you came," he said, his eyes filling, as if he would cry. But then he let go of me and stepped onto the polished wooden floor of the studio and faced the mirror again.

"I do not want you to worry about what you look like. Just copy. Come, come, come, stand behind me. One day soon, you will feel what t'ai chi is. I cannot explain it to you any more than I could explain Lisa to you. You will feel it for yourself. And then one day you will feel Lisa."

I stood behind him, heels together, toes to the diagonal, and shifting my body and then my legs and feet, ever so slowly, I found shoulder width. My arms lifted as if a string were tied to my wrists, gently pulling them toward the heavens, and I moved as Avram did, slowly through space, my dog lying at the edge of the tan carpet with only his front paws touching the light oak flooring of the studio.

Each time Avram stopped, I stopped, and we would begin again; sometimes repeating the same few movements over and over again; sometimes Avram would go ahead as I struggled to mimic him, clumsy where he was graceful, shaking where he was steady, struggling where he was authoritative, worried where he was calm.

After a while my legs were burning, especially the few times he spoke, asking me to hold a position while he looked at me. Several times he gently moved me, adjusting the position of an arm, a foot, straightening my spine or wrist, and afterward I felt something like a breeze, but inside, not on my skin, something cool and calming, something moving slowly, something wonderful, and when that happened, I wanted never to stop.

We worked from eleven to three in the morning, and finally Avram stopped and sighed audibly.

"I've forgotten everything already," I said in a panic.

"Go home, Rachel. You're tired. We're both tired. You couldn't possibly hold all the movements in your mind. Your body is learning t'ai chi. Your body will remember for you."

"But when will you—"

"Shh, shh, shh," he said, holding his head as if I had given him a headache. "Are you familiar with the parable of the tiger?"

No, I told him. I shook my head no.

"A man was walking alone in the country, and he came across a tiger. He began to run, but the tiger also ran. It pursued him. Finally he came to the edge of a cliff, and grasping a vine, he attempted to escape from the tiger by climbing down. As he climbed, he looked beneath him. There below him was another tiger, looking up, waiting to devour him."

What was he talking about? He might as well have been speaking Chinese.

"One tiger above, one below. Only the vine saved him. But when he looked back up, he saw two mice, one black, the other white, gnawing away at the vine. That's when he noticed, right in front of him, growing on the side of the cliff, a perfect strawberry. He plucked it and ate it. It was delicious."

He smiled, then shut off the light in the studio.

If the man had something to say, why couldn't he just say it?

"You'll be safe walking home," he said. Again, a question that wasn't one.

"I have Dashiell," I told him.

I slipped into my own shoes and put Lisa's carefully back where they had been, toes pointing to the wall. Everyone else's shoes were relegated to the hall. Only Lisa's shoes had a place of their own inside.

"Tomorrow night classes end at ten. Come at ten thirty. Bring your boy."

"Look," I said, standing in the doorway, "this was interesting, tonight's work. But I didn't come here to learn t'ai chi. I came—"

"First the t'ai chi. Then the questions. And Rachel, next time, don't take the elevator. Walk. It's good for your legs."

Meditation in motion. That's what one of Lisa's books had said t'ai chi was, a kind of Zen for people with ants in their pants. Okay. I had done it. Now what? Where was the brand-new world Zen was supposed to give me? Except for the pain in my knees, nothing had changed.

All the way home everything looked the same, homeless people sleeping in doorways, trash swirling about like tumbleweed when the wind blew, transvestites heading home after a long night, their false laughter echoing in the empty streets.

Where with each step was my connection to the earth? Where with each breath was my connection to the sky?

I unlocked the gate and followed Dashiell down the narrow passageway that led to the garden in which my cottage sat.

Where, I wondered, were the answers to all my questions? Where, in fact, were the questions?

I unlocked the cottage door, but I didn't go inside. Instead I sat on the cold steps in the skeletonlike shadow of the big oak tree, waiting unsuccessfully for enlightenment.

6

I Wondered If It Might
Have Been Lisa

THE NINTH LAW of private investigation says, Keep moving. This advice is meant to aid the operative during those unfortunate times when he or she is being shot at by one or more disreputable persons, but as a law to live by, it can't be beat. I had learned the wisdom behind it back when I was training disreputable dogs.

Keep an aggressive dog still while you berate him for his rotten nature and unacceptable behavior, and he'll have nothing better to do than figure out precisely which of your many body parts might be the most succulent. But keep a bully moving by walking fast, changing directions, appearing to all but ignore him, and your unpredictability will consume his mind. It's as effective as if he were a balloon and you had a pin.

Keep moving. It gives you a much better chance of keeping yourself intact, whether it's bullets or teeth coming in your direction.

Unfortunately, when I got up late on Thursday morning, moving seemed all but out of the question. I could barely lift my arms or swing my legs off the bed. With a gait so stiff that if I were a dog the word *euthanasia* would come to my owner's mind, I finally made it to the bathroom and into a hot bath. And much as I would have liked to stay there all day, I decided to obey law number nine. It was time to check out the boyfriend. His phone number was in Lisa's address book. But before I called, I looked through her appointment calendar and found two most curious things.

I reached Paul Wilcox at work. He listened politely to my request and said that if I could come by at one thirty, he could talk to me about my cousin Lisa.

Okay, I do sometimes stretch the truth a bit, but only in order to get the job done. I learned the hard way that revealing my occupation has a silencing effect on people, even those whose worst crime has been finding a quarter in a pay phone and failing to return it to the phone company.

I had time before my appointment, and time was what Dashiell needed. I cleaned and medicated his ear, then headed for the dog run at Washington Square Park. Dashiell needed to spend part of every day just being a dog, and I needed to spend part of every day watching him do exactly that.

It would be nice to imagine the dog run as a fenced outdoor area where dogs can safely run around and play in the fresh air. But this was New York City. There is no fresh air.

As for safety, just as in playgrounds reserved for human children, there's a microcosm of life, and life, my mother would be quick to point out were she here, is lots of things—but safe isn't one of them.

So while Dashiell played, I paid attention. Once I saw that things looked benign, I let my eyes wander, noticing a young man practicing t'ai chi on the grassy area just to the west of the run. I had once seen a young woman practicing there. I wondered if it might have been Lisa.

In China, Avi had told me when we took a break from practicing the form, people always practiced out of doors. Groups of hundreds of people gathered in the early morning, before going to work, and in the evening, on their way home, to do the form in a sea of shared energy. Most Americans practiced alone, as Lisa must have, Lisa who had wanted to go to China but had gone only in her imagination.

I got up, walked to a corner of the run, faced north, and practiced whatever I could remember from years earlier and the night before. An hour later Dash and I headed for the West Village Fitness Club, on Varick Street, a short walk from Lisa's apartment. The Club, as it was called, had a twenty-five-meter indoor pool. I suspected that it was where Paul and Lisa had met.

As I entered the cavernous space, the pool was down a flight of stairs on the left. I could smell the chlorine. The aerobic equipment and weight machines were in a large mirrored room off to the right.

The health bar, where Paul Wilcox had said to ask for him, was straight back.

I walked up to the young man who was standing near a display of high colonics making carrot juice and politely waited for him to notice me. To my surprise, he was practically naked, though if I looked half that good, I too might walk around wearing nothing but a tiny orange bikini. He was my height, maybe an inch or two taller, my age, maybe a year or two younger, and looked to be about 155 pounds soaking wet, which he was, his hairless body the color of jasmine tea.

"Would you like a carrot juice?" he asked over the sound of the juicer. His almond-shaped eyes, mysteriously hooded beneath epicanthic folds, were the color of melted bittersweet chocolate.

It was the voice from the telephone. Sounded like Queens. Must be ABC, I thought, American-born Chinese.

"Paul Wilcox?"

"The cousin?"

"Rachel," I said, reaching out my hand.

He didn't take it.

"Funny she never mentioned you," he said, pouring the hideous-looking brown juice into two glasses, "but I can see the family resemblance."

"Yeah?"

Cool, I thought.

"Yeah. It's really strong." He took off his round, metal-rimmed glasses and stared at me. "Your coloring is different. Lisa's was more extreme—whiter skin, darker hair. But you have the same body type, the same-shaped face, the same wild hair."

Apparently the ancient rules of politeness had gotten lost in translation.

He walked around to the front of the counter and stood next to me. "And you're the same height."

He was barefoot.

"The same shoe size, too," I told him.

"So, are you like her in other ways?" he asked, carefully putting his glasses back on.

"Yeah. We were identical cousins."

"Then you speak Chinese?"

"Not a word. How about you?" I asked.

"Not a word," he said. "I'm only half Chinese, in case you were puzzled by the name."

I shrugged one shoulder, as if to say, hey, you wanna be half Chinese, what's it my business.

"An identical cousin," he said. "Another swimmer?"

"Dog paddle. Olympic quality."

"You hide your grief well," he said.

"Thanks. According to the Talmud, the deeper the sorrow, the less tongue it hath." I emphasized the *th*.

"Ah, another scholar in the family. That's just the sort of thing she might have"—he took a swig of juice—"said," he said, studying me.

I studied him right back.

I remembered a trick Ida had shown me, the time she asked me to bring my family album to a therapy session. She had placed her hand over the top half of people's faces, my mother's, my father's, Lili's, and mine, to show their smiling mouths. Then she'd slid her hand down and covered the mouths, exposing the tops of the faces. Without the smile, something else showed. I looked afraid. Lili looked defiant. My mother's eyes looked angry. My father's eyes looked sad beyond belief. Like Paul Wilcox's dark eyes.

He handed me one of the glasses of rust remover and led the way to one of the little bistro tables next to the juice bar.

"My cousin and I weren't close," I confided. "You know how it is."

"For sure."

"Funny, you don't sound half Chinese."

"Born in the USA." He smiled, showing me his dimples. "Flushing."

I skipped all the obvious cheap shots and got down to business. "The reason I called, Paul, is that I was wondering if you could tell me about Lisa. What she was like, you know, as an adult. What might have made her"—suddenly feeling the weight of what I was saying, I lowered my voice—"make the decision she did."

He scratched Dashiell's nose-tackle-sized neck.

"He's huge, your boy," he said. "What does he weigh?"

"Is this where you met my cousin?" I asked.

"What is this all about? Lisa never mentioned you, and I don't mean to be rude, but what's the deal?"

"It's my aunt Marsha." I lowered my eyes. "She's not sleeping well. She needs—we all need—answers. Did you ever meet her, Lisa's mother?"

"No. I never did. Lisa said she wouldn't sic her relatives on a dog." He shook his head. "No offense meant."

"None taken," I told him.

He took another swig of the sludge in his glass. "You're not drinking your juice," he said.

I nodded. He was right. I wasn't drinking it.

"So you never met them?" I asked.

"What's the point of this, Rachel? She's dead." He began looking around as if he were bored.

"Look, I'm sorry to stir things up. But my aunt asked me if I could find out what the hell was going on that made Lisa, you know, kill herself. It's so hard to—"

"Swallow," he said. "Isn't it though? Lots of things in life are difficult to swallow. Don't you find that so, Rachel? Is it Rachel Jacobs?"

"Alexander. That branch of the family. Not the Jacobs branch."

"And the Alexander branch resembles the Jacobs branch."

"Exactly."

"How homogeneous." He drained his glass.

I picked up my glass of juice and set it right down again. If Lisa's boyfriend saw the family resemblance, perhaps the person at the desk would, too. Lisa's membership card to the Club was in one of the pockets of her calendar. Clearly my clever interview technique wasn't winning Paul Wilcox over. Maybe my dog paddle would.

"Did Lisa swim here?" I asked. "Is that how you met?"

Paul was looking away, and for a while he said nothing. "Maybe she got dizzy. It can happen when you exercise. Maybe she went to the window for a little air, and—"

"There was a note," I said softly.

He turned and stared at me. "A *what*?"

"A note."

He covered his face with his hands. They were clean and strong looking, his fingers long and graceful. He moved them to his lap when Dashiell got up and laid his head there.

"What did it—"

" 'I'm sorry. Lisa.' That's all. No one told you?"

" 'I'm sorry. Lisa'?"

I nodded.

Suddenly the top and bottom halves of Paul Wilcox's face were in concert.

"No way," he said, his fist hitting the table so hard the top jumped and then continued to vibrate for another minute. Dashiell backed up a foot and barked until I signaled him to lie down.

"No *fucking* way. Lisa Jacobs never apologized to anyone in her life."

"Is that a fact?" I said, cool as a Borzoi.

"Look, cousin, I found the first news difficult to believe, and now *this*. Give me a break."

He pushed his chair back and got up.

"Wait a minute here," he said, leaning over me, so close I could see his tonsils. "Are you telling me my name was on it?" he whispered. "That it was addressed to me? Is that why you're here?"

"No. Should it have been? Addressed to you?"

He just shook his head.

"Paul, were you and my cousin still going together when this happened?"

"No," he said, pushing the chair back against the table so hard it moved the table closer to me. He began to walk away.

Good, I thought. At least one of us was telling the truth. His name hadn't appeared in Lisa's calendar since January 11.

And that time, it had been crossed out.

"When did you break up?" I asked his back.

But he didn't bother to answer me. Without turning around or saying good-bye, he disappeared down the stairs that led to the pool.

7

How Long Will It Take?

AT TEN THIRTY that night, after I had practiced the form alone in the garden, Dashiell and I headed back to Bank Street T'ai Chi. Avi opened the door before we reached the landing, his finger to his lips. Without speaking, I dropped my jacket onto one of the couches, changed into Lisa's black cotton shoes, and followed him onto the floor.

Standing behind Avi, I could see the strength of his movements, as if he were moving not through air but water—not springwater, cleansed of all impurities, but ocean water, thick with salt and life. It was as if he were swimming in the air.

After three hours of work Avi stopped, and we walked to the couches in the area between the office and the studio and sat opposite each other.

"How did you and Lisa meet?"

"So late, and still your head is full of questions," he said.

"You said, first the t'ai chi, then the questions."

Avi sat silently.

"You didn't mean after I learn the *whole* form?"

Was he meditating, looking straight ahead like that at nothing, as if he hadn't heard my question?

"Or not even then, right? When I get to the end of the form, you'll tell me we need to do corrections, that I am not good enough yet to ask you questions. Is that it? I am working so hard, staying up all night learning t'ai chi, and you will never help me learn what I need to know."

He lifted his big hand like a stop sign.

"A student once asked his teacher, 'Master, how long will it take me to learn Zen?' 'Ten years,' the master told him. 'But what if I work extra hard, then how long?' 'Twenty years,' the master replied."

"Avi, I—"

"You are so busy thinking about the destination, you cannot keep your mind on the journey."

"Avram, my aunt and uncle have asked me to help them understand the death of their daughter. They are in pain."

"And they will not be in pain when you tell them why she is gone?"

Now I was the one who was silent.

"Avram," I said after a moment, "I appreciate what you're trying to do, but I don't have ten years for this."

"Then we should stop wasting time. Tomorrow come earlier, come at seven."

I stood and picked up my jacket.

"I am only trying to help you make room for Lisa," he said, "so that you will understand her."

"Yeah, yeah," I said. "It's like dog training."

"Like dog—"

"Some people approach a dog so full of themselves, there is no room for the dog. They are full of ideas, full of answers. They think they know everything there is to know. And without looking at what is in front of them, they are sure that when the dog misbehaves, it's out of spite. They are so busy grabbing, punishing, being angry, that they never wonder, Who is this dog, what is he feeling, what does he understand, what confuses him, and why is he confused, what are his special abilities, and how can I use these to teach him what he needs to know? They are so sure they are right, they never examine their insubstantial conclusions. No matter what the dog might be able to tell them, they cannot learn it. There is no place inside them to put the information."

"So tomorrow, when you come, you'll wear your Everything I Know About Zen I Learned from My Dog T-shirt?"

"I didn't say I knew anything about Zen. I was only talking about dogs. I used to be a dog trainer," I said, "until I came here."

"I understand," he said.

"I'll see you tomorrow, then."

He stood, reached for the jacket, and helped me into it. He put his warm hand on my cheek and looked into my eyes.

"I'll be here," he whispered.

Then he walked to the door and held it open for me.

"Lisa was here every day. This was her life."

He stopped and blew his nose.

I didn't breathe for fear he'd stop talking.

"There was nothing more important to her, nothing that took precedence over her studies. We spent many hours together, studying, talking, or silent, working on the form. One never stops trying to perfect one's ability to do the form. We do not think, Ah, now we have learned it. We pay attention to one detail at a time, taking pleasure in each. We do not think about what isn't. We pay attention to what is. Now, go, child. I will see you tomorrow."

He closed the door.

Here I was, obeying him again.

Well, he was the *master*, wasn't he?

I heard the lock turn.

So what did that make me? I wondered as Dashiell and I headed down the stairs.

And more important, what had it made Lisa?

8

I Took the Stairs

WHEN I WOKE up it was afternoon, three thirty to be exact. If I was going to be at Bank Street T'ai Chi by seven, I had to move. I cleaned and medicated Dashiell's ear, gave him his monthly heartworm preventive, and spent an hour in my office paying bills, now that I could, and taking care of paperwork.

Since I had to repark the car anyway, I drove five blocks to Lisa's street and in only forty-five minutes was able to find a legal spot. Waving to the concierge, I passed the elevators and took the stairs to the second floor. Paul Wilcox had made me more than curious about the strong resemblance to my *cousin*, and I wanted to look more carefully at the pictures of Lisa that were among the books in her living room.

I picked up one of the photos and took it over to the window, holding it so that the light would fall on it. Lisa's eyes were as blue as the Caribbean; mine were more the gray-blue of the Atlantic. Her skin was white, like her mother's. Mine was fair, but not pearly or translucent, not as delicate looking as Lisa's.

Lisa's hair was very much like mine, darker, but about the same length and also curly. In the photo she wore a little braid on one side. I put the picture back on the shelf and, taking a small strand of hair on the left side, braided it as Lisa had done; then, holding the end of the braid, I went into the kitchen, where I had seen some lavender string on top of the refrigerator. I secured the end of the braid, then looked for scissors to cut off the piece of string.

I ran upstairs and opened the closet door, zeroing in on a sheer black silk shirt, black velvet leggings, the Chinese-style quilted jacket, and those fabulous pink high-tops. Leaving my own things in the closet, I put on Lisa's clothes and shoes. Everything fit, so I took some soft black pants and a black T-shirt for t'ai chi as well, folding them carefully and putting them in a nylon mesh tote bag I found in Lisa's closet. Halfway down the stairs, I turned back. I needed a bathing suit, didn't I? Before leaving, I also borrowed some jewelry to go with my new clothes, a jasper heart necklace from Tiffany's and a pair of silver earrings that sounded like small bells when they moved. I left my small gold hoops in their place.

I dropped the clothes off at home, and once again Dashiell and I headed toward the heart of the Village, Washington Square Park. Radiating out from the fountain at its center were paths that led north, east, south, and west, to the hanging tree, an old elm once used for executions, to playgrounds, to enclaves of the down-and-out asleep or sitting up and smoking on the benches that were the closest things they had to home, and to the dog run. Dashiell began a hip-hop ballet with a broken-coated Jack Russell terrier, and I took myself to the southwest corner of the run and, listening to the crunching sounds of the dogs playing on the pea gravel, faced north, eyes on the horizon, and became meditation in motion in Lisa Jacobs's beautiful, expensive clothes.

Near the dog run, a mounted policeman was putting his horse through its paces. A nurse was pushing an old man in a wheelchair, a plaid blanket over his legs. A nanny pushing a baby carriage walked by, a handsome young man was headed in the direction of the NYU law library, people sat on the grass reading. No one was imitating Bob Dylan or Janis Joplin, and it was a bit early for the drug dealers. Later in the day, if I asked Dashiell to "find the grass," he'd go nuts.

It was quiet, so I stayed for a long time, watching Dashiell play and thinking about Lisa Jacobs. At six I stopped at the Cowgirl Hall of Fame for a burger, then headed over to school.

I took the stairs. Avi had said it would help me do the form. Lisa, he'd said, always took the stairs, never the elevator.

Avram looked startled when he opened the door, but said nothing. I slipped off Lisa's jacket, put on her black cotton shoes, and followed Avi into the studio. Dashiell had already taken his usual spot in the sitting area, his big white paws just touching the wooden floor where we worked.

As is tradition, we did the form without speaking. Then Avram began again, and I followed him. This time, as I continued, he came near me to make corrections, gently moving an arm or a hand or readjusting a foot by placing his next to where mine should have been and leaving it there until I'd lifted mine and placed it next to his.

Most of the form is done with knees bent, as if you were in a low-ceilinged room. Avi helped me to sink lower, until my legs felt as if they were on fire. He had explained that the burning meant that the blood was seeking new pathways, and so my legs were getting stronger. Unfortunately, so was the pain.

Suddenly I was flushed with heat. All I wanted to do was hang out the window and get some air, but Avi kept on working.

"Did you ever notice how clumsy people can be?" he asked, leaving me with all my weight on my right leg.

"When your step is empty, no weight at all in it," he said, taking the same posture he had left me in sometime back in the Iron Age, "you are steady *before* shifting your weight."

He flexed his knee, lifting his left foot off the ground. Then he placed his foot back down, heel, toe, and shifted his weight forward, as slowly as honey oozing off a spoon.

"Remember that t'ai chi is a martial art, Rachel. You must always be connected to the earth, both figuratively and literally. You do not want your opponent to be able to push you over."

It was long past dark, but neither of us stopped to put on the lights. Lit by the bright light of the moon shining in through the big windows, reflecting in the mirrors, and shining on our faces, we continued to practice, mostly in silence.

"Okay, shake out your legs," Avi finally said.

We stood quietly for a moment, neither of us speaking. Something was bothering me, jabbing away at the edge of my consciousness. I turned and looked at the windows. Then I looked into Avram's face.

"Which one?" I asked.

"The second from the left," he said. He turned and walked back to his office, leaving me alone.

I walked over, unlatched the window, and pushed it out, letting the cold, damp night air hit me in the face.

The street looked very far away, and just looking down made my knees turn to water.

The door had been locked, I thought, but the chain hadn't been latched.

I felt a wave of nausea as I pictured Lisa looking down, just as I was doing, then climbing onto the sill and falling into nothing.

I thought about the second curious thing in Lisa's calendar. All those appointments. All those plans. The days after her death were filled with things to do.

No handprint on her back, Marty had said.

Most jumpers were men, I thought, looking down. Female suicides usually used carbon monoxide or some other form of poison, not something that would disfigure them, like a gunshot wound. Or defenestration. Vanity at play, right up to the very end.

I thought about all Lisa's pretty things, about those roses, dozens of bouquets, hanging upside down from her ceiling.

I thought about her pretty face.

I thought, No *way* did Lisa Jacobs jump out of this window.

There was a reason none of this made sense. Lisa Jacobs hadn't killed herself. Someone had done it for her.

I leaned out and looked down.

Then, quickly, I straightened up and stepped back, bumping into Avram. He leaned past me, pulled the window shut, and latched it.

In those black cotton shoes, he had been so silent I hadn't heard him approach me.

I began to shiver. I had stood in front of an open window in a dark room in the middle of the night with a stranger behind me, a man strong enough to lift me and toss me out the window as if I were a sack of trash he was tossing into a Dumpster.

His hands were trembling.

So were mine.

When he moved, I felt myself jump.

He reached into the pocket of his soft cotton pants.

"Will you lock up after you change your shoes? I must go now."

"Of course."

He handed me a set of keys.

"Tomorrow, five o'clock?"

I nodded.

"Good," he said. "I'll have a surprise for you."

My heart was pounding so hard I thought I might have a surprise for him too, another of his protégés dead in the middle of the night, this one right in the studio, of a fear-induced heart attack.

But he never noticed anything.

He grabbed his jacket from a hook near the door, and in a moment he was gone.

I was going to leave, too. In fact, I couldn't wait to get out of there. But then I noticed the door to the office. It was ajar.

I walked inside and sat in Avi's chair, putting the keys he'd given me down and placing my hands on the smooth surface of his ruddy teak desk. The computer was to my left, the files to my right. The bookcase behind me covered the entire wall. On the wall to my left, in a simple oak frame, was a photo of Lisa frozen in the middle of doing Cloud Hands. I hesitated for only the briefest moment before turning on the computer.

"Insatiable curiosity," Frank Petrie used to say, "it's what makes you broads so damn good at the job."

I slid the chair closer, preparing to work. So many secrets, I thought, so little time. But then I looked back at the keys. I already had these. Lisa's mother had given them to me.

No one had taken Lisa's keys to lock up after the murder.

Whoever killed her already had a set.

9

Forever, She Said

THE LAST TIME in her life a woman feels really comfortable about being seen in a bathing suit is when she's six, and God knows, I hadn't seen six in a dog's age. Nonetheless, there I was in the doorway of the ladies' locker room at the Club, wishing I had a dog to hide behind. Unfortunately, I'd left him at home.

At least it wasn't rush hour at the pool. There were only three people in the water. One of them was the coach.

I stood watching him do laps for a long time. He seemed tireless, cutting through the water the way Avi cut through the air when he did the form, as smooth as a thread of silk being teased from a cocoon. When he reached the deep end, he curled around underwater and shot out in the opposite direction, not coming up for air until he was nearly halfway to the other side. A fish. But what kind of fish? I wondered.

I dropped the towel onto a bench, then stood next to it, trying to keep my balance as I wiggled the elastic band that held the key to my locker onto my ankle. Suddenly I saw feet, so close I could have reached out and touched them.

"Ah, the cousin."

I straightened up.

"I didn't expect to see you again."

"Out of my way. I'm trying to get a tan."

He smiled.

"So what are you doing here?"

He was staring.

Perhaps it was Lisa's black bikini bathing suit, which barely covered the stuff my mother said no one but my husband or a doctor should ever see.

Or maybe it was Lisa's jasper heart necklace dangling just below my modest but attractive cleavage. Or was it the cleavage itself? since that's where he seemed to be looking.

"If I want to compete in the next Olympics, it's practice, practice. Anyway, I'm here. So, hey."

"Hey, yourself," he said, finally bothering to look at my face. "So, let's see that stroke you're so famous for."

I turned and walked to the deep end and, one heart hanging around my neck, another in my throat, dove into the now-deserted pool. I began swimming laps, and just when I was really getting into it, I noticed that Paul was back in the water, hanging on to one side at the deep end. I swam over to hang out with him. After all, this was work. I wasn't here for my health.

"Hey."

He reached out and picked up the jasper heart, holding on to it for a moment before dropping it.

"Lisa had one just like this."

"No kidding?"

"If memory serves," he said.

"Well," I said, "sometimes it plays tricks on one. Instead of serving."

"You have similar taste to Lisa. It's interesting."

"It's a family thing," I said.

"Take that suit, for example."

I did, I thought.

"Lisa had a similar one. Not exactly the same. But very similar."

"Yeah? How are they different?"

"Hers had more cleavage," he answered.

Rule number whatever of private investigation is, Never take the job personally.

Yeah, right.

I pushed off the wall to swim away, but something stopped me. It was the coach's hand. He had hooked it into the back of the bottom of my bathing suit, what there was of it.

"You don't leave a person much dignity," I said, flailing around until I could turn and get a grip on the side of the pool again.

"How much do you need?" he asked.

"I thought saving face was a big deal with Orientals."

"I'm nowhere near your face," he said, finally letting go of my bathing suit bottom.

Clinging to the edge of the pool, chlorine wafting up at me and stinging my eyes, I wondered what Lisa had seen in this guy. Sure, he could swim. I'd give him that. But so could a fucking sturgeon.

Maybe it was the t'ai chi. Maybe they had that in common, too. "Did you meet Lisa through t'ai chi?" I asked him.

He shook his head. "What are you up to, Dog Paddle?" he said. "Why are you here?"

"I told you, Paul. I'm trying to help Lisa's parents. My aunt and uncle."

"Okay," he said, "let's talk."

"Here?"

I started to tremble. If my mother were here, she'd probably tell me my lips were turning blue.

"I'd rather we had more clothes on," he said, looking at me as if I were a pastrami sandwich and he were a starving Jew.

"What about—" I said, feeling as if someone else were speaking through my mouth. It was probably the echo from all the tile.

"What about this evening?" he said.

"I'm busy."

"Me, too. I have to take my grandmother shopping. But I could meet you afterward, at ten, say."

Apparently Paul Born in the USA Wilcox was no banana, the Asian equivalent of an Oreo.

"Should I come up or wait for you downstairs?" he asked.

"Downstairs?"

"Bank and West, isn't it? Two buildings in from the corner, south side of the—"

"Oh, *that* downstairs."

"That *is* where you'll be, isn't it?"

I nodded.

"I'm coming prepared to talk. Et tu, Dog Paddle?"

I could feel his breath on my face.

"I'll be prepared to listen," I said.

"That's a start," he said.

He put his hands on the edge of the pool and hoisted himself up and out of the water. I put my hands on the edge, too, but before I could propel myself out of the pool, Paul Wilcox did it for me. He had taken my wrists, and then there I was, standing too close to him, rivulets of chlorinated water running down my thighs and onto the wet tile beneath my bare feet.

"God," he said, his voice suddenly husky, "your hair does the same thing Lisa's did when it got wet."

His was jet black and thick. It stood straight up when it was wet, in spiky little clumps.

"Another family thing?" he asked, his voice soaked with sadness.

I pulled my hands away and brushed the hair off my face.

"Nah, it's a Jew thing. We all have curly hair and big noses." Big Nose was what the Chinese called Caucasians.

He smiled and ran his finger down my nose. "Your nose isn't so big. It's just about perfect," he said.

"Yeah, yeah," I said. Next thing he'd be telling me I was a hard-boiled egg, white on the outside, yellow on the inside, a Caucasian with an Oriental soul. Like my cousin.

I'd forgotten how dark his eyes were.

He turned and headed for the men's locker room.

For a moment in the pool, he'd seemed so angry, I'd been afraid he was going to push me under. But that couldn't have been my real fear. Hell, my sister did that all the time when we were kids. The real threat was becoming sucked in. The real fear was that something about this man was making me lose my objectivity, even my judgment.

"Wait," I shouted at his back.

"You bellowed?" He came back to where I was standing.

"About tonight," I said. Avi had said he'd have a surprise for me. I thought he might be ready to talk. "I can't meet you tonight. How about—"

"How about now? I'm ready for lunch."

"Lunch?" I said, as if I were a parrot.

He simply waited.

"Okay, lunch. That sounds fine."

I had to talk to the man. He was an important source. Lunch was better than the deep end of the pool. For one thing, I'd be dressed. Suddenly, lunch sounded safe, it sounded perfect. What the hell could happen at lunch? I asked myself, feeling smug now, as if it had been my idea all along.

"It'll take me ten minutes to get dressed. Can you wait that long? You seem to be a pretty impulsive person." He picked up a corkscrew strand of my wet hair, shook his head, then let it go and headed for the locker rooms.

"I'll meet you at the front door," I said to his back, watching his adorable little *tochis* as he walked away. "In seven minutes. Don't keep me waiting."

I'm not one for fussing. I was showered, dressed, and in front of the gym in six minutes.

"We can go right across the street," Paul said a moment later, not breaking stride as he joined me on the steps and swept me along onto Varick Street.

The mystique of perfect timing pervades the literature of dog training. Correct a dog precisely at the moment of his indiscretion, and he'll learn to mend his ways. Make your correction a minute later, and he won't. Had we come out of the Club a minute sooner, or a minute later, I never would have seen him.

I was supposed to look across the street, see the ordinary-looking luncheonette that, according to the Zagat survey, had the best fried chicken north of the Mason-Dixon line, and agree to have lunch there. That's all. But trouble never asks permission. Like that proverbial bad penny, it just keeps turning up.

There, across the street, standing right in front of Edna Jean's, was a middle-aged man I knew, a man who shouldn't have been there. It was Saturday, wasn't it? He should have been home, having lunch with his wife of twenty-four years, admiring his panoramic view, listening to his children bicker. Instead he was on Varick Street, so absorbed in the blond at his side that he never turned and noticed his sister-in-law staring at him from across the street.

Was she one of his models? She was all in black, of course, except for her perfect, long blond hair, which she wore loose, even on such a mild day. Didn't it make her neck too warm? *I* was certainly hot under the collar.

Not the blond. She looked cool holding his arm and smiling up at his face. Totally cool. Maybe you could do that when you had zero percent body fat, flawless skin, teeth that were probably perfectly even and actually white—but that was just a guess, because surely I wouldn't get close enough for the bitch to bite me. She might have rabies.

I thought about my sister and her big dimpled ass, her size-eleven feet, her mouse-brown hair. Until that moment, until seeing her husband hanging on every word of a stunning slip of a blond—or was that actually a *dress* she was wearing?—I'd thought of my big sister as beautiful.

Suddenly I began to panic. My brother-in-law was turning in my direction. So I did the only thing I could.

I grabbed Paul's shoulders and pulled him toward me, as if he were a Chinese screen I could hide behind. I moved my arms from his shoulders to his neck, then into his wet black hair, and keeping him between me and what I was still watching across Varick Street, I whispered, "God, I feel so terrible about Lisa," and buried my face in his neck.

I heard his voice, so close the words reverberated on my skin, heard him say, "Poor Dog Paddle," and when I felt him stepping back, what could I do, I had to keep him there, I lifted my face and found his lips. And then the most surprising thing occurred. Despite the fact that my only motive was to protect myself from being seen until I'd figured out what to do if I were, I found myself being kissed by a complete stranger, his long fingers in my hair, the tip of his tongue tracing my lips, a guttural sound like the one Dashiell makes when I scratch inside his ears coming from only God knew which one of us.

Then over his shoulder I could see Ted's arm up, waving for a cab.

"Hold me," I whispered, pulling him closer, so close you couldn't slip a slip of paper between us.

"Rachel," he said, "Rachel."

A cab stopped. I watched Ted and the blond get into it. Were they lovers? I wondered as the cab moved into traffic and pulled away, heading downtown. Maybe there was another explanation.

Yeah, right, maybe.

That's when I realized that something else wasn't right. The cab was gone, but Paul was hanging on to me, breathing audibly. And something was pressing into my leg, something hard. What the hell was it, an egg roll in his pocket?

No, I thought, not an egg roll, it felt more like a knockwurst.

I stepped back.

"Oh God, Rachel," he said, his dark eyes all gooey with lust. He sure did have a way with words.

"Look," I said, "something just came up. I have to reschedule our lunch."

He turned and looked the other way, his face now more the color of rose hip tea than jasmine.

"I'll call you," I said. "I'm sorry." And like a steak left out to defrost in the same room with an untrained dog, I was gone.

Walking home, thinking about my sister, I remembered another kiss. Well, it was sort of a kiss. That time I'd been a child, and the person I'd sort of kissed had been Lillian.

I was too young to know how ridiculous her original idea was. We were lying on the glider on Aunt Ceil's screened-in back porch, after a

day at the beach. We were face-to-face, so close I could see the finger-
prints on Lili's glasses.

Let's become blood sisters, she said.

How? I asked.

First you have to put a match under the needle, like when Mommy
takes a splinter out, she said. Then you stick your finger, and I stick
mine. Then we press them together, mixing the blood, Lillian said,
pressing her two pointers together to illustrate. That makes us blood
sisters, forever.

I began to cry.

Okay, okay, she said. There's another way. Stick out your tongue.

Wug iz dis thaw, I asked.

She didn't answer. She stuck out her tongue and made the smooth
tip of it touch mine.

Forever, she said.

Thawevah, I repeated obediently, afraid to pull in my tongue. God
only knew what germs were on it, I thought. Even then.

Could you even let your own sister's tongue touch yours nowadays?
Probably not. Not if her husband was maybe running around doing
God knows what with God knows whom.

The bitch wore black, a short, slinky thing that went in and out
wherever she did. Her hair was long and straight, shimmering where
the light hit it, moving as gracefully as seaweed in the ocean. I hated
her on sight.

But what could I do about this? Tell my sister? Mightn't she simply
kill the messenger?

Not tell her? Then what?

Confront my brother-in-law? And say what? Who was I supposed to
be, the sex police?

Was this even what it appeared to be? And if it was, mightn't it blow
over without Lili getting hurt?

Without Lili getting hurt, I thought. How could she not get hurt,
even if the thing was a one-night-stand? Doesn't infidelity, even the
briefest sort, always damage a relationship? Even if Lillian never
found out, wouldn't the very fact of it change everything? Forever.

10

Something Was Different

WHEN I GOT home, I made two urgent phone calls. Then I sat in the garden with Dashiell until it was time to see Avi.

As soon as I opened the downstairs door to Bank Street T'ai Chi, Dash knew something was different. His nose dipped down to the floor in front of him and soaked up information unavailable to mere humans. His head pulled up. It appeared he was looking up the stairs, but it wasn't his eyes that were working so hard. His nostrils flared as he tuned in on the scent cone hanging thickly in the air. Whoever had recently passed this way interested Dashiell greatly. He turned as if to ask if my hands had fallen off or my feet were nailed to the ground, and he whined. I unhooked his leash and watched him disappear.

A moment later, they were both standing on the landing, looking down at me. He, the Arnold Schwarzenegger of the dog world, a can-do machine, was all muscle. Except for the black patch over his right eye and the black freckles on his skin that show through his short, smooth coat, Dashiell is white. He has a broad head with great fill in his cheeks, a jaw so strong he can hoist his own weight, a chest as hot and powerful as a blast furnace, and a heart so elastic you'd think his dam was Mother Teresa.

She reminded me of Lisa's mother, refined where Dashiell was crude, decked out where he was no-frills, feminine where he was clearly one of the guys, champagne to Dashiell's beer.

The bitch wore black, a double coat of medium length, thick, lush fur, the splash of white at her front like a bib of pearls. Her feet were white, too, as if she had delicately dipped them in gesso. Her tail was tossed majestically over her back, the white tip resting lightly on her flank. A symbol of good health in the breed's native country, she radiated her own vigor. She stood above me, her head cocked to the side, her brow wrinkled, her intelligent brown eyes alive with light. I loved her on sight.

I looked at Dashiell. He had fallen hard and fast for the Akita, too. His eyes were absent of all intelligence. He had moved, lock, stock, and rawhide, into pheromone city.

As if on a signal from each other, the dogs turned, taking the stairs at a speed I couldn't even aspire to, and disappeared. I climbed to the fifth floor at my usual pitiful, human pace. Because Lisa never took the elevator.

"She's called Ch'an," Avi said. At the sound of her name, the Akita turned and looked at him. She was large for a bitch, probably about eighty-five pounds. "Outside," he said, waving his arm toward the windows, "they call her Charlie. But of course Lisa did not name her Charlie Chan."

"You mean she gave a Japanese dog a Chinese name?" *Ch'an,* I had read recently, was the Chinese term for Zen, or meditation.

Avi's eyebrows went up. "You've been studying. You are so like Lisa."

"It's just that I'm walking in her shoes, trying to understand her life so that I might, one day, understand her death." Avi winced. "I love the t'ai chi, Avi, but I don't know much more about Lisa now than I did the day I met you, certainly nothing that would explain in the slightest what happened."

"In China," he said, "if one wants to study t'ai chi, seriously study it, the way Lisa did, it is necessary to be accepted by a master. You cannot go to a school, pay your money, and be taught t'ai chi, the way you can here. Every family guards its secrets," he said. "They will not teach just anyone."

"I—"

He raised his hand to stop me. Both dogs, thinking his gesture was meant for them, lay down.

"In China," he said, "tradition dictates that the student follow the teacher, and that is how he learns. Here we place great emphasis on education. It is different. But even the way we teach here, giving our students helpful images and patiently correcting postures, we still count the time of study in decades instead of years. Even that may be optimistic. So we try to find peace and beauty along the way. Now, about Lisa"—he pointed to the black shoes, their toes touching the wall—"a few days, Rachel, would be on the optimistic side in this study, too, wouldn't it?

"Twenty years or forty years, there isn't enough time in the world to know someone after they are gone. It's just not possible to get a true portrait of a human being from the detritus of his or her life and the opinions of others.

"Zen teaches you who *you* are, Rachel. Once you know that, you will know everything you need to know."

Then why, I wondered, had Alan Watts said, "Trying to define yourself is like trying to bite your own teeth"? Or was that my grandmother Sonya, the night her false teeth fell into the split pea soup?

"And t'ai chi—" I interrupted him.

"Yeah, yeah, Zen in motion."

So what else could I do? I took off the pink high-tops, put on Lisa's t'ai chi shoes, and silently, standing behind my mentor, I practiced the form. Afterward Avi asked me to do a silent round, and this time, instead of working with me, he watched.

Something was different. Perhaps the study now had forged a link with the past, with the t'ai chi I had studied so long ago and thought I had forgotten. Or perhaps concentrating on what I was doing rather than on watching Avi was what made the difference. Now when I placed my foot in an empty step, it felt as flat as a sheet of paper. I felt at ease, my body remembering everything, energy moving up my spine, over my head, spilling down my chest, connecting me to the earth beneath my feet and the universe above and beyond.

"Better," he said, stroking one side of his beard and then the other with the back of his hand, like a cat cleaning its whiskers.

But the moment I stopped moving, all my confidence fled. I felt only the enormous weight of my ignorance. It was a familiar feeling. The work I do is like driving in heavy fog. Sometimes it clings to the windshield, and you can't see an inch in front of you. At best it rolls a foot or two away, or lifts for a moment and allows a tantalizing glimpse of the road ahead before closing in all over again. Most of the time I feel as if I were driving blind.

I slipped off Lisa's shoes and put on her sneakers. When I looked up, Avi was holding Ch'an's thick, black leather leash.

"Come in the morning Monday. We have a staff meeting. You can meet the others. Maybe *they* will answer some questions for you. And leave your boy at home. Only bring Ch'an with you."

I began to shake my head.

"Can't you do this one thing for me?"

He didn't wait for an answer. The master was used to obedience.

"Lisa—"

"Yeah. I know," I said. "Lisa never took the elevator. She always took the stairs. And I do, too. But *this* I can't do for you."

"But Lisa always brought Ch'an to school with her."

"Lisa always brought *her* dog to school. And I—"

But he wasn't listening. He was looking toward the big windows.

"Even on the night she died," I said.

He nodded.

"I was asleep when the police called me. They said there was an emergency and asked if I could come right away with the keys. They didn't say what it was. They didn't tell me what had happened here. I thought a pipe was leaking. I had no idea.

"There were so many people here, so many. I could see them from down the block. I got confused. I couldn't understand why. A fire, I thought. There must have been a fire.

"Then I saw.

"She was lying on the street, under a yellow tarp. I could see one of her hands, the palm up"—he turned his hand to show me—"sticking out from under the plastic.

"They asked me to look. They asked if I could identify her. One of the detectives slipped his hand around my upper arm and another one drew the tarp back, uncovering her face, her beautiful face."

Avi shook his head and began to cry. He took a wrinkled handkerchief from his pocket and wiped his eyes.

"We walked up the stairs," he continued. "The door was locked, of course. Lisa wouldn't have left it open when she was here alone late at night, even with Ch'an to protect her. I unlocked the door, and one of the two detectives who came up to the studio took my arm and pulled me aside. The other drew his gun, he shouted 'Police' and waited, but there was no sound, nothing. We stayed in the hall and he went in.

"For a moment I was just blank, just seeing the hand, turned up, like so, as if to catch rain. Then I remembered Ch'an and was polluted by the fear that the detective would be frightened of her and shoot.

" 'Don't be afraid,' I called out to him. 'Don't shoot the dog.'

"The second one opened the door wide, and we both stepped in. The room was dark, the way we worked last night, you and I, the studio lit only by the moon. It was empty.

"The first detective was just walking into the office, and I heard him gasp. I thought to myself, God, no, someone else is lying dead on the floor.

"We went to the doorway to see, myself and the other detective. But it was Ch'an who had startled him. That's all it was. She was lying on her mat, her head up, her front paws crossed, one over the other, looking at us, as if nothing at all had happened." He put a hand on his chest and rubbed it, as if by doing so he could erase his grief.

"What about the note, Avi? Where was the note?"

"It was on the desk, in front of the computer. 'There's a suicide note,' the first detective said. I am not ashamed to tell you, the tears were flowing from my eyes that night, too, Rachel. I don't know why, but the thought of her sitting at my desk and writing . . . Poor Lisa."

"Did you read it? Did they show it to you?"

"Yes, yes, I read it," he said. "First the second detective read it. They each leaned over the desk to read it. No one touched it. They asked me to do the same. To read it, but not to touch it. I did. They asked me if it was Lisa's writing. I told them it was." Avi took a few breaths. When he had calmed himself, he continued. "Even then," he said, "with all three of us in the room, Ch'an never moved. She just stayed on her mat, watching us. I guess she was in shock."

"She was just being an Akita," I said.

"What do you mean?"

If he didn't understand Ch'an after living with her, how could I explain her to him?

I looked at my watch. "I have to get up early," I told him. "I better go." I tapped my leg for Dash, but then hesitated at the door. "Will you keep Ch'an, Avi? I don't think Lisa's parents want her."

The Akita had gotten up when Dashiell did. She stood quietly next to Avi, looking off to the side, as if she were in another world and none of this had anything to do with her.

"She belongs here, Avi, with you."

"Go home, Rachel," he said. "It's late. Let me not keep you any longer."

11

Was There a Message Here?

I COULDN'T REMEMBER if it had been the homeopathic veterinarian or the holistic dentist who had told me about Rabbi Lazar Zuckerman, but he hadn't asked how I'd heard about him, so I hadn't had to lie to a man of God.

I had left a message for him yesterday afternoon. He had left one for me after sundown, when he could use the phone without breaking the laws of God. He said I could come the following morning. But since I hadn't spoken to him, I hadn't had the chance to say I was bringing a pit bull with me.

He was seventy-five if he was a day, but crouching so that he could embrace Dashiell, he looked about eight. His eyes, behind rimless glasses, were a faded hazel, but wise and full of light. I think it's a job requirement. He had a full head of hair, steely gray ringlets, a black yarmulke held onto the back of his head with a single bobby pin, and the obligatory rabbinical beard, long, full, and wonderfully unkempt.

"Rabbi Zuckerman," I said.

He stood and looked intensely into my face.

All the way here I had been expecting short and stout, perhaps because of his deep, rich voice, but the rabbi was as tall and slender as a young tree, if not quite as lithe.

"I hope it's okay about the dog?"

He waved his hand in front of me, as if he were saying hello, to stop the false apology. "Come, come, both of you," he said, leading me into a dining room off to the right, "we have important work to do."

We sat at a dark mahogany table on chairs so huge I felt my feet wouldn't touch the ground. Or was it the rabbi who made me feel as if I were a child? There were heavy velvet drapes on the windows, wine colored, swagged back with white curtains beneath, but still the light came into the room, showing the sheen of the much-polished table and the age of the faded, flowered wallpaper and worn oriental rug.

Rabbi Zuckerman placed his hands on the table and waited. After the long walk, Dashiell didn't need to be told to lie down. Sighing heavily, he plotzed right next to the rabbi's chair, showing his innate respect for such obvious authority. I reached into my pocket and drew out the copy of Lisa's suicide note and the samples of her known handwriting the rabbi's message had asked me to bring along, letters I had found in the briefcase her mother had given me what seemed like a hundred years ago, in Sea Gate.

He pushed his glasses up onto his forehead and into that mess of curls and brought Lisa's note up close to his face. I thought he was speaking to me, but realized he was humming—Bach's Sonata no. 1, if memory serves. He studied the three words for a very long time. Then he carefully placed the copy down on the table, smoothed it flat with both hands, and looked at it some more.

Next he picked up one of Lisa's letters. These had been written to her mother and father, and so, like anyone else's letters home, they were fairly egocentric, bland, and reassuringly cheerful. But it wasn't the content that the rabbi was studying. For him, the writing itself was the message. What I'd remembered hearing was that a Rabbi Zuckerman on Eldridge Street had a passion for graphology, that he'd been studying handwriting and the things it revealed about character for thirty or so years.

"Suicide, you said, yes?"

I nodded.

He began to hum again, this time keeping time with his foot tapping away on the threadbare carpet. By now five letters were spread out in front of him. He studied them and nodded.

"Su-i-cide," he said. "Hmmph."

"Rabbi Zuckerman, I was wondering if you—"

"Shah," he said. With one hand he reached up and brought his glasses back down to rest on his nose. He got up, causing Dash to momentarily lift his head, and disappeared into the kitchen. I could hear the water running. So could Dashiell, who got up and followed him. A moment later I could hear the sound of one dog drinking, considerably louder than the sound of one hand clapping.

The rabbi returned with two jelly jar glasses, which he placed on the table. He bent and opened the server at the wall behind the head of the table, taking out a bottle of sherry. As he poured, he hummed. Then, handing me one of the glasses, he said, *"So."*

"Rabbi Zuckerman," I started again, "I was wondering if you could tell if the same person, if Lisa Jacobs, who wrote the letters, also wrote the suicide note. I realize that the note only has three words, well, two and a signature, but—"

"There's a lot of energy in her writing. Strength of body, strength of mind. A remarkable woman. Remarkable."

He took a sip of sherry.

So did I. When in Rome, so to speak.

"Ambition. Optimism. Self-control."

"But—"

Dashiell had remained in the kitchen. I could hear his tags as he flopped over onto his side on the no-doubt-cooler kitchen floor.

"The hand holds the pen," the rabbi said, "but the brain controls the hand. Thus the writing reveals character."

He picked up one of the letters and pushed his glasses back up onto the crown of his head.

"You have never before used the clues from handwriting in your detective work?"

"No, never."

"But you are hoping for a definitive answer. She did. She didn't. If she didn't, who did?"

"No, not that much."

He took a sip of sherry.

"Rabbi Zuckerman, Lisa's parents—"

"Yes, I know," he said. "I can see from her letters. For the parents, there is no more sun to rise in the morning. The world is now dark for them. So, Rachel, what do you hope to give them?"

"What they asked me for," I said. "Some understanding of why."

He nodded.

I waited.

The rabbi hummed.

"This young woman," he finally said, "the woman who wrote with such a regular hand, everything in balance, the proportions pleasing, she was tenacious, self-willed, powerful, a determined person. The writing, you see, shows a person's hand."

I nodded.

"She was confident, more confident than vain. There are no flourishes, no embellishments, no hauteur. Do you know this word?"

I nodded.

"Young people nowadays," he said, "they have no vocabulary. They read only what is sprayed on walls. Do you own a dictionary, Rachel?"

"Yes, Rabbi."

"That's good," he said. He looked back at the letters. "I don't believe this was an empty person with an insatiable craving for attention. No, no, no, a focused person, a strong person, but a self-centered person too, someone who put herself first. A disciplined person, the writing up and down, up and down. Vertical. A thinking person."

"But Rabbi Zuckerman, did she write all five letters? Did she write the last letter?"

"Did she write the last letter? You think she did not?" he asked.

"What I think is that she did not kill herself, Rabbi. I think someone else did that. I can't buy suicide. It makes no sense. There was no history of depression—"

"Look here, Rachel, in these letters, the lines are straight or sometimes they rise ever so slightly, up, up, up, like so," he said, pointing, "and so and so, showing optimism, not depression. Depression makes the lines go down, sometimes off the page, as if the person were too weary of spirit to notice their writing had walked off the paper. Not your Lisa."

"That's what I mean. Her home is serene and lovely. She loved her work. Her parents doted on her. It doesn't seem she could have, would have killed herself. It—"

"So, forgery. Is that what you think?"

"I—I don't know any other way to explain the note."

"When someone forges another's writing, Rachel, they tend to pay attention to the obvious, in this case, the L in Lisa, the loops, the flourishes. But Lisa did not embellish. Her writing is small, neat, and simple. The forger tends to forget the smaller items, the little letters in between, and these areas can give him away. But we have so little to go on here. Three words."

"So you can't tell?"

"Can I tell? Can I tell?"

I watched quietly as he studied one of the letters again, his nose nearly touching the page. He was so focused, nearly obsessive in the attention he paid to each letter. Yet he was clearly sensitive, too, not the kind of man who would ignore the needs of his guests, even when one of them was a dog. He was old, but he was strong, the way a tree is, able to sway in the wind and not break. You could see that when he moved. But he was also soft. You could see that in his eyes, his yin and yang in perfect balance.

For a moment I pictured myself living here, making gefilte fish every Friday morning, going to the *mikveh* once a month. Was there a message here?

"The last letter was written more quickly than the other four," he said. "Forgery is almost always written slowly, deliberately." He stood and began to pace. "Even if the forger practiced Lisa's writing, one does not dash off a note in someone else's handwriting. When copying, one takes his time." He leaned over the table now. "Not only does the *L* look like Lisa's writing, Rachel, but the *I* in *I'm sorry* looks as if she wrote it. And the small *i*, see how straight, how precise, now look in her other letters, see, the same, the same, and here, the same."

The rabbi fished in his jacket pocket, came up with a magnifying loupe in a green leather case, and took his chair again, sighing as he sat. He held it over the suicide note, moving it slowly over each letter in each word.

"Here's something interesting," he said, holding the paper right up to his face again. "Look at the periods in her older letters."

I took the loupe and slid it over the letters. Magnified, Lisa's periods were tiny dashes that turned up at the end. I picked up the xerox of the suicide note. Again, a tiny dash that with the naked eye looked like a dot. A dash that had an upward movement, that told you the direction her pen was lifted off the paper. The same, the same, the same.

"And her *s*," he said, "in 'sorry' and in 'Lisa.'"

"The same, the same," I said.

He nodded.

"I don't get it. She couldn't have killed herself. I feel it so strongly."

"No one is saying she did, Rachel. We are just seeing that it seems she wrote, 'I'm sorry. Lisa.'"

"Oh, God," I said.

The rabbi nodded and began to hum.

"She wrote the note. But not necessarily for the purpose everyone assumed."

"She wrote the note," he repeated. "But unfortunately, the only person who could have told us the purpose is dead."

"Maybe not," I said. I picked up the jelly glass and downed the sherry. "Maybe one other person knows, the person who wanted us to *think* it was a suicide note. The person who killed Lisa."

The rabbi turned sideways on his chair so that he could look toward the window. He sat like that for a while, nodding to himself, his face and hair illuminated by the afternoon sun.

"Perhaps so," he said. "Perhaps so."

After a while, he picked up one of the older letters.

"See how the letter is framed, Rachel, the broad margins left and right, top and bottom, as if it were a painting. She had, your Lisa, a passion for beauty, did she not?"

I pictured the roses hanging upside down over Lisa's dining room table.

"Yes, I believe she did, Rabbi."

He sighed. *"Azoy gait es,"* he said.

"So it goes," I agreed.

I folded the letters and put them back in my pocket, wrote a small check to the building fund, called Dashiell, and suddenly remembered the black Taurus sitting down the block from my house. A true New Yorker, I was so used to walking I hadn't remembered I had a car this month, and now, having walked all the way to the East Village, I would have to walk all the way home.

I stopped for fresh hot bialys, giving the bag to Dashiell to carry for me, and then stopped at Guss's for a fresh, crisp pickle, the kind that gets fished out of a wooden barrel. This no one had to carry for me. This I munched noisily as we headed back to the West Village.

We walked along Houston Street, past the Mercer Street dog run, which you have to be a member to use, past the thirty-six-foot-high bust of Sylvette by Picasso, set on the grounds of University Village, and past Aggie's restaurant on the corner of Houston and MacDougal, which made me realize the pickle was only a first plate.

Across MacDougal from Aggie's was a large, fenced ball field. I went to a far corner, took the bag of bialys from Dashiell, and unhooked his leash. I sat on the ground, legs folded in front of me, eating a bialy and thinking about Lisa's dog, there with her the night she'd been killed.

The Japanese consider all their breeds to be more courageous than any Western breed. It is courage in the face of adversity that the Japanese most admire, a trait, by their own admission, of national character that they also assign to their dogs, the Akita, the Sanshu, the Shika, and even the cute but bratty Shiba.

If the note that I'd carefully put back into Lisa's jacket pocket had not been a suicide note, if Lisa had not climbed up on the windowsill and tossed herself straight into eternity, what, I wondered, would the Japanese say about the fact that someone had murdered her while her Akita stood by doing nothing?

The American standard for the Akita—*American* meaning the standard approved by the American Kennel Club, the main U.S. registry of purebred dogs—says the ideal Akita should be "alert and responsive, dignified and courageous."

Whatever the truth was, whatever had happened that night, Ch'an was living proof of the beauty of the breed. If truth be told, Ch'an, with her deep-set, triangular eyes, her powerful, wedge-shaped head, her thick, dark coat, was breathtaking.

And isn't beauty what most of us go for anyway?

Wasn't it what was motivating my brother-in-law's apparent indiscretion?

Wasn't beauty what killed King Kong? Just try telling any one of the single apes you know that you want to fix him up with a woman with a great personality. *See* how far you get.

At least the Akita standard says *something* about temperament. Many of the AKC standards have nothing at all written about character, as if a dog were an assembly of parts covered with fur.

Had Lisa been fooled by the words of the Akita standard, all that overblown, flowery stuff the national clubs write about each breed—loyal, dignified, courageous? Or, since she embraced things Eastern, had she merely wanted an oriental dog?

I opened the bag and pulled out a second bialy, giving half of it to Dashiell.

The same, the same, Rabbi Zuckerman had said.

But who's to say what its purpose was?

I'm sorry. Lisa.

It could have been about anything.

I thought about stopping at the Sixth Precinct on my way home, but what would I say—that I'd made the astonishing discovery that Lisa Jacobs had actually written the suicide note they already knew she wrote? Or that, despite that fact, I had a strong *feeling* that she'd been murdered?

You mean an *intuition*? Marty might ask.

Or would he say, "Handwriting analysis? Pretty flaky, Rachel, even for you. What's next, a Ouija board?"

Just thinking about it, I could almost hear them snickering.

No way. If their motto was Cover your ass, well, so was mine. I didn't need to be thought a fool by my local branch of New York's finest.

What, after all, did I have so far? Cops say the criminal always leaves something of himself at the scene, and that he always takes something away from the scene when he leaves. Could the note, written for another reason, be what was left? That could mean the killer had planned Lisa's death. So what might he have taken away? A hair? A thread? The scent of her perfume? But so what? Whatever he took, whatever he left, a fingerprint, some dandruff, even his damn wallet, couldn't he have been leaving things and taking things away from the scene for years? After all, he had the keys. Didn't he?

Or she?

It was way too soon to talk to the cops. All I had was Lisa's note. And the nagging idea that its purpose had been universally misconstrued.

12

Are You Seeing Anyone?

IN THE EVENING I walked Dash to where the car was parked and drove to Rockland County to visit my sister. Maybe there I'd discover something telling, like if my sister's husband had suddenly started wearing turtlenecks to cover up the hickeys on his lousy, philandering neck.

I made a mental note. Check bald spot for signs of hair transplants in progress. Check bathroom for Grecian Formula for Men. Get Lillian talking.

The gate was open, and I parked just outside the two-car garage. What a different life from mine my sister had—two children, an expensive suburban house, a fully stocked and equipped kitchen, a washer and a dryer, even a freezer. And now, or so it appeared, a cheating husband.

I walked down the long, skinny deck. The door was ajar. I called Lili's name and walked in. She was in the kitchen making soup, her sleeves rolled up, the chopping board deep in carrots, celery, parsley, and parsnips, a cut-up chicken in a bowl to her right.

"Oh, I didn't hear you," she said, her face without makeup, her hair uncombed and sticking out around her face as if she'd stuck her finger in a socket. She was wearing one of Ted's old shirts and what we used to call fat pants, baggy, wide-legged jeans. Maybe those were Zachery's. She had a dishcloth tucked into her waist with assorted stains in various colors on it, and she wore fuzzy slippers, black-and-white ones, in the shape of pandas. If not for the size of her feet, eleven, I would have thought the slippers were Daisy's.

I thought about Lisa's mother, perfect in her gray silk dress and simple pumps. My sister used to dress like that, fussing with her hair, wearing makeup and pretty clothes even when she was staying home. Then I thought about the blond and wondered what difference dressing up would make anyway.

Lili held her arms out to the side as I hugged her, so as not to get raw veggies on Lisa's gorgeous clothes. Since she always complained about the way I looked, I thought she'd notice the improvement. But she didn't. She just turned back to the cutting board and resumed her chopping.

"Zachery is bowling," she said, as if I'd asked. "Daisy is sleeping over at Stephanie's. Teddy had to go in to the city and take care of something at work this afternoon. Inventory? Was that what he said? Whatever. So it's just the two of us." She looked up now and flashed me a Kaminsky grin.

"Are you hungry? There's cold chicken in the fridge. Make some tea for us, too."

I filled the kettle and lit the stove, watching as the blue flames momentarily fogged the pot.

"I thought Ted would be home for dinner." Lillian shrugged. "He's such a workaholic, that man. You know, I thought he'd get better as he got older, but he's worse." She stopped cutting and looked at me. "Sometimes I worry that something's wrong," she said. She turned back to the cutting board and carefully began taking the skin off a clove of garlic.

"What do you mean?" I asked, feeling as if I hadn't taken a breath since Nixon made his Checkers speech.

"Like if the business is in trouble and Ted won't say. He's so good, Rachel. He's never wanted me to worry about our finances." She began to peel another clove.

I took two mugs off the shelf, put a tea bag in each, and began to make the sandwiches.

"Sometimes I think I should get a job."

"No kidding."

"The kids are always off with their friends, they don't even eat supper at home half the time. And Ted's been working late a lot, like last week the accountant was supposed to come at two thirty and he didn't show up until ten to five. Can you be*lieve* that?"

I didn't offer an opinion.

"It's always something. Maybe it would help if I earned some money, too. There'll be college to pay for soon."

"What would you do?"

"Well, that's precisely the trouble. It's a great idea, but what am I trained for? Who's going to hire someone my age with no real work history?"

"You could always become a detective," I told her, and then ducked out of the way as the dish towel snapped through the air.

"This is stupid. I have such a lucky life," she said, signaling that she'd had about enough. We took the sandwiches over to the table. "Are you seeing anyone?"

She was obsessed with me getting married. Well, I had, hadn't I? And where had that gotten me? Where, I thought, did anything get anybody—love, marriage, having a child? Where had it gotten the Jacobses? And where had it gotten Lillian?—all her ambitions to be a lawyer instantly put aside when Ted had gotten a terminal case of ring fever and insisted, even before she finished law school, that they get married and she stay at home and play house.

"There must be some job you could get," I said, deciding against telling her that my social life consisted of recently having kissed a total stranger in order to avoid being seen by her husband, who was at the time Velcroed to someone young enough to date her son. "Lots of women go back to work when their kids are older."

"You get so detached from everything," she said, "staying at home. Why am I complaining so much? I live in the most beautiful house in the world, on top of a mountain, with this wonderful"—Lili stopped and sipped her tea—"view."

"Still, a job might be interesting. Look, even if things are fine with Ted's business, working is not only about money."

"I know, but there is so much to do around here."

She pushed her half-eaten sandwich away. I picked it up and gave it to Dashiell. "Let's go for a walk," I said.

Lili changed to mud-stained sneakers and put on Ted's old leather jacket. I put on Lisa's quilted one. Dashiell rushed on ahead. We proceeded more slowly, following the circle from Lili's flashlight so that we wouldn't trip over roots or fallen branches. We went up the path that led into the state park that surrounded Lili's house, walking arm in arm where the trail was wide enough.

"Have you talked to Ted about it, about going to work?"

"I don't think he'd like it, Rach. You know how Teddy is. He wants his dinner on the table the minute he gets home. He wouldn't like the inconvenience of it."

"So you haven't discussed it with him?"

"He has his own problems, Rachel. I don't know if I told you, but a few months ago he seemed so tired all the time that I got really worried. Maybe you should join a gym, I told him. They say it really helps, you know, exercise. It's even supposed to reduce stress, and you know Ted's work, well, the garment district, it's ulcer country."

"So what did he say?"

"He thought it was a great idea. He found this gym right near work. He's already lost that big gut. He looks good for fifty."

Fifty. Maybe that explained it.

"With Teddy working so hard and making all these changes, how can I—"

"You need to talk. You guys are best friends," I said, as if I still believed it. "That's how you stay close, by communicating. That's what you told me, when Jack and I—"

"You're right. It's all my fault. I haven't been talking to him." My sister turned and headed back toward the house. I whistled to Dash and followed along behind her.

"I didn't say it was your *fault,* Lili. I was just repeating what you always told me, that good relationships are based on good communication," I said to her back.

Once inside, Lili picked up her lukewarm tea and began to drink it. Then she began talking about something she'd seen on television. I waited for her to use the downstairs bathroom so that I'd have an excuse to use the one off her bedroom. I quickly checked the hamper, finding it empty. That's when I got really depressed. I expected to find out that designer briefs had replaced my brother-in-law's baggy boxers. Instead I discovered that my sister had nothing better to do than the laundry.

13

Frank Would Be
So Proud

I WOKE UP early enough to make a much-needed raid on Lisa's apartment. Her workout clothes were getting a bit ripe, and unlike my sister Lillian, I had more pressing things to do than the wash.

I took Dashiell to the strip of land along the river, now gussied up with benches and called a park, and let him run for a while. Then we headed for Lisa's. When I unlocked the door, Dash made a beeline for the water bowl. I dumped Lisa's mail on the small table near the door and headed upstairs. I had brought along my leather backpack to use as a shopping bag.

I began my shopping in Lisa's bureau, taking a few more black tops and some leggings. Next I decided I needed a change of jewelry. I dropped the musical earrings back into the top drawer of the jewelry box and fished around to see what else I liked. I decided on little silver hearts, simple, with a dot in the center of each.

In the second drawer, in keeping with the theme, there was another heart piece, tucked into a robin's-egg-blue Tiffany bag, as the jasper necklace had been, a heavy silver link bracelet with a heart dangling from it. It was engraved, but not with Lisa's name or initials. It said, Be My Love. Pretty corny, but I wouldn't have thrown it away had someone I loved given it to me. I held it in my hand for a while, warming the silver and feeling its weight. In the end, I put it back in the little blue bag and left it.

I changed to one of Lisa's black sweaters and a clean pair of faded jeans. It was sort of like playing dress-up, only it was morbid. Still, I was just following Avi's advice, wasn't I? I was walking in Lisa's shoes. And her earrings, necklace, and clothes. I was reading her books and letters. I had just barely escaped from having to sleep with her dog. And in a short while I'd be back at Bank Street T'ai Chi, where it was possible I'd be meeting the person who had last seen her alive.

I put the rest of the clothes into the backpack and headed for the stairs. I planned to put most everything back, of course. I'm often a liar, but only rarely a thief. On the way out I snagged the book of Zen quotes I hadn't finished reading, tucking it under one arm. It was time to go, but first I had a guilt pang at the front door. The pile of mail was growing. One of these days, I knew, I'd have to look through it. But not this day. If I didn't hurry, I'd be late for the staff meeting.

I could see light coming into the hall as together Dash and I climbed to the fifth floor. The door had been propped open. I could hear their voices as I approached.

"—a matter of time," I heard Avi say impatiently.

"But you're not denying—"

"I am not denying. But length of time does not determine—"

"I have been here for seven and a half years. I have done—"

"Janet, there is something important you have *not* done. Now, could we discuss this, you and I, at a later time? I have something important to talk to all of you about today."

I was a few steps from the landing when I put my hand into Dash's collar to stop him. Someone had left an expensive camera, a Nikon, on the shelf where the shoes were stored, an odd thing to do in New York City. I wondered which of them was so trusting.

"But it's the same old story, Avram. Exactly the same. And I need—"

"*You* need. There is barely room for oxygen in this place with all this overblown ego. I, I, me, me!" There was a silence and then Avi spoke again, slowly and calmly. "The study we have all embarked upon is a lifelong investment in loss, letting go of ego, letting go of tension, letting go of fear—"

"Avi, you—"

"I have only taken on an apprentice. You act as if—"

"That's what you said last time."

"But *who*?" It was a man's voice this time. A young-sounding man. They were all young. Howard Lish, a massage therapist who worked out of his home on Bank Street, only a block and a half east of the school, I had learned by surfing around in Avi's computer files, was, at thirty-eight, the oldest on staff. Stewart Fleck, a social worker who apparently had no compunction about signing out to the field and then coming here to study or teach, was thirty-four, just two years older than Lisa. Hey, it'll be nice to meet a couple of young men for a change, I thought, even if at this point in time they were both murder suspects.

Like *I'm* perfect.

"You mean you've ignored my request again, Avram?"

That was Janet again, Janet Castle, thirty-three, a bodybuilder who earned her living as a personal trainer and, like the others, did t'ai chi on the side.

"Enough. I want you all to accept her. To help her learn."

They all lived in the neighborhood, all close to the school.

"Where did she come from? Where were you hu-hu-hiding her? Lisa's only been d-dead two—" A man's voice.

"*Enough.* This pushing, this ambition, this jealousy, where does it get you? Not where you say you want to go. You come here so full of yourselves, all of you, how can I teach you anything? Look at the sorry lot of you."

I could picture their heads hanging, like three reprimanded golden retrievers. If they had tails, just the tips would be hopefully beating against their chairs as they waited for some sign of forgiveness.

"I was hoping," Avi continued in a softer voice, "that when she comes, you would welcome her, teach her, embrace her."

"Em*brace* her?" Janet said.

I let go of Dash's collar, and together we sauntered into the staff meeting.

"Ah, it's Rachel and Dash. Come in, come in," Avi said, beaming at me as the other three all turned in unison and stared daggers in my direction. "I'd like you to meet the others."

"Hey," I said, offering one of my most dazzling smiles. "Great to be here."

There was an empty chair next to Avi, so I took it, dropping the full backpack and the Zen book next to it, then slipping Lisa's jacket off and letting it drape, inside out, over the back of the chair. I crossed my legs, adjusted the sleeves of Lisa's soft black cashmere and cotton sweater, and began to play with her jasper necklace.

Avi extended a big red hand. "Rachel Alexander, Howard Lish—"

"Hey," I said.

"Stewart Fleck—"

"Hey, Stew."

"And Janet Castle."

"Hey, Janet."

I might have gotten a more animated response from Mount Rushmore.

The phone rang, and Avi excused himself. It was the first time I'd seen him interrupt anything he was doing to take a call, and I could only think he wanted the others to have a chance at me. You could just see they were dying of curiosity. He'd probably sit in his office listening as they circled and closed in for the kill.

"Now I see what my problem is," Stewie said, staring after Dashiell as he followed Avi into the office. "I don't have a dog."

Janet smirked and ran her fingers nervously through her short hair.

"So, Rachel," Howie said, his big face flushed, his hands trembling, "wh-what did you do before coming here?"

That's New York for you. Skip the foreplay and get right down to it. I stared for a moment, making him even more nervous than he managed to be on his own. He was wearing a plaid shirt and jeans that both looked as if they had come from Goodwill, and I'd bet a day's pay he had at least one hole in his socks.

"I was a brain surgeon," I finally said.

I heard a chair scraping in the office. Avi had probably just fallen off it.

"Oh, great," Janet said in her Texas twang, "another one. Oddly enough, we were all brain surgeons before finding t'ai chi." She began to laugh. "Looks like the old man got a live one this time," she said, "got to give him credit." Her hair was boyishly short and blond, nearly white, with a small splash of green at the crown, a case of better living through chemistry.

"We all have d-day jobs, so to speak," Howie said, his forehead wrinkled as he waited for me to volunteer something. Good fucking luck on that one. I was only sorry I wasn't chewing gum. It was definitely the missing touch.

Fuss, fuss. Lisa had been heavily subsidized by daddy, five or ten thousand dollars at a time, for birthdays, Hannukah, Simchas Torah, whatever, in order to have the privilege of being Avi's apprentice. So what was this all about? Being teacher's pet?

"You live in the neighborhood?" Stewie asked.

Where were his manners? Next he'd be asking me what my rent was.

"I'm staying at my cousin's place," I told him, "for now."

"Your cousin?" Janet asked.

"My cousin Lisa."

Stir things up, Frank used to say; it makes the shit float to the surface.

"You're Lisa's cou-cousin?"

"Didn't Avram tell you?" I asked.

"I'm a massage therapist," Howie said, his bulldog jowls trembling as he spoke. "It's good to know, in case you ever get a crick in your neck or anything. So wha-what were you up to, before?"

Maybe he *was* a bulldog. He sure didn't know when to let go.

I looked into my lap and smiled. "Look," I said after a while, "Avi says now is all there is. Now I'm here."

No one spoke. Not one of them appeared to have taken a breath since Eve reached for the apple, sending the human race on its downhill slide.

Frank would be so proud.

"How long have you known Avi?" Stewie finally asked, as interested as if he were a cocker spaniel and I were holding a liver snap.

"It's hard to say."

"Just what we need around here," Janet drawled, "another bitch."

Stewie shot her a look.

Avi returned and with a motion of his arm called us for rounds. Howie, Stewart, and Janet went out into the hall to change shoes. I picked up Lisa's shoes from right behind my chair and slipped them on. We were off to an auspicious beginning, I thought as I took a place in the back so that I could watch them from behind as well as in the mirror.

Howard Lish, a sad-looking fat man, was off to the left. He was about five-eight, flabby, and had apparently found the very potbelly my brother-in-law had just lost.

Stewart Fleck was as small and chary as a rodent out on a raid in some street cat's territory. He was barely my height, on the gaunt side, and pale, as if he stayed indoors too much. I could see his dark, beady little eyes watching me in the mirror. Fuck *him,* I thought and watched him right back.

The only other person I knew with muscles like Janet Castle was my pit bull. She was wearing a shocking pink cutoff singlet that showed off her rocklike abs. You could see her perfect quads under the floral latex tights, and her glutes looked as if they were made of concrete. Holy steroids, Batman, what a construction site *she* was.

I looked around at the sorry group. Not one of them was quite what I'd expect to find if I opened the latest edition of Who's Who in Zen in America. Where did Avi find all these nerds?

But who was I to talk? I still cared far too much about what my family thought about me, even though most of them were dead. The strongest substance I'd abused lately was sherry out of a jelly jar with a seventy-five-year-old rabbi. And it had been a dog's age since I'd shared my bed with someone who wasn't wearing a flea collar.

14

Janet Gave Me a Wink

AFTER ROUNDS STEWIE and Howie left immediately, and Avi
went into the office and closed the door. Janet gave me a wink, as if
we were old buddies and we'd just pulled off another good one. While
I was changing my shoes, she came up to me.

"Listen," she said, "I'm sorry I came down so hard on you. It's not
your fault, what happened. It's just the way things are." She shrugged.
"I mean, Avram's great, I love him to pieces, but he does things his
way. Shit, it's his school, am I right?"

I nodded.

"So why don't we go have lunch, my treat, to, you know, make it up
to you for me being such a bitch?"

"Why not?"

"Great," she said, slapping me on the back and nearly knocking me
through the wall.

I put Lisa's shoes back where they belonged and, with Dash trailing
along after me, met up with Janet in the hall changing to her thick-
soled, multicolored cross-trainers. Was she figuring we'd run to the
restaurant?

"You like Chinese?" she asked. She'd covered her short hair with a
baseball cap, worn backward.

"Who doesn't?" Actually, I'd had a yen for it for days now.

"Great. We'll go over to Charlie Mom's. Did you ever try their vegetable dumplings? They're *fabulous*."

The waiter's erased blackboard of a face never changed as he regarded Dashiell's credentials and his yellow Registered Service Dog tag. I was pretty sure he had no idea what they meant, or what the law said, but he let him in anyway. We were led to a table in the back. Dash slid to the floor right behind my chair and fell immediately asleep. As usual, no one else in the restaurant seemed to notice he was there.

Janet ordered soup and dumplings for both of us. By the time we'd unfolded our napkins, the soup was in front of us.

"It's so cheap here. I come every chance I get."

"So why the fuss over Avi teaching me t'ai chi, Janet? He must teach lots of people. It's what he does, isn't it?"

"But there's only one apprentice," she said, picking up the baseball cap and placing it back on her head.

The waiter brought the dumplings even though we hadn't touched the soup yet.

"What's the big deal?"

"It means he thinks you have special ability. And so he gives you lots of time. What else do you think we're talking about? Sure, the man teaches t'ai chi, we get to work with him in *class*. It's not the same. His special student gets to spend time alone with him, I mean, hours at a time. That he doesn't do with everyone. And that's what this is all about, time with Avram. The man goes, Get that, will you? when the phone rings, and he changes your life. It's not what he does. It's what he is. And just being around him, I don't know. It does things to you, Rachel. The man's amazing."

"He sure is," I said, dipping one of the crispy noodles in duck sauce, then just hanging on to it. "Janet—"

She looked up from her soup.

"What do you make of the note?"

"The note?"

"You know. The one Lisa left?"

"Oh, *that* note. Here's how I see it," she said, taking a handful of noodles and tossing them into her soup bowl. She leaned forward. "We had talked, me and Lisa, what, a month ago. I mean, I was pissed."

"About Lisa being Avi's apprentice instead of you? But you were both at the school for *years*, weren't you? Why did you wait so long to tell her?"

"It wasn't *that*," she said. "I mean, in the beginning, when she came, well, I knew it wasn't *her* fault that Avi spent the time with her, not me. It was his decision, so how could I blame Lisa for taking a wonderful opportunity?"

"Of course. You couldn't," I said.

But of course, you could.

"So, what was it?"

"A few months ago, something changed. Lisa changed."

"In what way, Janet?"

"She got real la-di-da, like she was more important than the rest of us. So finally one day I got her alone, and I went, What got into you, and she goes, What are you *talking* about, Janet, and excuse me, but can't you see I'm busy here? and I went, This won't take long, it's just when are you going to stop being such a bitch, woman?"

"What did she say?"

"Nothing at first, you know. She just looked, well, shocked. I mean, we had been close, me and her," Janet said, holding up two fingers that appeared to be glued together at the sides. "So then she goes, Janet, I had no *idea*. There's a lot of stuff going on in my life right now, a lot to deal with. She looked like she was going to lose it, you know. I actually felt bad for her for a minute. But then she goes, I guess that's why I've been short with you people. You people! Give me a damn break. I mean, isn't that pathetic, not to know the effect you're having on the people around you. And to call us *you people*, as if we had just fallen out of her nose or something."

"What else did she say?"

"*Nada*. She just shook her head and walked away. And then, well, it happened. I mean"—she made an arc with her chopsticks and whistled—"out the window."

"I don't get it, Janet," I said, leaning over the table to get closer. "You're not saying she killed herself because of what you said to her, because you were upset—"

"Hell, no."

She drank some tea and picked up a dumpling with her chopsticks.

"So what *are* you saying?"

"I figured the note just took care of our unfinished business."

"Such as?"

"She'd explained herself, you know, a lot of stress, blah, blah, blah, like *that*'s an excuse. But she didn't really apologize, you know what I'm saying? Now she has. That's all."

"And you forgive her? Now."

"Absolutely." She popped the dumpling in her mouth and chewed thoughtfully. "She was perfect, you know," Janet said. "She'd never leave anything undone. It's like a dis-*ease*, being like that." She picked up her bowl and drank some of her soup.

"Why did she do it, Janet? She was so young, and she was doing what she wanted to do, wasn't she? I just don't get it. Did you ever find out what she was talking about, the stuff she said she was dealing with?"

"Not really. I figure there'd been big trouble with her boyfriend, because he'd stopped coming by to pick her up. But that had been a while before. Maybe there was some new guy busting her chops. Who knows? Or maybe she just got tired of having to be perfect. *That* can be a real drag."

"What do you mean?"

Janet shrugged, picked up another dumpling, and dipped it into the little dish of soy sauce before putting it into her mouth. I spooned up some soup.

"See," she said, pointing at me with her sticks. "That's how Lisa ate. She'd never pick up her bowl. Afraid she might drip a little soup on her chin." She wiped her mouth with the back of her hand. "Like it would be the end of the fucking world if she did."

"Janet, what did Avi mean when he told you there was something important you hadn't done?"

"We were that loud?" she said. "You heard us fighting before you even walked in?" Janet put both hands over her mouth.

"I did."

"No wonder you were such a bitch!"

"I couldn't help hearing you all, Janet," I said, leaning over the table and punching her playfully on her concrete arm. "The door was open, and I was walking—"

"Because Lisa never took the elevator," she said. Then she crossed her eyes and stuck her tongue out to the side.

"So, the thing Avi said—"

I picked up a dumpling and dipped it in the soy sauce. The strong flavor made my eyes tear.

"The bodybuilding." She lifted her right arm and flexed the most astonishing biceps I had ever seen. "Avi says t'ai chi makes learning everything else easier. And everything else you do, physical stuff, like sports or exercise, makes it more difficult to learn t'ai chi."

"Is that true?" I asked, thinking of all the hyperbole I had read in one of Lisa's books, particularly the sweeping statements about health and longevity.

The waiter arrived with the check. I reached for my wallet, but Janet shook her head.

"Yes," she said, looking down. "He gets really pissed when I come to class so sore from weight lifting that I can hardly move without groaning. T'ai chi, he goes, is about letting go, relaxing the muscles, strength from softness, all that shit. He goes, Ach, you know how he does that? So what do you do, he goes, you make rocks out of your muscles. You're not happy until you're in pain.

"What happens when the most pliable element meets the hardest? he goes one time. But he doesn't wait for an answer. He'd be one unhappy dude if you ever answered one of his questions. He has to ask and answer. Am I right?"

I nodded.

"The rock yields, he goes. It is worn away by the water. Nothing, absolutely nothing can withstand the force of water." Janet leaned forward and lowered her voice. "He got so mad at me once, he can be a cranky son of a bitch, you know, so he goes, How long are you going to go on trying to be superwoman? like one word from him and I'm going to burn my cape and throw away my shirt with the red S on it."

"What did you tell him?"

"Nothing. I didn't say squat. So he goes, Janet, haven't you noticed that it gets more and more difficult to find a phone booth nowadays? And when you finally do, someone's already gone and pissed in it." Janet covered her mouth when she laughed. "The man's a fucking riot."

"Have you ever thought of giving it up?"

"Shit, no. You done any? It makes you feel so *good*."

"Pumping iron? Not really."

Janet raised one eyebrow. "Never?"

I pushed up the sleeve of Lisa's sweater and flexed my biceps. She wasn't impressed.

"You're coming to the gym, woman, for a *real* workout. I want you to *feel* what I'm talking about. Hey, it's on me. No charge. Okay?"

She took out her appointment book and a pen, and we made a date for my bodybuilding lesson, for Thursday at five. She carefully wrote my name in her book, holding the pen with her left hand. This would have been a huge issue, perhaps even exoneration from my suspicions, had I not already seen Rabbi Zuckerman and heard his opinion that Lisa had written the note herself, the note that Lisa's parents, Paul, and now Janet thought had been an apology to them.

As Janet wrote, her tongue out to the side and moving with each word, I took a good look at her arms. She could have carried Lisa up the stairs and pitched her out the window without stopping to catch her breath.

"You coming to sword class tonight?" she asked.

I pictured myself as a *New Yorker* cartoon. The caption would read, "Oops."

"I'm sort of a klutz. I'd probably cut off my own foot."

"No problem, as long as you don't cut off *my* foot." She winked at me. "Everyone says that. Beginners use wooden swords. Your foot'll be safe."

"I have some stuff to do tonight," I told her. "Maybe next week. Hey, thanks for lunch. And for not holding a grudge."

"No problem," she said.

"Janet, you aren't going to get mad at *me* now, are you, because Avi—"

"Nah. I was pissed at Lisa for all of a sudden acting so nasty to all of us. Shit, Howie was in *tears* one day. Truth is, I wouldn't be the favorite even if you never showed up. Avi likes pretty girls. He says I look like a boy." She picked up the cap and ran her hand through her short hair. "I don't get my period anymore," she whispered. "Not enough body fat. Are you eating this?" she asked, picking up her chopsticks and pointing them at my last dumpling.

"No, go ahead."

"You sure, woman?"

I nodded.

She didn't have any breasts to speak of. She had well-developed pecs instead. Even her skin had coarsened, and her jaw was as square as a boxer's, the human kind.

She ate the dumpling, dipped the rest of the fried noodles in duck sauce and ate those, and then drank the rest of her soup.

"What happened between Lisa and Howie to make him cry, Janet?"

"I don't know. Neither of them would tell me. Say, that's your cousin's necklace, isn't it?" she asked after wiping her mouth and dropping the napkin onto her plate.

I felt for the jasper heart. It looked as if it had been molded from melted crayons and the artist had left a thumbprint dead center before it hardened.

"Like I said, I'm staying at her place for now."

"And using her stuff?"

I shrugged. "What's the big deal? It's not like *she* needs it anymore."

"Ain't *that* the truth."

She got up, and Dashiell and I followed her out. On Sixth Avenue she handed me a card with my appointment on it and a pass to the gym at the Archives building, on Christopher Street.

"I trained Lisa, you know," Janet said, nodding.

"Lisa? Even though Avi—"

"Look, Rachel, if you haven't found out yet, you will. The man's got a Napoleon complex. Everything has to be done his way, no exceptions whatsoever. You have to draw the line *some*where, at least if you're going to keep your sanity you do."

"So he knew that Lisa—"

"Nah. It was our little secret." She winked. "Lisa said it helped her with sword class. Those mothers are *heavy*. You need strength here," she said, slapping her left shoulder with her right hand. "You'll see." Then she feinted a punch toward *my* shoulder and took off.

That evening I took Dashiell for a long walk along the waterfront. Playing with a flirty husky bitch, he seemed to forget the rest of the world existed. Later, after reparking the car, I read unfathomable Zen stories to him as he lay snoring at my side.

15

This Is Going to Hurt

I COULD HEAR the rain tapping lightly on the roof when I woke up. I told Dashiell to find the cordless phone and, when he had, dialed Lili.

"I was just thinking about you," she said, the way she almost always does.

"Me, too," I said. "That's what I was calling to say."

"Ted's working late tomorrow, some buyers in from out of town, I think. Why don't you come out? We can go to that nice Japanese place in Nyack."

"Can't," I told her, in a rush now that I'd gotten what I needed from the phone call. "I have to work."

"Bummer," she said.

"Maybe next week." I hung up without waiting for an answer.

Wednesday. Excellent. I had the car. Now I needed a driver. I dialed again.

"Paul?"

"Rachel? Is that you?"

"I'm sorry about the other day, running off like that. It's just that I remembered something I'd forgotten. An appointment I'd scheduled."

"I thought it must have been something important, for you to run off like that."

"I was wondering if I could make it up to you, buy you dinner?"

"Rachel, you don't have to—"

"How about tomorrow night?"

"Tomorrow?"

"Just say *yes*, okay?"

"Let me check."

I heard him put the phone down, but I couldn't hear him walking away. Maybe he was barefoot. Or his appointment calendar was right near the phone. Or he was pretending to check his calendar in order to save face.

"Yes," he said. "Consider yourself lucky. Tomorrow's okay."

"Great. I'll pick you up at the Club. Is five okay?"

"Rachel—"

"It was all my fault. Five. Okay?"

Once again, I hung up without giving the person on the other end of the line a chance to say another word.

It was eleven fifteen. Stewie was teaching a noon class, so Dash and I headed over to Bank Street T'ai Chi.

Avi had just finished practicing the form. "Do you have a moment?" I asked him. "I need to ask you something, about the note Lisa left." Show him proper respect, I thought, and he'll be putty in my hands.

"Are you familiar with the story of the young man who wanted to study Zen?"

"Oh, *please*."

" 'Have you had your breakfast?' the master asked him. The young man nodded, just the way *you* always do. He had. 'Then wash your bowl,' the master told him."

"So, what does that mean?"

But didn't I know what it meant? After all, Avi had announced that I was his new apprentice, a role I'd had experience with. I had learned dog training as an apprentice to another trainer. That meant I would get lots of private lessons, a chance to assist in class, that I'd answer the phone, do the bills and mailings, lick the stamps, sweep up, dust, pinch dead leaves off the plants, run out and buy him cigarettes, and wash the coffee cups after class because he thought ceramic cups were more friendly to the environment than Styrofoam, a man clearly ahead of his time.

"Did you want me to sweep up out here?" I asked. "Or vacuum your office?"

Avi sighed.

"That won't be necessary. We have someone to do that, Rachel," he said, as if I were a few logs shy of a full cord.

"Then will you answer my question?"

He merely waved his arm impatiently and headed for his office.

"Or not?" I said after he'd already closed the door.

"Being a de-tec-tive sounds like *fun*," my nephew Zachery had said the night I'd made my official announcement to the family.

Yeah, right.

Thank God our mother is dead, Lili had added, because if she weren't, *this* would have killed her.

I sat down on the studio floor, against a side wall, to wait. The students began to arrive at ten of twelve for the lunch-hour class, changing shoes in the hall and then sitting in the area between the office and the studio until they were called to begin. Stewie arrived late, changed his shoes, and after nodding to his students, turned to face the mirror and began to do the form. I joined the class, taking a place in the back.

Stewie's eyes, which should have been half closed and half open, darted nervously from side to side, watching his students in the mirror. He was watching me, too, but when his eyes met mine, his moved away quickly.

He spoke softly as we moved slowly through the form. The empty leg is yin, he said, but when you shift your weight into it, it becomes yang, yin and yang, dark and light, soft and strong, these are constantly changing.

I thought about the way a bitch plays with her puppies, moving gracefully from her role of natural authority to a submissive posture so that the puppies can play at being alpha, then taking charge again when the game is over, never leaving them with a false impression of the way things are.

I was hoping I'd end up at lunch with Stewie after class, the way I had with Janet. Clearly I wasn't the only one of us who was curious, but before I had the chance to change my shoes, he was gone. I never did get to ask him any questions or find out how he felt about my cousin Lisa. Not wanting to waste the rest of the day, I got another idea.

I waited until I was downstairs to use the phone, calling information first, for Howard Lish's number, then asking to see him, for an emergency. My calf, I told him, was throbbing and cramped.

Come right over, he said, not stuttering at all. I'll take care of it.

I smiled as I hung up and, Dashiell at my side, headed east, just past the HB Acting Studio, to the building where Howie Lish lived and worked.

"The crick is in my leg," I said when Howie, wearing a white jacket as if he were a dentist rather than a masseur, opened the door. "Instead of my neck."

"You're pushing yourself too hard," he said, turning and walking toward an open door just down the hall and on the right. "You're trying to learn t'ai chi too fast, working too many hours."

I heard the sound of a television set from somewhere else in the apartment. Howie closed the door to his office.

"Hop up on the table," he said. "Let me have a look at it." I signaled Dash to lie down in a corner of the room. Then I panicked. Had I told him which leg it was? I hoped not, because I couldn't remember. Luckily, my normal rocklike tension saved me. Howie began prodding the muscles in my right leg, and before I knew it, I was screaming. Then he squeezed the calf on my left leg, pressing his fat fingers in so deep they could have touched each other. Again, I embarrassed myself.

"Hey," I said. "Easy."

"It's only a matter of time until the other one goes into spasm," he said, as serious as an undertaker. "You're very tense."

I guess he'd be eligible for Mensa now that he'd figured that out.

"I only have time to work on your legs today. I have a client coming in twenty minutes. But you'll need to do more than just this if you want to stay out of trouble."

He handed me a cotton smock, telling me to strip from the waist down. Right, like guys weren't telling me that since I grew tits. Leaving my underpants on is sort of a rule I have when I'm around strange men. And if ever there was a strange man, it was Howie Lish. Wearing the smock, I got back up on the table. Now what? Was I supposed to call him? Or just lie around in my skivvies hoping he'd eventually return?

Howie came back into the room carrying a thick blue towel, which he laid over one leg, and a bottle of lavender-scented oil. Standing at my side, he put a strong, gentle hand on my back.

"Howie, I can't tell you how—"

"Shh," he said. "This is going to hurt."

I heard him rubbing his hands together. When they landed on my bare leg they were warm, wet, and slippery. He began to massage my leg in long strokes, first up the back of the leg, then on the sides, and after it had gotten warm, the blood circulating nicely, thank you, he began to dig into the calf, and I heard someone cry out in pain and realized afterward that since it hadn't been deep enough to have been him, it must have been me. Again.

Saying nothing, his hot, slimy hands never stopping, going back and forth between the painful kneading and poking and the delicious long strokes that ended right at the edge of my tiger-striped underwear, Howie worked on my legs for over half an hour. At the end he took my feet, one at a time, in his big, strong hands and did exquisite things to them. I was sure it couldn't be legal to feel this good.

"Better?" he asked.

"Wonderful," I told him. "Thank you."

"I'll go out so you can get dressed."

I pulled on Lisa's leggings, then turned. Howie was standing in the doorway. Had he just come back? Or had the little weasel been there all along? I picked up Lisa's turtleneck and put that on too, breaking eye contact with Howie for the moment the shirt slipped over my head.

"When you get home, take a long, warm bath," he said, as if nothing untoward had happened. "Not hot," he added. "Hot baths make you more tense." His face looked hot. At any rate, his nose and cheeks were as red as if he had been in a sauna. "You're pushing yourself very hard, physically and mentally. Your body gave you an important message today, to lighten up on yourself. You ought to pay attention to that. And I'd like to see you again on Friday."

I bet you would, I thought.

"I can fit you in at three thirty."

"Perfect," I said. I could always call and cancel later.

I wondered what Lisa had said to make him cry. I didn't think it would take much.

"You're probably eating badly, too," he said.

"What am I supposed to be, a vegetarian or something?"

Howie smiled. "No, but raw, organic vegetable juice can really help give you the stamina you need for t'ai chi. You don't need to be a vegetarian, but you certainly should watch your fat intake—"

Look who's talking.

"But I'm not—"

"It's not for your weight. Your weight is good. Fat's been linked to—"

"*Stop*. I'm feeling too good to hear the list of diseases you get from each food group. I read the papers. The trouble is, they change their minds every week or so. You know, one week it's oat bran, the savior of the human race, then it's selenium, or green tea or beta-carotene. You know what I'm saying, Howie?"

"I do," he said, shifting his weight and looking uncomfortable. "Sometimes you sound just l-like her," he said, looking down at his Fred Flintstone feet.

"You mean Lisa?"

Howie's face got all splotchy, and his neck flushed red. He nodded.

"It's hard to get a handle on her," I said. "We were cousins, but I hardly knew her. And now I hear so much about her, being at the school and everything. But it's inconsistent. Sometimes she sounds so special, so smart, so graceful, the way her parents saw her. Other times—" Something in Howie's eyes made me pause. "You'd want to toss her out the window."

Howie blinked once.

The doorbell rang.

Dashiell stood, ready if needed.

"Do you miss her, Howie?" I asked as he headed out of his office to answer the door. "Were you and Lisa close?"

He turned to face me. "Of c-course I m-miss her," he said, his voice as flat as Kansas. "She was my teacher—and a client."

"That's all?" I asked him.

"I-isn't th-th-that enough?"

He ought to do something about *his* tension, I thought. The man looked as if he were ready to implode.

"How much do I owe you for fixing Mr. Leg?"

The bell rang a second time.

"I'll catch you next time," he said, a kind of pain showing on his face that couldn't be fixed as easily as a bogus spasm could.

16

You Think Too Much

WHEN I LEFT Howie's, I headed for Lisa's. I'd decided I'd sort through her mail and check her answering machine messages and then reward myself with a bacon burger and some fries. I was feeling really tired, probably a fat deficiency.

The concierge handed me even more junk mail than was waiting for me upstairs, the stuff too big to fit in her mailbox, catalogs and magazines folded and held together by a fat rubber band. Just the volume of stuff started depressing me. If I liked paperwork, I would have become a CPA. By the time I'd gotten upstairs, I'd convinced myself, just as I did at home, that I could pitch out Victoria's Secret and L. L. Bean one day later.

The answering machine was flashing, but instead of rolling it back and listening to the messages, I picked up the cordless phone that sat next to it, walked over to the black couch under the windows, and dialed my aunt Ceil.

"Hello?" she said, her voice strong and gravelly.

"Ceil? It's Rachel. I was wondering if I could come and see you tomorrow afternoon. I have a favor to ask."

"Of course, tootsie. Come early. Stay late. I'll make us a little lunch. When can I expect you?"

"Is two okay?"

"Two is perfect, darling. See you then."

Was Ceil the only one in my family I had an easy time with because she had been married to my father's brother, so she wasn't a blood relative? Maybe, like dogs, people just got along better with others that were not from their own gene pool.

I meant to get up and listen to Lisa's messages, I really did, because the tenth law of investigation work is, You never know. I thought again about dumping the junk mail and doing whatever was appropriate with the rest of it. But I felt almost drugged. Perhaps it was the massage. With some of my tension gone, there was nothing left to hold me up.

I'd heard Dashiell going up the wooden steps. I'd heard the bed creak as he'd gotten onto it. I thought of joining him, but the black couch was so soft and inviting, and I was already there. So I leaned sideways, pulled up my legs, and fell immediately asleep, Lisa's cordless phone still in my hand.

When I woke up, it was dark in the apartment, and for a moment I had trouble remembering where I was. Dashiell was lying next to the couch now, and when I sat up, he looked up at me, reminding me that a dog has needs, too. I looked at my watch. It was after seven. I pulled myself together, and we headed for the waterfront so that Dashiell could stretch his legs and use his muscles before dinner.

We crossed over at Christopher Street and headed north, Dashiell running far ahead, ecstatic to be free to move, running back to check on me every few minutes.

There was a Great Dane wearing an American flag bandanna waiting up ahead, and in no time they were jumping in circles, eyes dancing, feeling each other's strengths and weaknesses as they practiced a dog version of Push Hands.

When I felt someone right behind me, I turned.

"Stewie. Hey."

It was my lucky day. I was now looking into the small, dark eyes of Stewie Fleck. He was wearing a heavy black turtleneck and black jeans, a beatnik in the age of grunge. When I turned, he smiled, and I could see the strain in it.

"I was going to practice the form out on the pier," he said, looking at his feet now, "but it's too crowded tonight. Avi says to be careful practicing outdoors, because someone might see you and challenge you."

That seemed a remote possibility to me where we were. The Greenwich Village waterfront was a gay pickup area, especially after dark. People came here to make love, not war.

"I was just going out for a bite to eat. You feel like some food, or a beer?" I asked him, never one to let a serendipitous opportunity slip through my fingers.

"Well, if—" he said, looking like one of those Fresh Air Fund kids seeing trees for the first time.

"Sure you do," I told him. "I know a great place. Dylan Thomas used to drink there. Of course, where didn't he used to drink?"

Stewie smiled his nervous smile. I took that as a yes and led the way. Ten minutes later we were seated at a booth at Chumley's, drinking beer, Dashiell lying under the table on my feet.

"So I was working as a carpenter, making cabinets, fixing things," Stewie said, continuing the story of his life he had begun as we'd crossed West Street, "living in Ohio of all places, and I'm not exactly happy, but I have no idea what I want to do with the rest of my life. I'm all of twenty then." He flashed me his tense little smile again. Like a lot of shy people, once he felt it was okay to talk, there was no stopping him, which was just fine with me.

"So one night," he continued, "I go to sleep and I have this dream that I'm walking in the woods and I meet an ancient man, right, and we begin to talk, we just sit on the ground and talk, and he says he's going to tell me the secret of life, right? Just like in all those shaggy dog jokes, you know, life is a bowl of cherries, those jokes? But when I wake up, I know he told me the secret, but I can't remember what it was. Jesus, I thought. Maybe I can go back to sleep and ask him again. But then I thought, No, you can't do that, if someone tells you the secret of life, you can't go back to them and tell them you forgot it, right?"

I laughed and tried to look fascinated. "So what happened then?" I asked.

"Get this, Rachel. I'm sitting there and I'm really depressed, and then I think, No big deal, I'll have to find it out for myself."

"Wonderful," I said, thinking this guy would be talking to a lamp-post if he hadn't run into me, the way this stuff was pouring out of him. His last conversation was probably when he ran into Adam and Eve as they were leaving the garden.

"And that was the beginning," he said. I sipped my beer, and our food arrived. "That's how I found t'ai chi." He sat back, nodding, really pleased with himself. "You take a lot on faith here," he said. "It's too dark to see what you're eating."

He had ordered the vegetarian chili. I had gotten a bacon burger, the bacon and the beef so rare it must have been only moments since they had their own dinner. It didn't occur to me until the first delicious bite that the sight of a fresh kill might offend Stewie. On the other hand, on my list of things to worry about, offending vegetarians doesn't even show up.

"How long after the dream did you come to New York?" I asked, hoping to catch up to the present before arthritis set in.

"There was this girl I met, said she was moving to California, so I went out there, too. But I had to wait about six weeks after she left, to finish up the jobs I had started. And when I got to where she said she'd be, she wasn't there." He took a spoonful of his chili. "I tried to find her, and when I couldn't, well, I was out of money by then, so I stayed anyway, and that's when I began to study t'ai chi. It was really popular out there. The yellow pages were full of schools."

"How did you end up in New York?"

"I met this guy who was out on the coast on vacation, and he was taking classes where I studied t'ai chi. People do that all the time, if they're serious. They don't take vacation from going to class. And after rounds one evening, I overheard him talking to another student, about the school he studied at in New York, and he started to talk to him about Avi. Two months later I was in New York. And two weeks after that I was working for the welfare department and studying t'ai chi on Bank Street, living in Greenwich Village."

"What about the carpentry?" I asked, noticing how rough and stained his hands were. "Do you still do that?"

"Why? Do you need some work done?"

"I might," I said.

"I still make things—boxes, bookshelves. I made the shelves in Avi's office, and the supply closet. I did Lisa's shelves for her, floor-to-ceiling, in her living room. When I have time, and someone I like asks, I build for them. I like to work with my hands."

"Nothing for Howie, or Janet?"

"Howie's always tight on money. He has, you know, a lot of responsibilities."

"Like what?" I asked. "He's married, he's got kids?"

"I told him once, whatever you need, I like to do the work. You just pay for the materials, labor's free. But he couldn't do that," he said. "No way."

"Too proud?" I asked.

Stewie shrugged.

"Nothing for Janet?" I asked, realigning my bacon burger as I did. "She's got a cash flow problem too?"

"Janet? What would she need bookshelves for? She practically lives in the gym."

"Really?"

"You don't get to look like Janet lifting weights three times a week. That's dedication. She competes, you know. She was Miss Tex Pecs before she came to New York." Stewie began to laugh. "I'm not sure of the *exact* title," he said. Then he sort of lost it, tilting his head back and sounding as if he were sneezing backward.

I looked up from my fries. Fleck was loosening up. Maybe it was the beer. I signaled the waiter to bring another round.

"She talks tough, Rachel, but she's a good egg, Janet. It's just that she's like a kid. She likes to do what she's not supposed to, get herself into trouble."

"Yeah, she seems like great fun," I said, picking up my pickle. "She ever get you into trouble?"

"Me? No. Not really. I got other stuff to do in my free time."

"What about Lisa and Janet? Were they friends?" I reached under the table so that Dashiell could clean my greasy fingers for me. "Did they hang out? Put glue on the master's chair? Become juvies together?"

"I wouldn't necessarily say *that*. Lisa was a serious student. She didn't have much time to socialize. Like me. Anyway, Avi says it's not appropriate for teachers to form personal relationships with their students. He says it interferes with the teaching process if you become emotionally involved."

"Even friendships?"

Stewie nodded.

"Avi says we should rely on ourselves, not on each other."

"So Janet and Lisa didn't spend any time together outside of class?"

"Lisa was at the school until all hours. Always working. Or staying up half the night studying. This is my *life*, she used to say, there's no room for anything else. Or any*one* else. And Lisa, she wouldn't go against Avi the way Janet does, doing something he wouldn't approve of. Not Lisa."

"She must have been very disciplined," I said.

"What about you?" Stewie asked. "What were you doing before—" He stopped in the middle. "Never mind," he said. "I just remembered. Now you're here. Eating dinner with me at Chumley's."

"This is true," I said, finishing my second beer. "Stew," I said, waiting for him to look up from his dinner. "I'm seeing my aunt and uncle tomorrow."

"Lisa's parents?"

I nodded. "I feel so confused about what happened. I was wondering, I mean, you worked with her, Stew, were you shocked by what she did? Did she seem troubled to you? Do you know of any problems she was having? I don't know how to talk to her parents. I don't know what to say to them."

Stewie looked down at his plate. "When I told you the dream I had, well, I don't think Lisa ever found herself wondering what to do with her life. She was so focused, this was the life she seemed to want, and it was the life she was living."

"But what about her personal life? Was that going well, too?"

"She could have had anything she wanted," he said, his eyes shining in the dark of the former speakeasy. "I don't get it. The truth is, nobody gets it, Rachel. It's a mystery."

"So she didn't seem unhappy near the end? There was nothing—"

Stewie shook his head. "I would hate to have to talk to her parents, because what could you say to someone who lost the one person they loved most? There's no way they'll ever get over it."

I skipped dessert. Stewie had some obscene chocolate thing that seemed to grow larger as he ate it. He said he lived on Bedford, but he'd walk me home. Dashiell walked a few steps ahead, the leash loose, automatically turning right on Hudson Street, toward home. Without thinking, I turned right, too, until I felt Stewie's hand on my arm.

"Where are you going?" he asked.

Lisa's place was to the left. I looked toward Dashiell, who had stopped when I did. Now they were both looking at me as if I were crazy.

"I wanted to pick up a muffin," I said, "for the morning."

Stewie nodded and walked me to Sacred Chow, which of course was closed. Then we turned around and headed for the Printing House, where I got to see Stewie's crunched-up, embarrassed little smile once more as we said good night.

I walked in through the front door, greeted Eddie, and walked out the side door. A few minutes later, driving around looking for a legal spot for the Taurus, I was thinking about Stewie Fleck.

There was a Zen version of his dream. Avi had told it to me one day during a private lesson.

"In the middle of the form, having gathered your energy, you return to the mountain. There you seek the teacher, but the answers you seek," he'd said, late one evening, "are already within you."

"What about the answers I need about Lisa?" I'd asked him.

"You think too much," he'd said. Then he'd turned north, toward the window Lisa had been pushed out of, and begun the form again.

17

What Do You Suggest?

CEIL WAS DRESSED to the nines, all in black, her white hair slicked back in a twist at the nape of her neck, the only color her bright red lipstick.

"Come, darling," she said, swooping me into her arms and then leading me to her sunny kitchen. "Let's eat."

Dashiell sneezed at her perfume, then padded along behind us, wagging his tail.

Over the table were pictures of my cousin Richie as a little kid. He must be somewhere in his late forties by now. "What do you hear from Richie?" I asked, more to be polite than out of any real interest. In truth, I was thinking only of the reason why I had come.

"That kid," she said, "what a hoot he is."

"How's his writing going?" I asked, digging into my salad niçoise.

"Writing? Writing? Is that what your mother told you?"

I nodded. "She said he moved to Key West to become a writer, like Hemingway. She even emphasized the writer part, meaning why don't *you* do something that would give your mother *noches*?"

Ceil roared. "She always worried about what other people would think. She had a cover story for everyone, even my son. You know, before you got married, she always told people you'd been engaged, but your fiancé had died in a tragic accident, so of course they wouldn't ask you anything." She laughed again. I felt my face flush.

"Oh, darling, I didn't mean to upset you. Except for funerals, we never see each other. I hardly know you now."

"I—"

"I know. I know. You're a busy professional. So, today we'll get acquainted again." She smiled and took a sip of her coffee. "Richie's not a writer, Rachel. He's a drag queen."

My eyebrows must have gone up.

"A female impersonator. Come on, cookie, you know what that is. He dresses up in women's clothes, he sings a little, he makes a nice living."

"My mother knew this?"

"Of course."

"And Richie, what, he just told you one day?"

"He never had to tell me, Rachel. I used to catch him trying on my bras when he was a kid, putting on nail polish, falling all over himself in my high heels. He even bought me a wig once, for Mother's Day, so that he could wear it when I wasn't home. He's too much, my Richie."

"So where did my mother get this story?"

She pricked a tomato with her fork and held it aloft. "When Richie was at Yale, he *did* talk about becoming a writer. He also talked about becoming an architect, a veterinarian, an engineer. It was all talk. I did think he might take up acting. They had a wonderful drama program at Yale, and I thought that would be right up Richie's alley. But he didn't take to it then. Of course, he does all sorts of skits now."

"So my mother fixated on the writing?"

"Why not? He did write a poem once. When he was ten. Your mother didn't make up the story from air. She put together a little this, a little that, some imagination, and her enormous pride. Your poor mother. That was her obsession, that everything should look just so." She popped the tomato into her mouth and chewed.

"Did Richie go to Key West right after Yale?"

"No, he lived in New York for a while, in Chelsea. He worked in a restaurant, he was a singing waiter, darling. And every winter he went to Key West. One winter, he bought a little place. And that was that."

"Does he know you know?"

"Sweetheart, he calls me for advice. Mom, he says, my skin is breaking out from the base. What do you suggest? Would aloe help? And he gives advice. Tells me what to wear. Tries to get me to color my hair. Mom, he said, last time I was down, for my eightieth birthday, Mom, he said, if you dyed your hair, you'd look ten years younger." She roared.

She didn't ask about the Jacobs case, and I didn't bring it up. After lunch, she showed me pictures of my cousin Richie on stage, as Liza Minelli, Judy Garland, and Marlene Dietrich.

"He has fabulous legs," I said.

"Takes after me." Ceil pulled up her skirt and stuck one long gam out from under the table for me to admire.

After lunch she went rummaging around in a closet and came up with a lace and velvet shawl wrapped in tissue paper. "This was your mother's," she said. "She gave it to me once when she came to visit. I'd like you to have it now."

"Ceil, I can't take it from you. It's too beautiful."

"Of course you can. It should be with you." She handed me the shawl. "You know, darling, your mother was just a human being. One day, it would be nice for you if you let go of some of your disappointment."

"I—"

She lifted one long-fingered, bony hand to silence me. "Do you remember the summer you stayed with me for a month, when you were eleven?" I nodded. "And do you remember Margaret?"

"Of course," I said. "How could I forget? That was my first job."

"I'd met her late one afternoon, the week before you came. I was admiring the ocean, talking out loud to myself. You know how I am. She asked if, as long as I was looking anyway, I'd watch her swim. At first I thought, What chutzpah, what a loony request. And then I saw the white cane folded up and lying on the corner of her towel, so I said yes, I'd watch. Stand on the shore, she said, and shout to me if I'm headed in the wrong direction. So I watched her swim. And when she came out—"

"You said, I have a very responsible young woman coming to stay with me next week, for the whole month of August, my niece Rachel, and she'd be delighted to meet you here every afternoon at five and watch you swim."

"We all need that," Ceil said, "someone to shout and tell us if we're headed out to sea. But when you can see," she said, picking up her coffee cup, "well, most of us don't have someone responsible standing on the shore to make sure we stay headed in the right direction. Now, come, I know why you're here."

I was truly amazed. I hadn't said a word about Lillian and Ted, not even on the phone.

"So let's take that adorable creature of yours to the beach." She turned to Dashiell, his big mouth agape in adoration as she spoke. "Aunt Ceil knows why you came to visit. For the same reason your mommy used to come when she was little. She loved the beach, just

294 / CAROL LEA BENJAMIN

the way you do," she said to him. "Marsha told me you showed up *wet* for your meeting with them," she said to me. "That's the girl I remember, I thought when she said it. Come," she said, talking to Dashiell again, "we'll take our walk."

"You have to give him what he needs," Ceil said later, as we watched Dashiell running along the sand. "You're responsible for him."

Of course, I didn't for a minute think she was talking about Dashiell.

"He always loved dress-up," she said, walking next to me but with her thoughts far away. "He liked to pretend he was something he wasn't. Some*one* he wasn't. He enjoyed that. He still does. I never told him to try to be anything different. People are who they are. I never tried to tell him what to do or not do, how to live his life. It's harmless, what he does. It gives him pleasure. He's my son, and I love him. That's all there is to it. That's what I told your mother, too. She thought I ought to *do* something. Do what? I asked her. Beatrice, I said, all I can *do* is alienate my son. No one wants to be told what to do. People have to handle their own lives, their own way."

I had come to talk about Lillian.

"Do you believe in fate, Rachel?"

"I don't know," I told her.

What do you suggest? I'd meant to ask. But what with one thing and another, I never did get around to it.

18

Follow That Cab

I WAS NEARLY dry by the time I arrived at the Club. Paul wasn't out front, but as I got out of the car to go get him, he appeared in the doorway. I winced. He was wearing a black T-shirt, a black jacket, and black slacks. As soon as the car began to move again, it would be aswirl with white fur. Dashiell, who was sitting behind the driver's seat, was shedding.

Without saying a word, I walked around to the passenger side, and Paul got in on the driver's side. Some things are easy to arrange with men. You never have to ask them to hold the remote either.

He got in, fastened his seat belt, then checked to make sure I'd fastened mine. "I thought we'd be alone," he said, looking toward the backseat, "so we could talk."

"You can talk in front of him. He's tight-lipped."

"Where to?" he asked.

"Forty-fourth, between Fifth and Sixth."

He gave me a funny look and began to drive. I looked out the side window to avoid obsessing about his strong, beautiful hands.

When we got to Forty-fourth, I told him where to pull over.

"We can't park here," he said. "Not unless you want to get towed."

"We're not parking," I told him. "We're waiting."

"For another couple?" he asked, looking disappointed.

"Sort of."

He nodded, watching me as I slid down a little in my seat, my eyes glued to the door of 17 West Forty-fourth. Perhaps it was the expression on my face that kept Paul Wilcox waiting in silence. As we sat there, I had murder on my mind.

He wasn't even there yet, but already I could almost feel my hands around his throat, choking the life out of him.

I could push my gun into his chest, tell him why, make him beg, then pull the trigger anyway.

Or I could poison him, slowly, painfully, with something impossible to detect.

Fuck it, I thought. As soon as he steps out the door, I'll have the driver gun the engine and run him down. My sister looks stunning in black. Come to think of it, who doesn't?

When he finally appeared, *she* was hanging on to his arm, smiling up at his face. He *had* lost weight. Even scrunched down in the seat, looking past Paul, I could see he was thinner. And wasn't that a new sport coat the bastard had on?

He leaned over and kissed the blond on the mouth, then his arm went up, and a cab pulled over to the curb for them.

"Follow that cab," I told my driver. But he did nothing. Unless you call staring something. "Follow that cab," I repeated. "And don't spare the horses."

"Ah, so," he said, nodding. He pulled out and caught up to the cab, which was waiting at the corner for the light to change.

"Good *job*," I told him.

Dashiell's tail beat against the backseat.

"I'm quite experienced at covert pursuits," he said.

"Is that right?"

"Exactly. My grandmother is dying to know where her neighbor, Mrs. Chiang, buys fish. She always finds the freshest fish for the least money, but she refuses to tell my grandmother where."

"How frustrating," I said as the light changed. We followed the cab onto Fifth Avenue and began weaving in and out of traffic to stay behind it as it turned east, then south, heading downtown. "So you and your grandmother follow Mrs. Chiang's cab?"

I thought we were going to lose Ted and the blond when their cab went through a changing light, but Paul zipped right after it, risking a ticket.

"Not exactly," he said.

"Meaning?"

"We follow her rickshaw."

"Ah, so," I said as we careened toward the Manhattan Bridge. And me without my passport, I thought, but the cab kept heading down-town, turning a few blocks later into Chinatown. After an impossible final few minutes trailing behind the cab through the crowded, twisty, narrow, one-way streets, it stopped at 63 Mott Street, outside of Hong Fat. I ducked way down as the cab door opened.

"You can get up. They're inside now," my driver said.

He was a fast study.

"Thanks," I said, as casually as if, instead of going through a red light and driving like a maniac, he'd just held a door for me or lit my cigarette.

"Do you have anything to tell me?" he said, turning sideways to face me, an inscrutable expression on his face.

"Yeah," I said. "Pull in as much as you can and cut the engine."

"That's it?" He waited patiently, his eyebrows raised.

"We're eating Chinese," I told him.

"Let me guess. At Hong Fat?"

"Don't be ridiculous," I said, unzipping my teddy bear backpack and pulling out my cell phone. "We'd be towed in a nanosecond if we parked here." I called information for the number of Hong Fat and, before dialing it, smiled at Paul and in my sweetest voice asked him what he'd like for dinner. He laughed so hard tears came to his eyes.

"Surprise me," he said when he'd regained his composure.

"No problem."

I dialed Hong Fat.

"I'd like an order to go, please. No, delivery. Well, it's not exactly an address. I'm parked across the street in a black Ford Taurus. *T* as in *to go*, *A* as in *appetizer*. Taurus. A car. Car. *C* as in *chow mein*. Yes. An order of steamed dumplings with oyster sauce. Do you want soup?" I asked Paul. He shook his head. "We'll skip the soup tonight. One order of kung po chicken and one crab with ginger and scallions. White rice or brown?" I asked Paul, but he just waved his hand at me. "White rice," I said into the phone. "And chopsticks, please. Thank you."

"Chopsticks okay?" I asked him.

He merely stared at me.

"How about a drink before dinner?"

I didn't wait for a response. I reached back to the floor behind his seat and pulled out a plastic shopping bag. I handed him a bottle of merlot and a corkscrew, and I held the two plastic glasses.

As if he ate dinner in a car every night of his life, he anchored the bottle between his legs, peeled off the foil that surrounded the cork,

298 / CAROL LEA BENJAMIN

and began to twist the corkscrew carefully into the center of the cork, which a moment later came out with a satisfying pop.

He filled the glasses and took one for himself.

"To you, Dog Paddle," he said, touching his plastic glass to mine.

We sat back and sipped our wine. I thought about music, but Dashiell was asleep and I didn't want to drown out the sounds of his snoring. I had thought about candlelight, too, but there really wasn't anyplace safe to put candles. I'd checked it out.

When the confused-looking little man in the white jacket came out of Hong Fat and looked around, Paul rolled down his window and motioned him over to the Taurus. I leaned over with the money, but Paul brushed my hand away, taking some folded bills from his pants pocket and paying for the food himself. The waiter said something I couldn't understand, and then Paul nodded and laughed. He pulled the bag in through the open window and turned back to me. "So, how do you want to do this?" he asked.

"One course at a time, starting with the appetizer," I said, opening the bag and pulling out the dumplings and the little clear plastic container of dipping sauce.

"Would you like to tell me what this is all about?"

My mouth was full of dumpling. I shook my head no. "I thought we were going to talk about Lisa," I said around the dumpling. "You promised."

He took a bite of dumpling. "You want to talk about your *cousin*?"

"I do."

"This is delicious. How did you find this place?"

"It was recommended, so to speak, by someone I thought I knew."

He refilled our wineglasses.

"Seriously, Paul, I—"

"She wanted to marry," he said, leaning back and gazing out the windshield. "She said it was time to formalize our commitment to each other. I told her I wasn't ready." He turned toward the food, hoisting the final dumpling with his chopsticks. Then, chopsticks poised, as if he were about to conduct an orchestra, he looked at me. "Okay?" he asked. There was a flash of white between us. I could hear Dashiell swallowing the dumpling behind me.

"You said *okay*. It's his release word."

"The chicken next?" he asked, as if nothing untoward had happened.

"But you loved her, didn't you?" I asked, thinking about the jasper heart necklace and the heart bracelet, thinking about all those roses.

Paul turned away from me and looked out the side window. Sitting on the sidewalk, to the right of Hong Fat, there was an unshaven, disheveled-looking man leaning against the wall, a cigarette dangling from his crusty lips. He wore a purple sweater that was too big for him and was frayed at the bottom, stained, wide-legged brown pants, shoes without laces. In one hand he held a live crab.

He put the crab down on the sidewalk.

"Come here, Donny," he said in his gravelly voice.

The crab didn't budge.

"Goddamn you to hell, Donny," he shouted at the crab. "I said *come*. When the fuck're you gonna learn to mind me?"

He took the cigarette from his mouth and, holding it between two stained fingers, touched it to the rear end of the crab. I grabbed Paul's arm and squeezed it.

"Tha's a good boy, Donny," he said as the crab moved forward. "See," he said, leaning down into the crab's face, "it ain't so hard to be a good boy."

He picked up Donny by one claw and quickly dumped him into a paper bag that he had anchored under his legs, struggled to his feet, and holding the bag out in front of him, staggered down the block.

I didn't feel hungry anymore, and apparently neither did Paul, because neither of us picked up the bag to take out any more of the food.

"What did she say?" I asked. "My cousin Lisa?"

"That she had wanted to bring me into her family, to have my children, for us to grow old together."

"And when you told her you weren't ready, she didn't want to see you anymore?"

"No," he said, looking straight ahead again, as if he were driving instead of parked. "I didn't want to see her after that."

"Why not?"

"It had all been spoiled," he said. He looked back toward the street, but the little man with the crab was gone.

"But you still loved her," I insisted.

"Yes," he said. "She was . . ." He looked down, into his lap, the chopsticks still in his right hand. "I had hoped . . ."

He took off his glasses, placing them on the dashboard, and put his fingertips over his eyes. I don't know what got into me then. Maybe it was all the walking in Lisa's shoes. Once again, I reached over and slid my arms around his neck. But this time, it was different. When he moved his hands away and looked at me with those hurt, dark eyes, I leaned closer and kissed him. My lips gently brushed one cheek, then the other. When I kissed his eyes, I tasted the salt of a tear. Then I felt his chopsticks against my back as he embraced me, his other hand on my neck, his long fingers reaching into my hair. I felt a familiar heat starting and spreading quickly, as if someone had dropped a match in straw. Live in the now, Avi had said. So I did. I sank into it and let it happen.

That's when something caught my eye. Over Paul's shoulder, I could see them as they came out of Hong Fat and stood just across from where we were parked, kissing. They talked quietly for a moment, then Teddy's arm went up, for a taxi.

I pulled away from Paul and ducked.

He put his glasses on and turned.

"Why do I get the nagging feeling you're using me?"

"Because I am."

"I thought as much. Follow that cab?" he said.

"Wait until they *get* one," I told him.

You had to give him this. The man was a good sport.

Men like this don't grow on trees, my mother would have said.

But only if he were Jewish and a professional man.

A cab stopped. We took off after it. Ten minutes later, I knew where the blond lived. Had I been alone, I could have rushed in and told the concierge she'd dropped her pen on the street and gotten her name. Or I could have waited in the car for my brother-in-law to emerge.

And then what?

"Rachel?"

He touched my cheek with the back of one hand.

I had gone to Sea Gate to ask about my sister's situation, to find out if Ceil thought I should say something, or do something, to see if between us we could think up a way to prevent the shattering of my sister's marriage, of her life. Interfering, after all, was my family's stock-in-trade.

Leave them alone, Ceil would have said.

But, I would have said, in my usual articulate fashion.

Exactly, darling, she probably would have told me. Butt out. It's not your life. It's not your problem. Let it go.

What on earth had I been thinking?

"Let's go home," I said.

"And where is that?" Paul asked, his voice as soft as the fur between Dashiell's round brown eyes.

"I've been staying at my cousin's," I said.

"I thought so."

"You did?"

"You don't have anything on that didn't belong to Lisa. All finished here?"

I nodded.

Paul drove to Lisa's and found a spot that was good for the next day. On our way across the street to Jimmy Walker Park, we pitched the Chinese food into a corner trash basket. Let some poor homeless person who didn't know Donny eat the crab. I certainly couldn't.

Leaning against the fence, watching as Dash left notes for the other neighborhood dogs, *I was here, and here, and here,* I wished I were still a dog trainer and that the man whose shoulder was touching mine were really a date and not part of a criminal investigation.

I'm sorry. Lisa.

When I'd told him about the note, he'd thought it had been written to him.

But why would Lisa have been the one apologizing?

Of course, if it had been the other way around, if he had done the asking and Lisa had been the one to refuse, then her note might have been an apology to Paul for turning him down.

Why had she?

She hadn't brought him home. Had she been worried about Daddy's disapproval? She was still dependent on him, still taking lots of his money so that she could live the way she wanted to.

The Village, the Village, David had said, so he'd bought her a condo. But at what price?

None of the ubiquitous concierges was at the desk, so I used my key to get into the lobby. I picked up Lisa's mail. There were still bills coming in, postcards and letters from real estate brokers asking her to call them should she want to sell, coupons for a free car wash or half-priced lunch, and the usual pile of mail-order catalogs. Upstairs, I unlocked Lisa's door and dumped the new pile of mail on the little blue table to the right of the door, right next to the old pile, which looked tall enough to topple over.

Paul took off his shoes and put them against the wall, under the coat hooks on the wall to the left, then went to give Dashiell some dog biscuits and make us tea. I hung my jacket and backpack on one of the hooks.

I could hear Dashiell crunching loudly, the hiss of the boiling water as it was poured into the teapot, water being poured into the sink. The first potful was to warm the pot. The second potful brewed the tea.

"Honey?"

"What?"

He poked his head into the living room, smiling.

"Honey in your tea?"

"Oh. Sure," I told him.

I heard the spoon against one cup, then the other.

We sat on the black couch in the dark living room, neither of us touching the tea he had made us.

"Do you have a life of your own, Dog Paddle?"

"Not lately," I said.

I heard Dashiell on the steps, then I heard the bed sigh as he climbed on, circled, and lay down to sleep.

"You look tired," he said. "I should go."

I turned and looked at him, his eyes shining in the light that came in from the window. One thing about New York City, it never really gets dark.

"I had fun tonight," I told him.

"Me, too. You're"—he stopped and laughed—"you're not like anyone I know."

"Not even . . . my cousin?"

"Especially not your cousin."

"Well, we were—"

"*Distant* cousins," he said, finishing my sentence.

He leaned in and kissed me, gently, on my lips.

Okay, he was completely adorable, but no way was I going to bed with this man. I hardly knew him.

"How are we different, me and Lisa?"

"You have a sense of humor," he said, removing the lavender string from the little braid and undoing the braid with his long fingers. "Warped, but clearly evident."

If I were *truly* walking in Lisa's shoes, shouldn't I reconsider?

The trouble with sex was where it might lead.

First I'd go to bed with him, next thing I knew, I'd be letting him touch the parts of my body that never got suntanned, then I might start necking with him in the car until all hours, I'd let him hold my hand in the movies, and who knows, one fine day after that, I might give him my phone number.

What kind of a girl did he think I was?

"Come on," he said, pulling me up from the couch. He held my hand and walked me to the stairs. He led the way up and gently guided me to a spot near Dash. When he leaned down, my steely resolve took a powder. Even sitting, my knees felt weak. I closed my eyes. That funny brush fire had started up again and was spreading fast.

He picked up the pillow and fluffed it and then stood straight again.

"*Shuijiao hao,* Dog Paddle," he whispered. "Don't let the bedbugs bite. Stay put, *xiao yue.* I'll see myself out."

"What did you say?" I asked him.

"How would I know?"

He grinned, letting me see those cute dimples again.

"I better go," he said.

"See," I said in the dark, "it ain't so hard to be a good boy."

"That's what you think," he answered.

You had to love this man. Or was the delicious rush I was feeling just the *feng shui* of Lisa's apartment?

"Before you go . . ."

"You need?"

"Tea. That nice cup of tea you made me."

"It'll be cold by now. I'll make you a fresh cup."

I waited until I heard the water running before opening the night-stand drawer and feeling around in the dark for what I knew was there. When I heard him coming up the stairs, I quietly closed the drawer.

He put the tea on the nightstand.

I was waiting for him to kiss me again, but instead he just touched my cheek, turned, and headed down the wooden steps.

I ached to call him back.

I slid quickly off the bed and went to the top of the stairs, just in time to see Paul lean over the little blue table, pick up an envelope from the pile of Lisa's mail, and slip it into his jacket pocket. Then he put on his shoes, tied the laces, and reached for the door.

I heard the knob squeak. It needed oiling.

I watched the door open, then close.

Damn. Why hadn't I opened Lisa's mail? I had to see what he had taken.

At any cost.

I tore down the stairs, praying he'd still be in the hall. Not knowing what I'd do or say, only knowing I had to get that envelope, I pulled the door open. There he was, just standing there, facing me, his hands at his sides.

"I couldn't go," he muttered.

"I know," I said, my hands around his neck, pulling him back inside.

As I backed into the living room, he was kissing me, my eyes, my mouth, my neck. He took one of my hands from behind his head and pressed the palm to his lips. I could feel his heat on me, and my own, setting me on fire.

"We can't," I moaned into his neck.

There had to be another way to get that letter back, I thought. Hell, I could just ask for it.

"Of course we can," he said, "I'm a coach. I'll see us through."

And then we were on that soft black couch.

Was it my grandmother Sonya, right before Hannukah, who had said, To receive everything, one must open one's hand and give? Or was it Taisen Deshimaru?

Either way, I opened one hand and held it up for Paul to see what was in it while I slipped the other hand into his pocket. He took the foil-wrapped condom I had taken from Lisa's nightstand and put it carefully on the floor next to the couch, where he could easily find it when he needed it. Then he took off his glasses, folded them, and placed them there, too. While he did that, I stuffed the envelope that had been in his pocket between two of the couch cushions. Then, the lamppost light shining in on us like moonlight, he began to take off my clothes.

Later we moved upstairs. Dashiell grunted as I slipped into bed next to him. Paul said he had to go, but apparently he didn't mean immediately. Once again I opened my arms to him, even though it was patently clear that this time there were no pockets to frisk in his outfit.

No one could ever accuse me of not giving my all to the job.

It was past eleven when he finally got up to leave. I strained to hear his bare feet on the stairs. As he got dressed, Lisa's place began to seem so lonely I could hardly stand it.

I slipped out of bed and went to the head of the stairs, figuring I'd snag one more good-night kiss. But the door was already closing.

I thought of tearing after him again, leaving myself not a shred of dignity in the bargain, but something else happened, something that made me freeze in place.

I heard a key slipping into the lock. Holding tight to the railing, I was barely breathing when the tumbler turned over.

I suddenly felt chilled. I went downstairs and pulled the velvet shawl from my backpack, slipping it around me as I walked into the dark living room.

I walked over to the couch and slid the envelope out from between the cushions.

Lisa and Paul had been lovers, I told myself, trying to stop my heart from pounding.

Of course he'd have her apartment keys.

That didn't mean he had her work keys.

Did it?

19

She Rolled Her Eyes
When She Read It

SITTING ON LISA'S couch, I tore open the envelope I had retrieved
from Paul's pocket and by the light of the lamppost coming in through
the windows discovered what it was that Paul Wilcox had not wanted
me to see. As soon as I had, I went through the rest of the mail,
finding yet another real surprise.

I pushed the play button on Lisa's answering machine, listening to
the lonely sound of the dial tone as I got dressed. Then I woke Dashiell, locked up, and took the stairs down to the lobby.

"Ms. Alexander?" the concierge said as soon as he saw me. "Wait
up. I have something for you."

"For me?"

"Yeah. I'm sorry I didn't catch you on your way in. I must have been
on my break. I see he's back," he said, handing me a bouquet of roses.
"These came this afternoon. I guess he wanted you to have them, you
know, before."

"What are you talking about?" I asked, looking for a card and not
finding one.

"The old boyfriend. I mean, Mr. Wilcox. I guess he wanted you to
get those before he came over," he said. Then he began shining up his
brass name tag with the heel of his hand to distract me from the fact

that, according to his job description, he was out of line in commenting on my personal life. Since I didn't raise my eyebrows or inhale sharply, he looked back up after a moment.

"You mean *Mr. Wilcox* sent these, Eddie? There's no card."

"Wouldn't be the first time," he said. He leaned over the high desk. "After he and Ms. Jacobs split," he said, "he got pretty weird. Used to stand across the street, the other side of the ball field, so he'd like be out of the way, looking up at her window." He shook his head. "He must of had it real bad for her, to do that. No chick's worth *that,* far as I'm concerned, but, hey, not everyone thinks the same, am I right?"

"What are you talking about?" I asked him.

He leaned over the counter. "Well, I guess they had some kind of fight, you know, a breakup, like over the holidays. But he kept coming around for a while, asking if Ms. Jacobs was home. But when I went to ring her, he always said, Never mind, and he'd just leave. I was really embarrassed for the guy, coming around like that but not even calling up. It was pretty humiliating."

"And he'd go wait across the street, like until she walked the dog?"

"No, it was way later, like after midnight. Ms. Jacobs, she never walked Charlie that late unless she worked late and Charlie's last walk was the walk home. This was when my shift was over. Twelve thirty, one o'clock."

"When you were leaving for the night?"

"Yeah, right. I'd see him, not right here, you know, not so obvious, but way on the other side of the ball field, where the bums hang out?"

"You mean the boccie court?"

"Around there, right. I'd see him, you know, lurking in the shadows, like leaning on a tree, a baseball cap pulled low over his forehead, like I wouldn't recognize him, right? It was real dramatic, like something out of a movie, you know what I mean, the ex-boyfriend watching the building, standing there all alone, just staring like that. Gave me the creeps."

"But he never came late, used a key to get in?"

"No, ma'am."

"How do you know?"

"We're covered here twenty-four hours. If the night man is late, I wait. We never leave the door uncovered. I would have seen him."

Of course, he had missed me coming in with Paul.

"He just stayed there and watched? How long?"

"From, you know, after they broke up to until she died. Sad thing, about her dying, your cousin. Such a pretty girl. Always considerate, too. Not like some of them," he said, tilting his head toward the elevator doors to indicate those residents who were less considerate than my cousin Lisa.

"I meant, how long did he stand there? Ten minutes? An hour?"

"Oh, that I couldn't tell you, Ms. Alexander. I don't know how long he was there because I stay behind the desk, you know. So I only noticed him when I was leaving. But figure it was winter, right, so how long could he a stood it out there in the cold?" He shrugged his shoulders. "Musta been really stuck on her, your cousin, to take the breakup so hard."

"You mean to stand out there in the cold watching her windows?"

"Yeah, and all the stuff he sent."

"Stuff?"

"The flowers, for example. A half dozen roses, sometimes a dozen, two, three times a week. All like this, with no card," he said, pointing to my roses. "The delivery guy would have his slip with Ms. Jacobs's name and the address, but there was never one of those little envelopes pinned to the cellophane. Like Ms. Jacobs was fooled. You know what I mean?"

I nodded.

"There were presents, too. I mean, money was no object. Little packages used to come, UPS, just her name and address on them, never a return address. She worked late sometimes, Ms. Jacobs, so I'd hold them here for her. Once she opened one in front of me. It was, you know, from Tiffany's, in that little blue box they have, with a white ribbon tied in a perfect bow on top, kind of thing you women go crazy for, am I right? But Ms. Jacobs, she didn't go crazy for it. She was *pissed*. 'Can I leave this with you, Eddie?' she said, and she left the box and the ribbon for me to put in the trash, but, you know," he leaned over again and whispered, "I didn't. I took it home. I'm saving it for my girlfriend's birthday. I'll get her something, put it in the Tiffany box, you know what I mean?" He winked.

I forced a smile. "So what was in it? What'd he send her?"

"A silver bracelet, with a heart on it, and some writing. I didn't get to see what it said, but she, your cousin, she rolled her eyes when she read it, put it back in the little blue bag, and stuffed it in her pocket. There was some other stuff too, but that was the only one she opened here. That was the last one," he said. "That one came right before she did it, a day or two before."

"And then afterward, Mr. Wilcox wasn't around? You never saw him again?"

"Not until tonight, forty, forty-five minutes ago, when he left."

"Thanks, Eddie."

Lisa's daddy had done well by her. The Printing House was like living in the fucking Plaza. They had maid service, if you wanted it, and you could drop off your laundry and dry cleaning at the desk and have it back, clean and ready, by the time you got home from work. If you needed gossip, protection, opinions about your private life, that was available, too. I wondered if you could put your shoes out in the hall at night and find them back and polished in the morning.

"Can you hold the flowers another minute for me, Eddie. I forgot something upstairs."

"Sure I can. Anything you say, Ms. Alexander. Anything to help."

Back at Lisa's apartment, I took the steps two at a time, opened the second drawer of Lisa's jewelry box, and took the silver bracelet out of the robin's-egg-blue bag. I opened the clasp and put it on, feeling the silver warm up where it was touching my skin.

I turned the heart over and read the inscription.

There wasn't a scratch on it, no patina from use. Lisa hadn't worn the bracelet. But I would. Like it or not, I had taken over where she'd left off.

Down in the lobby, I picked up the roses. Outside, where Eddie could no longer see me, I lifted them to my face and inhaled their perfume.

Never, I remember Frank saying, holding my shoulders and looking into my eyes as he spoke, never go to bed with a suspect until you find out who the murderer is.

I had nodded dutifully.

And it's someone else, he'd added.

Right, Frank, I'd said. And what number law is that?

Sex is no laughing matter, he'd said, shaking his head. In this job, it can kill you.

Who did I think I was, walking down Hudson Street with a dozen roses in the crook of my arm, fucking Miss America?

When I got to the corner, I pitched the bouquet into the trash basket. Then Dashiell and I headed home.

20

I Don't Know Anything for Sure

I OVERSLEPT ON Thursday morning. There was barely time to call Lisa's mother and check out my landlords' house before getting to school for a noon instructor's session with Avi.

Once a week or so, Dashiell and I went through the Siegals' town house to make sure that no homeless person had noticed it was empty and decided that sleeping indoors under crisp percale sheets would be preferable to sleeping in a cardboard box on a grate on the sidewalk. I even checked the smoke alarm, which was admittedly ridiculous since, should it go off, no one would be there to hear it. But Norma had a thing about smoke alarms, and in New York City you don't argue over an easy job that gets you a terrific place to live at an affordable rent.

Everything was covered with dust and grime. When I got back to the cottage, I called the cleaning service and arranged for them to come the first of May, which is when the Siegals usually showed up to spend a month or two in the city before heading out to the beach. And in an extravagant gesture, I told them I'd like my house cleaned as well this time.

Wearing my own clothes, and nothing of Lisa's, I headed for Bank Street. Once inside, I ran up the stairs, following behind Dash. Rounds had started, and I walked in on a startling scene. There were

Janet, Stew, and Howie, each with a string of bubble gum running from the tip of the nose to the *t'an t'ien*, a spot a couple of inches beneath their belly buttons.

"Nose-navel alignment," Avi said without turning. I watched him watching me in the mirror. "Gum's on the coffee table. Chew it first." Just like my mother, I thought, always assuming I had the mental prowess of an idiot.

"The gum will remind you to keep your nose where it belongs," he added, rather personally, I thought. My nose was everywhere, usually in someone else's business, and that was precisely where I wanted it.

After class the other teachers all went to change their shoes and get back to work. "Gotta run," Janet said, looking at her watch. She caught my eye and winked, mouthing, "See you at five." When they had all gone, Avi motioned me to follow him into his office.

"How is your project coming along, Rachel?" he whispered, even though we were all alone.

"I don't know anything for sure," I said.

"Excellent," he said, then he sat and turned his full attention to his computer.

It was one thirty. If I was going to get to Sea Gate on time, I had to hustle. After passing muster with the guard at the gate, I headed not for the Jacobses' house but to the beach. Marsha was already there, standing by the gate, a scarf covering her hair, a bag of groceries in her arms. I parked the car and went to join her.

"I told David I had to do some shopping," she said, hiking up the bag of food and looking terrified. "What did you want to tell me?"

I took the bag of groceries and set it down on the ground. "Walk with me," I said, looking down at her stockings and heels after I did so. She slipped off her shoes, leaving them next to the bag of groceries. I took off my running shoes and sweat socks and gave them to her to put on, feeling the coolness of the sand as I did.

She took my arm, and we walked down the beach, then headed to our right, where the spit of land that is this private community abuts Gravesend Bay.

"I wanted to see you without David because I thought that if you were alone—"

"David would be very upset with me if he knew about this. Very angry."

"Why is that, Marsha?"

I felt the envelopes I had brought with me in my pocket, all that was left of Lisa's mail after I'd pitched the catalogs and junk mail and filed the bills for her parents to deal with later.

"Certain things, he says, belong in the family, only in the family." She lifted her free hand and wiped her cheeks. "But I know you can't really help us if you don't know the truth. Your aunt Ceil said we should trust you completely. But we haven't done that. We've kept secrets from you."

I took the envelopes from my pocket, the one I'd slid out from between the couch cushions after Paul had left and the one I'd found in the pile of mail I'd gone through later.

"What is that?" she asked.

I showed her the contents of both envelopes.

"I knew that one day I would have to talk to you myself. I am only ashamed that I waited for you to call."

For a moment, there was only the sound of the seagulls, their beaks wide open as they cawed loudly to each other.

"When you asked about Lisa's note to us—"

"The suicide note?" I asked.

Marsha nodded. We walked past the jetty, where there was a small pool of water caught between the rocks and the sloping shore. Dashiell began fishing for crabs, and I called him to follow us as we slowly headed toward the bay, the light so bright it was difficult to see.

"We had seen her several times in the months before, and there had been many phone calls, more than usual. She was usually so busy, she'd only come on the holidays, and only call once a week. Sometimes less. Her father would try to call her in between, but he would only get the answering machine. She worked such long hours at the school, she couldn't return her calls the same day. Sometimes not for several days. David would get impatient and call her at school, too, but there they do not answer the phone when they are teaching or practicing t'ai chi, and Lisa told us they were always doing one or the other."

"But then something changed?"

"Yes. She started calling more often, then she came to see us, because she had something on her mind."

I stopped walking, loosened my arm from Marsha's, and turned to face her.

"China," she said. "Again, China." She began to weep, covering her face with both hands.

I put the airline ticket, one-way, to Beijing and the signed contract to sell the condo back into my pocket, then took off my jacket and spread it on the sand for Marsha to sit on so that she wouldn't ruin her good coat. And for a while, my arm around her, she cried against my shoulder. When she sat back up, eyes swollen and pink, her lips were shaking, her hands, too.

"Tell me what happened, Marsha."

"Lisa came to visit us, at the holidays, for Hannukah, in December, and she told us she was going to go to China."

I reached for her hands.

"Not to visit," Marsha said, her voice cracking. "To live."

When I'd first seen the envelope from a travel agent, I had assumed it was like the ones I get, junk mail, a brochure touting a guided tour to Africa or a discount trip to Rome with Mr. Italy. I'd assumed, even though the fifth law of investigative work is, Don't jump to conclusions. I'd also assumed all those letters from real estate brokers were like the ones my landlords always got, letters that started, "Dear Owner, If you've been thinking of selling your apartment, if you've ever wondered what it would be worth in today's seller's market . . ." But one of them had been a countersigned contract to sell the condo Lisa's father had bought for her so that she could walk to work.

"This didn't make her father very happy, did it?"

"He was wild. Just like the first time. Saying the same things. Only now Lisa was a woman, not a child. She didn't *need* his permission, his approval. Perhaps that's what she *wanted*, for her father to approve of her decision, to give her emotional support. But that is not what happened."

Her head was down, the scarf covering part of her face; her arms clutched each other, and she rocked as she spoke.

"She, too, flew into a rage. 'Daddy,' she said to him, 'I'm a grownup now. This time you can't force me to do what *you* want me to.' 'It's for your own good,' he said, just like before, when she was a student, a young girl, 'for your protection.' She jumped up from where she was sitting, Rachel. 'This time I'm going,' she said, cold, like the inside of a refrigerator. And she was gone. Out of the house. I thought we wouldn't hear from her or see her for a long time. Or ever. I thought she might just go, and never write us. But she called, she pleaded, she explained, she wanted so much for David to let her go with his blessing. She was not so grownup that she didn't still need this from her father."

"What did *you* say to Lisa?"

"I gave her my approval. Of course, I thought my heart would break, that if she went to China, that would be the worst tragedy that could occur to me, to have Lisa so far away. What did I know then about tragedy?"

She looked away for a moment, toward the shore where gulls were landing and taking off and Dashiell was constructing a long, curvy trench, shoveling the sand with his big front paws and backing up as he dug. When she turned back to me, her cheeks were flushed, her eyelashes wet with tears.

" 'David,' I told him, 'you have to let her go. She's not a child.' When we were alone, he wouldn't talk to me, not about this, but I said to him, 'David, if you let her go, you will still have her. And if you don't, if you make her defy you in this, you will lose her.' "

"What did he say when you told him that?"

"He said, 'How could she do this to me?' You see where it is, was, between them?"

I nodded.

"It didn't get resolved?" I asked, thinking of the sad way things can be in families.

Marsha shook her head.

"And that's why you thought the letter was written to you, or to David?"

"Yes. I feel my daughter was torn in half, wanting so much to study in China, to live there. And wanting so much to please her father. To have his love. I believe we did this to her, Rachel, this terrible thing. That the apology she wrote was for hurting her father so much. I don't think Lisa could do that. She was never able to defy her father. So, I think, perhaps she changed her mind, but that made her so unhappy—"

"And you hired me—?"

"We were hoping," she said very slowly, "that you would find out—"

"Something else," I said. "Another reason for this tragedy."

"Another reason," she repeated. "So that we could begin to make peace with this one day." She looked back toward the ocean where Dash was now racing back and forth where the waves hit the sand.

More than anything, I wanted to help. But what could I say—that the note may have been written to her and David, but that I didn't believe it was a suicide note? That I felt this, I didn't feel that, or I thought this happened, or this didn't happen. Not knowing how to comfort her, I sat there biting my lip until I tasted blood.

"It took courage for you to be able to say what you did. A lot of courage," I finally said. "This should help me find out what we need to know."

"Do you really think so?"

I nodded.

I followed her back to the gate where her groceries and shoes sat.

" 'Why did she want to go over there to live with those goddamn Communists?' he asked me a few days ago. 'To ride a bicycle to work. Here she could have had a car. I would have bought her a car. She knew that. I would have given her anything she wanted.' "

When she handed me back my shoes, I put my arms around her.

"I'll call you as soon as I can," I said.

She nodded, picked up the groceries, and headed toward home.

When I turned around, Dashiell was pleading with his eyes. I waited until Marsha was crossing the street, then, leaving my shoes and socks near the gate, I headed slowly down the beach, toward the surf. We headed back to the point, where the bay flows into the ocean and where you can see the Verrazano Bridge looming over the narrows, connecting Brooklyn to the once isolated Staten Island.

I stopped and picked up a short, fat driftwood log, which I swung back behind me and let fly into the ocean. Dashiell dove into the chilly water, all his attention on the task at hand.

I sat where the sand was hard but not wet, rubbing my hand on the cold sand and feeling it adhere to my skin. It's not only at a crime scene that we leave something and take something away. I had come here with Lillian and Ceil after my mother had died, to scatter her ashes in the ocean.

"She always wanted to travel," Ceil said as the ashes arced gracefully across the surface of the water. "But with two young children and no money, you can't go far. Then with your father dying so young, poor man, only fifty-two, where would she go by herself? And then," Ceil sighed, "the cancer. So she traveled to the hospital and back. And now here."

I picked up a broken shell and began to write in the sand.

I'm sorry. Lisa.

"The same, the same," Rabbi Zuckerman had said.

I wished he hadn't. I wished I had been able to tell the mother that her daughter hadn't written the note. One way or another, I was always wishing for things to be different, the way I had wished last night, first in the park, next in Lisa's bed, that the beautiful young man at my side were not connected to a criminal case.

But he was. He was right in the middle of it.

Last night, sitting on Lisa's couch, my fingers trembling, my mother's soft velvet shawl wrapped around me, I had opened the envelope I'd slipped out of Paul's pocket. There, with the ticket, I'd found the list of immunizations required for bringing a dog into China. Lisa hadn't abandoned Ch'an. She had planned to take her along.

I thought about Beatrice again, the way her ashes hadn't floated out to sea, as we foolishly thought they would, but had come right back to shore with the next wave. We could see them lying still and sodden on the wet sand in front of our feet. I hadn't known there were so many shades of gray. Lillian, ever the hostess, had brought a bottle of wine to the beach, and plastic cups.

"To Mom," she said, lifting her cup and draining it.

"To Beatrice," Ceil and I said as one, and we drank our wine and thought our private thoughts.

I hadn't made peace with my mother before she'd died. Now it was too late. I'd left her remains here, but I hadn't left the bitterness I'd felt, nor the sadness. Those I had carried away with me. Those I still held on to.

For a while I just sat there, looking out over the ocean, toward the horizon. Then, scratching at the hard sand with my broken piece of shell, I began to dig a little hole, watching it fill with water from beneath. When Lili and I would dig in the sand, back when we were kids, Beatrice would poke my father to get his attention. Look, Abe, she'd tell him, they're digging to China.

I called Dash, dried his ears carefully on the end of my shirt, and following the lacy footprints of the gulls along the shore, we headed back to the car.

21

I Thought I Spotted a Sadistic Gleam in Her Eye

ON MY WAY to the gym to see Janet, I stopped at Lisa's. When I had gone through her drawers and her closet, I had noticed a Lycra bodysuit, like Janet's, and a pair of cross-trainers. Leaving Dashiell there because the gym with all those machines moving and heavy weights swinging around was too dangerous a place for a dog, I changed quickly and headed out.

Janet, wearing men's boxer shorts and a cutoff T-shirt with the logo of the gym on it, was on the phone, making faces as she listened.

"Go warm up on the treadmill," she said, as if I were a hamster. Minutes later she came to fetch me.

"Most women have more strength in their legs than their arms and chest," she said. She had a clipboard with her and a form with my name on top of it. "Let's start with your legs and work up."

"What?" I said. The music was deafening.

She took me over to a machine that you lie down on and took the pin from where it was, moving it down for more weight. I would have thought the other direction more appropriate. Getting on the machine, I was squinched into a little knot, my knees practically inside my mouth. When I pushed against the plate my feet rested on, I was propelled backward and my legs, which felt as if the bones might shatter, partially straightened out. Janet positioned my feet and told me to begin. I thought I spotted a sadistic gleam in her eye, but I couldn't be sure. It might have been a trick the fluorescent lights played with reality.

"This hurts," I said, after a dozen or so leg flexes.

"It's supposed to," she said. "If it doesn't hurt, you're not going to get stronger."

Just about when I thought someone had set fire to the whole damn gym, Janet looked up from her notes to offer some encouragement.

"Okay, Rachel, you're doing good, now let's see three more. Five, four, okay, good form, woman, keep it up, four, three, two, let's do it, don't give up now, three, two, one, excellent."

The woman, besides being an admitted and practicing sadist, couldn't count her way out of kindergarten. My legs felt as if someone had torn them out of my body and sewn them back in without anesthesia.

Janet stopped counting, but when I stopped, she flicked her hand at me, a motion that I assumed meant I was to continue.

"So how are you doing with Avi?" she asked absentmindedly, but instead of waiting for an answer, she resumed. "It's like I said, isn't it? Just being around him. Okay, rest," she said, but by the time I'd taken one breath, she was flicking her hand for me to push again.

"You can tell him anything," Janet said, sighing. "He's like the parent you always wanted and never had, very wise, and really interested in you. No one listens like that man. Okay," she said, "three, two, one. *Good*."

To my surprise, when Janet expressed her approval, I wanted to double the weight and do twenty more reps. Fortunately, she was off to the next machine before I got the chance. I got up and trailed after her, as imprinted as Conrad Lorenz's geese.

All around us, half-naked, muscle-bound men were grimacing in pain, grunting even louder than the earsplitting music, lifting weights as big as compact cars, and looking at themselves in the mirror any chance they could. There were females at the gym too, thin, pretty young girls reading magazines full of new hairstyles as they rode their stationary bicycles, others with earphones running on the treadmills, and some passing through on their way downstairs to step aerobics class. There were heavy women, too, two of them, both working on the thigh machines.

"Come on," Janet said, "we're going to work on your butt."

I followed her across the gym to yet another torture machine and listened carefully while she told me how far back to push the lever and how long to squeeze my glutes before releasing the lever so that it could come forward again.

And here I thought this would be mindless.

"He's such a stitch," she drawled. It took me a second to realize she was talking about Avi again. "Like he always says, 'You talk too much,' the minute you finish." Janet shook her head and laughed. "You talk too much," she repeated, and laughed again. "But only after he'd listened to every word you had to say, and only as a way of telling you it was time to do the form, to get your energy moving again."

She began to count, "Only three more, woman, let's do it," reminding me of the dentist my family used when I was a kid, always saying "Almost done" as he was about to set the all-time world record for drilling without a pause.

"You're going to be wearing that butt of yours behind your knees if you don't work it," Janet said on one of her many breaks in the middle of counting.

"What did you say?" I asked, the blood pounding in my head, my breath sounding like the ocean during a storm.

"Your butt, woman. It's going to sink if you don't work it. Five, four, three, good work, Rachel, hold it, hold it, okay, bring it forward, three, two, one. Other leg."

"My butt's going to sing?" I asked her.

"Yeah, but please don't let it do that until I'm out of the way," she said. "Just keep working."

We did shoulders, arms, back, chest, calves, quads, abs, and a few dozen parts I didn't know I had. When Janet's six o'clock showed up, I wanted to offer him a car. I thought we were finished. But I was wrong. While he warmed up in anticipation of *his* torture session, I got to stretch. It would have felt terrific to stretch out the muscles I had just worked so hard to tighten up, except for Janet, who pushed each limb a few inches farther than where I took it on my own.

"Doesn't that feel *good*," she drawled. "Don't forget to keep stretching later today and tomorrow. Don't you feel just fabulous?" She began to laugh in a way that made me think she knew *exactly* how I felt.

I left Janet in her world of grunts and groans and headed back to Lisa's. I had taken off the silver bracelet in order to work in the gym. I reached into my pocket and put it back on, feeling the cold weight of the metal first in my hand and then on my wrist.

Be My Love.

It had arrived *after* Paul and Lisa had broken up. After he had proposed. After she'd told him she was going to China and turned him down. Rejected him.

Had this been his way of asking again?

I had hoped, he'd started to say in the car.

I had hoped.

What? That Lisa would change her mind and stay? That she'd marry him after all?

He had reversed the truth, telling me that it was Lisa who had wanted to marry when it was he. And he had tried to take away the proof that his story had been a lie. To save face.

Big deal. Everyone had a story, the facts skewed to fit his own needs. They were probably *all* lying to me. Even Avi.

Everyone lies, my shrink used to say. People need to puff themselves up, she'd said, to make others believe they're more special than they themselves *feel* they are. Maybe there's something they want they wouldn't get with the truth, she'd said. Or maybe they're really lying to themselves. It's something they need to believe, and you're almost beside the point.

Lisa had been scheduled to leave the day after tomorrow.

Who else knew that?

A little while ago, I had wondered what the questions were. Now I had too many that needed answering. As I stood in Lisa's shower, the hot water pounding my sore muscles, they were swimming around in my head like fish. I needed to get dressed, take my dog for a long walk, and think things through.

22

Be Prepared

EARLY THE NEXT morning I took Dashiell straight to Bank Street, climbed the stairs, unlocked the door, and taking off my shoes, walked onto the polished studio floor and just sat. There wasn't a sound in the place, not even the ticking of a clock. I sat still, my thoughts still spinning like the specks of dust swirling in the sunlight.

I don't know how long I was there by myself before Dashiell heard him on the steps. He stood and wagged his tail.

"What are you doing?" he asked, pushing up the elastic that held his ponytail.

"Nothing," I told him.

"Good," he said.

He went into his office to change his shoes, then came back to where I was sitting.

"How long have you been doing nothing?"

"Long," I told him.

"Excellent," he said. "May I join you?"

"Suit yourself," I told him.

He sat next to me. Now we were both doing nothing. Well, truth be told, I wasn't exactly doing nothing. I was watching those dust motes twirling in the air, wondering what made them move so fast.

Avi wasn't doing nothing either. He was scratching Dashiell's thick neck. Dashiell began to moan.

"There's a saying that trying to understand Zen is like looking for the spectacles that are sitting on your nose," he said after a while.

"I don't wear spectacles," I told him.

"Give it time," he said with a wicked grin. "You will." He pushed up the band around his ponytail again. "Come," he said, "let's get to work."

We practiced the form twice without speaking. The third time, Avi stopped working to correct me. Suddenly he grabbed one wrist and pulled me off my feet, into him. "T'ai chi is a martial art," he said. He spoke softly, but he was still holding on to my wrist. "When someone wants something, you give in to them."

I thought he would yank me into him again, to illustrate the lesson, but he didn't.

"Watch," he said, releasing my wrist as suddenly as he'd snatched it and taking the position I had been in. "Take my wrist and pull me toward you."

I closed my fingers around his wrist and pulled him in to me. Where I had gone crashing into his chest with my other hand, Avi's other hand bent against my shoulder. I felt his wrist, then his arm, then his shoulder as his arm melted against me.

"Again," he said, taking the position I had been in when he'd pulled me off balance. "Slowly," he said, "see how I give in, I fold my hand, my wrist, my arm, like so. I give you what you want, but what have you accomplished?" When he grinned, I could smell the woody odor of bancha tea. "The same holds true if you fall, if you trip, if you are pushed to the ground. Fold. You won't get hurt."

"When you talk about folding with dogs, it means giving up," I said. "When you work a nasty dog, a miscreant, you need to get the dog to fold, to give up, to demonstrate that he knows you are top dog. Otherwise, he is. And he'll use his teeth to prove it."

"That sounds like a dangerous battle."

"This is true. Some dogs won't give up. They'd sooner die than fold."

"Some people, too. But in t'ai chi, the goal is to win without ever fighting. T'ai chi is an art of peace."

"So is dog training," I said, "properly done. But sometimes an owner only calls for help after the war has already started."

"In that case, it's best to be prepared. As in t'ai chi. Come, I'll show you."

He stood facing me, his arms in front of his chest. He merely looked at my arms, and I raised them up, as his were, understanding what he wanted in the way I know to fill Dashiell's water bowl when he indicates with his eyes that it's empty.

Avi placed the backs of his hands next to the backs of my hands, not touching, but close enough so that I could feel the heat of his skin, and slowly we began to shift, small movements that changed the balance of our relationship, back and forth, like the glider on Ceil's back porch, yin and yang, as graceful as a dance, but, as Avi had just reminded me, not a dance, a martial art. His hands began to push lightly against my wrists, against my arms, my shoulders. Moving slowly, we felt each other's strengths and weaknesses, we felt each other's total beings, without speech, using only touch, the way a human and a dog telegraph the facts of life to each other up and down the leash.

If you looked casually at what we were doing, it resembled the way Lili and I used to fight when we were kids, hands everywhere, pushing, shoving, circling round and round, each trying to get the upper hand. But if you looked carefully, the same, the same, only ritualized, like the dominance displays among dogs or wolves, each posture full of significance and information, each touch revealing the strength or lack of strength, both mental and physical, of the opponents.

For a single moment I thought about Paul, about the way his lips brushed my skin, barely touching it. In that instant Avi pushed, catching me so completely off guard that he sent me flying backward across the studio.

"Keep your mind *here*," he said, waiting for me to approach and begin again. "Concentrate on getting out of the way." He motioned for me to push him and he turned his body slightly to the side, deflecting my push and letting my own force take me off balance, using my own force against me.

The next time I felt my attention drifting, I was able to bring it right back. I'd once let myself drift for a split second when working with a scoundrel of a dog. I had the scar to remind me that, in dog training, the time is always now.

But then, despite trying to remain as riveted to the task at hand as Dashiell always was to a stick I was about to toss for him, I thought about Lisa, at the window. Once again, Avi threw me off balance. When moments later I tried to do the same with him, I failed to budge him. He was as rooted as a great oak, as difficult to capture as the wind.

My legs were burning, and I was out of breath. Avi motioned for us to sit, leaning against the wall of the studio. We sat quietly for a moment, just resting.

"Avram, were you aware of Lisa's plans?" I asked, trying to catch him off balance with words where I had failed to do so with my *chi*.

He didn't respond.

I pushed again.

"Did you know she was planning to leave? She did tell you everything, didn't she?"

"You have made room for Lisa," he said, not looking at me, not looking at anything. Maybe he was seeing Lisa. "You have been working very hard," he said.

"Yes, I have."

"I knew she was planning to go to China. I knew for a long time, Rachel, since the first day she came to study with me. Only then, then it was just a story, a dream."

"When did it become more than a dream, Avi?"

"Day by day," he said. "Slowly. Then all at once."

"Did the others know, too? The other teachers?"

"No. Lisa had planned to tell them herself, privately, at the last possible moment. She thought that if I announced it, there'd be a feeding frenzy, that they would all be scrambling to take her place, to become, she said, the favorite. She loved them, Rachel. She was, oh, the dearest person—" He reached to wipe his cheeks. "She couldn't bear to see them all lose their dignity."

"And would they have?"

"Ach," he said. "You've seen them. You've heard them. A gifted student, that might happen once in a teacher's life." He stopped and looked at me. "Maybe twice, if you are really lucky. You do your best with what is sent to you," he said as the door opened and Stewie Fleck walked in. He was wearing a shiny orange baseball jacket with plaid polyester pants, and his shoelaces were open and dragging on the carpet. When he dropped the jacket over the back of the couch, his wallet fell out of the pocket.

How did this man get through life?

And how would Avi, now that he'd lost Lisa?

I looked at my watch. It was five minutes to the lunch-hour class. I was supposed to stay, but I knew I'd be unable to concentrate. There was too much on my mind.

It's best to be prepared, Avi had said.

Frank always said that, too. Be prepared for surprises, he would warn me, and I don't mean good ones. He had that annoying habit of pointing when he was, by his own admission, making a brilliant point.

Yeah, yeah, I'd tell him, prepared, like a Boy Scout.

But he was right. It was a dog-eat-dog world out there.

Whoever had killed Lisa had caught her off guard. So when push came to shove, if Lisa hadn't been able to defend herself, what chance would I have?

With t'ai chi, Avi had told me, you can defeat your opponent by starting after him but arriving before him.

Yeah, right, I thought on my way down the stairs. Tell it to Lisa.

23

Did I See What I
Just Saw?

DASHIELL AND I walked over to Hunan Pan on Hudson and Perry.
I parked him under a table near the window, and when the waiter
arrived with a menu and tea, I conferred with him about an urgent
point concerning my case.

Then, just to be polite, I ordered a bowl of hot and sour soup,
steamed pork dumplings, and some chicken and broccoli. Out of respect for Donny, I didn't order crab.

After I'd eaten, instead of lingering over tea, I pocketed the fortune
cookie and headed over to Washington Square Park. Dashiell was
looking stressed, and I thought an hour of hip-hop with some other
friendly dogs would chill him out nicely.

Dashiell had no trouble living in the moment. As soon as I opened
the double gates to the run, he was in ecstasy, rushing into the group
of playing dogs, bumping them with his big, strong butt, racing back
and forth, engaging in good-natured humping, the whole canine en-
chilada. Watching him play was usually a beatific experience for me,
sort of a dog lover's meditation. But not this time. I was too busy
obsessing about Paul.

Why had he told me he didn't speak Chinese? And what other lies had he told me? What was he up to, anyway? And most important, when would I see him again?

It was probably a good idea that I had a massage scheduled for three thirty. I was as tight as the curl of a pug's tail.

At ten after three Dashiell and I headed for Bank Street. When I got to Howie's, I rang the bell and waited to be buzzed in. But nothing happened. I checked my watch. I was right on time. I waited another minute, then gave it one more try before leaving, leaning on the bell a little longer than usual.

I heard the intercom crackle, but I couldn't make out the words.

"Rachel," I said into the speaker. "I'm here for my massage."

He didn't respond, but the buzzer sounded, and when I leaned on the door, it opened. Dashiell and I walked straight back down the dimly lit hall to Howie's apartment, and when we got to his door, we rang again. This time we didn't have long to wait.

She filled the doorway. At first, I thought it was Howie, suddenly much older, and in drag.

Her face looked like melting ice cream, formless and sagging, as if there were no bones or muscles beneath the vanilla-colored skin. Or maybe that was powder, making her look as white-faced as a mime. Her eyes were a bleached-out blue, splotches of red from broken capillaries crisscrossed her cheeks, and smack in the middle of the whole mess she had a purple ginger root of a nose. Her face was like a hide-a-bed that had been left open, stuff showing that should have been hidden away, preferably under the sink.

She was short and heavy, leaden looking, as if she were glued to the ground beneath her Minnie Mouse–sized Nikes. Her sparse orange hair puffed out all around her head, making her look like an angry bird. But when she spoke, she was no bird. She barked like a big, cranky dog.

"Wha'd you want?" she asked, a cloud of Scotch and tobacco coming at me.

"I have an appointment with Howie, for a massage," I told her, trying not to make the mistake of inhaling again.

"Not here," she barked, about to close the door.

She was holding a cigarette and now took matches out of the pocket of her sweater and lit it. Dashiell sneezed.

"He's getting one, too?" she asked. "Don't look tense to me."

"No, he's cool. I'm the one who needs help. Howie says—"

"Howie says, Howie says, that kid don't know his ass from the hole in his head. So what're you standing in the hall, c'mon in."

Watching her tree-trunk legs shuffle slowly forward, I followed her down the hall, past the room where Howie worked, toward where I'd heard the sound of the television set last visit. The TV was on now, too. Some lady with iridescent fingernails like the wings of things that live in pipes and drains was moving her hand from side to side so that the ruby ring she was selling for sixty-nine ninety-five would catch the light.

"Sit down," she said, the cigarette dangling from her lips bobbing up and down when she spoke. "If he said he'd be here, he'll be here. He went out to get me my medicine."

There was an empty glass on the coffee table in front of her, the last ice cube down to a shaving now, sitting in cloudy amber liquid.

"What a good son he must be," I said, looking around the dismal room. The little bit of light coming through the windows hit the threadbare green wall-to-wall and the worn, dirty couch that faced the television set. There was one of those aluminum walkers off near the wall and newspapers and magazines stacked everywhere. The room looked and smelled as stale as the old lady's ashtray, overflowing with butts, a crunched-up empty cigarette package lying on top of the whole mess.

"What a good son he must be," she said, snorting as she did. "A lot you know. Dora Lish," she said. "*How*ie's mother."

"Rachel Alexander," I said.

She ignored me, and I sat watching the ashes from her cigarette land on her lap. "Howie's mother," she repeated. "The kid still comes crying to me when someone hurts his feelings, just the way he always has. He's thin-skinned." She looked at me with one eye as the smoke from the cigarette dangling from her lips went up toward the cracked ceiling past the other. "Thin-skinned."

"You mean he's sensitive?" I asked.

"Sens-tive my ass," Howie's mother said. "He's a damn crybaby, is what he is. Always was. Always will be. Whines ever' time I need something, s'if he had to trudge ten miles in the snow 'stead of around the corner." She puffed on the cigarette without removing it from her mouth and stared at me. "You're not from the school, are you?"

"You mean the t'ai chi school? Yes, I am. I'm studying there, too."

"*You* the one made him cry?" she asked, looking confused for the moment.

"No," I said, a little too quickly. "I just started there. I'm new. But I heard—"

"That bitch!" Dora said. She took the cigarette and pointed toward me with it. "Wasn't you, you sure it wasn't you? Say, what's your name anyway?"

"Rachel," I told her. "Rachel Alexander."

"No, that's not her name. Not Rachel Alexander. She had a completely different name."

"How did she make Howie cry," I asked, "that bitch?"

"Don't take much."

"So what happened, she hurt his feelings?"

"Feelings? She was going to *fire* him. That's nothing to do with feelings. It's to do with money." She rubbed her thumb and forefinger together. "Like we're rolling in it," she said, indicating the room we were in with a sweep of one hand. "Like we don't need every damn penny he can make."

"Did she say why? I mean, did Howie say what the reason was?"

I took a peek at my watch. Howie was already twenty-two minutes late for my appointment.

Dora Lish suddenly got up and started beating on the couch cushion. I guess she'd lost the ash of her cigarette. The cloud of dust came at me like nuclear fallout, and suddenly I was having a sneezing fit.

Satisfied she'd found the culprit and had beat it into submission, Dora sat and relit her cigarette. It was then I heard the familiar pop and looked up to see Dashiell, a huge paw anchoring the Kleenex box on the cluttered coffee table between Dora Lish and myself, a tissue dangling from his big, wide mouth. He walked over and dropped it into my lap. I blew my nose and patted his big head.

"Wait a minute here." Dora started to get up and then sat back down. She pointed at Dashiell with her cigarette. "Did I see what I just saw?"

I nodded.

"Naw. You're pulling my leg, trying to fool an old lady. Bet he wouldn't do it again," she said, suddenly as excited as a child.

I opened my mouth, but before I had the chance to say a word, Dora Lish, who apparently didn't live next door to the HB Acting Studio for nothing, lifted one big nicotine-stained hand toward her face and faked a rhinoceros of a sneeze.

Ever alert, Dashiell turned back to the coffee table and crushed one side of the tissue box with his foot so that it wouldn't fly up, then pulled out half a tissue, which he dropped into Dora's lap. He backed up and waited.

Dora began to cackle.

Dashiell went back for the other half of the tissue. But this time he didn't bring it to Dora. This time he dropped it right on the coffee table, and pop, pop, pop, three more tissues were out of the box.

"Enough," I told him. "Good boy."

Left without praise, like most of us, he finds a way to thank himself, in this case with the heady pleasure of snapping tissues out of the box until it's empty. After that, he'd discover how tissue boxes are constructed. And if his best efforts on behalf of the human race were further ignored, he'd make tissue-colored confetti, blue in this case. Hey, you never know when there's going to be a parade.

Howie was now forty-five minutes late. Dora had seen me check my watch this time.

"He musta got held up at the grocer's," she said, dropping the end of her cigarette into the whiskey glass. "I'll tell him you were here. What'd you say your name was?"

"Rachel."

"Oh, yeah. I remember. Rachel. Got a cigarette on you, hon?"

I shook my head.

"Mrs. Lish—"

"Dora. Everyone calls me Dora."

Everyone? The place didn't exactly look as if she entertained much, but you never know.

"Dora," I said, but she had turned her attention toward the television set. There was a faux pearl necklace being shown, and Dora watched the hand holding it move across the screen.

"You never told me, Dora, why was Howie going to get fired?"

"I'll tell him you were by," she said without turning to look at me. She fished a butt out of the ashtray and lit it. "I'll tell him about the Kleenex, too," she said, the smoke from her cigarette rising in a thin stream, then widening as it headed for the ceiling.

"Just pull th' door closed on your way out, will ya, hon?"

So I did. I closed the living room door, waited a minute, Dashiell and I frozen in place, my hand still on the knob, and when there was no sound other than the drone of the TV, I looked around the narrow, dark hallway and headed not toward Howie's office and the front door, but the other way.

Dora's ashtray of a bedroom was on the left side of the narrow hallway, a small, dark, cluttered hole of a space, its one window facing an air shaft. She had her own bathroom, though. I poked through her medicine cabinet, filled with enough antibiotics, Tylenol with codeine, Valium, Ex-Lax, and Tums for her tummy to start her own pharmacy. I even found her favorite medicine, hidden behind the six-pack of toilet paper under the sink for those times when Howie was too slow getting back from the store. Before leaving Dora's suite, I stopped at her bureau to look at the photo hanging over it, a round-faced boy, already overweight at seven or eight, standing next to a little girl, her dress so starched the skirt stood out, a ribbon in her curly hair, her face as round as Howie's. A sister? So where was she when Mama needed so much care?

Next door to Dora's room was a second bathroom, and across the hall from that was Howie's bedroom, the door so warped it didn't even close all the way. I pushed it open slowly and turned on the light.

Howie slept on what looked like a cot, or a youth bed. It was as neatly made as if Howie were in the army, the single pillow fluffed, the striped blanket pulled tight and tucked in with hospital corners. Howie's slippers were lined up next to the bed on a little mat. I walked in, waited for Dashiell, and closed the door behind us as well as I was able.

There was an old upright bureau on one wall and a small desk on the other. I sat at the desk, turned on the lamp, and opened the top drawer, looking at the neatly lined up pens and pencils, the checkbook, the little packet of rubber bands, the small dish of paper clips, and the box with stamps in it, all carefully torn from their sheets and stacked in neat compartments, everything just so.

The drawers to the left held Howie's business files, every payment and expense neatly recorded. And envelopes of receipts, all marked and ready for tax time. Behind the receipts were letters. I pulled the file and looked through the lot of them, all from patients and doctors relating to the conditions Howie was supposed to treat. And behind that a folder with photographs in it, only three of them, Howie kneeling with a bunch of other boys, perhaps a team shot but without the identifying paraphernalia, Howie's grim little high school graduation picture, and one really good photo, a black-and-white enlargement of Howie doing t'ai chi. It reminded me of the photo of Lisa in Avi's office, the way the subject was off center, the way the light hit the hands, caught in a graceful pose as the subject moved slowly through the form. Howie looked through the Tiger's Eyes, loose circles made by his powerful hands, which in the photo looked as chiseled as the David's.

I checked my watch. It would be nearly halfway into the next appointment, if there were one. Still no Howie. But for how long, I couldn't say.

I became aware of my breathing then, shallow and quick, my head clear, my ears alert to any sound from elsewhere in the apartment. I shut off the desk light and was ready to go when I got one last idea. I knelt and looked under Howie's neat bed, then slid out the magazines I'd had the feeling would be there, carefully sliding them back when I had seen enough silicone and whips to last me a lifetime.

I stopped in Howie's office on my way out. His appointment book was lying open on the cabinet near the head of the massage table. I checked my watch. It was four twenty-eight. Someone was due in just two minutes, on the half hour. Just then, the bell rang. I signaled Dashiell, and we made it out the door before the second ring, a longer one, had summoned Dora.

There was a tense-looking young man waiting to be buzzed in. Walking past him, I thought about her, about Howie's mother. She had looked as if she'd fall asleep, mesmerized by the TV. I wondered what would happen to the cigarette, but whatever would, it had happened countless times before, and Dora the lush was still here to tell any stranger who'd listen what a fucked-up loser the son who cared for her in her old age was.

24

There Ought to Be a Law

LEAVING HOWIE'S, I felt that crick in my neck he had warned me about the first time we'd met. I had thought about going over to the Club to see Paul. I could say I'd lost Lisa's work keys, ask if I could borrow his set, see what he said, watch his eyes while he said it.

Then I thought about the envelope. What had he thought when he'd reached into his pocket and found it missing, when he'd realized I knew that it had been he who'd been so anxious to get married, not Lisa? All she had wanted was to go to China, no matter what it cost her. So I thought maybe I shouldn't go and see him. I thought perhaps he needed some time.

But then I found myself thinking about the way his skin smelled, about the long, smooth muscles of his back, about the warmth and softness of his hands, about the way he'd said my name, over and over again, like a mantra. Then I *knew* I better not go see him, because the sixth law of investigation work is, Don't get caught with your pants down, and I didn't want to break it again. I cared much too much for this man, considering all I didn't yet know, and I didn't want to break my heart either.

I could hear the phone ringing when I was still in the garden, but by the time I got the door unlocked, it had stopped. It was probably just someone asking me if I wanted to switch back to AT&T. They call at all hours. There ought to be a law.

I went upstairs to run a bath, and while the tub was filling with water too hot to dunk anything in other than a lobster on its way to becoming bisque, I checked my answering machine and found that an unusual number of calls had come in since I'd left home that morning. Eleven. But when I rewound the tape, I discovered they were all hang-ups. As if someone were trying to find out whether or not I was home.

I was tempted to dig my revolver out from the shoe box on the top shelf of my closet where it had been for over a year, but I told myself that that was too paranoid, even for me.

I turned off the phone and turned down the volume on the answering machine. Soaking in the steamy hot water, without the agitating noise of the telephone, I quickly fell fast asleep and stayed that way for over an hour, until the water had cooled off enough to wake me.

It was nearly eight o'clock when I got out of the tub, turned the phone back on, and, still feeling exhausted, plodded downstairs to feed Dashiell. When the phone rang again, I grabbed it on the first ring. This time the person on the other end didn't hang up.

"Rachel?"

"Marty?"

I looked out the small kitchen window into the garden, a tangle of dark shadows at this hour. "What's up?" I asked.

"I need to see you, kid. Can you come over for a minute?"

"Now?"

"It won't take long." Sounding like a cop.

"Sure," I said, looking at the kitchen clock. Eight twenty now. What was Marty even doing there at this hour? He worked days. "Is anything wrong? You okay? Are the dogs okay?"

"I'll wait for you at the front desk," was all he said. And then I heard the click. He had hung up.

Had he made all those other calls? Had he been waiting, for some reason, for me to get home and pick up?

I pulled on one of Lisa's black sweaters and some leggings, stepped into a pair of clogs, combed back my wet hair, and poured some dry dog food for Dashiell. In less than five minutes I was out the door.

Marty was standing near the front desk, and when he saw me, he took my arm and led me to a desk in back where there was no one else within earshot.

"There's been a murder, Rachel. In the neighborhood. Close by." I felt my heart start to race. Who was I, for the Sixth Precinct to suddenly be filling me in on their most up-to-date bad news? "The victim was found on Bank Street, in that outdoor area at Westbeth." He

334 / CAROL LEA BENJAMIN

paused, as if the location of the body would be so pregnant with significance I'd burst out with the name of the killer.

"And?" I said.

He was watching my face. I watched his, not blinking, waiting for the other shoe to drop.

"Across from the school," he added, "where your clients' daughter used to work."

"Yes. But what's—"

"He had your name on a card in his shirt pocket, Rachel."

"You mean my card? Maybe it was someone who needed help, you know, a work contact."

"It wasn't *your* card, Rachel. It was actually *his* card. He'd written your name on the back of it. And there was something else written there, too."

"Something else? What else?"

"Something in Chinese."

Suddenly I got a strange rush to my head, as if I were breathing pure oxygen, and the air tasted metallic, the way it does when you take antibiotics.

"*Xiao yue?*" I asked.

But he didn't reply. Instead he took my arm and backed me into a molded plastic chair next to the empty desk. He pulled the desk chair around so that he could sit in front of me, so close our knees were touching.

"Paul Wilcox is dead, Marty?"

He nodded.

I looked back toward the desk, at the uniforms milling around, at the line of civilians, there at any hour of the day or night to report the kind of minor irritations that build up in a city like New York, things that drive people to the brink of insanity, or over it. I reminded myself where I was and what was at stake here.

"How? What happened?" I asked him, as if we were talking about some stranger and not a man I'd gone to bed with, my voice sounding as if it were coming from far away, or from the other side of a closed door.

Marty took my hands.

"A couple of the detectives want to talk to you. I came back in so that I could do this." He squeezed my hands. "So like I said, he was carrying a card with your name on it, Rachel. Looks like you were pretty important to him."

I felt my face flush, but the rest of me was as cold as a corpse. I had come out without a coat, and my hair was still wet, I thought as I felt myself shiver, my fingers like icicles in Marty's hands.

"Rachel?" he said. He stood, slipped off his jacket, and put it around my shoulders.

"How, Marty? Help me out here, will you?"

"ME says broken neck, unofficially, of course, pending autopsy. They're working on him now."

"When did it happen?"

"Mid to late afternoon. Best guess? Weather conditions weren't unusual, so by the deceased's temperature, he figures four to five, give or take."

I winced, thinking of the medical examiner slipping the thermometer next to Paul's eyeball. Keep your mind *here*, I told myself.

"Who's on?" I asked him. "Who do you want me to talk to?"

"Talk to me," he said.

"He was Lisa Jacobs's sweetheart," I told him, "until a few months before her death, her suicide. I met with him in connection with the case, to try to find out what I needed to know about Lisa, for her parents."

Marty nodded.

"So that I could help them to understand what had happened, I mean, why what had happened had happened, so that I could give that information to her parents."

"And?"

"He wasn't very forthcoming when I first went to see him. He just seemed angry. Turned some of that on me."

"So you tried another approach? Something less threatening, more friendly."

"Swimming," I said, feeling my throat closing.

"Swimming?"

"He was a swim coach. I went over to the gym where he worked, the Club on Varick Street, and went swimming."

"And?"

"And then he was more forthcoming. He opened up," I said, swallowing hard, "about their relationship. I guess that's why—"

"He had your name in his pocket, over his heart?"

I nodded. "How did it happen, Marty?"

"Looks like a mugging. The sort where you not only take the individual's credit cards and cash, you also inflict as much damage as possible, given the constraints of time and place. Sometimes the mugger gets scared off in time, and the victim lives. No such luck this time."

"Was there anything else on him, Marty, besides the card?"

"Handkerchief, key ring, driver's license, small change, nothing much."

"Show me."

"His belongings? What for?"

"Please, Marty. This has to do with my case. It's really important."

"I don't—"

"You don't think *I*—"

"Rachel—"

"So show me."

A moment later I was looking through a plastic bag at Paul Wilcox's handkerchief, driver's license, two quarters, a dime and two pennies, and a key ring with eight keys on it, three of them Lisa's, three of them for Bank Street T'ai Chi, one for downstairs, two for upstairs, though nobody ever locked the bottom lock.

"That's it?" I asked.

"Just what you see," he said.

"Rachel, you know anything about this man's life, any enemies he might have had?"

"No," I said. "No friends either. We only spoke about Lisa, about his feelings for Lisa."

"If you think of anything—"

"Right," I said. "Can I go now?"

"Rachel—"

"What? You don't want me to leave town?"

"I want you out of this."

I nodded.

"Unless you *think* of something he said, anything he said that might—"

"Yeah, yeah," I said. "I'll call you first thing. I'll beep you. Whatever."

"Or Matthew. He and Dave are in charge of this. They might want to talk to you, but I'll talk to them for now."

"Thanks, Marty."

"Sure thing, kid."

I started to go, but Marty took my arm and stopped me.

"Hey, I meant to tell you, Rach. You were right on the money about Elwood's thyroid." He made a fist and pointed to the floor with his thumb. "Way down. He and Gluck are taking the same pills now. We keep telling Gluck he better watch it, he'll be out of a job, we're going to put Elwood on the phone. The doc says it'll take a few months for his weight to go down, but his energy is way up. You gotta see him. He's like a new dog," he said. "I'll call you as soon as he gets back."

The bomb dogs worked one week, then had two weeks off, what a lot of their fellow officers considered an enviable work schedule.

"You okay?"

I nodded.

"Good. That's good. You take care now. And call me if you think of anything."

It was nearly ten when I got back home, and I couldn't remember having just walked across from the precinct. There were two more messages. Both hang-ups. Of course the calls hadn't been from Marty. He would have left a message.

I sat in the living room for a while, thinking about Paul. There wouldn't have been a wallet. When he'd paid for the Chinese food, his cash had been loose in his pocket. He wouldn't go out without money. No one would. So the mugger had taken whatever cash he'd had on him.

I made a pot of tea, heating the pot with boiling water the way he had. But when it was ready and I'd carried my cup back to the couch, I just let it sit there, untouched.

He'd had the keys to the studio. Had he used them that night? No, of course not. He wouldn't have been so surprised to learn about the note if he had.

The phone rang, and I picked it up, but oddly, whoever was on the other end had nothing to say. That's when it occurred to me that I couldn't remember if I'd locked the garden gate. I grabbed my keys, put Lisa's jacket back on, and walked outside, Dashiell following. We headed toward the dark tunnel that led to the gate. I was going to try it, to make sure it was locked. I was going to shake it, to see if it held, then finally go to sleep. But what I saw stuck in a curlicue of the wrought-iron gate stopped me dead in my tracks.

There, wrapped in floral paper with a layer of waxy green tissue paper underneath, were yellow rosebuds, twelve of them, each perfect. Their perfume filled the night air.

After making sure the gate was locked, I looked at the bouquet very carefully, even turning it upside down and shaking it. But no matter how hard I looked, I couldn't find a card.

25

We Don't Need the Money, He'd Said

THE PHONE RANG again. I could hear it as I carried the flowers back toward the cottage and laid them on the steps.

Someone had been sending roses for a while now. Someone had waited across the street from Lisa's, watching her windows. And someone knew that I didn't live at Lisa's house, that I lived here. That when the time came, this is where I was to be found.

But it hadn't been Paul. Then who was it? And what was he after now? Or who?

Leaving the roses on the steps, Dashiell in the garden, and the door open, I went upstairs, took the little stool from my office, and carried it into the bedroom closet. Then I climbed up on it and pulled down the Joan & David shoe box, a relic of my eight-month marriage to Dr. Fashion, a box much too heavy to have shoes in it, and put it on the bed.

Under some circumstances, my shrink Ida used to say, paranoia is not such an inappropriate response.

I went down to the basement where I had the formal dining room table I never used and all the cartons of stuff I'd never opened from when I split with Jack and moved here, saltcellars and linen napkins, a dozen sterling silver iced-tea spoons, stemware, Rosenthal china, wedding presents from people who apparently thought Jack had married Martha Stewart. I squeezed my way past a mountain of boxes to the sideboard against the far wall, which held only bullets for my gun and the boxes of gadgets Bruce Petrie used to give me, so full of formal dinner parties was my life. With a box of thirty-eights in hand, I began to pick my way back to the stairs. But then I stopped.

Why was this stuff still here, still part of my life? More to the point, how had I fooled myself into thinking I could be happy spending my days hanging up the clothes someone else tossed over the dresser the night before and finding new things to do with cilantro?

I had moved into Jack's Victorian house in Croton, overlooking the Hudson River, a sort of mirror image of Lili and Ted's modern house on the other side of the river. Lili, cradling her morning coffee, could watch the sun rise over Westchester, pink turning to gold, all brightness and hope. I could watch the sun set over Rockland County, brilliant orange and flaming red, the colors of dying leaves in fall.

Having closed my dog school in the city, I'd figured, no problem, I'd train in Westchester, closer to home. But when I told Jack my plans, he became as still as marble and just as cold.

We don't need the money, he'd said, as if that were all that work was about. Then, after a long frost, he spoke again. He wanted me home when he got home, not running around at all hours of the night getting myself bitten. He wanted to sit down to a nice, home-cooked meal with me and discuss his day. That's what marriage was, wasn't it, for chrissake, he'd said. He hadn't married me, he added, to come home to an empty house.

Where, I remember wondering, was the man who'd found my occupation quirky and endearing? Get a load of this, he'd told his cretin brother Alan, she trains *dogs* for a living. And while I'd answered all his brother's inane questions, he'd looked proud. But as soon as we were married, he'd changed.

The price of my poor judgment had been a divorce. Lisa's may have cost her her life.

I put the box of bullets on the bottom step and began to open those other boxes, cartons containing carefully wrapped champagne flutes, a soup tureen, a fish poacher, grape shears, lobster forks. At three in the morning, having set aside only a hand-thrown planter I could use for herbs in the winter and a small, flowered bud vase, I resealed the cartons and stacked them neatly under the windows. Then I shut off the light, dropped the box of ammo in the kitchen, and went back out into the moonlit garden.

Alongside the house were the logs I had gathered last fall in the woods surrounding my sister's house. The smaller pile, the split logs, was nearly gone. I tossed the jacket over that pile, lifted the heavy tarp from the larger wood pile, and unwrapped the sledgehammer and wedge that lay on top of the wood.

Dashiell lay peacefully on the rich, loamy earth near the oak tree that stretched skyward from the center of the garden. It was taller than the cottage. The moonlight, filtered through its branches, made his white fur look pearly, almost iridescent.

A mugging. Yeah, right.

Mid to late afternoon, I thought, lifting a log from the wood pile. Where had Howie been? It didn't take an hour and a half to pick up a bottle of cheap Scotch for your mother, did it?

I stood the log on the tree stump near the wood pile and tapped in the wedge. Where had Stewie Fleck been between four and five? In the field, meaning anywhere he damn well wanted to be, the little creep?

What about Janet? Had she been at the gym, where Stewie said she practically lived, torturing innocents?

Come to think of it, where had Avi been? The news was full of reminders lately that no one is immune to human frailty, not judges, Nobel laureates, or even holy men.

If Paul had been killed across from the school, didn't that mean he'd been on the way to the studio, to find me?

If so, why hadn't he called to see if I were there?

But what would be the point? Surely he knew that no one ever picked up the phone. If someone doesn't have the patience to wait for us to call them back, Avi had said once when I was going to answer the phone in the middle of working, they're not going to have the patience to learn t'ai chi. Not answering the phone was a weeding-out process for him, the first in a long string of character tests.

Why Paul? I thought. But the answer to that question hit really close to home. Too close, if you ask me.

I looked back at Dashiell, still lying under the tree. Between his paws, right under his nose, he had serendipitously discovered a scent worthy of his complete attention. I could see his nostrils moving.

I turned my attention to the wood pile and began to split logs in earnest now, tapping the wedge into the next log, swinging the sledge-hammer back and then high over one shoulder, bringing it down hard, hearing the satisfying clang of metal on metal and seeing the log cleave in two, opening like a flower that had suddenly decided to bloom, the outside darkened by the weather, the inside raw and vulnerable looking as a wound. I worked until I developed a rhythm, until

I was drenched with sweat, until I no longer knew where the sledge-hammer ended and I began, nor did I care, until there were no more logs to split. Then I sat quietly on the steps, my dog on one side of me leaning in, those perfect roses on the other, until the stars began to disappear, the color of the sky lightened, the first bird began to sing. And when it did, I sat some more.

26

Be Not Afraid

WHEN THE GARDEN was filled with the sweet, clean light of morning, I spread the yellow roses under the bushes across from the cottage to mulch. Then, sticking my sore hands into my pockets, I felt the fortune cookie I'd never opened. I broke it in half and held the pieces for Dashiell to eat while I read the message. It was a proverb. *Be not afraid of going slowly, be afraid only of standing still.*

I went inside and gave Dashiell food and water, ran a bath, and while the tub was filling, put my gun and bullets on the top shelf of the closet. Later, dressed in Lisa's comfortable black workout clothes, I called Goodwill to arrange for them to pick up the physical evidence of my brief marriage in exchange for a generous tax deduction. When I hung up, I saw that Dashiell was fast asleep on the couch. He was so tired, he hadn't finished his food. I gave him a kiss and headed for Bank Street T'ai Chi alone.

I took the stairs, walking slowly. I had, after all, been up all night. The door was locked, but when I unlocked it, I found Avi there with Ch'an. He was at his desk paying bills.

"Ach," he said, "I hate this. Lisa used to do this for me. Now the bills pile up, and I have to sit glued to a chair for hours to take care of them."

"I'll do that for you," I told him, one hand on his shoulder. "You shouldn't have to do this. Go. Go for a walk. I'll leave everything ready for your signature when I finish."

I picked up Ch'an's leash and held it out to Avi. He opened his mouth as if to speak, but changed his mind. He merely waved it away with one big hand.

"You keep her," he said, his eyebrows pinched together, his brow tense.

"Okay," I told him. "No problem."

"And give her a little walk before you leave, Rachel," he said without looking at me. "I won't be back for her until this evening."

I waited to hear the door close and the tumbler turn over. Then I pushed the stack of unpaid bills aside. While the computer was booting up, I rolled back the tape on the answering machine and began to listen. Avi rarely picked up the phone, even when he was at his desk.

There were five messages on the machine, all inquiries about beginning classes, requests for brochures. I rolled the tape back and played it again, addressing the five brochures, then began surfing Avi's files, looking at the dates and times the computer automatically adds to each directory. Avi had been working on-screen yesterday, starting at one thirty. Unfortunately, I could see only when he logged on, not when he'd finished working.

There were no classes on Friday afternoon or evening, no way of knowing if Avi had been here or not. I slit open the envelopes in the pile of bills, checked each against last month's billing, and wrote the checks I'd promised I'd write, leaving the stack for his signature when I'd finished, even stamping the envelopes for him. Then, before closing down the computer and shutting off the light, I checked one more thing, Avi's personnel files. I copied down the addresses I didn't already have, making sure to check my own as well. I was listed as living at Lisa's apartment, with Lisa's phone number. I wasn't in the phone book. Still, somebody knew where I really lived.

I patted my lap for Ch'an, and she came and laid her big head across my thighs, sighing as she did. I put one finger inside one of her ears, and she began to moan, the way Dashiell always does. That's when I noticed the tag on her collar. I picked it up and looked at it. It wasn't her license. It was her ID tag, complete with Lisa's name, address, and phone number.

Like Lisa, I would never risk losing my dog. Dashiell too had an ID tag on his collar, a brass plate attached to the leather collar with two rivets, for complete security. His had only my name and number on it, no address, because my life's mission was to raise paranoia to a high art. So my secret admirer had had to be extra clever to have both my phone number *and* address.

No problem. Whoever stood across from Lisa's apartment, looking up at her windows, could have followed me home. But it hadn't been Paul, had it? It had been someone else, someone who had nothing more important to do than to wait, hoping for a glimpse of the person he so longed to see. Not Lisa. Lisa was gone. Now it was *me* he had waited to see, me looking out over the dark street or up at the white face of the moon. It was me, one night when the weather was mild and his patience long, who appeared not in the window, but on the front steps, leaving with my dog.

Was I just giving him a walk? That would be easy enough to find out. At that hour, even in New York, there aren't many people around. You could follow someone from Hudson and LeRoy to Tenth Street, staying far enough away to remain undetected yet still not risking the chance of losing them. Even when your unsuspecting prey turned the corner onto Tenth, there'd be no problem. Dashiell, like any intact male, was infinitely more conscientious about leaving his scent near home than far away. The closer he got to where we lived, the more urgent and time-consuming was his need to mark, and, lucky mutt, he had an owner who had an understanding of and a soft spot for hormone-driven canine necessities.

I left the office, slipped off my shoes, and walked onto the studio floor in Lisa's white cotton socks. Facing north, I did the form, keeping my concentration in the raging furnace beneath my navel. Something was chewing away at the edge of my consciousness, but I didn't know what it was. When I finished, I walked over to the windows, opening the one someone had pushed Lisa out of, and once again looked straight down at the street, so far away.

The first time I'd imagined Lisa doing this, I'd supposed she'd stood here alone and miserable. I'd pictured her climbing up on the sill, then pitching herself forward, into eternity.

Now I was sure she'd had help.

But not from her ex-lover.

Before I closed the window I looked at the courtyard across the street, where Paul's body had been found. Formerly the research facility of Bell Labs, Westbeth was now housing for artists. There was a security guard inside with closed-circuit TV watching the elevators, the hallways, the entrances and exits, the courtyard.

Was the killer someone Paul knew, someone who could have rested an arm over his shoulders in friendship? Two men walking or standing that way wouldn't alert a security guard, not in this neck of the woods.

Or were they shielded from the camera's eye by one of the trees planted in rows across from the entrance? Perhaps the guard was checking another monitor at the time of the murder. No one can watch everything at once. How long would it take to snap someone's neck, slip the money out of his pocket, then disappear? Not long. A life, a complex being, a family, and a future, destroyed in an instant.

I went back into Avi's office and picked up the phone.

"Can you meet me at the studio in half an hour? It's important. Good. Lunch is on me."

I put on my shoes, grabbed my jacket, picked up Ch'an's leash again, and headed for the door. Ch'an got up slowly, stretched, and followed me, looking elsewhere, as if it were merely a pleasant coincidence that we were both going out at the same time.

On the way to pick up lunch, I thought about my companion, walking along untroubled at my side. If trouble came, would her demeanor change? Had it changed during the last moments of Lisa's life, or had the dog remained asleep in the other room, oblivious to what was going on in the studio?

Wouldn't there have been loud voices, accusations, recriminations, something to rouse the sleeping dog and make her curious enough to pad out into the studio to see what all the fuss was about, something to make her understand her owner was in jeopardy?

After all, Akitas are reputed not only to be loyal and courageous but to have astonishing powers of reasoning as well. In fact, those very characteristics, one owner had told the *Times,* had enabled his Akita to save his life. The dog had wisely neglected to alert him to a crime in progress the night thieves stole his Lincoln from his driveway. "He didn't want to see me come running out of the house in my underwear and into a dangerous situation," the proud owner said. "And, besides, I didn't really like that car anyway."

Sometimes what seems like a clever ploy on the part of a dog is merely a case of an owner who loves his dog, as many of us do, beyond all reason, and the ability of the human half of the partnership to tell a good story, saving face not for oneself but for one's dog.

Talk about stories, how about the O. J. Simpson case? Here again an Akita was present during the commission of a crime, the double murder that captured the attention of the entire nation. In Simpson's first trial, the dog was part of the case. Since she had been found afterward, wandering the streets wailing, the prosecution attempted to use her cries to establish the time of the killings.

Akita lovers could not understand why Satchmo, formerly Kato, hadn't protected Nicole Brown and her friend Ron Goldman. But if they secretly doubted her courage, no one could doubt the dog's loyalty. There had been blood on her legs and paws when she'd been found, and on her undercoat as well, as if she had in her grief lain down beside her beloved mistress's body.

Days after the crime, the dog's behavior became an issue again. When Simpson returned to Rockingham after the much-televised slow-speed chase, the bitch had cowered as Simpson stepped out of the Bronco. Some thought that was an accusation, the dog's way of telling what she knew. Some people even suggested the big dog take the stand.

But why had the dog failed to protect the victims?

She had the motive—she clearly loved her mistress. She had the means, didn't she? She was a powerful animal with big teeth. And as far as anyone knew, she had the opportunity. She was out, not locked up in the house.

But the man accused of the double murder had been powerful, too. And he had a knife. In next to no time he slaughtered not one young, healthy person but two, nearly decapitating one of them, the woman with whom he was obsessed, the woman who thought, for one heady moment, that she had finally broken free of him.

Any dog worth its feed would know its owner's feelings toward another person, would feel the fear. Moreover, if accusations and suppositions were correct, in line with the second trial rather than the first, the killer had not been a stranger to the dog, someone to back down, an enemy to be dispatched without hesitation. Just a short while before, he had been the dog's master. So long before the night of the murder, she had seen him enraged, perhaps starting when she'd been a pup and no one had remembered to take her out on time. She'd been there when Nicole was beaten. Perhaps she'd been beaten, too. If Akitas were half as smart as their owners claim, perhaps she kept away to protect *herself*.

Two cases in which an Akita failed to stop a crime. Yet in both instances, the Akita people could only sing praises for the breed that bores so deeply into the human heart that all the dogs have to do to win the boundless love of their people is be themselves. And this the Akita can do with remarkable self-assurance.

Now there was a third case involving an Akita. Hadn't Lisa's dog been present when her owner had been murdered? Had the dog been complacent because she knew the killer? Someone who had the keys.

Be not afraid.

Had Lisa been writing when the killer arrived?

I'm sorry. Lisa. Not a suicide note.

Was it an apology to someone whose feelings she was about to hurt? Someone who was coming to hear the news of her departure? She'd told Avi she wanted to tell the others herself. One at a time. Had one of them been here?

If so, which one?

As of now, only the killer was privy to that information. And once again, the Akita knew. But sadly, she had no way of telling the rest of us the answer we so desperately sought.

27

His Eyes Were Pinched
and Small

WHEN I GOT back to school, he was sitting on one of the couches, his eyebrows pitched with worry. Ch'an didn't greet him. Instead, she quickly disappeared into the office. I heard her at her water bowl, heard her lie down with a sigh.

"I'm s-sorry about yesterday," he said. "Really s-sorry. I j-just forg-g-got about your—"

"Bullshit," I said, taking a seat across from him. "I've had enough lies, and I'm ready for the truth now. The appointment was in your book, your book was open, you didn't forget. And you didn't go shopping for Mother Teresa either. So where were you?"

He had his mother's eyes, washed out and saggy, and her fleshy cheeks, already losing their battle with gravity. They were trembling now, as if he were frightened. Good, I thought, exactly the effect I'd been looking for.

"I f-forgot," he said, petulant as a child. "Is th-that a c-crime?" His eyes were pinched and small, like a pig's.

"It's not a crime. It's a lie."

"What m-makes you—"

"You can tell me, Howie," I said, my voice now soft and nurturing,

the voice he'd never heard at home. I didn't live that far away from
the HB Acting Studio myself.

I pushed the t'ai chi magazines aside and put the bag of food on the
low table between us, opening the bag and taking out the juicy ham-
burgers and fries, then the sodas, and putting one portion in front of
Howie.

"You can tell me anything. You know you can. What happened
yesterday?"

"I w-went for a walk. And I l-lost track of time. Th-that's all."

"Doesn't sound right to me, Howie. I'm trying to believe you. Honestly, I am. Hell, I *want* to believe you. But it just doesn't come together for me, Howie. It doesn't jive, does it, that you lost track of
time and missed *two* appointments. Doesn't sound like you, Howie, a
responsible man who cares for his mother in her old age."

Howie, who'd talked to me about a low-fat diet, always a dead
giveaway, eyed his burger like a hungry wolf.

"Howie, you know you'll feel better if you're honest, if you tell me."

"It was my m-mother," he shouted. "Ha-happy now?"

And then it happened, the tears, first one, rolling down his doughy
cheek, then a double. Thin-skinned, she'd said. Mother knows best.

"She was after me a-a-again."

"About money?"

"About everything, how inadequate I am, how insufficient a human
being I t-turned out to be, how I d-d-disappoint her, in every way.
'You have a f-fine mind, Howie,' she said yesterday. That's how it
started. She was st-standing in the doorway of my office with a ci-ci-
cigarette even though I told her not to smoke there because it's not
fair to the pa-patients. 'You have a fine m-mind, Howie,' she said, 'so
how come you n-never *use* it?' That's what I li-live with, Rachel, and
sometimes, every once in a while, I can't st-st-st take it, and I just have
to get away from her. But I am so sorry that I had you come for no-
nothing. There's no excuse for me not calling you. None wh-whatso-
ever."

"It's no big thing, Howie."

"But it is. You're being so k-kind to me, and I *lied* to you," he said,
picking up his napkin and starting to shred it.

"About forgetting the appointment? Forget it, Howie. It's no big
thing." I took a bite of my hamburger and salted my fries. Like an
Akita, I knew how to pay attention without seeming to do so.

"No. About Lisa. About, you know, us n-not having a relationship."
He opened one of the sodas and drank as if he were at the twenty-
mile marker of a marathon.

"You had a relationship?" I asked, incredulous, but using the same neutral look I'd used as a dog trainer when someone told me about the "little game" they played with their dog that had "gone wrong." "You were lovers?" I asked, as if it were the only obvious conclusion an intelligent observer could draw, as if I'd known it all along.

"No. N-not l-l-like that," he said, his neck all red and splotchy, color flaring in his cheeks and chin. "We were friends."

"Friends? Your mother said Lisa was going to *fire* you."

Howie looked down at his shoes.

"Talk to me, Howie. The bitch was going to fire you. That's what your mother told me. So you tell me, Howie, what kind of a person fires a friend?"

"That's not what happened," he said, looking sadly at his hamburger, as if he thought I'd take it away once he spoke.

"That's what your mother said happened. Why did she tell me that, Howie? What's going on here?"

"Sh-she was m-misinformed," he said.

"Yeah? By whom?"

"She saw me," he wiped at his eyes with his hand, "crying," he said, almost inaudibly. "I mean, she heard me, pushed into my room, the way she always d-does, put on the light, almost blinding me, stood there making f-fun of me, why was I crying, what the hell was wrong with me, like she always does. I couldn't tell her the truth, so I told her, you know, what she told you, that L-Lisa said she'd fire me."

"You must have been pretty mad at Lisa to say that, Howie."

"No, I—"

"I guess, given the circumstances, anyone would be upset. Here you thought you had a true friend, and she was going to desert you, wasn't she?"

Howie shrugged.

"You told Lisa everything, Howie, didn't you? Then you can talk to me, Howie. I'm her cousin. Howie?"

"I guess," he said. Four years old.

"So you were crying because Lisa was going away?"

Howie nodded.

"And when your mother got after you, you gave her a good reason for the tears, one that would shut her up."

He nodded again. "She didn't know about Lisa and me being friends. She wouldn't have much liked it, so I never told her."

"What would her objection have been?"

"She says I don't do enough for *her*," he said. "She doesn't want me wasting my time on other people when my own mother is sitting alone all day, rotting out, as if she didn't have a son to take care of her in her old age. She's not even that *old*," he said. "People still work, they live alone, at her age."

"Oh, Howie. No son could do more than you do."

He looked surprised, then pleased. "You look so much like her," he said, "it's almost like she's s-sitting here with me."

"Lisa?"

He nodded.

"I used to talk to her here, just like this." Howie ate some fries, then picked up his hamburger and just held it in his hand.

"When no one else was around?"

He nodded.

"Yeah. Lisa worked late a lot. Sometimes I'd come over and help her out, and then she'd let me"—he stopped and looked around—"unload. That's what she used to say to me, Rachel. Howie, you're carrying a building on your shoulders, you need to unload. Sit here and tell me your troubles." The tears began in earnest, but Howie didn't seem to notice. "When I'd talk to Lisa about my mother, it wouldn't seem so b-bad. She'd tell me, like you did, how good I was to take care of her, and I'd feel better, feel I could d-do it. But now, now with Lisa gone, sometimes I can't stand it, and I don't know what to do. There's no one else to d-do it but me. What choice do I have? And I do it, I do the best I can, but nothing s-satisfies her. The b-b-bitch won't let me breathe, she's on me day and night."

"How'd you get stuck with her, Howie? What happened to your father? Where's he?"

Howie stood so quickly, the couch moved back and hit the wall with a thud. His eyes were burning holes in me, his face a tapestry of rage.

I heard another noise, coming from the direction of Avi's office.

Then Howie began to come around the table toward me.

Ch'an came slowly toward us, her head down, her small, triangular ears alert, staring at Howie.

"Sit down, Howie," I whispered. "*Now.*"

Howie sat trembling on the couch, unable to take his eyes off the Akita.

"N-never l-liked me," he said.

Did he mean Ch'an? Or his father?

Ch'an lifted her nose in the air, then headed straight for the hamburger in Howie's hand.

"Tell me about it," I said, breaking off a piece of my burger, taking a bite, and offering the rest to Ch'an. For a moment, my whole hand disappeared into her mouth, but she took the food gently, releasing my hand unharmed. "Come on, Howie, talk to me. You know you want to."

He took a wad of tissues out of his pocket and wiped his eyes. "He left when I was s-seven. Just w-walked out."

"And you never saw him again?"

Howie flushed.

"Did you ever see him again after that, Howie?"

"Once," he said. "He came b-back a year later, just showed up at the d-door. 'Tell your m-mother I'm here, son,' he said. So I left him there, in the doorway, and went to tell my m-mother. She said, 'You go tell that b-bum we're not interested. Tell him to go away and this time, don't come b-back.'"

"And what did you do?"

"What she said. I always do what sh-she says," he shouted at me. "You met her!"

"So you did what she said?"

"I d-did. I told him to go away. And not come b-back. Only now," he said, tears falling from his basset hound eyes, "now she says to me, 'Who's to take care of me but you, Howie? You're all I've got, son. Thanks to you!'"

I was going to ask why his sister wasn't sharing the responsibility of taking care of Dora. But hadn't I been too busy with work when my own mother had needed care? Doesn't the burden of a sick or aging parent often, for one reason or another, fall to one person instead of being shared?

"Then yesterday," Howie shouted, before I had the chance to ask him anything, "I couldn't take it anymore. It was too much pressure. I ran out of the house. I didn't even take my jacket. I walked all the way up to Forty-eighth Street before I noticed where I was. I went into some bar, a real dive, McCann's or McKay's, and sat there drinking beer until it was dark out. Then I felt so bad, I walked over to the Winter Garden and got tickets to *Cats*. She loves that show, my mother. She's seen it three t-times already. No, that's another lie. I got the tickets not to please her, but so that I could get into my own fucking apartment without her savaging me all night. I got the tickets to *shut her up,* and now I have to see fucking *Cats* again." He reached into his back pocket, took out his wallet, and held out the tickets for me to see. Two balcony tickets for *Cats*. "The old b-bat won't walk a step outside alone, even though the doctor says there's no reason on earth for her to stay inside the way she does. She says she's afraid, unless I'm with her. I bought her a d-damn walker, to steady her. But does she ever use it? No, she d-doesn't. She waits for me. I'm not a nice person, Rachel, you can see that. She's right about that. Only Lisa, she didn't care about the horrible stuff I said. She l-liked me anyway. I used to c-confide in her, tell her things I couldn't tell anyone else. I n-never had a f-friend like L-Lisa. I probably n-never will again."

"Of course you will," I said, reaching over and stroking his hand. "Anyone would be lucky to have you for a friend, Howie."

"Do you really think so?" he asked. Looking at nothing in particular, he began ferrying pickle chips and cold fries into his mouth, one after the other. I doubt he would have noticed if the place caught on fire. I watched his big, strong hands, delicately lifting each morsel and moving slowly and steadily between the paper plate and his mouth, as if he were performing a religious ritual.

"Howie," I said, after he'd finished the last of his food, "what did you make of the note Lisa left? The suicide note?"

"At first I thought she'd written it to me, because of the way I cried when she told me she was leaving." Howie took the wet tissues and blew his red nose. "But I know that's stupid." He ran his finger across his empty plate and licked it off. "It couldn't have been to me," he said softly.

"Why not?"

"Because I'm not that important to anyone," he said. He took a swig of soda and just looked down into his lap for a moment. "Except, of course, my mother."

28

I Tried to Imagine It

I COULD HEAR the music out on the street, the pounding beat that apparently helped people do enough reps to tear their muscle tissue so that, during the repair process, the muscle would grow larger. I could see Janet through the window, doing her own workout, her mouth twisted in agony as she hoisted her own weight with the strength of only one arm. I stopped at the desk and asked for her, and the guardian of the lobby, a budding bodybuilder who introduced himself as Skip, told me to wait while he went to find her. Perfect, I thought, because what I was after was not Janet. It was her appointment schedule.

As soon as the door to the gym closed, I leaned over the desk and did some hoisting of my own. I hoisted the trainers' schedules, kept in a three-ring binder, turning to yesterday and checking Janet's appointments between four and six. According to the book, Janet had been working when Paul was killed. I wrote down the names of her clients—Barb Lefrack at four, Sandy Stiller at five, Mike Farley at six. Each name had a phone number beneath it, in case the trainer needed to cancel or reschedule. I copied those down, too.

When I'd come for my session, Janet had been busy on the phone. That's how I'd led three lives for ten minutes, one as myself, Rachel Alexander, private investigator, a second as Lisa Jacobs's smart-mouthed cousin, and a third as Chippy the hamster, working out on the treadmill and hating it, thank you.

She could have easily disappeared while I was warming up, couldn't she? Suppose she'd had to answer a call of nature or run out and take care of some urgent business?

Paul had been killed only blocks away, and the murder itself probably took less than a minute, maybe a full minute if you left time for a quick "hi" before the deed got done and a hand slipping into his pocket to remove his cash afterward, so that the murder would look like a mugging that had gone too far.

Had the killer in fact approached from the front or the back? I couldn't recall Marty specifying that.

I tried to imagine it, a strong arm coming from behind, circling around the front, the other hand snapping the neck. I pictured his hands reaching up to pull the arm away, but it wouldn't have happened like that. There wouldn't have been time for Paul's face to register surprise. At least that was a merciful thought.

For a moment my mouth tasted sour, and I thought that one small piece of burger I'd eaten was coming back up my throat. Then young Skip returned to the desk, catching me with my nose in the appointment book.

"She's booked solid, huh?" I said, looking disappointed. "I was hoping she could squeeze me in."

"She said if you could wait," he said, turning the book around so that it faced him, "her six canceled. But what she wanted to know was if you wanted to go get something to eat maybe, instead of working out?"

I looked at the clock on the wall behind him. It was only four forty-five.

"Great idea. Tell her I'll wait for her at her desk," I said, picking up a fitness magazine and looking toward the corner where Janet's desk sat, partly hidden behind a screen. From where I was standing, I could see Janet's chair, her jacket draped over the back.

"You got it," he said, heading back into the gym.

"Thanks," I said, hightailing it to the desk and picking Janet's jacket pocket before he could return to say, "She said, 'Cool.'" A moment later, Janet's keys in my hot little hand, I was at the front door before Skip had skipped back to the front desk to notice I had changed my mind. But when I opened the door, the buzzer sounded, and I heard him behind me.

"Aren't you staying?" he asked. "I told her you'd wait."

"I thought I'd take a walk. I'll be back by six."

He nodded and started fiddling with the tape deck, probably turning up the volume; there were still two or three people in the gym who hadn't suffered significant hearing loss from the music yet.

Janet lived on Grove Street. On the way there, I was hoping she didn't have a roommate.

She was on the top floor of what had once been a glorious town house, and now, like so many others, had been divided into small apartments and treated with not so benign neglect, inside and out.

Janet's apartment was in the rear. Keys in my hand, I knocked first, just in case, then waited and listened. I thought I heard something inside. I knocked again. This time I waited longer but heard nothing. I slipped the key into the lock and gave it a turn. Then what I saw gave me a turn.

Standing a few feet in front of me, square in the middle of a pretty, colorful handwoven carpet, her pretty, feminine head cocked to one side, her dark eyes curious and cautious, was a large white Akita.

I stood completely still. Even the sort of dog who wouldn't alert its owner when his Lincoln was being stolen might, at some given moment, feel it was her turn to save the day.

But once I'd had a moment to look at the Akita, I could see that she was just a big puppy, six or seven months old. She wagged her curled tail in slow motion, first to one side, sweeping over her back and leaning over her flank, and then, ever so slowly, to the other.

"Who's my good girl?" I said, kneeling down, arms to the side, my voice animated.

Head down, eyes squinchy, forehead wrinkled, the Akita came into my arms to be hugged. I confirmed her gender with one hand, using the other to scratch her neck. I kissed her small, triangular ears and read the tag on her collar, "Pola Bear." Then I checked my watch and got to work.

I started with Janet's desk, going through her receipts and bills, looking for something, I didn't know what. I didn't think Janet was sending those roses, but hey, this was the Village, anything was possible. Still, I didn't find receipts from a florist. Janet's receipts were all from the Foot Locker, Paragon Sporting Goods, or the Athletic Attic. But before I left the desk, I did find something interesting. Apparently Janet, like most other trainers, spread her services around in order to make more money. What I found was a 1099 from the Club. The world was rapidly becoming a smaller place.

I walked through Janet's apartment, looking at her stuff. Stewie had said Janet lived in the gym, but her place was warm and homey, particularly for me, since it had the two things I needed to call a place home, a dog and plenty of sunlight. I looked in the closets and found exactly what I would have expected—workout clothes, running clothes, cross-trainers, running shoes, and sweats, nothing much in the way of taffeta dresses, no sexy lace teddies in the dresser drawers.

There was lots of food in the small kitchen, mostly gross-tasting stuff that was supposed to be good for you—millet, apricot butter, and tofu mayonnaise. There was a juicer on the counter, the same kind that Paul was using at the Club the first time I'd met him. Instead of finding parts of dead animals wrapped in aluminum foil in the freezer, I found a twenty-five-pound bag of organic carrots in the fridge, just waiting for the juicer to turn them into sludge.

I refilled Pola's water dish and gave her a couple of biscuits for being such a decent hostess, checked my watch, and quickly locked up and headed back to the gym to get Janet's keys back into her pocket before she noticed they were gone.

"Oops. She's still busy," Skip sang out as I passed the desk. "Someone came in for a makeup session. You got to squeeze those in," he said, rolling his eyes. "House rules. She said if you would stay, she would *treat* you to dinner, you know, for making you wait so long. Or you could work out meanwhile, if you want."

"I don't know."

"She said to tell you your abs needed work. And there wouldn't be no charge," he added in a stage whisper, even though no one else was within earshot.

"I'll leave her a note," I said. "I have to go home and walk my dog."

"Tell me about it," he said, rolling his eyes. "She's so busy, busy, busy, but sometimes she's got to sneak out and do the same thing. You gotta go, you gotta go, am I right?"

I nodded.

"Too bad you can't stay. She'll be very disappointed," he said. "But even if you did, another person might show up with an aerobic emergency, who knows, right? She's very in demand," he whispered. "She's the favorite. It's a lot of pressure on her."

Not as much pressure as *not* being the favorite, I thought. I went back to Janet's desk to return her keys and write her a little note, but when I slipped my hand into her pocket, I felt something else, her wallet. I'd been so anxious to get my hands on her keys, it hadn't occurred to me the first time around that a wallet can be rich with things other than money.

Don't stop digging until you know *for sure*, Frank used to say when I'd come running to tell him I knew who did it before I'd checked out everything.

But it's so *ob*vious, I'd said, two days into my second case.

He'd looked down at his paperwork and smiled. Ring a few doorbells, he told me. Ask a few questions. Stick your hands in people's pockets. Snoop some more, kid. *Then* come back and tell me who did it.

Who did it? he'd said, shaking his head. Who did it is only the tip of the iceberg. You gotta know why. You gotta know how. You gotta have proof, Rachel, he'd said, because there's too many lawyers and not enough people out there willing to serve time for killing them. You get my meaning?

I had. So I angled myself away from the front desk and slipped the wallet out of her pocket and onto my lap. And in it, behind a picture of Pola, I found two very surprising things.

I slid the wallet back into Janet's pocket, wrote her a note saying I'd see her on Monday, and rolled my sore shoulders a few times before heading home. Dashiell did need a walk. And I needed sleep. There was no way to fight the exhaustion any longer, and all I could think of all the way home was how safe and wonderful it would feel to get home, take off my clothes, floss, and crawl into bed with my dog.

As my eyes were closing, I thought I could smell those yellow roses, dying under the bushes, returning to the earth from whence they came, but it was probably just a trick of what my mother used to call my overactive imagination.

You ought to be a writer, she'd said once. Like your cousin Richie.

Yeah, right.

I closed my eyes and pictured the photos Ceil had shown me of Richie in drag. But then I was thinking of other pictures, the ones in Janet's wallet.

The first one behind the plastic window was Pola. She was lying on that handwoven carpet, a rawhide bone between her big white paws. She wasn't looking at the camera, the way Dashiell would have. She was looking off toward the windows, the sun filling her dark eyes with light.

Behind the picture of Pola, there was a photo of Lisa Jacobs, her curly hair loose about her face, her cheeks flushed, as if she'd just been running, or working out. She too was not looking at the camera. It looked as though she didn't know her picture was being taken. She was laughing, looking beautiful and full of life.

And behind the snapshot of Lisa, there was another familiar face. This picture wasn't a drugstore print. It had been cut from a magazine or glossy newsletter, the kind a gym might send to prospective members to entice them to join up.

His dark hair was wet and spiky. He was smiling. Thinking about him now, I could almost smell the faint odor of chlorine that used to linger in his hair and on his skin.

I buried my face in Dashiell's neck and, for the longest time, tried in vain to sleep.

29

Feeling As If My Heart Were Breaking

EVEN THE SUNLIGHT slipping between the slats of the shutters didn't wake me until two in the afternoon. Feeling drugged instead of rested, I got dressed in whatever of Lisa's I found thrown on the rocking chair and headed over to the waterfront.

I passed the Christopher Street pier where there were dogs playing *hey, it's spring, let's chase the bitch and maybe we'll get lucky* and where some of the most gorgeous guys in the world were catching rays on the narrow strip of pier beyond the fencing, some of them naked, all of them gay, and headed south to the deserted Morton Street pier, where I could be alone and think.

The Morton Street pier was in such disrepair that it had been fenced off to keep people from using it. But this was New York, so there was a place where the chain link had been cut. I held it open for Dashiell, stepping through the opening and walking down toward the end of the pier. Standing there, watching the Hudson flow south toward the Atlantic Ocean, I thought about Paul Wilcox and played with the silver bracelet he'd sent to Lisa after they'd broken up.

Be My Love.

Or had he?

Wasn't the lovesick stalker someone else? And whoever it had been, sending presents and posies and watching her window, wasn't he now watching me? After all, the last bouquet had been left not at Lisa's but in the gate on Tenth Street, where no one was supposed to know I lived. And wasn't Paul killed after I'd been seeing him?

I turned north and breathed in the fishy air that wafted over the Hudson and across the old pier, then began the form. Dashiell, who had been scrutinizing the weeds that grew between the broken paving stones that covered the pier, came close and sat.

When my hands formed the Tiger's Eyes, once again I felt the presence of something I needed to remember but couldn't grasp. Twice I backed up and started again, but still, nothing.

Still tired, and feeling as if my heart were breaking, I climbed back through the space in the fence, held it for Dashiell, and together we headed home.

30

And Then It Came to Me

SUNDAY NIGHT DASHIELL and I slept for twelve hours, waking up with barely enough time to get to the noon class at Bank Street T'ai Chi, a class I couldn't afford to miss because I had plans other than practicing the form.

Class had already started. Stewie's jacket was tossed over the back of one of the couches. You know, I thought to myself, throw your jacket around like that instead of hanging it up and your damn wallet could fall out of your pocket.

Or worse, your keys.

So I picked up Lisa's black practice shoes and sat on the couch next to Stewie's jacket to change my shoes, sliding my hand into the pocket, hooking his key ring on one finger, and slipping the keys into my pocket before I got up. Then I went to join the class in progress.

Moving slowly, as if in water, rooted to the ground, as if I were the great oak that stretched its arms heavenward from its place in the center of my garden, thinking now of nothing but what I was doing at the moment, I stepped into Single Whip and, following Stewie's lead and direction, continued along with the rest of the students.

Janet was there. After Stewie spoke, she took over, asking us all to stop so that she and Stewie could come around and make corrections. We froze, waiting, our legs burning, and after each of us had been checked, we continued with the form. We moved backward, doing

Repulse the Monkey. We walked sideways, doing Cloud Hands. We opened our hips to do Fair Lady Weaves at the Shuttle. We stepped forward, folding our wrists before our chests, our hands closing into loose fists, the Tiger's Eyes.

Suddenly I was not seeing the polished studio floor beneath the circles formed by my hands, I was seeing Dashiell, days earlier, lying at the base of the oak tree, giving his full attention to the ground beneath his paws. I froze in place, my mind spinning, struggling again for whatever was just beneath my consciousness, looking through the Tiger's Eyes at the ground beneath me, giving it my full attention, as Dashiell had.

And then it came to me.

And when it did, it seemed so obvious, I couldn't believe I hadn't thought of it before.

After class Janet invited me to come to sword class at seven. I told her yes, I'd come. I thanked her, nodded to Stewie, changed shoes, signaled to Dashiell, and, feeling Stewie's keys in my jacket pocket, headed out the door.

I went first to the Sixth, asking for Marty at the desk.

"What's up, kid? You think of something?"

"Sort of. Marty, can I see the photos of Lisa Jacobs?"

Marty raised his eyebrows. "At the scene?" he asked.

I nodded.

He looked at me for a moment without saying anything, then told me to follow him. We passed the maps in back, near the arrest processing room. One had the locations of robberies, each marked with a pushpin. These fanned out all over the Village. The second map was for narcotics arrests. All those pushpins, sixty or seventy of them, were jammed into one small space, Washington Square Park.

I followed Marty up the stairs to the detectives' squad room, where he sat me down at one of the empty desks. Two detectives were working at desks over near the windows, and Marty went over to talk to one of them. I saw him hook his thumb in my direction twice, and when the detective he was talking to leaned back so that he could look past Marty and see me, I decided to skip being a wiseass and just looked away instead. When Marty came back, he had a folder in his hand.

"Is this going to jog your memory, so you'll have something to share with us?" he asked, just a tinge of sarcasm in his voice.

"It might," I said. "I had a thought this morning."

"Congratulations," he said.

The other detective—mid-thirties, thin, red hair, freckles—was doing the looking now.

"Well, more of a question than a thought," I said, deciding to ignore both Howdy Doody and Marty's tone. "I need to see the photos of Lisa. Okay?"

"Since you're in the middle of this now, and you're doing this to help out, as any good citizen would, why not?"

He laid the file on the desk and opened it. I leaned over the desk, took a good look, and winced. At first glance, except for the odd position of her legs and the fact that she was lying on the sidewalk and not in bed, Lisa Jacobs might have been asleep.

But of course, she was not asleep. A small dark stain had seeped out on one side of her head. The way her hair fanned out, you could hardly see it.

Her arms looked relaxed. One hand, as Avi had mentioned, was turned up toward the sky, as if to see if it were raining. The other arm lay still, palm down, across her chest, as if she were thinking of turning over.

She'd been wearing black leggings and a plain black sweater. You could see an inch of her white socks at her ankles. And beneath that, what I came to find out—whether or not she was wearing shoes. And she was—soft, low black suede oxfords with a leather sole, the sort of shoe Lisa Jacobs never would have worn walking, or running, across the pristine floor of the t'ai chi studio.

Unless, perhaps, there were some emergency, some reason to get to the window as fast as she could, without a thought to anything else, even a custom she had abided by faithfully for all the years she'd worked at Bank Street T'ai Chi.

"Lisa never would have walked across the studio with her street shoes on," I said to Marty.

"Rachel," he said, as patient as if I were more than a little bit slow, "when someone decides to end it all, they don't care about shit like that. You wanna tell me she was religiously neat, too, she never would have littered Bank Street? You're grasping at straws here. None of the rules count at this stage of the game," he said, pointing to the picture of Lisa dead on the sidewalk beneath where she'd taught and studied.

But I thought the rules you lived by *did* count up until the end. People folded their clothes neatly before a suicide. Or carefully buttoned up their uniforms and made sure their shoes were shined before eating their guns. What was the point of living your life with certain standards if you were just going to abandon them all at the last minute? And anyway, whether Marty believed it or not, I was still sure

Lisa's death hadn't been a suicide, any more than Paul's had happened during a random mugging.

I took one last look and closed the folder, turning my attention to the big windows that looked out over Tenth Street. Had I walked over to them and looked out, I would have seen the wrought-iron gate that led to my garden, just across the street and a few doors west of the precinct.

"Is that it?"

I nodded. "I thought—"

"Suppose someone killed her," he said, his voice low, his back turned to the detectives so that neither of them would hear what he was about to say.

"Okay," I told him. On second thought, I might not have been able to see my gate, had I walked over to the windows. The precinct had moved here from Charles Street in the late sixties, and it appeared that no one had had the time to get the windows washed since then. They were practically opaque.

"Might you then suppose the ex-boyfriend, Wilcox, was killed by the same individual, not by a mugger?"

"I might," I said, turning back toward Marty.

"And is there any particular individual you have in mind? Is there someone you suppose it might be, or haven't you gotten that far yet?" Sounding just like my brother-in-law, the *mamzer*.

"Look," I said, but Marty held up a hand to stop me.

"In order to make an arrest," he said, "we need more than suppositions. We need—"

"Yeah," I told him. "I get it. Evidence. Not hunches. Something concrete, airtight. A bloody glove. Particularly helpful if it actually fits the suspect. Bloody footprints leading away from the scene, preferably right to the suspect's house. Or a signed confession. Something of that sort."

"We don't need a signed confession. It could be videotaped. That would be acceptable, too."

Okay, I thought, so we were both having a bad day. It happens. "I'll get back to you," I said.

"You do that," he told me.

How much pressure was the precinct under, I wondered, with an unsolved murder in the area? Like Marty really wanted to up it to two, go tell the detectives they'd made a little mistake about Lisa Jacobs's death, tell the press, inform her parents. That sure sounded like a half an hour alone with a box of Twinkies and a quart of chocolate milk.

"Look, I know you're busy. Thanks a million for showing me the photos."

"No problem, kid," he said. "Sorry I jumped all over you."

I shrugged my shoulders to tell him it was no big deal, water off a Labrador retriever's back. He picked up the folder and turned to go.

I almost stopped him, but decided against it. He was right. I didn't have evidence. I only had a hunch. And the terrible feeling that time was running out.

31

He Couldn't Get In, Could He?

I GOT TO Stewie's apartment much later than I'd hoped I would, wondering as I knocked and waited exactly how early he left work. The welfare system was corrupt on both sides: people who should have been taxpaying, productive citizens getting checks, sometimes in more than one location, and employees signing out to the field and going to the Bronx Zoo, teaching t'ai chi, or merely going home.

Someone was playing with me now, letting me know he knew where I really lived, sending me flowers, calling up to see if I was home. I had to move fast, I thought, slipping the first of three keys into the first of the three locks on Stewie Fleck's apartment door, because whoever had killed Lisa and Paul was clearly playing for keeps, and it wouldn't take a genius to guess who might be next on his list.

I opened the door and quickly followed Dashiell in, closing the door behind us and locking the middle of the three Medeco locks. Then I waited, letting my eyes acclimate to the dark before feeling around for the light switch.

Stewie's studio apartment was on the first floor in the rear of a six-story tenement building on Bedford Street, a block and a half from Chumley's, where we'd had a couple of beers while he'd told me the story of how he found t'ai chi. Stewie was apparently one of those people who straightened up but didn't clean, as in, "I'll straighten up the bathroom." Whose husband hasn't said that? But there was no exasperated wife in Stewie Fleck's life to utter sarcastic epithets under her breath while handing him the Comet, Fantastic, Soft Scrub, and toilet brush. Everything was in order and covered with dust, to say the least.

Stewie didn't have a desk in the small room. There was a Murphy bed, and it was closed, locked up against the wall. There was a small Formica table with wrought-iron legs and one chair near the pint-size kitchen appliances in what was called a Pullman kitchen, maybe because it could fit in one of those miniature rooms you could get on a train. Stewie's breakfast coffee cup was in the sink, but the rest of the dishes were in the drainer. I'm sure if Beatrice were here she'd rewash them, but I had more urgent things to do.

It was after four, and Stewie could be home at any moment. I was hoping not to be here when he discovered his keys were missing, just in case the super had a set for emergencies such as this one.

I poked through Stewie's closet, checking out his inexpensive and tasteless wardrobe, finding nothing but small change and used tissues in his linty pockets. I looked at the vegetables in his refrigerator, feeling that sour taste in my throat as I did. Perhaps I should have left the Fantastic out, to give him a hint, but there probably wasn't any. Maybe it was made with animal products and he couldn't use it, for political or moral reasons.

I looked through a pile of magazines on the floor near Stewie's ratty couch, wondering why *he* wasn't on the dole. Surely he lived as if he were hovering at the poverty line. But the magazines were expensive ones, all photography journals, and his books were mostly photography books. The expensive Nikon I'd seen at t'ai chi school was nowhere around. Maybe, like Diane Arbus, he liked to photograph life's losers, so he took it to work with him. Maybe not. I wondered now if the wonderful photos I'd seen of Lisa had been his, or the one of Howie doing t'ai chi. No way those were drugstore prints. Anyone who did work like that had to have a darkroom, but dark as the apartment was, he wasn't using the kitchen. There were no chemicals under the sink, no stores of paper, no enlarger in the small closet. And even if Stewie could have made do in the tiny bathroom, covering the window with thick black paper and laying a board over the tub to have a surface for the chemical baths and enlarger, still, the equipment just wasn't there.

I went back to the books. Sure enough, several were about developing and printing black-and-white film. I looked around again to see if I had missed a place where Stewie could have stashed an enlarger, trays, and chemicals, but the place was small, and the storage practically nil.

I can't recall who started sneezing first, me or Dashiell, but once I started, I kept going until there were tears coming out of my eyes.

I never heard the first few pops. I was probably still sneezing. By the time I realized what was happening, there were tissues everywhere. Like an idiot, I began to pick them up before separating Dashiell from the box, but no matter, he'd destroyed it already. One side had been mashed down by his big paw to anchor the box so that he could pull the tissues out. Now he was shaking the empty box violently from side to side, having the time of his life. I'd have no choice but to take the thing with me, ditch it in a garbage can on the street, and let Stewie figure he forgot he used his last Kleenex.

That's when I heard it, the ping of something metallic and small hitting the dull parquet floor.

"Take it," I told him, not seeing what it was, a coin perhaps. Or the rabies tag falling off his collar. I knew I had to find out what it was before leaving.

Dashiell's mouth was right on the floor for a moment, which meant he was scooping something up with his tongue, something too small to get his teeth around. Then I heard it against his teeth as he chewed on it, trying to determine if luck were on his side and he'd picked up something edible, because don't all dogs believe in their hearts that they aren't fed nearly often enough?

I called him over, whispering in case someone were in the hall. It was a quarter to five now, time to get out of here.

I heard someone outside and froze in place. Dashiell was approaching me, and the sound of his nails click-clacking on the wooden floor seemed as loud as hailstones on the roof of a car. I signaled him to lie down by raising my arm over my head, then crept up to him and cupped my hand under his jaw.

"Out," I whispered, hearing the footsteps in the hall stop just outside Stewie Fleck's door.

But he couldn't get in, could he?

Unless the super had his keys.

Or he had an extra set over the jamb or under his ratty welcome mat.

Could he see light coming from under the door?

Crouched next to Dashiell, whose breathing seemed as loud as a respirator, I looked down into my hand at the saliva-covered key Dashiell had dropped there. It must have fallen out of the tissue box as he was annihilating it.

When the doorknob turned and rattled, my heart jumped, and while I was nowhere near as paranoid as Stewie, having only one lock on my cottage door, I was grateful I'd been paranoid enough to lock Stewie's door behind me.

He rattled the knob again, which was about as effective as kicking the flat tire you found on your car. I heard his footsteps as he walked away, then the click of the front door closing.

I opened my hand again and looked at the key that Stewie had hidden in his own home. What did he think, that just because he lived in New York City someone would break in and paw through all his worldly possessions?

I stuffed the torn tissue box and all the tissues into a dog pickup bag, waited an extra minute, heart still pounding, shut off the light, and let Dashiell into the hall, slipping out after him and locking all three locks, the key Dashiell had found in my other sweating hand. Then I looked for the stairs, because his darkroom would be in the basement, wouldn't it?

We didn't meet anyone downstairs. The building probably only had a part-time super. I tried to keep my eyes up; this was water bug territory if ever I'd seen it, and while I'd face a snarling dog or walk into a lion's den, so to speak, bugs were a horse of another color.

There were eight doors in the basement, all but one locked. I dumped the remains of Stewie's tissue box in the compactor room and went back to try the key Dashiell had found in each of the other locks, hoping one was a utility closet, with water, that Stewie used as a darkroom. At the fifth door the key moved and the tumbler turned over. I felt my heart start to pound again.

I found a light switch on the left, and as soon as the light went on, I inhaled hard enough to pull the whole room down into my lungs. There on the wall, over the sink and shelf full of trays for chemicals, and hanging on a wire, pinned up to dry, looking eerie in the glow of the red safety light, were photos of *me*.

Dashiell and I squeezed into the small room and, not knowing how Stewie would react to having lost his keys, or how soon after the locksmith let him in he'd notice his tissue box was missing, I locked this door behind me too.

Dashiell sat, and I began to look at the photos, one hand leaning on the counter for support.

I had been captured doing t'ai chi on the Morton Street pier, then holding the fence open for Dashiell as we were leaving.

There was a shot of me walking on Hudson Street, Dashiell heeling at my side. And several shots of me entering and leaving Lisa's building, even one of me looking out the window, at night. It seemed Stewie had more than just a Nikon with a telephoto lens.

There were close-ups, too. And shots at the dog run, most of me practicing the form, but some of me sitting on the bench and watching the dogs play. And one of me holding someone's cute Jack Russell puppy on my lap. There were even shots of Dashiell, but those were off on the little piece of wall to the right, opposite the side where Stewie kept his enlarger.

Then I noticed something else. The pictures of me all over the wall seemed to be tacked over other photos. In several places, I could see the edges of other pictures sticking out.

I leaned forward and pulled out some pushpins, carefully taking down a photo of me frozen in the middle of Cloud Hands, my arms moving from one side to the other in front of my chest, eyes on the horizon, knees bent, in Lisa's black leggings and sweater, her heart necklace dangling from around my neck. Under it, there was a similar photo. At first glance, it looked identical. But it wasn't.

There was a pull chain hanging down in the center of the tiny room. I gave it a tug and turned off the safety light. Then I leaned over the counter and looked at the picture again. Not me. It was Lisa.

I took out the rest of the tacks, exposing the prints underneath. There was Lisa dressed in black, doing Cloud Hands, wearing the same black shoes that I now practiced in, her hands moving like nimbi across the afternoon sky.

Under each picture of me, there was one of Lisa, sometimes two or three—Lisa walking in the Village, talking on the phone, walking her Akita, at her window late at night. Lisa, that little braid in her long curly hair, a smile on her pretty face, walking arm in arm with Paul. And in the pile of prints near the enlarger, me with Paul and Dashiell, and Paul leaving the Printing House alone.

The last two photos in the pile were pictures of me. In one I was leaving Lisa's building, Dash at my side, carrying a bunch of roses, twelve of them to be exact. And in the last, I was tossing those same roses into the trash basket on the corner. He must have used high-speed, professional film; every petal was in focus.

T'ai chi had certainly taught Stewie Fleck patience. No hunter had more successfully captured his prey.

I listened for a moment and, hearing nothing, opened the door and looked out into the dimly lit hallway. I shut the light, locked the door, and dropped the key in front of it, pushing it as close to the sill as

possible with my foot. Then Dashiell and I moved quickly and quietly
out of the basement and out of Stewie Fleck's building, blinking when
we emerged into the comparatively fresh, clean, bright air of Bedford
Street.

Unused to the light, I didn't see him leaning against the building,
just to the side of the door, until he'd actually grabbed my arm.

32

"Rachel," He Said

"RACHEL," HE SAID, surprised, but not half as surprised as I was, "what are *you* doing here?"

He looked pleased, the fool.

"I came to see you," I said, "to see if you were here, you know, if you felt like a beer or something." God bless adrenaline. "I didn't even see you standing here. I must have passed right by you," I said, thinking no one, not even a vegetarian, could be stupid enough to believe *that* lie.

"I didn't see you either," he said, frowning. "I must have been looking the other way."

"So, how about it?"

Stewie looked lost in thought.

"A beer? My treat."

"A beer? Oh, no, I can't. I'm waiting for the locksmith. I lost my keys somewhere. I'm locked out."

"Bummer," I said, his keys as heavy as an anvil in my jacket pocket. Dashiell was sitting now, and I reached down to touch his head, for my own comfort as much as his.

"You're wearing it," Stewie said suddenly.

I looked at him and followed his eyes down to my wrist. Then I lifted my arm, as if I were about to do Push Hands, or defend myself from a blow, and Stewie's hand closed around the silver heart.

"It was Lisa's," I said.

"But I never saw her wear it," Stewie said.

"No," I told him, "I don't think she ever did. It was still in the little bag from Tiffany's, brand-new, not a scratch on it. It's so beautiful," I said, "such an extravagant gift. I thought someone should wear it."

Stewie beamed at me. "Yes," he said.

And that's when I thought of a Chinese proverb I'd found in one of Lisa's books. He who asks a question is a fool for five minutes; he who doesn't ask a question remains a fool forever.

So I asked.

"Did she write that note to you, Stewie?"

He dropped the heart and I dropped my arm, putting my hand back on Dashiell's head. Stewie took a step to the side, away from me. "What do you mean?"

"What happened, Stew? Did you tell her you loved her, that it was you sending the flowers, not Paul, that you'd sent the bracelet, hoping that since Paul was no longer in the picture—"

"No!"

"What did she say, Stewie? Did she laugh at you?"

"I don't know what you're talking about."

"I think you do, Stewie. I think you know exactly what I'm talking about."

"I don't. I don't know."

"There's something you want to tell me now, isn't there?"

"You're out of your mind," he said, a little on the loud side.

I felt Dashiell's head move. He was looking at Stew now, too.

"You don't know what you're saying. I never—"

But he didn't get the chance to finish, because that's when the locksmith arrived, and I wasn't sure if I should be annoyed or grateful, because it was pretty quiet on Bedford Street and Stewie Fleck was looking more than a little bit crazy.

"Mr. Fleck?" He was carrying a metal toolbox, and the patch on his navy blue work shirt said "Hudson Hardware."

"That's me," Stewie told him.

"Too bad we couldn't have that beer," I said. "I think we need to continue this."

But Stewie just turned, and he and the locksmith headed inside.

"Catch you later," I said. But the door had already closed, and at that point, I didn't know if Stewie Fleck would have heard me if it hadn't.

33

Better Safe Than Sorry

BACK AT MY cottage, sitting on the steps that led upstairs, just staring at the front door, I decided to add another lock or two. Better safe than sorry, as the condom ads say.

Not wanting to move, or unable to, I took the names and numbers I needed from my pocket and sent Dashiell for the cordless phone.

"Barb? Hi. This is Michelle, from the gym? Fine. Just great. Okay, I'm wondering if you can help me out here," I said, lowering my voice to a hoarse whisper. "Yeah. I spilled my Coke. . . . Right. She told me exactly the same thing. And I'm trying like hell to get off it, drink Water Joe instead, yeah, springwater with caffeine in it. Right. She told me that very same thing. Carrot juice. And make sure the carrots were grown without pesticides. So, Barb, here's the thing, I spilled my Coke on the appointment book, and we can't do Janet's check, so I'm calling to verify, it looks like your name here in the book, but I can't see if it's checked off or what, so did you make that training session with Janet last Friday? Four? Great. Thanks a bunch."

I dialed the next number.

"Sandy? Hi. This is Michelle from the gym. How are you? Yeah, me, too. Listen, Sandy, I wonder if you could help me out here. There's been a little mix-up at the gym. Well, the truth is, I spilled my coffee on the appointment book. Yeah. That's what *my* mother used to say, too. Anyway, we're doing payroll, you know, and I need to verify if you were in for your five o'clock with Janet on Friday, because the place where she'd check it off is like rotted out from the coffee. You were? Great. Oh? Oh? No, of course she'll still get paid. Twenty minutes late? Because she had to what? Oh, right. Take her puppy out. Tell me about it. Half the time she sends me. So was she like all sweaty when she came back? She likes to run with Pola, get her tired fast so she can get back to work. Yeah, right," I said. "No, no problem. We don't dock the trainers for lateness. Yeah, she is the best, isn't she?"

But, of course, she *could* have run home to walk the dog. Just because she had the opportunity to do the killing didn't mean she did it.

Did it?

And just because Howie had tickets to *Cats*, that didn't mean he bought them on Friday afternoon.

And just because Stewie Fleck was stalking Lisa—Jesus, and now me—that didn't mean *he* had killed Lisa and Paul.

Did it?

After all, hadn't O. J. Simpson stalked his wife? Yet at his first trial, he got off. Apparently those jurors didn't think there was much of a connection between stalking and murder. Even though lots of other people did.

And when push came to shove—and I had every intention of pushing and shoving Stewie Fleck again—wouldn't he vehemently claim that what he'd done had been perfectly harmless? Whom, after all, had he hurt, taking pictures and sending presents?

But just the thought of that revolting little creep watching me, photographing me, following me, made me feel sick.

When I checked my watch, I saw it was almost time to go. Sword class was at seven, and I had to get there before any of the others arrived.

Climbing the stairs, I couldn't see light coming out into the hall from an open door, nor could I hear anyone talking. There were no jackets hanging on the hooks in the hall, no street shoes in the little cubbies that, except during class, held people's t'ai chi shoes.

The door was locked. So far, so good. I opened it, turned on the lights, and, out of habit by now, changed to Lisa's black shoes. I went to see if Avi was in the office, because sometimes he'd be holed up in there with the door locked and the rest of the lights off. But not this evening.

I dropped Stewie's keys next to the couch where he had tossed his jacket before the lunchtime class and pushed them with my foot so that they were half under the couch and half sticking out. Then I sat on the floor against the wall with Dashiell at my side, wondering how a nice girl like Lisa got herself mixed up with so many people who had the motive, means, and opportunity to do her in, wondering which one had, wondering whether—no, not wondering, fairly sure that—whoever the killer was, was already looking hard in my direction. It was only a matter of time now until the cousin shtick was going to wear thin, thin enough to see through, if it hadn't already. At least one of them already knew where I lived.

Janet came first. I could hear her on the stairs. I could smell the organic chamomile and aloe shampoo I'd seen in her bathroom, and anyway, by now I knew her footfall. I heard her plunk down a heavy backpack and put one shoe up on the top of the shelves where the shoes were to unlace it, then the other, and then she walked into the studio and called Dashiell for a head scratch.

"Sorry you couldn't wait," she said. "I was going to treat you at Charlie Mom's again."

"Did you go already?" I asked.

"Uh-uh. Truth is, it would have been a bust anyway. People show up," she drawled, "they don't even call, and the policy is"—Janet sighed—"the policy is never to let a dime walk out the door. I might look elsewhere soon, you know."

"Where else have you worked?" I asked, pulling my socks up tight and smoothing my leggings over them.

"Oh, I was at the World Gym two years ago, and last year I worked on Christopher Street, where I am now, but I also taught classes at the Club, on Varick."

"Where Lisa's boyfriend worked?"

"I heard about that," she whispered. "It was on the news. Jesus," she said, shaking her head. "You know, when I moved here from Texas, everyone I met said the Village was the safest neighborhood in New York City. I don't know. What is this world coming to, you can't walk around the neighborhood anymore without getting killed? Is that hers, too?" she asked.

"Excuse me?"

"That silver bracelet you're wearing. Was that Lisa's, too?"

I picked up the heart and let it drop.

"Yeah. I found it with her stuff. But I don't think she ever wore it. It looks brand-new."

Janet held the heart and read it.

"I don't know why not. I sure would have. It's nice. Don't you think so?"

I nodded.

"I guess Paul got it for her," she said.

"I guess."

I watched the muscles in her cheeks jump.

"Are you staying for class?" she asked.

"I think I'll just watch. I don't think I'm ready for this."

"Sure you are. You can do it. You can do anything you set your mind to, don't you know that, woman?"

"I'm going to pass," I said.

Janet shrugged. "Suit yourself. But we can still have dinner if you want. Charlie Mom's, after class?"

"Sure. Sounds great."

Then she turned, because we heard someone on the stairs, someone walking slowly. "Howie," she called out.

"It's m-m-me," he answered.

A moment later Howie and Avi walked into the studio. Avi had a bag from Staples with him. Howie looked at me and smiled, then sat across from me. Avi put his package down on the couch and joined us all on the floor, sitting in a circle around Dashiell. Then three other advanced students arrived and greeted us, a really skinny guy with a ponytail like Avi's, a short, muscular black man whose biceps rivaled Janet's, and a woman of seventy or seventy-five, thin and lithe, there perhaps to prove the point that t'ai chi helps you to live longer.

Avi stood, and everyone went to the supply closet and got swords. I sat with Dashiell watching the ritualized movements, the sword as an extension of the hand, an extension of one's *chi*. And while I was watching, I heard Stewie Fleck on the stairs, heard the squeak of his sneakers, heard him changing his shoes, and then he was there, a few feet away, looking around the couch. I turned to watch the class, hearing the jingle of Stewie's keys being scooped up from the floor and dropped into his pants pocket, waited while he got his sword from the closet, then turned to look at him as he passed where I was sitting to join the class, making a point, it seemed to me, not to look at me.

But then he didn't join the class. He came back to where I was sitting and squatted, sitting on his haunches the way Avi always tells us to.

"I know what you did," he said, his eyes hard.

"And I know what *you* did," I said back to him.

He glared at me. "I don't have time for this now," he whispered, standing up quickly and going to join the class.

The moment class ended, Janet pulled on my sleeve and nodded toward the door. I changed my shoes, grabbed my jacket, and picked up Dashiell's leash. Out in the hall, I noticed a baseball cap hanging on one of the hooks, but Janet didn't take it, and now I wouldn't be there to see who would.

Good thinking, I told myself. Like it would be terrifically significant to see who took the cap, like it was even legal to live downtown and not have at least a few of them. Besides, no matter who owned this one, I already knew who stood across from Lisa's in the weeks before she died.

Walking over to Charlie Mom's, Janet was quiet.

"When did you get Pola?" I asked her, wanting to get something going.

She turned and looked at me.

"Skip," I said, watching her face harden. "He said you sometimes had to run home to walk her. I was surprised you never mentioned her."

Janet shrugged. "I missed Ch'an. After Lisa"—she paused, as if looking for the right word—"well, Avi doesn't bring her in all that often. Not the way Lisa did. There's something about Akitas, I don't know, but I just missed being around one. I was able to find one, a female like Ch'an, only white, that a breeder in Jersey had held on to and then decided to sell. She's seven months old, a real peach of a dog. I've only had her since, well, just a few weeks. That's why I sometimes run out to give her an extra walk. She'd been a kennel dog, so I wasn't sure about her housebreaking, but she's doing real good, she's real clean in the house."

I nodded.

"They're pretty popular," I said, "Akitas."

Janet nodded.

"Paul said he liked them, too."

I felt her tense, the way I could always feel the tension surge in some male dogs when there was the perceived threat of another intact male approaching.

"So did you know him before Lisa?" I asked. "I mean, since you worked in the same gym with him. Or had Lisa met him before?"

"I introduced them."

Bummer, I thought.

"Lisa came over to train with me, and Paul came into the gym to ask me something, so I introduced them."

"And what? Rockets went off? Soft music started playing, you know, like in the movies, to indicate two people are falling in love?"

"Something like that," she said.

"Did they start dating right away, or what?"

"Lisa started swimming again."

"What do you mean?" As if I didn't know.

"She hadn't been swimming for a long time, except in the summer, when she'd visit her parents. And after she met Paul, she began swimming regularly again. He used to call her *xiao yue*."

We stopped on the corner, neither of us speaking as we waited for the light to turn green.

"It means *little fish*," she said as we crossed Seventh Avenue.

The waiter at Hunan Pan had looked away when he'd told me, not wanting to embarrass me by paying attention to how I might react. Such a nickname is given in great affection, he'd said, looking toward the other side of the restaurant, to family members.

"Did Lisa stop training with you after she met Paul?" I asked Janet when we'd reached the safety of the other side of the street. She didn't respond. "I don't guess she had the time to do both."

We'd arrived at the restaurant. Janet stopped and turned to face me. "You know, I'm going to beg off, Rachel. I wasn't thinking. It's late, and Pola's been alone all day. I'd feel like such a bitch, staying out even later. I'll catch you another night," she said and, not waiting for a response, turned and headed in the direction of home.

It was quiet for the Village. Even weekday nights, there are people everywhere, going to plays and clubs, going to or coming from restaurants, walking their dogs, or just hanging out at the coffee bars that have suddenly cropped up like weeds, one to a block. Some sit inside, reading the newspaper or a magazine. Others sit outside, on a bench, watching the passing parade, as if they were in Rome or Paris. But tonight was sort of peaceful, and Dashiell and I walked slowly, enjoying the quiet.

How should I feel, I wondered, about Paul using the same term of endearment for Lisa and me?

He'd loved her. That I knew. What harm would it cause to think the obvious, that in the short time I knew him, he had come to love me, too? What difference could it make anyway, I thought, now that he was dead?

Suddenly a hand grabbed my arm, and someone was in my face.

"You were seen," he said, his seething rage barely under control. "What the fuck is going on, that's what I want to know."

"You were seen, too, you little creep," I told him, turning slightly so that I all but disappeared. Stewie stumbled forward.

"What are you talking about?" he said, catching himself, trying to act as if nothing had happened.

"You were seen standing across from Lisa's every night, skulking around in the dark, staring at her window, watching to see who came

and went," I said, stepping forward. "What the fuck was that all
about?"

Stewie Fleck looked off to the side, took off his baseball cap, and
smoothed his hair forward.

"I . . ."

"What? You what?"

I grabbed the front of his jacket and pulled him back toward me.

"Quit that," he said. "Get your hands off me *now*."

And with that, he pushed back. Hard.

As I caught my footing, I felt Dashiell brush my leg as he stepped
between us. We both looked down at him, his tail, rigid now, level with
his back, moving ever so slightly from side to side, just stirring the air.
He was facing Stewie, who this time stepped back without being
pushed.

"What were those pictures all about, pictures of Lisa, now pictures
of me?" I said, my voice much too loud.

"You were in my darkroom?" he said, seething, but trying not to
shout, trying not to inspire Dashiell to anything more than what he
was doing, watching to see what would happen next, as if he had all
the time in the world and absolutely nothing better to do.

"I was," I said. "So are you going to tell me what this is all about,
Stewie? Or would you rather just cross the street"—I indicated the
Sixth Precinct with a tilt of my head—"and tell them what the hell you
had in mind when you decided to stalk Lisa? And Paul. Both of whom
are dead."

"You bitch," he said, forgetting Dashiell and shoving me back.

Then several things happened nearly at once.

I heard Dashiell's growl as I caught myself, one foot behind me, and
as Stewie Fleck slipped between two parked cars and ran for his life,
crossing the street on an angle so that he'd get to the other side as far
away from the police station as possible.

And Dashiell, never one for wasted action and clearly understanding that the shortest distance between him and Stewie Fleck was not
around the car but over it, in one move landed on the roof of the
Mercedes-Benz parked just to our left, setting off its alarm.

"Leave it," I told him.

So instead of leaping into the middle of the street and chasing down
his prey, my designer wolf stayed just where he was, the car's horn
blaring on and off, the headlights flashing, while across the street,
heading for the corner, was Stewie Fleck, moving as fast as the desig-
nated dinner in the middle of a caribou hunt.

34

I Listened to the Dial Tone

INSIDE THE COTTAGE, Dashiell asleep on the couch, I could hear the car alarm, still going off. No matter that it was a few steps away from the Sixth Precinct, no one would do anything about it until the owner showed up. And that might not be until tomorrow.

I began to pace around. It was too noisy to sleep. Unless you were a pit bull. And I was too unhappy with the way my case was going to sleep, even if it had been quiet. The more I learned, the less I knew.

Talking it out sometimes helped, I thought as I picked up the phone. I was just thinking about you, she'd say. I listened to the dial tone, but I never dialed. What had I been thinking? I had so successfully filled myself up with Lisa Jacobs that I had all but forgotten about Lili and Ted. For just a moment I thought about him, my brother-in-law, kissing the blond, and then I consciously withdrew myself from the problem. It was theirs to solve. I didn't call. Instead, I closed my eyes and pictured the bouquets of roses that Lisa had hung over her dining room table. I thought about the sound of her earrings, the smell of her perfume, the soft feel of her sheets, and the gentle touch of her lover, when he became my lover. And I put down the phone, because I was back where I belonged.

Avi had been telling me to rely on myself. That was exactly what I needed to do. Leaving Dashiell sleeping on the couch, I grabbed Lisa's jacket and headed for someplace where I could be alone and think, someplace far away from the noise of the car alarm.

Walking toward the waterfront, I began to think about how weird it was that nearly everyone in Lisa's life had a motive to kill her. It was more like a made-for-television movie or a novel than real life.

Real life, it's the husband, the boyfriend, the business partner, ba-da-boom, the cops go after one person, the schmuck usually ignores the Miranda warning, places himself at the scene, changes his story five times, then confesses.

Or no one seems to be guilty. The person was wonderful, his friends were wonderful, everything was wonderful. Until you start to turn over the rocks and watch the worms crawl out.

This case was driving me crazy. There was no one I *didn't* suspect. Maybe it was because she had so much. Everyone who knew her had reason to be envious.

It would be only human, wouldn't it?

Lisa did everything well. She was beautiful. She had money. Her father bought her this gorgeous apartment, full service, great light, all paid for.

But that wasn't half of it. She was smart, I thought, now heading north along the waterfront area, the Hudson dark and forbidding to my left, the wind going through Lisa's thin jacket. She was talented, focused, and lucky too, I thought, but then I began to shake my head. Lucky? Well, she was lucky until the end. Then she got very unlucky.

I thought about the people in her life, all of them in *my* life now. Any of them could have done it.

The only one I really *liked* in all this was Avi. So I began to wonder if I was being blind, no one to shout from the shore and head me in the right direction, blind because I liked him so much, admired him, as if that meant he weren't capable of murder.

I had been sort of skipping over him because I thought he was so special. But all kinds of people commit crimes, and he *could* have done it. I thought about how sweet he'd been to me. Not sweet, really—generous would be more to the point. I guess I'd prefer it if it were one of the others. And then I found myself talking out loud, a typical New Yorker. Is this pathetic, I said, or what? I'm supposed to be a fucking detective.

Jesus, I was cold. I crossed West Street again, but instead of getting out of the wind, I walked along the other side of the traffic, finding myself headed toward Bank Street. I crossed the street and walked into the Westbeth courtyard, across the street from the studio, the place where Paul was killed, and sat facing the school and looking up.

It was late now, very late, but the studio lights were on, the only ones on in the whole building. I wondered who was there. For a moment I had the eerie feeling that if I went upstairs, it would be Lisa, sitting at Avi's desk, the way she used to, doing the paperwork, Ch'an at her side. I shivered at the thought.

It was probably Avi, catching up on the work Lisa used to do for him.

From the very beginning, I didn't want it to be him, so I kept looking for ways it could be the others. But now that I was thinking about it, it occurred to me that the tradition in t'ai chi—no, not just t'ai chi, all the martial arts—is for serious students to remain with their master for years and years, and not go off on their own, not leave or anything, until the master dies. And Lisa had told him she was leaving, she was going to break with tradition and go off to study in China.

Of course, I thought, standing up, then sitting down again. Her note. It was on *his* desk. What was that they said in real estate? Location, location, location. How could I have missed this?

I could go upstairs, I thought. We need to talk, I could say. Of course, he'd say, looking at me the way he always did, as if there weren't anything that might happen that could be more important than whatever it was I had come to say, as if there were no tomorrow and nothing existed but now.

He'd wait. All I would hear would be the sound of my own breathing.

It's not going well, he might ask, your search for answers? You haven't learned anything? And I could shrug and say, oh, I've learned a lot, just not enough.

I've made a big decision, I could say, just to make sure I had his complete attention. What is that, Rachel? he'd say, and then I'd tell him that my intention had been to learn about Lisa, to understand her life so that I might understand her death. I could tell him how arrogant a notion that was, to think I might become privy to the complexity of another human being by meeting her colleagues, her mentor, her sweetheart, as if, by looking through her books, wearing her clothes, or sleeping in her bed, I would suddenly know who she was, how she felt. What happened, I could say, is that I only learned more about me, who I am, how I feel.

Rachel, he'd say. But I'd hold up my hand. Let me finish, I'd tell him. Something happened to me, something got started that I need to finish. So I've decided to leave here. I've decided to continue my studies in China.

What are you saying? he'd ask, shocked. Lisa's dead, I could say. What difference does it make why she killed herself, when you think about it? But walking in her shoes, reading her books, studying t'ai chi, that's what became important to me. And if Lisa felt the way to do that was to do it in China, then that's what I'm going to do.

But why not stay here and study? I can teach you, he'd tell me, not wanting to let me go. And I'd just say, I can't. I have to follow through with this.

Would he look away? Would there be tears?

I never meant . . . , he might say. And I'd tell him, it doesn't matter what you meant. Or what I meant. It's just something that has to be now. My aunt and uncle are letting me use Lisa's ticket, so I can take Dashiell with me. Everything is paid for. And there's nothing to keep me here, no husband, no job. This was meant to be, Avi. It was fate that brought me here, so that this could happen. Do you believe in fate? I'd ask him.

Now that I was letting in the dark thoughts I'd been avoiding, something else occurred to me. I'd assumed Paul was on his way to see me at the studio. What if he'd been on his way *from* the studio, after being told by Avi that I wasn't there? What if Avi had followed him out?

But why? I searched my mind and couldn't think of a time I'd mentioned him to Avi. If he'd view Paul as a threat to our master/slave relationship, how did he know? And then I remembered the first time we'd met. Avi had picked up the scent of Lisa's perfume from her scarf. Surely he'd noticed the stronger scent of chlorine. Surely he'd understood its significance.

Did he want to make sure that this time nothing would distract his new apprentice from her studies? Like Lisa's father, was he able to give Lisa anything under the sun, except her freedom?

Zen, I'd read in one of Lisa's books, is simply a voice crying, Wake up, wake up. That was exactly what I had to do, before it was too late.

If I had something to ask Avi, there was no time like the present. I looked up at the studio windows. The lights were still on. I got up, walked across the street, and, taking a couple of deep breaths, prepared to take the stairs, as Lisa always had.

35

I Could See His Aura

SHE WAS STANDING in the doorway, a thin woman in a worn-out coat. "You going in?" she said, pushing her brown bangs off her sallow face.

I nodded.

"I usually clean of a Sunday, when no one's here," she said, the keys in her hand, "but my sister's daughter is getting married, thank God." She opened the door for me. "You people work so late," she said, "no one else in the building. The old man was just leaving when I got here," she said, ringing for the elevator.

I walked in but didn't turn on the lights. Instead, out of habit I guess, I took off Lisa's jacket and changed to her shoes, then, standing in the center of the studio floor, slowly began to do the form. Stepping into White Stork Spreads Its Wings, my right arm bent, my wrist above my eyes, so that I would be able to see the enemy, all I could see was myself reflected in the mirror, wearing Lisa's shoes, Lisa's black workout clothes, and Lisa's bracelet. It dangled heavily from my wrist, reminding me of the weight I had taken on, the obligation to see this through and find out why Lisa, and now Paul, were dead.

Instead of paying attention to what I was doing, I thought about Stewie Fleck, of how guilty he'd acted.

But then I remembered three dogs I was training years ago. When the owner came home and found something wrong, he'd shout, Which of you hoodlums did this? One never looked guilty, even if she was. One only looked guilty if he'd done it. And one always looked guilty, no matter who tore the pillow, ate the defrosting chicken, or left a dump on the rug.

Hadn't Janet managed to keep alive the resentment she'd felt for Lisa when she'd come to the school and immediately become Avi's favorite? Lisa had stolen not one but two treasures from Janet. Then she'd tossed them both away, the way the alpha dog might take the best bone, only to drop it a moment later, having taken it as an object lesson, just to prove he could.

Push, push, that's a dog's world, a way of finding out who's who and what's what. Is that what Janet thought Lisa had done, taking Paul and then throwing him away? And did Janet change her rationale with the second killing, leaving the person who stole from her alive to suffer the sting of loss, as she had?

I heard the whine of the elevator. My spine straight, my eyes forward, I moved from my center, continuing the form as the door opened and a moment later closed again. I saw him out of the corner of my eye, just standing there watching me. I finished the form, slowly lowering my arms as I came back to my full height, then turned to face him.

"What are you doing here so late?" I asked. "Couldn't you sleep?"

He shook his head.

"Me neither," I told him.

He looked awful, pale and tired. His shirt looked as if he'd slept in it. His hair hadn't been combed.

"Do you come here often, this late?" I asked, thinking about what the cleaning lady had told me.

"No," he said. "I saw you."

"You saw me?"

"In the courtyard. I often s-sit there. It's so peaceful," he said, his voice flat, his arms hanging down at his sides. "I saw you sitting there. Then I saw you c-come up here. So I f-followed you."

A chill passed through me, as if maybe a window had blown open, letting in the cold night air. But I could see them in the mirror, and they were all closed and latched. Still, I was so cold I thought if I didn't do something fast, I might start shaking. So I did something. Like a dog, I pushed.

"It must be hard for you," I said. "You must get so frustrated. And so lonely."

"It's not so bad when I have someone to talk to," he said, no emotion showing on his face. Or was it just too dark to see?

"Too bad there's no one else to share the load?" I said, picturing the little girl with a round face, like Howie's, the pretty little girl who was clearly her mother's favorite. "No other siblings?"

Howie blinked.

"What about your sister?" I asked, hackles up, teeing up on him now.

"What do you m-m-mean?" he said.

"Your mother said—"

"No. She told you about *that*? She's a liar," he shouted. "It was *her* fault, not m-mine."

"Tell me about it."

"Didn't *she* tell you already?"

"Do you think I'd believe *her*? Come on, Howie. Talk to me."

"I was only seven," he said. "She can't hold me responsible. It was *her* job to watch her, not *mine*."

"But she'd been drinking?"

"A lot," he said, taking a step closer.

"Had she passed out?"

"I don't *know*. I was playing with my miniature cars, on the floor. I had my *back* to them. I didn't s-see. I was only a kid, for chrissake."

"And your mother? What did she say happened?"

"*She* was the one should have been watching. But she blamed *me*. She said I could have prevented it, if I wasn't such a d-dummy. That's what she told the p-p-police. 'My son was supposed to be watching her.' She'd never told *me* that. She never."

"And exactly what was it that happened when no one was watching?" I asked, even though part of me didn't want to hear the answer.

Howie took another step toward me.

"She must have climbed up on the s-sill," he whispered, his face alive now, "and somehow the cord of the venetian blind must have gotten wrapped around her neck. And then she lost her b-balance and fell out. At least th-that's what the p-police said happened. It was very tragic."

In the dark, I thought I saw him smiling.

Was it after that tragic accident that his father had left the first time?

"I guess that's why we live on the ground floor now."

Had little Howie stopped playing with his miniature cars long enough to speed his baby sister on her short flight to nowhere?

Had he done the same for Lisa? Surely it wouldn't have been the first time a man killed a woman because if he couldn't have her, he'd make damn sure no one else would either.

With Lisa gone, he'd latched on to me.

And sitting in the courtyard one afternoon, he'd seen Paul on his way to the studio. Surely Howie would have understood the significance of that, and the threat implied in it. Wouldn't the thought of losing me make him beside himself with rage? Mightn't it even make him furious enough to kill?

Don't ask me why, but even as I wondered if I'd be able to defuse the bomb that I myself had armed, I made things worse. Once set in motion, some things are impossible to stop.

"So, Howie, were you also present the night that Lisa lost her balance?"

"She had no right to do that to me. She had to be punished." He looked at the windows, then back at me. "How else would she learn?"

Had Lisa been writing to him, because he'd cried so when he'd heard her plans? Had he left and come right back, his tears turning to rage on his way down the stairs? Was it Howie, then, not Lisa, who had opened the window, Howie saying he couldn't go on without her friendship? And then what? Had he climbed up on the sill? Of course. And Lisa, her heart pounding, had run across the studio floor in her street shoes to stop him.

He was just standing there, between me and the door, so close I could feel the heat of his body, his eyes as glassy as if he were a dog with rage syndrome. In the dark I could see his aura, red and shooting out around him, like those telescopic photos of the sun. Howie Lish was looking like something that was about to explode.

36

I Don't Believe You, He Said

SUDDENLY HOWIE CAME to life, grabbing both my wrists in one big paw and, with the other, slapping me hard in the face. "B-bitch," he said, "you're just like h-her, only pretending you care."

"You're wr-wrong, I *d-do* care," I said, desperation in my voice. Now I was the *hikavater*.

T'ai chi, Avi had said, teaches you who you are, and when you know yourself, you can understand others. But I've always known who I am, a person who sees the world through dog-colored glasses. Now I remembered those magazines under Howie's bed. And I knew who he was, too.

My cheek was on fire, and fear had risen in my throat like a bad meal. No one else here, I thought, pushing the fear away. Rely on yourself.

"Ooo, you like it rough," I said. "You have no idea how that turns me on."

"What did you say?"

"Holding me so that I can't get away, slapping me around, it really turns me on," I told him, looking right into his eyes. I began to laugh. "I mean, it *really* turns me on."

He stopped moving.

I was standing in the middle of the studio, my hands numb from the pressure on my wrists, and the only sound was Howie Lish's heavy breathing.

"Couldn't we do this with less on?" I said, hoping he'd think I was trembling from desire and not fright.

"I don't b-believe you," he said.

"Try me," I told him.

I felt the grip on my wrists loosen a little. I could see the beads of sweat on his cheeks, and running down his neck.

"Let me take my clothes off, slowly, while you watch," I said, someone playing kick-the-can with my heart. "And then you can take yours off, Howie. And I'll watch."

He tightened his grip again.

"You've been thinking about it, haven't you?" I asked him. "I have. Ever since the massage."

Howie smiled. "Go ahead," he said. "Undress."

"I can't, with you holding me. Plenty of time for that later. We have all night, don't we?"

And then I was free, but Howie was so close and the door so far away.

As slowly as if I were doing t'ai chi, I pulled Lisa's black sweater over my head and dropped it onto the floor.

I could feel Howie's breath on my bare skin.

I unhooked my bra, holding it out to him on one finger and then letting it slip into his big hand.

"You, too," I said, stepping back one step and slipping off Lisa's leggings. "I want to see you, Howie." And as a final sign of good faith, I slipped my underpants down and stepped out of them.

Howie dropped the bra and began to undress, quickly unbuttoning his shirt and pulling it off. Then he opened his pants and let them drop and began to pull down his underwear. Looking in the mirror, I could see the big, white moon of Howie's ass shining back at me. I could see myself, too, no longer in black, naked now, except for Lisa's t'ai chi shoes and her heavy, silver bracelet hanging from one wrist like a handcuff.

Howie's erection had popped loose and was staring me in the face; his pants and shorts were around his ankles. As he lifted one foot to jettison them on the pristine oak floor of the studio, I remembered Avi telling me that in martial arts, unless doing something gives you a clear advantage, it's better to do nothing at all. For a moment, that's what I did—nothing. Then slowly I reached out for Howie, as if to embrace him, slipping my hands around his sweaty neck, and using a martial art even older than t'ai chi, I too lifted a foot, driving my knee as hard as I could into Howie's naked crotch. And when he'd doubled over, folding at the waist, his head coming forward, I lifted my knee a second time, even harder, and heard it crack against Howie Lish's forehead.

That's when the door opened and Avi walked in, Ch'an trailing behind him.

37

He Seemed to Be Smiling

HE LOOKED SLOWLY from my head to my feet. Too slowly, if you ask me.

"Ah," he said, focusing on Lisa's black cotton shoes. "You've been practicing. Excellent."

He seemed to be smiling, but it was too dark to be sure.

He turned away and headed for his office, Ch'an padding along at his side. "I forgot my keys," he said, "good, good, they're on the desk." I heard him dialing as I quickly got dressed.

I looked down at Howie. His eyes were still closed and there was a large red bruise on his brow. "Thinking," O. J. Simpson had once said, "is what gets you caught from behind." I'd say in his case, and Howie's, it was *not* thinking that had done them in.

After the police left, taking Howie with them, Avi and I sat on the couches and talked until the sun came up. Then I made a phone call and headed home to change to my own clothes, pick up Dashiell, and get the car.

A thin dusting of sand, carried by the wind, covered the street where I parked the Taurus. When I opened the car door, Dashiell headed straight for the ocean, and before I'd locked the car, he was out of sight.

I slipped off my shoes, rolled up my jeans, and swimming in the sea of now, stood in the surf with my dog, just listening to the roar of the waves. Then the yin and yang of private investigation went to see the Jacobs family one last time, to tell them that what had happened to their beautiful daughter had not been their fault.